T H E

AMAZON
CHRONICLES

BY
JANE E. M. ROBINSON

Clothespin Fever Press
San Diego 1994

ISBN: 1-878533-12-6
No part of this work may be reproduced or transmitted in any form or by any means, electronic or mechanical, including photocopying and recording, or by any information retrieval system, except as may be expressly permitted by the 1976 Copyright Act or in writing from the publisher, Clothespin Fever Press 10393 Spur Ct., La Mesa, CA 91941

Many years ago the realm of Amazonia was begun by the ordinance and enterprise of diverse women of great courage, who despised bondage, so as the histories bear witness.

—Christine de Pisan,
The City of Ladies (1405)

This story takes place around 1240 B.C.E.

To Julie

Characters

Abba-Bashti	Trader woman from Harran
Adad-Duri	Father of Abba-Bashti
Aegista	Trojan slave; belongs to Hesione
Aella	Apprentice smith; Telkhinia's oldest daughter
Amynome	Amazon; rides for Ariona
Antiope	Amazon; daughter of Thalestris; pretender to throne
Anuphey	Palace servant
Ariona	Amazon; chief of noble house
Artatama	Brother of Abba-Bashti
Athaia	Apprentice smith; Telkhinia's middle daughter
Batteia	Servant in Adad-Duri's house
Belit-Selim	Mother of Abba-Bashti
Brimus	Achaean
Celano	Temple steward and and advisor of Thalestris
Chalcodon	Achaean
Cleothera	Winemaker
Cletê	Palace servant
Damisos	Trojan slave; belongs to Hesione; flute player
Delphica	High priestess of Apasas; Myrtho's mother
Dione	Winemaker
Dirce	Little girl; Telkhinia's youngest daughter
Ennomos	Captain of the Trojan palace guard

Eriboea	Peasant woman; Penthesilea's wet nurse
Eripha	Myrtho's younger sister
Feodissia	Amazon; rides for Ariona; Penthesilea's friend
Glaucia	Wife of King Laomedon
Gubarnu	Man of Harran; master of Abba-Bashti
Hesione	Daughter of King Laomedon of Troy
Hippolyta	Amazon; chief of noble house
Ido	Amazon; rides for Hippolyta
Iphinoë	Priestess
Jason	Trojan slave; belongs to Priam
Kaptia	Man of Harran; slave; scribe
Klymene	Amazon; rides for Ariona
Laomedon	King of Troy
Leokadia	Amazon; Penthesilea's mother; rides for Ariona
Lysippe	Amazon; rides for Hippolyta
Marpessa	Amazon; rides for Thalestris, later Ariona
Melanippe	Amazon; daughter of Naunamé the just; pretender to throne
Merope	Temple kitchen girl; later chief cook
Miminousa	Amazon; leads city patrol during trading season
Molpadia	Peasant woman; Eriboea's cousin
Myrtho	High priestess; beloved of Leokadia
Nihtesaru	Woman of Harran
Oebala	Amazon; rides for Thalestris
Oenanthé	Arrowmaker
Omaïa	Oldest Amazon; dean of riders
Orthaios	Trojan charioteer
Penthesilea	Amazon; foundling
Perseia	Amazon; rides for Hippolyta
Philippis	Temple steward
Pirothous	Achaean
Priam	Son of King Laomedon
Proto	Child discovered by Abba-Bashti
Ribat	Son of Zakir
Soloön	Achaean
Tashmetum	Slave woman of Harran
Tecmassa	Amazon; rides for Ariona
Tehip-Tilla	Man of Harran

Telkhinia	Blacksmith; chief of artisans
Thalestris	Amazon; chief of riders and high judge of city
Thalia	Farmer
Theia	Dione's granddaughter
Thersandra	Potter
Theseus	Achaean
Tomiris	Amazon; rides for Thalestris
Zakir	Merchant from Babylon

Chapter 1

Leokadia the Amazon rode over a trail littered with rocks and surrounded by steep hills. She was patrolling terrain a tedious two hours from the walled city of Themiscyra, which stood on a rocky steep facing the southeast and overlooked a valley that stretched from the direction of the winter sunrise to that of the lingering summer daylight. The river Thermodon, having risen in mountains to the south, flowed northwest past the foot of this elevation, watering pastures where horses grew sleek and sheep thick-fleeced, fields where barley and emmer sprouted in profusion, and orchards where the branches of apple and cherry trees bent heavy in their seasons.

The city of Themiscyra and its valley and pastures were the women's domain, known to foreigners as the realm of Amazonia. Many had heard of it in Troy by the sea and in the mighty cities and mighty empires to the east and south. Men whispered wild stories about the place, where none of them was allowed to dwell for long, and, although it was out of the way of the principal caravan route, traders who could have crossed to Troy more directly took the trouble of calling there, for its women forged iron ornaments and wove red cloth that were worth the visit. The traders also lingered there, for the women went down to the tents of the male strangers to share their couches and make babies. There were also babies to be bought, the boy children born as a result of the inhabitants' nocturnal visits. The women bartered these tots as soon as they were weaned, for girls or for goods.

Hills hemmed in the fertile territory on all sides. To the south and east rose low elevations on the slopes of which grew row upon row of vines. Beyond these rises stretched steppes that ended a week's trek away at a ridge of mountains where the royal road of the great Hittite empire began. These powerful neighbors were content to leave the Amazons untouched: they paid their tribute and formed a buffer against northern marauders. A few days to the west along the Hittite road stood their capital of Hattusas; a fortnight farther on lay the warm sea and its rich cities, Apasas and Miletus. From Hattusas too, far, far to the south, were the mighty kingdoms of Babylon and Assur. Northeast of Thermodon's valley, unwelcoming heights rolled for days toward the region of the savages, the Kaska people, who came suddenly, stole women and livestock, and disappeared, leaving burned fields and bleeding bodies.

North and west of Themiscyra loomed tall wooded eminences that bore iron and silver in their bowels. To the north, too, flowed the river Lycus, which separated the Amazons' possessions from the littoral belonging to the men of Amisos. These hostile neighbors bore an old grudge against the women, whom, they claimed, had founded the Amazonian domain by stealing land from Amisos. They would send their infantry into the Amazons' holdings on any pretext to rape, torch, and slaughter.

Finally, in the direction of the setting sun, more than six weeks' journey from Themiscyra, stood the rich lands and high walls of Troy, with whose rulers the Amazons had generations before formed an alliance against the Amisos raiders and the Kaska savages. Until that time, both had raided Troy-bound ships and caravans with impunity.

Leokadia, one of the riders who kept watch over Themiscyra's marches, was patrolling the northeast trail. Without consciously seeing them, her restless eyes took in a burrow practiced under a rocky overhang from which glowing yellow eyes followed her; a few tiny bones, a curved beak, and a handful of bloody feathers where a new carcass had lain earlier that day; the hint of a path heading off from the trail—a lack of vegetation—which the moving airs only now made visible.

She had made the same tour on horseback for eight years now, each day that the weather allowed. And it would not allow much longer. She smelt snow, and her head tingled with the dark clouds that almost touched it. Now and again her thick-legged pony shrugged and exhaled a double stream of white vapor. The Storm God would close in before the daylight went away and within days would drive huge drifts into the passes around the city. After that, not a soul would get in or out of the valley. Leokadia could warm herself by the fire and rest then. She would not have to patrol the passes.

More than a month had gone by since the last traders had led their caravans of pack donkeys away from Themiscyra. Most of the merchants who stopped to bargain in front of the gates had stayed on for weeks. But the men were gone now, and it was a good thing, too. It was hard enough to keep an eye on the trails and passes, without them to worry about. When the wine was in them, they would shout and raise their fists— their knives if they could. That's why the riders always took their weapons from them as soon as they got there. Not that some didn't sneak in blades and try to use them. Well, babies had to be made.

A blast of air made Leokadia's brown wool mantle flap around her legs, revealing faded homespun leggings and the skirt of a knee-length tunic made from the same fabric and colorlessness. She had on heavy leather shoes, their straps crisscrossing her calves. Out of sight, under her cloak, a cuirass of horse hide covered her chest and back and a broad band of the same leather circled her waist. From the girth's right side hung a two-headed iron axe and from the left a long dagger of the same metal. The blade's handle was an elegant curve of bone inscribed with the constellation of Shaushka, the Mare Goddess. A horn bow and a quiver made of stiffened goat pelt, which slung diagonally across the Amazon's back, bobbed up and down with her horse's gait. A close-fitting leather helmet, almost egg shaped, completed the Amazon's apparel, the back of this head piece hanging like a veil over her neck. She sat easily on a sheepskin tied around her mount's belly, a saddle without stirrups that served to protect the rider's backside from the animal's spine and ribs.

Leokadia kept her pony to a slow walk. She had a sharp eye out for stones newly rolled down from the surrounding slopes. It was foolish to risk her horse's hooves (which were unshod). The northwest gale also hindered the Amazon's progress. It pounded on horse and rider with a malign strength that made both of them lower their heads and gather in their shoulders.

As Leokadia guided her horse through its evolutions, her thoughts dwelt on finishing her rounds as quickly as she could and heading back to Themiscyra. At least it was the last leg of the patrol; she would have only to circle the hill on her right before turning home. "And I'll welcome the shelter from this wind," she thought. "It cuts you in two. Oh, for a hearth and hot wine to warm my insides."

She sucked in the frigid air and slowly blew out a cloud of steam, which dissolved to nothing in the wind as she exhaled it. She glanced behind her. Another Amazon, Tecmassa, rode a few paces to the rear. Tecmassa was dressed similarly as

Leokadia, in a rough wool cloak and tunic and a leather helmet. A bow and shafts bounced across her back, and a dagger and labrys were suspended at her side. But the resemblance ended there. Tecmassa's apparel was of different colors and in different states of repair. And Tecmassa's face, the color of dark leather, and her big height and build set her apart from Leokadia, whose bronzed visage and middling frame were those of the city dwellers from these parts.

Tecmassa cupped her hands around her mouth and shouted, "This looks like the last patrol before the snows." As if to prove the point, the airs sliced at the women without mercy. Leokadia looked again at the sky. The clouds had grown heavier. She shouted to her companion, "Once more around the hill, and then we go home."

Tecmassa grinned and waved in reply. Leokadia gathered her mantle around her, hunched over her pony's neck, and touched its side with her heels. The horse turned smartly to the right and scrambled up a nearly invisible path that led to the other side of the hill. Tecmassa continued in the direction that Leokadia had just abandoned.

Leokadia and her pony rounded the hillside when a freezing gust slammed into them. Here, facing the northeast, the brownish green of the juniper bushes gave way to lighter verdance, scrub pine that clung to the steeps. On the ground lay shining dark pellets, goat droppings—fresh ones. So the goatherds had just passed by. They must be making a run for the winter pastures. But why were they still roaming the hills so late in the season? It would be days before they reached the pastures near the sea, and cold going all the way. "Well," muttered Leokadia, "good luck to them." She breathed into her mittens and rubbed her hands together.

The rider heard nothing except the wind whipping around the slope and pebbles clattering under her horse's hooves. But once, when the air died, a strange noise, like a small spirit's moaning, seemed to come from above and to the right. "A crazy turn of the wind," thought Leokadia, and she did not stop to listen. The air became agitated again, and, when it subsided, the wailing came to her once more. "What's this?" she thought. "I'd swear it's like a baby crying." She halted her mount, but the sound had disappeared in the renewed gusts. She stood still and waited. The blast ebbed again, and another thin plaint sounded. "Is the Storm God playing tricks on me?" she wondered.

She did not budge. The wind howled anew and drowned out the unaccustomed noise. When the air abated, the sound reached Leokadia another time.

No. There was no mistaking that. It was no joke.

The rider urged her pony to the right. The animal left the trail. Leokadia reined in her mount and cocked her ears. When at last she was sure where the sound came from, she nudged her horse forward to the base of an exposed steep. She dismounted and scrambled up on all fours. At its summit, on the ground near its single bush, squirmed a wee, squalling baby wrapped in filthy rags.

Leokadia unfastened her cloak and took it from her shoulders. She picked up the babe and wrapped the fabric around it. The creature bawled less frantically. The Amazon held the baby to her belly and, sitting on the ground, twisted her way down the slope to where her pony stood. She did not try to clamber onto the stirrupless horse, for she would need two hands to do that and was holding the baby. Instead, in one hand Leokadia took up the reins, which were hanging on the ground, and with the other she kept the infant close to her. She headed into the wind toward the spot where Tecmassa was bound to appear once her own tour of the opposite hillside was accomplished.

The infant yelled louder. Leokadia marveled at the noise the tiny creature could give off. The thing was so small. It must have been just born. Left by the goatherds, no need to bet on that.

Leokadia often saw them when she was on patrol. They had wandered in the hills since the beginning of time, from when Arinna made the world. They fled the cities and their ways. They moved around all the time with their livestock in search of mountain pastures. They heeded only their own gods and their elders. And they left the newborn babes they did not want to the beasts and the weather. Leokadia always rode past these folk when they came into sight. It was what she had been told to do, what the riders always did. Else the goatherds would fade into the hills before a woman could look again. But they stole nothing and harmed no one. Not like the Kaska folk and the men of Amisos.

Leokadia reached the point where she usually met Tecmassa. Leokadia looked at the sky and smelled the air. The snow would fall any time now. She stamped her feet with the cold—her mantle covered the infant's bones and not her own; she growled in impatience—Tecmassa had not yet ridden into sight.

It was not long before Tecmassa rounded the curve. As soon as she spotted her friend, Tecmassa urged her horse into a run and hastily covered the ground separating them.

"What's this? What's this?" she asked, reining up.

"A baby. I found it on the hillside. The goatherds must have left it. And not very long ago. Did you see them?"

"I saw some droppings."

"I did, too. Likely they had to wait until the babe was born. And then they left it. Judging by its cries it's not weak or sick. It must be a girl, then. Here." Leokadia handed the screaming bundle to her friend and walked to the right side of her mount. She bit off her mittens and, holding them in her teeth, grabbed the animal's mane and withers. She bent her knees, sprang up, and straightened her arms to hoist herself over her horse's back. When she had settled on the sheepskin and tucked her hands back into their covering, she took the baby from Tecmassa. Leokadia clutched it to her belly with her right forearm and fist. Her left hand held the reins. She turned her pony homeward and dug her heels into its ribs.

The Storm God shrieked after her.

Sheltered from the same wind by the summit of Themiscyra's hill lay the walled precincts that belonged to Hebatê the goddess of the land. Her temple stood at their highest point, and, below it, Her granary, barns, and sheds, as well as the limestone palace wherein dwelt the twenty-eight keepers of Her worship and the scores of women who oversaw Her household. The palace was a rectangular building measuring sixty paces by forty-five. A square-pillared room with a circular hearth at its center took up much of the building's ground floor. Warrenlike corridors that followed the palace's outside walls connected its front entrance and vestibule to the rear of the building, leading past the high priestess's private apartments, the chambers where the servants of the Goddess lived, and the storerooms that held the temple's wool and metal to sell when the weather was fair and the merchants set up camp.

A large kitchen, which had its own entrance, occupied the rear of the edifice. Under the cookroom lay a cellar, which was half as spacious as the ground floor and served as a storage place. It was here that the high priestess, Myrtho, was seeing to her tasks for this time of the year, inspecting the food, drink, fuel, and cloth that had been laid aside for the months to come, when the Storm God covered the earth with snow and lashed at it with icy wind, so that the women had to stay close to their fires and live off what they had put aside during the months that the Goddess walked free in the fields and forests.

Myrtho, who held an oil lamp in front of her, was slowly advancing through the sacks, baskets, gourds, kegs, and huge clay jars that cluttered the earthen floor or rested on pallets. She was a woman of more than middling height whose straight bearing made her seem taller than she was. At twenty-three, she was slim and easy in her movements. The folds of her long blue robe undulating around her haunches accentuated her graceful walk and dignified stature. Auburn hair that now and again glinted wild red in the uncertain rays of the lamp flowed over her shoulders, and her large blue-gray eyes set off a wide brow. Intelligent suspicion had drawn Myrtho's lips tight. It often did. Still, her eyes gave the lie to this skepticism, for, despite their cinereous color, they glowed with curiosity and goodwill. She was making her way through the stores under the guidance of the temple steward, Philippis, a short-legged, vast-framed woman, who grasped a reed stylus in her right hand and a flat tablet of moist clay in her left. Each time that Myrtho, having scrutinized a bag, bushel, or container, saw fit to dictate some observation, Philippis scratched oblique lines on the piece of clay.

The priestess and intendant were standing next to a tall jar of emmer wheat when they heard someone pound at the outside entrance of the kitchen. The floor above vibrated with light steps and the door groaned open. A voice talked in urgent tones, a baby cried, the door slammed shut. Myrtho raised her eyebrows in a question, Philippis shrugged her shoulders in answer, and the two resumed inspecting the supplies. More footsteps above their heads; Merope, a kitchen girl, poked her head through the door at the top of the stairs.

"Please ma' am," she said to Philippis, "can you come up? A rider just brought a baby in from the cold."

"Do go and see," said Myrtho in a lilting intonation unlike that of the women of Themiscyra.

The big-girthed woman placed her scribe's materials at the foot of a sack, gathered her skirts, and flitted upstairs with a light tread that always astounded Myrtho.

Philippis' voice and an unknown one exchanged brief sentences. The baby screamed again and set to crying. More low utterances. The priestess decided to see for herself. But first she tiptoed to a recess of the cellar, knelt, and pulled a straw mat over an area of floor that could not be seen from the stairs. She returned to the flight of steps and climbed to the kitchen.

A rider to whose face Myrtho could attach no name stood near the hearth. The Amazon's complexion was drained under her tan. Her dark eyes glowed with worry, but her lips were set in calm patience. She shivered, for she had on only her rider's tunic, whose faded wool and frayed hem meant that she was poor and, certainly, chilled to the bone. Wet dark spots—they must be melted snow—covered her headpiece and shoulders. Her hands, enclosed in rough wool mittens, clutched a babe to her chest. The babe was wrapped in the mantle that the rider should have been wearing.

The infant screamed. Judging by the noise it made, it still had plenty of life in it. Myrtho approached and took it in her arms. Its white face was beginning to glow pink. It shrieked again and started to thrash and squall.

Philippis interrogated Myrtho with her eyes.

"A wet nurse? Fetch Eriboea," answered Myrtho.

Philippis snatched a cloak, draped it around her, and hurried out.

During this time, the Amazon had plucked off her mittens and headpiece, edged closer to the fireplace, and began waving her arms and stamping her feet.

Myrtho found a cloth remnant and dipped it into a jar of goat's milk that lay on a table not far from the outside wall. She put the piece of fabric into the baby's mouth. The creature stopped crying and sucked. The rider, having repeated her gymnastics several times, folded in on her haunches and eyed the scene around her.

"Where?" asked Myrtho.

"About an hour's slow ride into the northeast passes," answered the rider. "Some goatherds passed there today."

"They abandoned it?"

"Yes."

Myrtho carried the infant to the table nearest the hearth and unwrapped the rags in which it had been swathed. It wailed with leather lungs.

"It's a girl child," Myrtho announced. "And it's sound of limb." Of course, it was always like that. When they exposed a healthy newborn, it was always a girl.

But the Storm God had been deceived and His prey snatched from Him. That was a triumph of the Goddess and a stroke of good luck for the rider. Myrtho again looked at the Amazon, who blinked her eyes and raised her brows like someone awakened from a dream that she had trouble recalling. Still, her lips suggested a smile.

Philippis soon ushered in the woman whom she had been sent to find: Eriboea—short, big-boned, with deep black eyes and immense, cracked hands. She was a peasant who worked land belonging to the Goddess. She said nothing as she removed her cloak and picked up the baby. She opened the front of her frayed garment, cupped her full breast in her hand, and nudged the baby's mouth to her nipple. The infant's mouth found it. The child sucked, gurgled with contentment, and sucked again. Eriboea's eyes grew warm. The Amazon stared with pleasure at the babe's greedy lips and with envy at Eriboea's white bosom and brown teat.

Philippis' gaze questioned Myrtho, and Myrtho whispered an answer. Philippis took the oil lamp that Myrtho had lately carried and stepped into the cellar. In a few minutes she came back bearing a length of wool and a bulging sack. Once the baby finished her frantic sucking, Philippis gave the fabric to Myrtho, who took the infant, wrapped her in the new warmth, and handed the newborn back to the peasant. Philippis tendered the bag to Eriboea and Myrtho addressed her. "The sack contains three measures of lentils. It is for you, as is the cloth. Take care of the new girl child. The Goddess must want her to escape the storms."

Leokadia stood up. "Begging your pardon, ma' am," she said. "It was I who found the newborn. So I get to pay for her food and shelter. I can . . ."

Myrtho made sure not to glance at Leokadia's worn garment as she lay her index finger over her mouth. The rider pursed her lips to protest, but Myrtho's expression silenced her. Myrtho turned once more to the peasant and said, "The Goddess must wish you well, for She has brought you this good fortune."

The hint of a smile played across Eriboea's walnut brown lips. She turned to go out but, remembering something, stopped and looked back. "What's the child to be called?" she asked.

Myrtho's glance interrogated the rider. The girl was the Amazon's to name. But the rider said nothing despite her objections of a moment before; puzzlement contracted her face.

Myrtho asked, "To whom among the women who no longer walk the earth do you want to give a second life?"

This time the rider answered without hesitation, "Penthesilea."

"Penthesilea?" repeated the priestess.

"Yes."

The peasant departed. Myrtho conducted the Amazon to her own sitting room.

A glowing brazier warmed it; a flagon, two cups, and a pile of barley cakes waited on a low table near the warmth. Two armchairs were drawn close to it. The priestess seated herself in one and bade the rider take her place in the other. Myrtho poured a goblet of wine for the Amazon and handed her a cake.

The woman nodded in gratitude, ripped off a huge piece, and gobbled it up. She dipped her finger in the drink and flicked a drop of it on the table in honor of the Goddess. The libation over, she gulped down half the vessel's contents without taking a breath. Then, still not talking, she bit and chewed, sipped and swallowed until there was nothing left.

Myrtho, who had been waiting for the hunger and thirst to leave her guest, now asked, "What is your name?"

"Leokadia."

"I have not seen you before."

"I'm not much in town. I patrol the northeast when the weather's fair. That's where we found the girl child."

"We?"

"My partner, Tecmassa, and I. She's the rider with skin as dark as leather."

Myrtho nodded in recognition. "But it was you yourself who discovered the girl child?" she asked.

"Yes. And not a bit too soon, I tell you. The snow was closing in right then. But the Storm God didn't get her, no He didn't. The Goddess didn't let that happen." Leokadia grew silent and tilted her head as though she were hearing her words for the
first time. She looked at her hands. Their fingers began to drum on her thighs.

"The Goddess has smiled on you," said Myrtho.

Leokadia stared back, astounded.

"She has. She has caused you to steal a girl child back from the Storm God. It is a sign of great favor."

Leokadia opened her mouth to say something but changed her mind and snapped it shut. She shook her head in disbelief. Myrtho searched Leokadia's face. "What makes you believe otherwise? What makes you believe that Hebatê does not look kindly upon you?"

Leokadia said nothing. She closed her eyes and wrinkled her brow. Then she answered.

"Seven years ago . . . don't you know the story about seven years ago?"

Seven years before. "Few knew me then," Myrtho said. "I had just arrived here from my native city of Apasas, whence I had fled." She shuddered.

Leokadia gazed at her with renewed interest.

"But go on," urged the priestess. "Go on."

"Seven summers ago, they sent me down to the tents. But I had no child of it. It was the same thing the following year, too. I had no child of it. The Goddess did not want there to be a rider to take my place. Every day I made sacrifice to the Goddess. I gave Her everything I possessed. That's what the high priestess then told me to do."

Of course, thought Myrtho, of course. That is how Anactoria seized so much wealth.

Leokadia continued. "Still, no new Amazon came of it. Hebatê did not smile on me. I was not pleasing to Her. I do not know why." Leokadia turned her head down.

"Did you not purchase a girl child from the itinerant merchants?" asked Myrtho.

Leokadia hesitated and then said, "I was never in town. And I . . . the Goddess did not want it."

Could it be that she was too poor? That she had given whatever she possessed to the Goddess and was not able to buy the girl her womb could not conceive?

Myrtho poured Leokadia another goblet of wine. Leokadia, who did not raise her face, took the cup and drank slowly. Then she turned it around in her hands and stared at it. Her knuckles were cracked and tanned.

At length, she said, "I was sent to the tents as a reward."

"A reward?"

"They wanted a daughter from me as brave as they said I was. Hebatê did not." Leokadia looked around to see if someone might be listening. She leaned forward: "It was after the three barrels of gold powder were found."

The priestess glanced at her sharply. The existence of the barrels was a great secret. Except for the Amazons who had captured them (all of whom were now dead, Myrtho had supposed), only the ruler of the city and the high priestess knew of their presence in Themiscyra.

The three casks of precious powder now lay hidden underneath the kitchen storeroom, in the vestibule of a tunnel leading to the other face of Themiscyra's hill. A wooden hatch separated the cellar floor from the treasure room. It was this trapdoor that Myrtho had stooped to cover one hour before.

Myrtho raised her eyebrows in curiosity.

"Seven springs ago," said Leokadia, "I was on the patrol that found the barrels. Four of us were together that day— Penthesilea, Alcippe, and Tanaïs me, of course. We were riding near the base of a hill away from the trail, in lands belonging to the Goddess, near that boulder that Texobos split throwing the lightning bolt at Shaushka. There was a cave. Some branches had been broken off from near the mouth, so we went inside to look. It was strange. No birds or animals lived there except some bats. Something had frightened them away. People must have done that. Even so, we weren't really sure because there was no trace of fire. But all the way in the back, we found barrels. They were very heavy. We opened one. It had powder in it, and we took a handful to where there was enough light. It was gold dust. Bandits working the Trojan road used the cave. That's where they hid what they stole.

While we were making sledges to bring the barrels to Themiscyra, an arrow struck the ground near Alcippe. We took cover. The robbers had come back. They must have been watching us for a while. Before we had a chance to shoot, they came for us, six of them. We fought. We fought. We got two of them. One struck me to the ground and was about to knife me, but Penthesilea threw her labrys. Right after she did, another one came on her from behind. I shouted at her to watch out. But I was too weak, and Penthesilea didn't hear me. She fell. I tried to get up, but everything went black on me. My friends put me on a sledge and dragged me back to Themiscyra. They told me I had the fever and screamed all the way. I don't remember any of it."

Myrtho looked hard at Leokadia. Her courage in the fray must have been immense. Had she not spoken of a recompense?

Had not the chief of the riders, the young Orythia, wanted to produce a daughter of equal bravery? Leokadia's reticence was unusual. Most riders would have taken advantage of the opportunity to boast of their prowess. Did this silence come from her strange fantasy of heaven-sent disgrace?

"Penthesilea was my companion." Leokadia's voice trembled. "We rode together ever since we were girls. Ever since we were initiated. I always wanted to name. . . ." Leokadia threw her hands over her face. When she dropped them, her eyes shone with tears. "No one except me is left of the four who found the gold. The Kaska men got Alcippe, and Tanaïs died two springs ago. The fever took her."

Myrtho scrutinized Leokadia anew. She was a sinewy woman with black hair, almost blue. Her locks were twisted into a braid that hung in front of her left shoulder, Amazon-style. A single white streak growing out of her left temple twined through the tress like a strong current through a jet-colored bay. A thin strip of flesh, lighter than the bronze of the rest of her face, extended from her left temple to the corner of her mouth. Was that where she had been wounded? Her lips were brown and wrinkled and drawn in a firm line. But it was her eyes that most impressed Myrtho. They were small, set deep, and their blackness glowed out at you. They never evaded yours, never, but looked out with sturdy courage. The crow's-feet at their corners told not only of a hard outdoor life, but of uncomplicated goodness.

Myrtho realized that she was looking at Leokadia with pleasure and closed her eyes. When she opened them she saw Leokadia staring back, concentrating on her face so intensely that Myrtho asked, "What is it?"

"It's strange. I've never seen gray eyes before. And your skin is pale. And that little line across your neck, what is it?"

Myrtho did not reply. The silence folded in. She hugged her thoughts close to her. Leokadia's face broke into a childlike grin, and Myrtho laughed.

"So you see," she said, "the Goddess does not hate you. But many times Her ways are unpredictable." Myrtho smiled to herself and then at the Amazon.

Eriboea ducked into the snow. It was falling hard. She was happy to take the newborn. Her breasts ached. She had lost a six-month-old girl child three days before. Young ones died as often as they lived, and the one before that was a boy, so she had to let them snatch him from her once he was weaned. She glanced back in the direction of the temple, her lips and brow set stubbornly, anger glowing in the depths of her dark eyes. Still, if this one held on, the priestess and the rider who found it would take good care of her. She felt the weight of the sack on her shoulder and the roughness of the wool in her hand. And it was great good luck for a woman to suckle a baby rescued from the Storm God. It would help the harvest. That's what the farmers here said. And the crops had been good. She had not gone hungry even once since she had run away to the women's city.

So maybe it was better that she had. Else they'd have made her marry her dead man's older brother, because that was the King's law they told her—once her own husband was in the ground, she had to take her pots and jugs to the brother's house and lie in his bed. She recoiled. The brother had beaten his first wife from the day that her father led her to him and, when the newborn came out from between her legs, left it on the mountain that night because it was girl, and the wolves got it. So maybe it was better that Eriboea had come here. But—the picture of her smiling baby boy rushed up in front of her eyes— maybe it was bad. Sharp claws dug into her chest and stomach.

Eriboea neared a squat dwelling of sun-dried brick that stood in the shelter of the wall amidst a jumble of similar habitations linked by narrow alleyways and cramped passages. She pushed aside the curtained door and stepped over the threshold. Her cousin, Molpadia, a dark, thick-armed woman, was leaning over a black cauldron set on the stone hearth in the middle of the room. She saw what Eriboea carried in and smiled. It could only be a rider's baby. That meant good treatment. Molpadia's five-year-old daughter jabbed her thumb in her mouth.

Penthesilea was to spend her first seven years with Eriboea, who carried the baby on her back to the fields until the girl could walk there on her own and who, as soon as the child was fit to work, put her to scattering seeds, pulling up weeds, and feeding the goat that Leokadia gave Eriboea, for there were no idle hands in Themiscyra, even those of a rider's girl. Eriboea was not quick to strike Penthesilea, either, the way women sometimes were, although she once thrashed her soundly for letting the hearth fire die out. And the warmth of Eriboea's strong arms and of her deep eyes set in her dour face commanded

Penthesilea's love, so that, years later, she always visited the little field where Eriboea lay under the earth to pour honey and tears over her still bones and wonder in whose body her soul had found its new resting place.

During the summer, Leokadia was not much in the city, but, whenever she was, she would leave gifts of beer or wool or even game at the nursemaid's little house and find Eriboea and her daughter in the farmlands. Winters, Leokadia would call regularly and take the child with her for a while. Sometimes she would lead Penthesilea to where she had her quarters, the house of the Noble Ariona, for whom she rode. Other times, she would take her to the temple palace, where she now came and went as if she lived there, for, without her being able to say at what moment and how it had occurred, Myrtho had opened her arms to her, and Leokadia had devoted herself to the priestess with the unquestioning honesty that was her way in all things. And Myrtho, too, watched over the child, occasionally calling at Eriboea's in person but most frequently assigning this task to Philippis, who spoiled the girl with gifts of honey-cakes, and barley candy, and plum tarts, and dried figs.

One late summer day, Leokadia appeared in the fields and asked to take the girl with her. Eriboea lifted the four-year old into the saddle in front of the rider, who wrapped her sturdy forearm around her waist and pressed her against her breathing belly. Leokadia clucked the mount into motion and set off for the terraced rises that faced Themiscyra from the same side of the river. The lass giggled at being so high off the ground, smiled at the friction of the animal's back against her body, and delighted in the feel of Leokadia's arm and stomach. Leokadia kept silent while the pony ambled up the slope, although, once or twice, she squeezed the little girl closer.

They came to the crest of the first elevation. Beyond it, arid steppes rolled southward as far as the eye could see. Leokadia turned the pony around and faced Themiscyra. Downhill, a shimmering ribbon of black and citrine, the swift-flowing river Thermodon separated fields of corn. Burnt yellow ears undulated now and then in the unpredictable breezes from sloping pastures whose brown-tipped grasses shivered fitfully in the same airs. A wooden bridge standing on ash wood piles spanned the waters where they flowed beneath the steep on which Themiscyra had been built. Stone walls that the afternoon sun transmuted to soft beige climbed up the hill and

surrounded the town, except at its highest point, where the
height's abrupt summit of jagged, black stone took over the job
of safeguarding the women. One hundred feet below lay the
temple grounds—their limestone sanctuary and palace blinding
alabaster in the sunlight. Below the sacred precinct, which a
twelve-foot-high stone barrier marked off from the rest of the
city, were the spring, the marketplace, and the ruler Orythia's
palace, a vast rectangle of wood and sandstone. On either side
of these, hundreds of low-built mud-brick houses fanned down
the hill, following the city's tortuous streets to its massive,
beamed gate. Two large dwellings rose amidst the modest ones:
one, a square of wood and brick, was the palace of the noble
Hippolyta, whose wealth and power were almost as great as
Orythia's; the other, an uneven, timbered oblong, was the
house of Ariona, who was far less wealthy and powerful than
Orythia or Hippolyta, but whose vineyards were their envy.

Here and there wisps of smoke snaked up from brushwood
roofs, hung in the air, and then, unaccountably, were swept
away by a breeze that was growing more balky as the day
retreated. In some places the leafy tops of apple and walnut
trees spread dark green smears against the burnt umber and dun
brown of the city.

The azure sky behind Themiscyra's summit vibrated and
grew darker. The wind picked up suddenly and brought the onlookers the sound of waters gurgling and hissing, plants rustling
and shaking, and, once, of a woman wailing out a doleful tune.
Leokadia kissed the crown of her daughter's head and pressed
her tight against her. The child rubbed her head in her breasts
and grinned at her over her shoulder. Leokadia beamed at the
girl before urging her mount back toward the fields.

Chapter 2

Leokadia stood at the door of Eriboea's house hugging a cloth packet to her chest. Her seven-year-old daughter strode into sight, intent on tossing a clay cone into the air so that it landed with its apex in the palm of her outstretched hand, which she shifted from left to right to prevent the toy from toppling. As soon as she noticed her mother, she pocketed the plaything and loped up to her.

"Here it is," said Leokadia, showing the child what she held, the brown tunic that apprentice riders wore. Penthesilea yelped with delight and began to jump up and down. But she remembered her new estate and tried to keep still. She did so for as long as a child of that age is able to. Then her dignity fled from her entirely, and she choked down sobs when she took her leave of Eriboea (who wept without apology).

Leokadia led her daughter to the temple, where Myrtho purified her and told her the first secrets of the riders. Then Leokadia took Penthesilea to the house of Ariona, where the girl was admitted to the sleeping-chamber and table shared by the youngest apprentices: Charope, Ariona's daughter; Amynome, whose favorite pastime was juggling anything she could get her hands on, and Klymene, a short child, who was always ready to break her neck scaling high walls and forbidden fences. For the first year, too, until she graduated to the older girls' quarters, the gawky, good-natured Feodissia took part in their bed and board.

The apprentices went about barefoot and uncloaked in all but the fiercest weather. Sometimes they feasted sumptuously, sometimes on bread and water, and sometimes not at all. Sometimes shouting women shook them from deep sleep to pass the night out-of-doors. They were made to run, and climb, and hide, and ambush, and trap until they thought nothing of spending entire weeks on foot or horseback ranging among the rugged hills in search of the others or in flight from them. Ariona herself taught them how to handle the bow and arrow, although later Feodissia took over the job, for she was known even then for her sharpshooting. Leucippe initiated them in the art of riding; rumor had it that this slight, bowlegged woman was descended from the Mare Goddess. The sinewy Andro who, even at forty, could outsmart and outwrestle any Amazon alive, instructed them in hand-to-hand combat. And all the riders gave the young ones lessons in throwing the axe and wielding the long knife. The older apprentices jumped them and laughed at them and vied with them, until no one could easily catch them off balance.

The daughters of the house knew by heart the songs in praise of the fearless rebels who, under the leadership of Marpasia, first delivered the women from the foreigners bent on enslaving them; the girls chanted the deeds of the noble chiefs who followed her—Lampedo, Sinope, Myrinne, Antianeira, and Orythia, who left this world for the glorious West when Penthesilea was five years old.

They danced the pantomime of Hebatê's imprisonment and fight for freedom, and of Shaushka's escape with the secret of taming swift steeds and riding them toward liberty. They fixed in their hearts and minds that the Amazons feared the Goddess and despised bondage. They learned which actions pleased Her the most—to bear a girl child, to rescue one from the Storm God, to free a slave. They knew that the rider who gave her life to keep Her women from thrall would be carried to the West and would feast on sweets and spiced wine. They understood that the woman who spoke the truth and gave to everyone her own was a pleasing sight to the Goddess, who would comfort her in her darkest hour.

At twelve or thirteen, when the young ones could run their horses through treacherous obstacles and over tricky hurdles, when they could hit the bull's-eye with the arrow at twenty paces and with the axe and knife at ten, and after their first moon's blood had flowed down, Myrtho's attendants cleansed them in the sacred bath and shaved their heads. Then the high priestess apprised them of still other mysteries, and they put on tunics of green and black and joined the older girls' table and sleeping quarters. Now, too, they sometimes followed full-grown riders on their duties and, when they were judged ready, were cast out one by one to live in the hills far from everyone's sight from the Day of the Year—the day when the hours of light catch up with the hours of darkness—to the Longest Night. Each girl carried only her tunic, cloak, and one bronze knife into exile.

The apprentices of Ariona's house competed in feats of skill with those raised in the two other noble establishments. Sometimes the older Amazons put the young ones up to it, and other times they improvised their own scrimmages. But whatever the motives for the girls' rivalries, and however furiously they contended with each other, fairness ruled their struggles. Their opponents were, after all, the women with whom they would one day ride and on whose goodwill and sure hands their lives would depend. And, in those days, their encounters had not yet been poisoned by dynastic quarrels.

One such contest pitted the older girls against each other in equitation, wrestling, and archery. After a morning's competition, Feodissia came up against Melanippe in the last round. The latter, a small, nervous, heavy-thighed girl of the same age as Feodissia, was the daughter of Naunamé, the ruler who had succeeded Orythia. Melanippe, whose daredevil riding made many girls envy her, had easily outdistanced Feodissia in that engagement; still, Feodissia bested her in the hand-to-hand that followed. Now the shooting contest would decide the outcome: whoever won it would win the day and the glory. Few thought that Melanippe had a hope of coming out ahead. Feodissia was the surest shot of all the apprentices and perhaps of all the Amazons.

The youngsters who had taken part in the day formed a semicircle around the two remaining contestants. A skinny, rosy-cheeked girl from Hippolyta's house said she would bet any comer that Melanippe would beat Feodissia. She found many takers; no one believed that Feodissia could lose at archery.

Feodissia and Melanippe took the regulation distance from the target, a purse of woven straw no bigger than a woman's hand fixed to the trunk of a walnut tree thirty paces away. The referee handed each player an arrow. Each sighted down the shaft of the missile that had been given her and ran her fingers over the feather. Each in turn nodded her head. The bolts were true. Melanippe planted her feet and squared her torso perpendicularly to the target. She placed the nock of the arrow in the bowstring and drew the bolt back to her chest. Silence fell. She peered down the length of the shaft, hesitated, and loosed it. It hissed as it flew through the air. It impaled the purse, slammed into the tree, and vibrated there together with the target. Melanippe's eyebrows fluttered in triumph. Her friends cheered. The rosy-cheeked girl whistled.

Melanippe's chances of beating Feodissia were not as slim as anyone had imagined.

Feodissia set her lanky frame at right angles to the mark. Before taking aim, she pivoted her lantern-jawed face toward her cohorts and grinned shyly. She turned back to the target. As she did, Melanippe said something to her under her breath. Feodissia's long limbs stiffened imperceptibly. Then she positioned herself, pulled back the bowstring, and centered her vision on the bull's-eye ninety feet away. She let fly. The bolt whizzed past the target and drove into the tree beside it. Her friends groaned. Melanippe's bow lips sketched an arrogant smile and, without looking at her opponent, she sauntered toward those who had wagered on her. The mole above her right lip trembled.

Later that evening Penthesilea asked Feodissia, "What did she say to get you so angry?"

Feodissia, whose big-fisted, huge-footed body measured a head taller than Penthesilea's, confided, "It was something she thought of while we were swimming last time."

"Naked?"

"Yup."

"What?"

"I don't care to repeat it."

Penthesilea lowered her head in thought. She looked up and said, "Why ever would Melanippe do a thing like that?"

"Maybe she can't stand to lose. Maybe she got something out of it. There was betting."

"Why didn't you say something?"

"To the referee? Folks would have thought I was a crybaby or a sore loser. Anyways, I don't care to argue with the daughter of the chief of the riders. One day she'll be ruler herself."

"But Naunamé is as fair as any woman alive."

"What does that have to do with it?" said noble Ariona, who had overheard her apprentices' conversation. She folded her muscled arms over her thin chest and said, "She won't be alive forever." Ariona pronounced these words in the even tone tinged by cynicism that had earned her the name "the dry Ariona," although some said that it came from her having given up strong drink years before.

Ariona's words came true sooner than most women wished. Naunamé ruled for only eight years. During that time, she earned the epithet of "the Just," for, no matter what their station, women seeking fairness found it at her hands. But even before she ascended to her high position, the Amazons respected her for her bravery and tactical skill. She had proven them as a young rider when she improvised and led a sortie against surprise raiders from Amisos that shattered their forces. She had also shown scrupulous evenhandedness in distributing the spoils captured in the action. For these reasons the riders named her chief immediately after her mother, Orythia, went to the West. And they did so without the bad blood that might have poisoned their counsel, for authority over them was elective, although they always picked their principal from the direct lineage of Marpasia, and Naunamé had a younger sister, Thalestris. The riders' choice of Naunamé proved right: while she was dealing equity to all women, Thalestris was drinking with some and dallying with others. Only her courage and prowess redeemed her. Thalestris was a skilled fighter. Brave and daring. Women admired her for it. Her distinguished ancestry helped her reputation, too.

She fought with boiling vigor in the action that cost Naunamé her life, a foray against Kaska raiders who had chosen the longest days of the year to fall on merchants journeying from Themiscyra toward Troy. Not long after Naunamé fell, a throwing spear impaled Thalestris' thigh and she was put out of the fight.

In later years, the puckered scar left by the wound made her limp a little and, if the wine added to the unsureness of her gait, use a walking stick. Thalestris was dragged home on a sledge. She lay raving on her couch for two months after the battle. Many thought she would succumb to her wound. A palace servant, Celano, volunteered to care for her. Celano let no other woman minister to Naunamé's sister, sleeping across the threshold of her chamber and performing all tasks, no matter how noisome, to comfort her. She even prevented Thalestris' fifteen-year-old girl from visiting her for more than a few minutes at a time. Often during the first weeks Thalestris thrashed at the covers and screamed out in her delirium that it wasn't her fault Naunamé had been killed. Celano held Thalestris down, wiped her brow with a cool cloth, and assured her that she had done no wrong.

The summer had long since ended when Thalestris got up from her bed and, leaning on Celano's arm, made her entrance into the great hall of the palace, the huge room in which the chief of the riders called the Amazons together and heard women's complaints and petitions. In Naunamé's day riders, votaries, women of the plow, and women of the tool flocked there day and night. Now only a few members of the palace staff waited for Thalestris. Amazons who rode for her house had not bothered to attend her, although she was Naunamé's sister; and, she, too, was a direct descendant of Marpasia and should be the next ruler. Even the regent who had taken over while she lay shuddering with pain and fever, noble Hippolyta, had not troubled to call and pay her respects. Nor had the eighteen-year-old daughter whom Naunamé had left behind, Melanippe. She had abandoned the palace and taken up residence at Hippolyta's during Thalestris' illness.

At the sight of the near-empty room, rage exploded in the depths of Thalestris' dark eyes, and the blood drained from her narrow face. Celano took her arm, whispered in her ear, and conducted her out. That evening, Thalestris moved into the apartments that Naunamé had once occupied. The next morning, Thalestris called together the household staff and announced that from then on Celano was her steward, in charge of her palace. Everyone was to take orders from her. Then Thalestris sent for Omaïa, the oldest of the riders, and conferred with her for a long while. Their interview over, she summoned Leokadia.

Leokadia left her presence to discover that Myrtho was waiting to visit in turn. Leokadia widened her eyes. Myrtho's face became blank. Leokadia made hers expressionless, too. Myrtho stepped into Thalestris' quarters.

"I'll wait here," said Leokadia to the short, weasel-eyed woman with a brow the color of wax who had shown her out of the chief's rooms.

"Of course, of course," intoned Celano in a nasal monotone. She stretched her skinny fingers toward the long table that occupied the back of the hall. She bowed low and tiptoed back into Thalestris' rooms. Leokadia seated herself, and an attendant appeared and set a flagon and goblet before her.

Leokadia poured, made her libation, and sipped. She put down the cup and slowly turned her head. Her blue-black hair had grizzled over the years, and the white streak that cut through it had widened. Her scout's eyes, into whose corners the crow's-feet had dug deeper, peered around her restlessly. She had seldom visited the great hall.

It measured a full twenty paces by fifteen. A profusion of dried blossoms covered its floor, except at the midpoint, where a large stone hearth full of huge logs gave off waves of warmth. Above the fireplace, two openings cut in the roof gobbled up the smoke and welcomed the daylight. But the windows were so small that only half-shadow bathed the hall on the brightest afternoons, and scores of oil lamps atop bronze stanchions placed along its sides gave off flickering, ochreous twilight and a salty odor that was dulled only by aromatics smoking in censors set everywhere. On the walls, countless swathes of scarlet and night blue fabric alternated with a myriad of iron knives and axes that glimmered canary yellow and lustrous gray, innumerable alabaster-feathered arrows that ended in glinting triangles, and an abundance of leather headpieces and shields buffed so brightly that they trembled and flushed in the wavering lamplight. Stools and benches covered with cloths tinted jonquil yellow and madder orange stood near the walls, as did dozens of chests made of wide, ruddy planks girded by strips of brilliant bronze. One of these coffers gaped open, and the cups and platters that it enclosed pulsated blinding silver as if they possessed a source of light all their own. The long, red oak table at which Leokadia sat stretched from near the room's back partition almost to the hearth; benches of the same timber flanked the board, which could seat fifty women; for banquets, three others of that size were carried out and assembled. Behind stood a beechwood armchair carved with figures of the beasts of the forest. The copper-colored pelts of red deer and the dun-colored skins of mountain goat surrounded the throne's feet, which were modeled in the form of lion's paws.

A few yards in back of the throne, an inner wall pierced by a curtained entranceway separated the hall from the chief's apartments and those of her family and from the narrow steps that led downstairs, for half of the great hall's floor formed half of the ceiling of a vast, irregular lower story that spilled farther down Themiscyra's hill. The living quarters of the chief's fourscore riders and numerous household retinue were found on this level of the palace, in addition to its kitchen, storerooms, and stables. Clustered around these, as well as stationed near the walls of the city, were the mud-brick huts and shops of the hundreds of peasants and artisans attached to the household, for the fruits of many fields and hillsides belonged to Themiscyra's chief.

Celano pulled aside the curtain and, bending almost to the floor, held it open for Myrtho to pass. Leokadia left with her.

A glowing brazier awaited them in Myrtho's private chamber. She neared the warmth, opened her cloak, and let fall her cowl. Time had rounded her frame and tamed her tresses to dark rust streaked with lifeless gray. A triangle of fine wrinkles fanned out around her eyes.

She sank into an armchair. Leokadia lowered herself into the one facing it and drummed her fingers on its arm.

"Thalestris is neglecting no possibility," said Myrtho, "to ensure that she has enough Amazons in her favor to elect her chief instead of her sister's daughter, Melanippe. That is why Thalestris convoked us, and separately, I suppose, so that we could not consult beforehand. She has already conferred with the dean of the Amazons, Omaïa. That is the intelligence that Philippis imparted as I left for the palace."

"Omaïa? Now there's someone we listen to hard in Amazon counsels. She's been around longer than anyone else, and she speaks good sense. I wonder what Thalestris told her to convince her to speak up for her."

"And what she offered her," said Myrtho.

"But even if Omaïa backs her, Thalestris still can't count on many women to do the same. The riders who were loyal to Naunamé have little to tie them to her, and many don't think much of her wine-soaked ways. The women who ride for Hippolyta will be against her. Only those of us who ride for Ariona have no choice but to back her. But our number isn't big enough to carry the day."

"But that," said Myrtho, "is Thalestris' goal—to sway a sufficient number of riders from her sister's house to choose her instead of her sister's daughter. And from what I have seen— conferring with Omaïa and then summoning us—she is doing everything in her power to achieve her ambition. She believes that I have influence with many Amazons."

"She's right," said Leokadia. She stared hard at Myrtho. "And what's she offered you?"

"To intercede with the Goddess and beg Her to pronounce in favor of Thalestris' aspirations? Something that She has coveted since the beginning. A field adjacent to the heath; it will round out our croplands."

"It's not Thalestris' to give away. It belongs to the chief of the riders, and we haven't named anyone to take Naunamé's place."

"Not yet," said Myrtho. "But if you Amazons choose Thalestris to ride at the front of your column, the land will be in her gift. She has also assured me that her generosity will surpass that of her late sister, if she is the one to make the offering for the Longest Night."

"That duty is the chief's, too. We Amazons have to name her first."

"Yes. That is why Thalestris makes these offers."

"It's easy to promise things you don't have," said Leokadia.

"That may be. But what the Goddess says is of great import to many riders."

"You mean what *you* say She says. Don't say anything."

"I cannot do that. I cannot easily refuse the presents that Thalestris has promised. They will greatly augment the Goddess' wealth."

"That doesn't mean you can't turn them down."

"Should I refuse them, Thalestris would make sure that word of this reached the other votaries. Their anger would be immense. My authority over them would be diminished."

"Only if Thalestris is named chief," said Leokadia. "And if you don't help, she might not be. Many riders don't think much of her."

"Pray look at the other choice."

"Melanippe?"

"Yes, Melanippe," said Myrtho. "I am obliged to do all in my power to prevent her ascension. I do not have a high regard for her character."

"That's what Penthesilea says, too."

"And Melanippe is Hippolyta's protégée. As ruler, Melanippe would be Hippolyta's close ally. I do not need yet a second enemy among the great nobles."

Leokadia nodded in agreement. Five years before, Hippolyta's winemaker had complained that Ariona's was working a hillside that didn't belong to her but to Hippolyta's woman. Hippolyta took the grievance to Naunamé. Ariona protested. Naunamé asked Myrtho for a record of this land tenure, for the keepers of the temple always wrote down such arrangements. From Hippolyta Myrtho understood that not producing the archive, or changing what it contained, would greatly benefit her. But Myrtho read the original deed to Naunamé, who decided against Hippolyta and for Ariona, even though Hippolyta was the most powerful woman in Themiscyra after herself (sixty Amazons rode for Hippolyta and the benefits of many fields were hers) and Ariona counted only forty riders in her following, a few fields, and some wine-growing hillsides. Hippolyta blamed Myrtho for her defeat and swore that she had secretly plotted with Ariona to ruin her. Hippolyta added this reproach to a family grudge against the high priestess, who had been named to her eminent post instead of their kinswoman Herminia. Now Hippolyta would do anything she could to confound Myrtho.

"And if I withhold my efforts on behalf of Thalestris," continued Myrtho, "and she is named ruler nonetheless, she will intrigue against me and the temple. It would be imprudent to call down her enmity when I must constantly parry Hippolyta's."

Leokadia pressed the tips of her fingers together.

A silver spark glinted in Myrtho's eyes. "But pray, my love, what did Thalestris offer you to influence me? Something that you, too, cannot rebuff?"

"Maybe so, maybe not," allowed Leokadia. "Thalestris wants Penthesilea to finish her apprenticeship in her house. She's the same age as her daughter, Antiope."

"The rewards for Penthesilea will be great, if Thalestris ascends the throne. That house is rich: it has much treasure and many lands. And as chief, Thalestris would be entitled to one part in four of all the booty the Amazons captured when they rode out to defend the territory. She would have much wealth to distribute to her followers. And Antiope herself might be chief of the riders one day. Then your daughter could be her right-hand woman. There is prestige and recompense to be gained from that." A thought drew Myrtho's lips tight. "This offer would also provide a pretext for Thalestris to compensate Ariona richly for depriving her of a rider. In that, too, I am certain, Thalestris will be generous in the same way that she has been with us."

"You mean offering something we'll only get if she's chosen?" asked Leokadia.

"Precisely."

"Penthesilea's just an excuse to get your help," declared Leokadia. "And once she's in the palace, she'd be a hostage to make sure you kept in line."

"Especially since, one day, Thalestris' daughter and Naunamé's will compete for the throne."

"I'm going to say no," affirmed Leokadia.

"Say no? But you cannot decline Thalestris' offer anymore than I can."

"I will."

"If you do, troubles will assail you whichever way you turn."

"What?"

"Your demurral would be an affront to Thalestris: it would signify that you do not think she is a good enough Amazon to supervise Penthesilea's apprenticeship as a rider."

"That's not why I'd do it," asserted Leokadia.

"That would be of little import. Such a decision would shame her in other riders' eyes. She would never pardon the injury to her reputation. And if by some chance she were named chief without our assistance, she would avenge herself for your aversion."

"How could she? Anyway, I don't ride for Thalestris. I take my quarters at Ariona's and share my booty with her. So will Penthesilea."

"But your refusal would also set Ariona against you. For once she learned of it, she would attribute your disinclination to a hidden alliance with Hippolyta."

"Bah!" said Leokadia. "She knows me better."

"What other motive could she think that you had for turning down such an honor for your girl, save that you knew of a better one? What other motive could you have for frustrating her of what would doubtless be a rich recompense? She would conclude that you were secretly in favor of Melanippe's ascension, which would put her at the mercy of Hippolyta. You do not imagine that we have seen the last of Hippolyta's attempts to encroach on Ariona's land?"

"The women I ride with know that I don't like Hippolyta."

"One must never be sure of public approval, much less understanding. Riders would impute your reluctance to pride. Thalestris would make sure of that. They would think that you had declined the honor, because you thought that Thalestris had not promised you enough, you, the dear friend of the high priestess. They would whisper that you had grown overweening because you come and go in my house as in your own, although you are a rider of no great lineage and no wealth. Have you yourself not told me that many are jealous of you? Is that not what Tecmassa has said to you more than once?"

"Damn Thalestris!" exclaimed Leokadia. "I don't like being ambushed!"

"Does anyone?"

"She never had a grain of shrewdness before. She rode the fastest horses, yes. She led the attack, yes. But keen wits, no. No one ever thought that about her. Some of us even swore that the wine had dulled them."

"The astuteness is probably not her own."

Leokadia's eyes questioned Myrtho's.

Myrtho answered, "The domestic who cared for her while she was ill is doubtless behind these machinations. Her name is Celano. She saw you out of Thalestris' presence. She was in attendance when I met with her and listened to every word. Thalestris has named her steward of her lands and palace. Many will fear and obey her."

"Only if we riders choose Thalestris."

"Precisely."

Leokadia sank back in her chair. "And what am I to say tomy girl, Penthesilea?"

"The truth. One cannot allow her to enter that house without warning her."

"I don't like this one bit, Myrtho, not one bit. And Penthesilea has a way of telling the truth that will get her in trouble."

Chapter 3

The gatekeeper, a stocky woman with short gray hair and lifeless eyes, rubbed them and heaved open the massive portal. The fifteen-year-old Penthesilea thanked her and rode into the darkness. She reached Thermodon and guided her mount onto the path that followed its curve downstream. On her left, columns of steam rose from the grumbling river and pressed against the slate of the sky. Far to her right, feeble light outlined the somber iron hills. It spread and brightened as she rode on. A flat cloud materialized, its top canary yellow, its underside deep gray, and stretched over the tallest crest. In back of it, fragile pink began to color the heavens; pale blue vivified the firmament behind the dawn hills; burning orange traced the contours of the summits. Vapor rose in front of them, turning the hill's flanks into smoky masses. To the west, the leaden night was fast retreating before less heartless indigo, and, although the southwest elevations were still veiled and uncertain, they, too, began to sketch their shapes against the new sky.

The track that Penthesilea was riding down met one that cut eastward and uphill through the pastures. She took it. She faced the new day. The firmament above the heights shone brilliant ivory that hinted at delicate purple. She glanced behind her. Smoke from the river twisted up to heavens that were only a little darker than daylight. She looked ahead. The mist blanketing the wooded eastern heights had thinned in the space of a heartbeat and spread down from the summit like a diaphanous throw. Streaks of hyacinth pushed out from behind the hilltop; a finger of alabaster reached upward; a blinding, uncertainly contoured disk rose from behind the slope; the ether embracing the peak stunned Penthesilea with its whiteness.

Dawn. The contest would begin.

Penthesilea and her new comrade, Antiope, Thalestris' daughter, were playing an old amazon game, pursuit and evasion on horseback. It was a good sport for those whose strength lay in slipping past their enemies' surveillance and setting traps for them. The apprentices had drawn lots to de-

termine who would chase and who flee. Antiope was the
stalker, Penthesilea the quarry. Penthesilea had started at
first light. Now, at sunrise, Antiope would ride out. She would
do everything she could to track Penthesilea down and
Penthesilea would exercise all her skill to elude her. If
Antiope laid eyes on Penthesilea before sunset, she would win
the contest; if day's end came without Penthesilea's being
spotted, the match was hers.

Penthesilea had set her mind on taking cover in the forest
on the side of one of the iron hills. There were many paths
through the slopes and many thickets in which to hide.
Antiope would have to figure out which height Penthesilea
had chosen and then which track. The main thing was to keep
from her sight while making for cover. To get to the hills,
Penthesilea had to cross an expanse of treeless land. That was
risky. She might not get to the iron hills without being
observed. But she knew an out-of-the-way path that would
shorten her route.

Her chest tightened in anticipation. Tala, the mare that
Leokadia had given her just weeks before, sensed her mood.
The horse's nostrils dilated; she whinnied and shook her head.
Penthesilea loosened the reins and leaned forward. Tala began
to lope diagonally toward a slight incline. Penthesilea kept
her to an easy run. There was no use tiring her out so early in
the day. She would need every bit of endurance she had to
keep out of the way of the magnificent black stallion that
Antiope rode, Melanthus, the chief's present to her girl.

Penthesilea neared the little hill, veered off the trail, and
guided Tala up. A bleat sounded from the other side of the rise.
Then another. Then three flat claps of wooden bells. Tala
crested the slope. A putrid smell tightened Penthesilea's
throat. The flock of goats ambled toward her. The billy—his
unkempt gray coat balding in spots—flattened his ears,
lowered his horns, and bleated a warning. Tala snorted back at
him. The livestock footed forward under the urging of two
women whose faces and stature were those of the goatherds
who roamed the hills. Penthesilea's build and countenance
were similar: an elongated head, straight, raven hair, coal
black eyes in the shape of huge almonds, a nose almost turned
down on itself, pouting lips, square shoulders, and a wiry trunk
and legs.

The herders waved and wished Penthesilea a good day.
She gesticulated back. Once she had passed them, her face

sank. She had not foreseen their presence here at dawn, although she might easily have guessed that they would take their beasts down to drink at first light. That was stupid of her. Antiope, who had doubtless asked the gatekeeper which direction Penthesilea had taken, would surely come this way and just as surely ask the women if they had seen another rider. They would show Antiope where Penthesilea had been headed. Penthesilea berated herself, even as she worked out a new plan of action.

The goatherds disappeared behind the hillock that Penthesilea had just ascended, and she reined Tala in the direction opposite the one that they had observed her following. Now, when Antiope inquired where she was headed, they would show her the wrong place. Still, Penthesilea was forced to approach the iron hills obliquely and so cover twice as much distance to reach her hiding place than she had first calculated. She hoped her feint worked. If it did not, she would have lost the time that she needed to get safely into hiding.

After an hour, she reached a stand of alder that grew at the foot of the heights. In the center of the copse stood a tiny altar devoted to the spirits of these trees, who had blessed the women with wood that burned as hot as the sun in the flames and grew as hard as the iron in the water. She halted Tala and dismounted at the edge of a rivulet that ran down from the heights. She swung herself up into an alder and settled on a branch from where she had a clear view of the pasture she had just crossed. A brilliant white cloud stretched like a blanket from mountaintop to mountaintop. She shaded her eyes and made out a faraway blotch, a horse and rider, emerging from behind a rise. The form was crossing Penthesilea's view from right to left. It stopped moving. After a pause it headed straight toward Penthesilea.

She jumped down, her knees bending like springs to absorb the weight of her fall. She hastened to the mare, untied her, and, grabbing her mane and withers, vaulted up and pulled herself over her back. Tala gathered her legs under her to run, but Penthesilea held in the horse's head and whispered soothing words. She needed time to think.

A trail free of obstacles that started an arrow's shot away led to a cluster of black pine halfway up the hillside. Penthesilea could hasten to the protection of the evergreens and then, instead of continuing that way, as Antiope might expect, slip downhill and backtrack over the pasture land. She would then have a straight run across the bridge and over the trail that led to the hills bordering the other side of the valley. She would have no trouble finding a cave to hide in on the far slope. But what if Antiope once more guessed right? What if she foresaw that Penthesilea would make for the opposite bank of the river? Antiope could easily overtake her on the run. Tala was smart and surefooted, but Melanthus was full of fire and ran like the wind.

There was too much risk in that. But nearby lay a goatherds track that snaked past the hill the city sat on and eventually joined the northeast trail. It would be slow going, because Penthesilea would have to pick her way painfully along so as not to risk her horse's hooves. Still, if Penthesilea got a good start before Antiope figured out where she was headed, she would win back the time that she had wasted because she had not foreseen running into herders. She cursed herself again.

To deceive Antiope, she first sought the start of the easier trail and guided Tala along it for several hundred yards, making sure to steer the mare over the path's softest earth so that her hoofprints would be plain to see. Then Penthesilea dismounted and led the mare back through woods and bushes to the alders. She reached them with no time to spare: when the wind died for a brief instant, she heard muffled hoofbeats near the alder. She sprang onto Tala's back and steered her toward the goat track.

It was tricky work once she got there. She led Tala forward with tireless attention. The narrow way twisted back and forth; bushes growing out of the rocks grabbed at her; stones seemed to be strewn in the path to trip whoever was foolhardy enough to come here and to destroy the hooves of horses or donkeys. The wind blew harder and colder; rain clouds closed in. Then chill drops pelted Penthesilea. Though the storm passed quickly, the rocks were now slippery, and the path more treacherous than before. For the last miles, the track consisted of the bed of a tiny stream. Icy water dripped from Tala's pasterns; cold numbed Penthesilea's feet. But she dared not rush: one false step, one inadvertent fall, and Tala's hooves might be injured forever.

Their slow progress took them to the northeast trail. The glare behind the clouds meant that it was noon. Penthesilea led Tala up one of the steeps bordering it and hid behind a large rock next to a thicket. She sat down and let Tala nose under the bushes. Weariness made her bones heavy. Hunger pinched her stomach. But she was not allowed to eat or drink until the day ended, much less to bring along some of the leaves that riders chewed during their long forays.

A faint neigh from down the trail startled her. She crawled to where Tala was standing and put a hand over the mare's nostrils. She crouched as low as she could. She must not be seen by anyone, for the exercise mimicked evolutions in lands held by an enemy. The sound of three walking horses reached her. She quickly glanced over the rock. The amazons rode single file. Leokadia was in the fore. Feodissia came next; she now accompanied the older riders on their rounds. Tecmassa rode rearmost. Penthesilea ducked. When she dared look up, Tecmassa, whose face was turned in her direction, swiveled her head back.

Penthesilea's cheeks burned and the back of her eyes pounded. But she decided to continue. There was no telling what Tecmassa had seen, although Penthesilea's failure—the second that day—would eat at her until the game was decided. She waited until the sound of horses died away. She led Tala down the hill and inspected her hooves. They were in good shape. She leaped onto her back and steered her down the track toward the river. She went slowly. She still wanted to spare Tala, even though Antiope might have discovered the route that Penthesilea had taken and might be on her trail.

Horse and rider emerged from the track and followed it past the apple orchard toward the city. Across Thermodon, rectangles of bare earth sloped toward low hills behind which gleamed a bright gray sky streaked with white wisps. Scattered groups of women were tending piles of burning straw. The breeze turned, and Penthesilea heard voices and laughter. Acrid smoke dizzied her. The picture of Eriboea rushed up before her mind's eye—her deep-brown eyes, her weathered brow and cracked lips, her look of calm, of patience, of love never spoken. How hollow that face had seemed and how absent those eyes that last time, the summer before. It had been hard to say good-bye. The old woman's callused hand had grown so thin, that when . . . Tala snuffled. Penthesilea started. The mare had been standing motionless. Penthesilea had been daydreaming. How long? How long had she been burning the daylight? Asking to be caught? Her jolt of surprise roused Tala, who broke into a run.

The shadows, such as they were, had begun to slant when Penthesilea reached the bridge. Tala loped onto its planks. Her hooves resounded against them. She panicked and reared; she had never done so before. Penthesilea threw her weight forward, put her arms around the mare's neck, and gripped tight with her thighs. Tala calmed down only when she stepped onto packed earth, and no echo sounded. Penthesilea let her run off her nervousness before putting her to a gentler pace. The light was growing flat as they ascended one of the low hills facing the city. The path turned right. Penthesilea continued straight. The way was narrow, and fist-sized rocks littered it. If Antiope had surmised what she was doing, she would have crossed the bridge by now and would have set her stallion into a run. But if she came this way, she would have to slow her mount to a walk or risk ruining its hooves or breaking her neck.

Penthesilea dismounted again and grasped Tala's bridle. "Come on, baby," she said in a tone that Tala had learned was meant only for her. "Let's hide." Penthesilea led her over the hill to its far slope. The chilly air made her shudder. Before her stretched steppes that extended far southwest to other tiers of hills. She struck out along a ridge that led around the hillside to the caves. She passed the entrances of three. She decided to double back to the first. The move was smart: Antiope would not think she had hidden in so obvious a place.

The move was risky: Antiope might crest the hill at any time and see Penthesilea before she had concealed herself. Penthesilea took the gamble.

She reached the first cave and led Tala in. She left her there, doubled back, and obliterated the prints of hooves and feet. She returned to Tala and grabbed her bridle above the cheekpiece. She unsheathed her blade—who knew what beast lived in the cavern's depths?—and, keeping the mare's muzzle next to her ear so that she could hear her breathing, penetrated farther inside. The tunnel turned sharply and blanketed them in darkness. Penthesilea stood still and listened.

In time a horse walked past the cave entrance without stopping. Penthesilea exhaled in relief. Sure that she had fooled Antiope, she advanced back to the entrance. Antiope was waiting for her there. Antiope had tricked her.

Still, the daylight had just turned purple. The sun had gone down without Antiope's setting eyes on her. Purists would say that the game had ended in a draw, although, in Penthesilea's mind, she had lost it three times over.

Penthesilea and Antiope stumbled into a small room on the downstairs level of the palace. Here fires heated the air, cauldrons steamed on top of the flames, and standing lamps illuminated whitewashed walls. On them, the red and black figures of unclothed women promenaded around the chamber. They were votaries, and the heels of their hands stretched to the heavens in supplication.

Two young serving women were waiting for Antiope and Penthesilea. As soon as they entered, the servants emptied the heated liquid into oaken vats.

The vaporous air dizzied Penthesilea; hunger made her head throb. One of the domestics, Cletê, a plump, pink-cheeked, cheery young woman, handed her a cup of warm wine in which herbs had been soaked. Penthesilea gulped it down. The pangs that gnawed at her insides quickly ebbed, as did the pulse that assaulted her brow. Her arms and legs loosened. She breathed deeply. She reached for the skirt of her tunic to pull it over her head.

"No, no!" chided Cletê, grabbing her arms. "You forget where you are now. Let yourself be waited on!" Cletê was right. Penthesilea had not yet gotten used to the luxury of Thalestris' house. Penthesilea let Cletê strip her garments off her and then sank into her bath. Warm waves caressed Penthesilea's skin; perfumed mist dissolved her weariness. Cletê's strong hands oiled and scraped and rinsed her. She helped her up, toweled her with hot cloths, and smeared cool unguent on her backside, lips, and thighs. Sweet tingling followed her agile fingers. Penthesilea murmured thanks; her eyes met Cletê's, who was smiling. She grinned back weakly.

The other serving woman had finished bathing Antiope, who refused her help and without assistance pulled her slender, leggy body out of the tub. Once upright, she meshed the fingers of her hands, turned their heels outward, and slowly stretched her olive-complexioned arms toward the ceiling. Her supple spine and slim shoulders arced backward. Her small, firm breasts glistened in the torchlight; their berry red nipples pointed upward. It was the same pose as that of the painted figures on the wall. The servant handed Antiope a towel.

The young riders entered the great hall just as Thalestris was getting up from table. She walked up to them with the careful tread that, as Penthesilea had learned this first week, spoke of one flagon of wine in her belly. She stroked Antiope's hair, inquired about their game, and did not listen to the answer. Celano took her arm and led her to her quarters. A full-bosomed, radiantly healthy serving woman followed.

The girls took their place at the older apprentices' table. The others had retired, and they sat alone. The servants who had bathed them now brought them food and drink and, when the hunger and thirst had gone from them, asked to take their leave.

"No. No. Stay with us," said Antiope, turning her handsome, heavy-eyebrowed gaze on Anuphey, the woman who had washed her and served her dinner. Anuphey was a slim-hipped girl with huge, sloe eyes and copper skin. She had taken refuge in Themiscyra two years before. Thalestris had chosen her as a retainer on the strength of her exotic looks. Anuphey avoided Antiope's glance, but sat down at her side and folded her long-fingered hands in front of her. Antiope's slanted, dark glance caressed them. Anuphey closed her long-lashed eyes. Cletê seated herself next to Penthesilea.

"Have some wine," said Antiope.

Cletê poured herself a goblet, lifted it to her lips, and, fixing amused, brazen eyes on Penthesilea, sucked at the dark liquid. Blushing, Penthesilea turned away and focused on Cletê's arms. They were solid and muscled.

"Are they as powerful as yours?" asked Cletê.

"Are they as powerful as *mine*?" asked Antiope.

Cletê's rose-hued lips traced a broad smile.

Anuphey giggled.

Antiope planted her right elbow on the table, held her forearm erect, and opened her hand to challenge Cletê to an arm wrestling match. "Well," repeated Antiope, "are they as strong as mine?"

Still beaming, Cletê rolled up her sleeve, set her forearm in the same position as Antiope's, and grabbed her hand. The women locked grips. Cletê's arm pushed against Antiope's. Antiope struggled against the thrust. Her face whitened; her muscles nearly ripped her sleeve. She grunted and bore down. Incarnadine flooded Cletê's cheeks. She frowned, gritted her teeth, and—the veins in her wrist beating blue against the skin—shoved back. Antiope groaned. Beads of sweat poured down her brow. The girls' arms teetered this way and that, this way and that. Cletê yelped and bore down. Antiope's arm wavered and slammed onto the table.

Red crept up Antiope's neck and face. She looked at her lap.

"Cletê grew up milking goats," said Penthesilea.

Antiope glanced at her furiously. "But I'm a rider, and riders are better!"

"You should have figured out her strength before tangling with her."

Antiope vaulted over the table, locked her arms around Penthesilea, and pulled her to the ground. She pinned her there. Penthesilea lifted her knee and drove her foot against the floor. She hoisted her hips sideways and threw Antiope off. Penthesilea sprang to her feet. So did Antiope. Penthesilea locked Antiope's left arm. Antiope wriggled free, threw Penthesilea, and dove on top of her. Penthesilea gasped. Antiope's breasts, belly, and thighs pressed against Penthesilea, whose heart now beat so hard that it hurt. Antiope's face was directly above hers; fierce joy glinted in her eyes. Antiope's breath wet her cheek. Suddenly, a helpless look invaded Antiope's expression. Her respiration came deeper and longer than a moment before. Blood filled her lips. She laid them against hers. Penthesilea closed her eyes and opened her mouth like a a baby bird in search of sustenance.

Antiope yanked herself off and, lying on her side, exploded into laughter that shook her until she wept. Cletê placed her fist on her hips, threw her head back, and guffawed. Anuphey widened her large eyes and tittered.

Penthesilea lay on her stomach, stunned. She remembered only a plunge on the floor, a few fast holds, and a sensation in her guts that drained her determination. It frightened her that her will to fight had fled from her like water into the thirsty earth.

She got up and Antiope handed her a goblet of wine. Penthesilea raised the vessel to her lips; Antiope pounded her shoulders. The purple liquid drenched Penthesilea's shirt and chilled her overheated thighs. Antiope exploded into peals of merriment.

"What is the meaning of this noise," rasped a nasal monotone. The four girls froze in place. Celano stood in the entranceway. Her weasel eyes glowered.

Antiope murmured, "Let's go." Hatred burned in hers.

"Come with me," said Cletê to Penthesilea, when the four young women reached the sleeping chamber that Antiope was supposed to share with Penthesilea.

"What?"

"Come with me. You can sleep in our room."

Penthesilea looked over her shoulder at Antiope. Antiope was paying no heed. She stood in the shadows, pressed against Anuphey.

"Come," said Cletê. "She'll be pleased if you do."

Cletê took up an oil lamp and led Penthesilea downstairs through tangles of passageways to a small room, not more than a closet, located near the stables. Two cots occupied almost all the floor space. Cletê placed the lamp between them, yanked her robe over her head, and seated her buxom form on one of them. The bottoms of her round young breasts shone like yellow half-moons in the light of the flame, which drew a fleshy halo around her thighs.

Penthesilea sat down opposite and began to peel off her tunic. It caught in her amazon braid, and she struggled with it until she felt someone pull it off. Cletê's naked form stood above hers, her pelt directly in front of her nose. Attar perfume and the aroma of woman's flesh turned Penthesilea's head. She slid into Anuphey's bed. Cletê did not return to hers but stood watching.

"Well?" said Cletê.

"Well what?"

"Aren't you going to make room for me?"

"In this bed?"

"Where else?" said Cletê.

"But I've never . . . I mean not with anyone else."

"What? Oh, come on. How do they spend the winter nights in Ariona's house, anyway?"

"It's a fine house! And Ariona sets a better example than Thalestris."

"How so, honey?"

"With all the drinking and sharing the couch."

"Well, what's wrong with that?" Cletê leaned over the lamp. Her breasts shimmered in the light it gave off. She blew it out."

"You're sweet, you know," she said. "And you're not spoiled like Antiope."

She slipped into bed; her flesh glided the length of Penthesilea's. Penthesilea's neck warmed, and the tingling inside her thighs shivered up her vulva and belly.

Chapter 4

In the middle of summer two mounted Amazons were slowly making their way along the northeast trail. The sun battered them from the sky and glanced off the stones to smite them again. Their horses' hooves raised sour-tasting dust that scratched the riders' throats into a frenzy of thirst. Once in a while a current of air, a fluke, a mistake, would blow aside the grit that made the riders' lungs and eyes itch.

Instead of their usual leather headpieces, coverings of cloth shielded their necks and eyes from a fire that could addle a woman's brains in no time. Blue-green paste was smeared on their eyelids and lashes. Light-colored tunics shaded their frames. Sweating gourds hung at the withers of each mount, but neither animal nor human had drunk since midday, when they had halted to rest by the side of a miserly trickle that had been a wild torrent three months before. Water would cut the beasts' limbs and destroy their own stamina.

Tecmassa walked her horse beside that of Feodissia; the other member of their patrol, Leokadia, had left her comrades to have a look at the other side of the hill they were passing. The three were combing the northeast passes in search of Kaska marauders. The night before, goatherds who had led their flocks to the summer pastures at the base of the iron hills had sighted a tiny glimmer on one of the slopes, a fire where none was ever expected. One of the herders scrambled back to the city by the light of the moon, and Amazons rode out before dawn, among them Feodissia and Tecmassa, who had come into town for supplies. Leokadia, who was waiting for them near the entrance of the territory that they regularly watched over, joined the search.

Feodissia peered around. Her eyes were swollen with lack of sleep. She pouted contritely.

Tecmassa was muttering at her, "Who d'you think you are, anyway? I could have got into trouble that I didn't have coming to me."

Feodissia's ears burned.

"The last time we talked about it," Tecmassa continued, "you were spending your nights with Cleodice the dyer. So, halfway between midnight and dawn, I went to her place and knocked. No one stirred, so I knocked harder. After I'd pounded for a while, Cleodice came out, rubbing her eyes. I asked for you. She asked me if I was crazy and then hollered at me what to do. She also told me that Pelopia the farmer could do it, too. Then another woman came out. Whoever she was, she was a head taller than me and looked like a plow woman, you know, big, strong arms and shoulders, like an ox. She put this huge fist under my nose and told me to get lost. So I did.

"I went down to Pelopia's house and called your name. Nobody answered. So I called it again. Not a soul. So I stuck my head in the door. A chamber pot comes flying at me. I duck. Then someone from the back yells that if she ever sets eyes on you or Phoebe the tanner again, you'll get the same.

"I took it on the lam. I went up and banged on Phoebe's door. And then you take your sweet time. . . ."

The object of Tecmassa's wrath suddenly reined in her horse, closed her eyes, and listened hard. Tecmassa shut her mouth and halted her mount. Faint whinnies reached her, but she could not tell from where and frowned. She wet an index finger and raised it. She shook her head gravely and swept her hand in an arc. Feodissia dug her heels into her horse's side and ran it farther down the trail to where it curved around the base of the hill. She would guide her horse uphill from there and climb diagonally. Tecmassa wheeled her mount around and returned to a shallow, rocky stream that circled the foot of the elevation. She followed its course toward the top. Soon frantic neighs sounded. She reached a thicket and dismounted to lead her horse around it. When she came to the other side, she saw Leokadia's mount standing riderless in the water. She pivoted her head everywhere but saw no trace of Leokadia. She swung herself into the saddle and went farther up. Bushes grabbed at her; exposed roots tried to trip her horse.

The swift-running water turned around on itself. Its glistening loop framed an emerald-grown clearing. Buttercups littered it; light drenched it. In the middle Leokadia lay on her right side. Tecmassa waded her horse across and looked down. Leokadia did not move. Her head was turned sharply to the left. Her chin touched the tip of her shoulder. A purple welt covered her left temple. Two strips of blood traced thin lines from the corners of her mouth. She was dead.

Tecmassa clenched her fists, roared like a wild beast, and ran her horse breakneck around the perimeter of the clearing. She spotted a tiny piece of homespun impaled on a low branch. A yard away a passage that no horse could penetrate cut into thick brush. Broken twigs shook in the wind at this break in the foliage. Tecmassa jumped down, threw herself on her hands and knees, and, snarling, followed a trail of broken branches. The man she was pursuing began to crash through the heavy growth. Feodissia, who was now twenty yards away on the other side, heard a thrashing that no animal could make. She slipped her bow off, plucked an arrow from her quiver, and drew back the bowstring. The Kaska man bolted into the open. The shaft drove home.

At this moment, high-spirited laughter rang through the iron hills west of the scene. Antiope and the older apprentice riders of Thalestris' household—Oebala, Tomiris, Marpessa, and Penthesilea—were returning to Themiscyra, singing and laughing as their mounts ambled forward. The adolescents had spent the previous night on the forested slopes, sharing a gourd of Thalestris' wine and belting out raucous songs. The Goddess must have been watching over the riders, for—although Kaska raiders were bivouacking on the next hill—the enemies saw and heard nothing, the forest masking the women's campfire and chants. In the twilight before dawn, the girls had hunted on foot with bow and arrow, their chase ending only when the light and heat drove the beasts back to their lairs. Antiope had felled a magnificent doe after she had stalked it for the better part of the dawn hours. Pride shone in her eyes when she slung the beast over her horse's croup. The saddlebags of the other hunters bulged with smaller game.

The sun had begun to descend toward the western horizon when the members of the party rode onto the sloped pastures that separated the iron hills from the river. Downhill, shepherds lounging in the shade next to their beasts looked up and waved. The riders waved back. A temperate breeze blew up from the river. Antiope, who led the column, threw back her good-looking head and warbled a verse of "The Buxom Lady who Sold Dried Figs." Then she giggled.

"I don't blame you," said the rider behind her, Oebala, a long and slender woman with curly hair wrapped tightly around her crown and thin lips forever pursed in an ironic smile.

"It's a beast any hunter would envy. The venison will feed many a woman. And the coat is handsome."

Antiope agreed, paused dramatically, and added, "I'll have a fur throw made from it for Anuphey."

"For Anuphey. That's news, isn't it, girls?" said Oebala, batting her long, lazy eyelashes. "The intrepid huntress will have a beautiful mantle made of this exquisite pelt by the best hands in Themiscyra to present to the comely, the lovely, the oh-so-fertile Anuphey."

"She's a fine breeder," said the stocky young woman with high cheekbones who rode beside Antiope. That was Tomiris, and she was alluding to Anuphey's having given birth to yet another girl child that spring. "And what a girl!" snickered Tomiris, her vixen eyes lighting up. "She's got leather lungs. Tell me Antiope. . . ."

Antiope swiveled and beamed.

"Does that baby keep you and Anuphey awake with her screaming? She keeps everyone else up, all the way downstairs."

"Or is it that you're not sleeping anyway?" asked Marpessa, who rode next to Oebala. As Marpessa spoke, her flame-colored mane shook in the bright sun. She turned her pale face back to Penthesilea, who rode last, and winked.

Oebala grinned, "Is it true what they say about the women who've already had babies? That their skin gets red and hot the minute you touch them?"

"And what's it like to kiss the breasts of a woman who's nursing?" taunted Tomiris. "Does the milk taste good?"

Antiope kneed her horse and lunged at Tomiris. Tomiris laid the reins of hers on its neck and, snickering, sidestepped the mock attack.

Penthesilea, who had witnessed the play from a distance, bent her head and sucked in her lips. Marpessa glanced over her shoulder, saw her friend's distress, and waited for her to catch up.

"You're sad about Cletê, aren't you?" asked Marpessa, turning her pale, delicate face to her friend.

Crimson spread over Penthesilea's cheeks. She had not said a word to anyone about how she felt. How she had spent an entire winter in Cletê's arms only to be followed by nine months' exile in the hills. When she had returned, exhausted, famished and aching for caresses, she learned that during her absence Cletê had become pregnant by a merchant from Troy

and had run away with him. Nights that Penthesilea had
fantasized full of moans of delight and sobs of bliss were lonely
again. And, lacking Antiope's luck in such things, she found no
friend to take Cletê's place.

Penthesilea protested with fierce, youthful justice.

"There is nothing we can do to keep her in Themiscyra if
she wants to leave. That's not our way. We don't keep any
woman here who doesn't want to stay."

"Still, it's a sad thing if you like someone."

The party rounded a rise. Downhill, a rider on a gray
horse, who had been following the river, reined her mount
toward them and goaded it into a run.

The woman was tall and fair-skinned. Tomiris was the
first to recognize her. "It's Perseia," she sneered, "Melanippe's
fond friend."

Antiope curled her lips in distaste. "Melanippe," she muttered. She hated Melanippe: Melanippe would one day
compete with her for the chiefdom, and might well win.
Melanippe was more skilled than she in the arts of riding and
shooting, and was the daughter of Naunamé, whom most
Amazons remembered and loved. Melanippe returned the
loathing: Antiope had displaced her as the chief's chosen
daughter and was, to boot, long-legged and pleasing to look at.

"Now why would Perseia be seeking out Melanippe's great
rival, Antiope?" asked Marpessa.

Perseia came close. Antiope set her face in haughty frigidity, Tomiris smirked, and Oebala raised her eyebrows.
Marpessa and Penthesilea looked at her in a straightforward
manner. Perseia did not spare a glance for the detractors, pronounced a curt hello to no one in particular, and directed her
horse to Penthesilea. She whispered a few words to her.
Penthesilea stiffened. She dug her heels into Tala's sides and
began to rush for Themiscyra without looking back.

The heat of the day had passed, and the houses threw blue
shadows over streets that had lately shimmered in blinding
sunlight. Myrtho draped a white cloth over her head and set
out down the hill. Philippis lumbered alongside, grumbling
and swatting away the insects that buzzed around her face.

Myrtho was bound for the tent of Zakir, a merchant who set
up his pavilion each summer on the slope west of Themiscyra.
He came from Babylon. He had called at the women's city for
more than a decade; the scales on which he measured out spices
and perfume were honest, and he left behind girl children. But

Zakir had not appeared for the past two years. When Myrtho inquired of other travelers, she learned that raiding parties from Assur had made his land's northern marches dangerous to cross. And so she was glad to hear that he had once again arrived.

Zakir's men had set up his quarters in the best position that the shade trees near Thermodon afforded. The pavilion, a large, round, purple-striped affair, stood several paces away from the temporary quarters (which were made of undyed canvas) of Ammunas the Hittite, another regular visitor. A stone's throw away were three squat, walnut brown shelters that housed men from the other side of the warm sea, who had journeyed to Themiscyra by way of Troy, whither long wooden ships had carried them.

Pleasure lit up Zakir's eyes when he set them on Myrtho. He stood waiting at the entrance of his dwelling. He was Myrtho's height. Thick, opal black hair curled around his ears and temples, and piercing eyes and a large hooked nose made his face shrewd and disarming at the same time. A knee-length robe of sky blue linen draped his body. A midnight blue sash that ended in tassels hugged his waist. His stomach, once prosperously round, had lost much of its protuberance since Myrtho had last set eyes on him. A fez-like hat and finely worked leather sandals completed his apparel. He smiled with gleaming teeth, crossed his arms over his chest, and bent from the middle. Myrtho put her hands on Zakir's shoulders and kissed his whiskered cheeks. Zakir pulled open the tent flap and made another obeisance. Myrtho stepped inside. Philippis followed. Zakir seated his guests and beckoned to a skinny youth who stood in the shadows at the back of the tent. The lad did not move. "Come now," said Zakir, "come now. You must serve the women."

The boy started as if awakened from sleep and carried them a tray bearing thick glass vessels. He was a short, skinny, beardless replica of Zakir. He sucked in his lips as he offered the priestess and her steward tiny cups full of sweet-smelling liquor. At a barely perceptible gesture from Zakir, he stepped back. He did not cease gaping at the female visitors as they made their libation and raised the drink, chestnut-colored date wine, to their lips.

After the host and his guest had traded ritual niceties, Myrtho said, "My old friend. It's good to see you once more. I did not know what to imagine when you did not visit two years ago. When I learned the news of your kingdom's troubles, I feared for your safety. Travelers told me how insecure the northern border has become."

"Thank you, my friend. I missed you too. And I give thanks to Marduk that I am alive and can be with you this season."

"And I praise the Goddess," said Myrtho. "But that you are *alive*? What happened that you should pronounce words of thanks that you are alive?"

Zakir wet his lips and let forth a singing sound that blended horror with relief. "Two years ago I set out from home, as I often have after the floods have fallen back. When the caravan I traveled with neared the northern border, a large force from the hills of Assur fell upon us like a pack of hungry wolves upon a herd of innocent sheep. We are men of peace, and so did not stand a chance against those ruthless savages. They took everything. Everything." Zakir's voice grew flat. "They killed my oldest son, Zakir, the light of my years, the hope of my nights, the comfort of my days. He was to be the staff of my old age. He was sixteen." Pain contorted Zakir's face.

"I am sorry, Zakir. I am deeply sorry."

"The barbarians took me hostage, and the ransom nearly ruined me. That and the new taxes to pay for the king's war against them. They understand only war and force. But at least I was not sold into slavery—I, Zakir, a free man and the son of a free man. And to lose a son, my son. . . ."

"Do you have other children?"

"I have two other sons."

"And daughters?"

"Two or three."

Zakir pulled himself up straight in his chair. "Yes, I have other sons, and my boy Ribat will journey with me from now on." Zakir indicated the youth who had waited on them. "And this year was not so bad. The road through the northern lands was calm. The king sent foot soldiers with us, and chariots, although they left when we began to climb the hills.

"But you must get another look at Ribat. Come here, my son."

Blushing, the youth shuffled forward, bent from the waist, and muttered embarrassed salutations. Myrtho inclined her head graciously; Philippis nodded, once.

"Look at him," said Zakir. "He is fast becoming a man. He is glad to make this journey with me. He has looked forward to visiting the city of women since he heard about it from other traders. I have told him that if he is sound and healthy like his father—and he is, he is—a beautiful girl will choose him so that he can lie with her while we pause before the gates of Themiscyra."

Philippis narrowed her eyes and inspected him like a herder inspects sheep. Myrtho examined him without changing her expression.

"Like me," continued Zakir, "he will plant some of my seed here, to put the life it contains into the women's fallow ground so it may ripen. He, too, will leave the tribute of my likeness to pay you women for your kindness to me."

Zakir's smile gleamed in the half-light of the tent.

Philippis wheezed.

They spoke of this and that until Myrtho's posture told Zakir that she wished to leave. He rose, bowed low, and held the tent flap open for her. A cool breeze was stirring from the river. They stood for a moment enjoying the fresh air and gazing at the sky, whose pale blue now ran before a tide of azure.

"And do not forget," he said bending from the waist yet again, "that my chief man wants to look at your she-donkeys. Their bloodline will improve that of my beasts."

Myrtho and Philippis began to walk uphill. A blonde-bearded man emerged from one of the squat tents nearby. He was naked. He yawned and stretched. A young woman, also nude, came out. They began walking down to the river. The man whacked the girl's rump.

"Hmmph!" sniffed Philippis. "Hmmph! And did you see Zakir's boy? A runt. Who'd get babies out of him? He's still one himself."

Myrtho's eyes closed halfway.

The women began to climb the road that led to the gate. Philippis continued muttering. Hooves echoed from below. Their thuds grew louder and did not slow when the rider began to ascend the hill. That was unusual. Myrtho stopped and turned. Feodissia was running her steed toward them. Her horse's neck and mouth dripped lather. Sweat covered its withers. Dust coated Feodissia's hair and masked her face. She reined in her mount and gazed at the earth.

"What is it?" Myrtho asked.

"Leokadia," gasped the rider.

"Leokadia?" Myrtho's voice had lost its assurance.

"Tecmassa is bringing her in," answered Feodissia, still not raising her head.

"Is she wounded?"

Feodissia looked up. Two black lines spilled from her eyelids and incised the white coating of her jowls.

Myrtho dropped to the ground.

By the time Penthesilea reached Thermodon, the sun touched the peaks of the low hills west of the valley. Ariona, who had ridden down from the city, reined up next to her. Ariona's face was grave.

"You must wait here," she said, clasping Penthesilea's forearm. "They'll be along soon with Leokadia's body."

"How did it. . . ."

"A Kaska marauder got her with his sling. His stone struck her head. She didn't suffer."

"I see," whispered Penthesilea.

"They say you were out hunting with Antiope and her crowd. Your saddlebags are full, too. Have you washed the blood from your body?"

"I have."

"Someone from Thalestris' house will be along soon to give you mourning clothes." Ariona pointed a stone's throw down-river. "There's where they're going to build the pyre."

Ariona took her leave. Penthesilea dismounted and led Tala down the riverbank to the spot that she had indicated. Penthesilea settled on the ground and pulled her knees to her chest. She hid her eyes and sobbed and sobbed. At length, she felt a hand on her shoulder. She looked up. Gray-purple dusk had followed the half-light of sunset. Anuphey stood over her, her baby girl strapped to her back. Penthesilea wiped her tears with her forearm and sprang to her feet. Anuphey's large eyes, the corners of which seemed to wrap around her temples, deepened. She caressed Penthesilea's hair, kissed her on the mouth, and handed her a tunic of brownish red. She knelt and unfastened the young rider's shoes. Eriboea's cousin, Molpadia, came up, shot a sad glance at Penthesilea, and clucked her tongue in pity. She snatched the hefty saddlebags from Tala's croup, tossed them over her shoulder, and trudged upstream to where two kitcheners from Thalestris' establishment had planted tripods and were kindling cooking fires.

Women were streaming down from the city. Telkhinia the smith, her flaxen locks streaming over her broad shoulders,

sauntered toward her, followed by a gang of big-muscled women
of the tool. Some bore large branches, others shared the weight
of logs, and two carried axes. Telkhinia stopped. The women
behind her lumbered to a standstill. She pointed to the place
that had been chosen for the pyre. With sparing and
purposeful gestures, her followers laid out a well-ventilated
square of lumber.

Women of the plow, some still bearing scythes, arrived in
twos and threes. Merope and another temple kitchener came
down, supporting a pole between their shoulders from which
was suspended a huge skin filled with barley beer that swung
from side to side with their steps. Antiope, Oebala, and
Marpessa reached the river from the pastures. Eager hands
snatched their saddlebags and carried them to the cooking
fires. Antiope walked her steed up to Penthesilea. Without
dismounting, she smiled weakly and opened her lips to speak.
She could not think of anything to say and closed them. She
trotted her horse off. Oebala led Tala away. Marpessa came
up to Penthesilea, alighted, and kissed Penthesilea's
forehead.

Cymbals and chimes sounded in the distance and grew
louder. A double column of votaries filed into sight, Myrtho
leading them. She walked forward like someone newly risen
from sickness, placing one foot in front of the other with great
care lest pain impale her again. The swarm of women who had
gathered fell silent. The keepers of the temple reached the
pyre and turned toward Themiscyra.

Hooves thudded and bridles jingled. A score of Amazons,
all the riders who could be found in the city at this season,
paraded down, two abreast, wordless and somber of
countenance. Thalestris rode at their fore, bodefully handsome
in her red ochre tunic. In the middle of the cortege, between the
two files, Tecmassa, who was on foot, led Leokadia's pony, over
whose back her body had been strapped. Tears rushed down
Tecmassa's cheeks like springwater over polished leather.
Feodissia followed. She blubbered shamelessly. Thalestris
raised her hand. The Amazons stopped and dismounted.
Penthesilea joined Tecmassa and Feodissia.

One by one the stars glimmered into view. A gibbous moon
was rising from behind the eastern hills. Three bonfires threw
their dancing brilliance on the sad scene. The perfume of roast-
ing meat and of cakes grilling on heated rocks wafted through
the air.

Tecmassa led the pony bearing Leokadia to the crematory heap. Telkhinia effortlessly plucked up the stiffened body, placed it on the chest-high square of lumber, and straightened it by sheer force. She closed Leokadia's eyes and, running her huge fists over her own, took her place among the crowd.

Myrtho proceeded with slow steps to the body. She cradled Leokadia's face in her hands and bent her head and shoulders over her like a mother over a sleeping child. Indistinct words fell from Myrtho's lips. When their sound died, Philippis handed Myrtho an egg, half of which was painted black and half yellow. Myrtho laid it on Leokadia's chest, above the rider's folded hands. Philippis gave Myrtho a jar of honey and a jug of springwater. Myrtho placed them by Leokadia' side and raised her worn visage to the moon, which was now fully visible, and intoned a long prayer. Then she grew mute. She did not budge for a long time. Women stared in pitiful silence. Finally, Philippis put her hand on Myrtho's shoulder and guided her away.

Tecmassa moved forward. For once her rolling, confident gait was constrained and hesitant. Clutching a tiny clay pot containing red earth, she drew next to her dead friend and smeared her brow, cheeks, and lips with a double line of the tellurian color. When Tecmassa had finished, she swerved away and dropped the vessel. Then, as if drunk, she teetered back to where she had been standing.

Penthesilea scooped up the jar. She advanced to the pyre and stared at the motionless face. There could be no mistake. It was Leokadia—still, intense in her sleep, blotches of blue showing under the earthborn pigment, a mask, a peaceful mask, not the real woman and yet, without a doubt, Leokadia. Suddenly her lids, brows, and lips trembled. Hope electrified Penthesilea. Then, against her will, she realized that the liveliness was a trick of the flames that flickered nearby. She felt the warmth drain from her. She sank her fingers into the moist earth and daubed it on the countenance of the woman she revered. Leokadia's skin was cold, like a serpent's. Penthesilea shuddered. Tears blinded her when she stepped away.

Feodissia performed the same baleful duty, groaning and hiccuping as she did. She turned from the body and threw herself into Penthesilea's arms.

Merope the cook sobbed out the high-pitched "aam, aam, aam," the women's lament for the dead. Amazons who had looked on the scene with dry eyes burst into tears. Women bawled, cried, keened, moaned, and wailed in a turbulence of pity that deafened Penthesilea. They formed a single line behind the four mourners, who—clasping one another and grieving and weeping as one person—led them with halting steps past the lifeless form. As each inhabitant of Themiscyra moved alongside the pyre, she laid a lock of hair on the wood. Amazons who had fought at Leokadia's side wrung their hands and beat their chests when they stepped up to their dead comrade.

The funeral feast took place on a level spot near the fires. The women sat on the ground in small circles, keeping a considerate distance from the mourners.

Myrtho wrapped her ample blue robes around her and reclined on the earth. When attendants came to pour hot water over her hands and give her cloths to wipe them with, she acquitted herself of the ritual act as befitted her station. Still, Myrtho's cheeks were drained, and she kept her eyes lowered. She made a pretext of partaking of the food and drink set before her, but ate nothing.

Penthesilea, who sat next to her, did not know what to say. She wept softly while she feasted on succulent meat and steaming cakes with all the appetite of her young years. She drank a brimming cup of the wine Thalestris had sent, and its perfume invaded her head. She once more saw Leokadia's rigid face in the wavering firelight and felt her cold skin. She shook with sadness. Then the image of a radiant spring morning rushed into her soul. Leokadia led the newly acquired Tala by rope and halter. Penthesilea threw her arms around Leokadia's warm waist and poured out confused thanks. Leokadia's cheeks reddened with pleasure. Penthesilea smiled. Then Leokadia's lifeless visage chased away the happy picture. The young woman sought the bottom of her cup again and again.

Tecmassa, who sat facing Penthesilea, did not talk at all as she turned joints of game in her thick hands, carefully selected pieces to bite off, and chewed with slow, thorough method. Now and then she would take up her goblet, lift it to her lips, and dribble its contents over her tongue. When she was done eating and drinking, she stretched out and began to snore. Feodissia polished off her food in no time and lay back. She put her hands under her head and stared at the stars. Tears rolled down her cheeks.

The fire faded to embers, and the talking of feasters ebbed to nothing.

At first light, Penthesilea sat up all at once. Her eyebrows throbbed, and her temples burned. Realizing where she was, and why, was like plunging into icy waters after basking in the warm sun. Myrtho lay a few feet from her, her eyes wide open. Tecmassa, who was stretched out exactly where she had lain down, shattered the dawn hour with her snoring. Feodissia was nowhere to be seen.

Myrtho hoisted herself to a sitting position. "You slept?" she asked Penthesilea.

"Not well," answered the young rider. "I . . . I . . . my head hurts. And you? Did you sleep?"

"Leokadia came to me last night," whispered Myrtho. "I am not sure exactly at what time of night. The fires were dying. Silence surrounded me. The mist had risen from the river."

Myrtho's eyes focused on something far away. "Leokadia came to me from out of those mists. I cannot say that she walked, so ethereal was her step, as though she already had no substance, no weight to secure her to the earth that we mortals tread. A dark cloak covered her head to foot. Its cowl kept her face in the shadow. I could not see her eyes, their sockets were black ovals without light, her face was gaunt, emaciated, her cheeks hollow, her mouth thin."

Myrtho shook her head. "Leokadia spoke to me in a windy whisper that was more like a moan than a woman's voice. I recognized it nonetheless. She said, 'Myrtho, dear friend, I am sad. The sun! My body has not gone back to the sun! Please send me to the West.'

"I told her that we would do so this very dawn, that the women would send her spirit up to Arinna so that She might carry her to the West.

"Leokadia seemed appeased and spoke again, 'I will wait for you,' she said. 'I will be sad until you come. Do not forget. When you look at the sunset, do not forget.'

"I told Leokadia that I would remember her all the days of my life.

"She fell silent, but I realized that she had more to say. She was so sad! So sad! I would have asked her what made her grieve so, but I suddenly had no voice to pronounce words. At last she spoke again, 'And the girl I stole from the Storm God,' she said, 'tell her to keep her heart pure and listen to its truth. Tell her to follow the ways of the Goddess. The Goddess saved her from the snows. The Goddess loves her. The Goddess wants her to. . . .'

"Leokadia never finished, for her shade began to dissolve into nothingness." Tears filled Myrtho's eyes. "I reached out to embrace her one final time. But my arms clasped at a shadow that slipped away when I tried to enfold it.

"When I looked about, I saw that everyone slept."

Around Myrtho, women stirred to their feet. Philippis took her wrist and guided her to waiting attendants.

Penthesilea turned onto her belly and propped her cheek in her hand. Leokadia's words echoed in her head as she pondered both her own sorrow and Myrtho's—but most of all her own.

Tecmassa's snort shattered Penthesilea's meditation. Tecmassa sat up and blinked. She pulled herself slowly to her feet. Her scout's nose sniffed the air; her red-rimmed eyes reconnoitered the scene around her. "Feodissia must be down at the river," she muttered, "Let's go there ourselves." Tecmassa ran her hand over her jaw. "It'll do us good." She squinted at Penthesilea. "Especially you. You're looking a little worn." Tecmassa rubbed the top of her head. "It was good wine. Thalestris always pours good wine." Her voice turned gruff. "There's more of this funeral to come. So let's shake the cobwebs out of our heads." She scratched her head and flashed her gleaming teeth with the black square in the middle where an incisor should have been. "Course," she said, "they can't start without us."

Penthesilea and Tecmassa made their way to the bathing place.

"Leokadia came to Myrtho last night," said Penthesilea.

"Yeah, I knew she would. What'd she say?"

"That she longed to go to the West, that her soul wasn't happy trapped in her body, that she would wait for Myrtho, that I. . . ." Penthesilea fell silent.

"What did she say, girl?"

"Leokadia said that I was dear to the Goddess, and that the Goddess wanted something for me."

"Yeah, Leokadia said that to me, too."

"But Leokadia never told Myrtho what it was. She vanished into the air before she could."

Penthesilea and Tecmassa reached a clump of willow trees situated half a mile upstream from where the feast had taken place. An expanse of sandy earth separated this grove from Thermodon, whose current here slowed and grew less treacherous than in other reaches. A little girl and a grown woman were wading in the river. The child, a pear shaped stripling with prominent ribs, puckered dots for breasts, and a hairless body (how naked she seemed to Penthesilea) giggled and pushed armfuls of water at a laughing grownup who stood waist-deep in front of her. The woman's face, forearms, and hands were as brown as berries; so were her bursting nipples and the puckered flesh around them. The rest of her dazzled with its whiteness—solid arms, muscular shoulders, and the full bosom of a nursing mother. Nearby, on the riverbank, four unclothed women lounged in the rays of a sun that was spilling molten gold into a cloudless, robin's-egg sky. Two women basked with their hands behind their heads, the tips of their breasts pointing to the heavens, and the two others lay on their sides, their faces in proximity, chattering and laughing. Farther from the water, an old woman sat propped up against a willow tree. She cradled a babe in her arms and hummed.

Penthesilea smiled and gloried in the warm rays that caressed her back. Tecmassa grinned. The supine women abruptly ended their happy buzzing, and moved away.

"Bah!" said Tecmassa, "you'd think we had the plague." She yanked the funerary tunic she wore over her head and struggled to pluck it off her husky body. Her voice complained from within the garment, "This is the damned most uncomfortable getup I've ever worn. Who'd they make it for, a rider or a runt?"

Tecmassa tugged hard, something ripped, and she snatched off the piece of apparel. Her big-breasted, large-hipped, walnut-brown torso made Penthesilea, who had also shed her tunic, ashamed of her pale and scrawny frame.

Tecmassa plowed into the Thermodon. Her powerful shanks made great splashes as they pushed through the water. When it reached her shoulders, she disappeared under the surface, leaving a circle of ripples that spread and dissipated. After a while her head emerged halfway toward the opposite shore. She shook it violently, and the drops it flung outward glowed like a halo. She spat a long jet of silvery liquid at the sun and shouted, "Come on, you'll never get the wine vapors out of your head if you don't."

Penthesilea waded forward and, with quick strokes, glided like a beetle to where Tecmassa was alternately treading water, dunking, and blowing streams of it at the brilliant orb.

"You've got to keep your head under if you want to clear the fog from it," said Tecmassa. "Dive down and stay there for a while."

Penthesilea let herself sink until her toes touched bottom. A blanket of light shimmered above her, and Tecmassa's big legs were like logs paddling the water, their thickness exaggerated by the trembling luminescence. When Penthesilea could no longer stand the burning in her lungs, she came up and panted.

Tecmassa laughed. "Feel better?" she asked. Her mouth spat a silvery jet at her young friend.

They swam to the far shore, returned, and began to wade out. Tecmassa stopped when the water reached her thighs. Her belly glistened gold and her fleece silver in the morning light. She stretched her thick arms above her head and rolled it from side to side. Argent drops trickled from her big, carmine-tipped breasts down her round belly onto her shining pelt. "Sure feels better," she said. "Sure feels better. And the other good thing to know," she said, continuing some unspoken chain of thought, "is how to ride when you've had too much to drink. You've gotta do exactly what the rider at your side does and you've gotta look smack between your horse's ears. D'you know who taught me that?"

Tecmassa's arms fell limp, and she whooshed out air as if someone had hit her in the middle. "Leokadia did," she whispered feebly. Her eyes brimmed with tears.

Feodissia strolled out of the grove and hailed them. A woman whose face they could not make out slipped back into the shadows. The three returned to the funeral.

The sun had begun its siege. Leokadia's body lay pale and toylike on top of the pyre. Tecmassa, Feodissia, and Penthesilea held themselves a stone's throw away from it. Myrtho stood like a lifeless doll at their side, with Philippis hovering close. Nearby, two rows of mounted women held their horses in place. Thalestris paraded her beast up and down the ranks. When Thalestris reached the head of the column, she proffered a few words to a gray-haired, thick-set woman of stately posture and movements who always rode at her left on solemn occasions—noble Hippolyta. She nodded curtly in reply. Behind her, Melanippe sat her dancing steed. Antiope was stationed next to her. Unlike their elders, the two young women did not pretend to converse but avoided each other's eyes.

Thalestris raised her hand, dropped it, and dug her heels into her mount. The steed reared once, ran toward the pyre, and wheeled around it. A score of horses broke into a run, and the Amazons hurtled around their fallen comrade three times at breakneck speed. They howled like hungry wolves; their horses' hooves beat an ominous percussion. A cloud of dust rose and concealed the living riders and the dead one. Then, from the middle of this pall, a tongue of transparent yellow shot up into the air. Soon smoke climbed toward the heavens. The Amazons pulled away from the body as suddenly as they had ridden on it. A puff of wind dissolved the dust and fanned the blaze. Great flames leaped around Leokadia's remains, which flared, became glowing cinder, and crumbled abruptly into a formless heap.

The fire hypnotized Penthesilea. She had not thought that it would consume Leokadia so quickly. Sobs racked her; she covered her tired eyes with her fingers and tears tumbled out between them. Someone touched her forearm. Myrtho, her face locked in a mask of pain so great that she smiled like a madwoman, had brushed close to her. Penthesilea lay her hand on her shoulder. Myrtho did not notice.

Tecmassa shaded her weeping eyes and, half to herself, said, "Now Leokadia's soul can go back to the sun." She looked up at the western sky. "Well, old friend," she whispered, "I'll join you soon enough."

Feodissia gasped and moaned.

Thalestris waited until a crowd formed around her. As soon as it did, she touched her feet to her horse's flank, and the beast pranced and reared, but Thalestris seemed not to notice or to change position in the saddle. She scowled nobly at the onlookers and, when she judged that her words would have the most effect, mouthed, "As death follows life, so life must follow death. Let the games begin."

Chapter 5

Tecmassa halted her horse. Penthesilea did likewise. The steps of Antiope's mount slowed and stopped, then those of Feodissia's pony. The riders looked back. In the distance, dark clouds poured toward them from the ridge that separated Themiscyra's territory from the plain skirting the cold sea and lands belonging to Amisos. They had spent the night near the elevation's easternmost defile and now rode slowly home. Thalestris had sent Antiope and Penthesilea to reconnoiter the northeast under the supervision of the seasoned scout.

The air was heavy; it would rain soon. "Just one more stop before we head for home," said Tecmassa, setting her mount into motion again.

The riders progressed in silence for hours. The cold wind stiffened and sliced at their backs. The trail snaked through juniper bushes whose dark leaves vibrated in the breeze. On the left a scrub-covered steep towered over the rough ground. The hill protected a stand of black mulberry trees from the northeast winds. The trees spread their bare branches to the sky; all the leaves had disappeared weeks before, and the fruit months before—plucked off by hungry birds or by white-kerchiefed women who carried full baskets back to Themiscyra. It was time now to seed the winter barley, and, when Penthesilea had crossed the bridge two days before, she had seen oxen dragging plows through the fields to turn over the earth.

Six weeks before, when the hours of darkness equaled the hours of light, the last of the traders, men from the south, had folded their tents, and riders had escorted them to the waste-land that stretched between Themiscyra's domain and the Hittites' royal road. Some women blubbered unashamedly when the travelers departed; others sighed with relief. The men brought goods and babies to the city and comfort to many dwellers. But the visitors' presence stretched the riders' ranks to the limit. A dozen horsewomen had to keep an eye over the tents during the men's sojourn. At the same time, scores of fighters had to watch the plains and hills around Themiscyra. Fair weather invited hostile soldiers.

Penthesilea remembered the relief written across Leokadia's face whenever she returned from accompanying the last traders to the border. "And good riddance to them!" she would blurt out as she plucked off her headpiece and wrapped her big hand around the goblet Myrtho offered her.

Penthesilea flinched. Memories of Leokadia still pained her. But no sooner had the grief seared through her, than a happy recollection made her smile—the rest of the scene that invariably took place. After Leokadia's outburst, Myrtho would explain why the men had to be there, and that their presence was not only divinely ordained but a practical affair. Philippis would corroborate Myrtho's lesson by drawing her big form up to its full, short height, and sniffing. If Tecmassa were present, she would flash her patched smile (whose origin in scaled walls and an irate lover Leokadia had one day inadvertently hinted at) and laugh so hard that her wine would almost spill. Leokadia would grin triumphantly, and Myrtho purse her lips.

The way veered left at the same time as a path took off from it diagonally. At the end of this track loomed a cluster of ragged heights that the chill light made gray and surly. The riders halted. Tecmassa turned and, pitching her voice under the wailing of the wind, said, "We're going in there to have a look."

"*In* there?" asked Antiope.

"The cliffs make a circle around a notch, and there's fresh water in there. It's the hottest damned place in the whole territory during the summer—even if," self-satisfaction flickered across Tecmassa's face, "it's not as hot as where I learned to ride. The hills keep off the breeze, and the rocks soak up the heat. Of course, it's an advantage at this time of the year, especially if you take shelter at the foot of the northernmost cliff. That's what the herders do.

"Anyway, we've got to go in there and have a look-see. The last time we did was six days ago."

The mounted women reached the defile's entrance, a cleft between two cliffs, and Feodissia separated from the other riders and took up station beside a clump of spruce surrounded by heavy brush.

"With only one way in and cliffs on all sides," explained Tecmassa, "the valley's a good place to be ambushed in. That's why Feodissia has to stand watch outside. As for us, we have to go in single file. There isn't a whole lot of elbowroom."

Tecmassa guided her mount into the passage; Antiope and Penthesilea followed, their shoulders brushing the hard walls. They stopped when they emerged from the corridor. The cold gusts no longer slashed at them, and the whine of the breeze had subsided into a far-off murmur. The air was bluer and warmer than on the outside. It was late in the day and the light was flat. Penthesilea reminded herself that she had better be careful of Tala's hooves.

Hostile bluffs hemmed the gap in. The riders faced a seventy-foot precipice, much of whose flank hung perpendicular to the valley floor. Horizontal strips of duller stone laced the height's surface, some exuding fingers of water that reached down to gather in a rock basin. Three stone pines flourished near this trough. A narrow path snaked to it from the way in. Shining black and dull gray rocks, some the size of a fist, others of a grown woman, littered the valley floor. Protrusions of gravelly earth, out of which shot pugnacious little conifers, rose and fell like freshly turned furrows, except that there was no sense to them.

The riders separated. Penthesilea turned Tala along the south-facing cliff. Stubborn brush and haphazardly strewn stones formed an obstacle course for the smart little mare. Rustling exploded underfoot; a blackbird streaked upward. Horse and rider reached a vertical groove scored in the precipice, a natural chimney. Traces of fire and smoke blackened it. The cleft widened at the base. A pile of charred branches cluttered it.

Penthesilea dismounted and walked over. The remains of two-dozen pieces of wood lay there. She knelt and fingered the burnt residue. It was cold, but neither moist nor pasty. She scanned the ground that surrounded the fireplace. The earth was newly trodden on, shallow furrows dug into it here and there, and a sapling had been pulled out of it. Penthesilea felt the tree's roots. The soil that clung to them was damp. People had recently camped here. She measured the space with her eyes: eight at the most could sleep around the fire. But who?

Penthesilea opened her mouth to call out just as she heard a horse bellow and a body thud to the earth. Tala neighed and reared. Penthesilea lunged for the reins and caught hold. Then she turned. Tecmassa's mount wallowed on its side, its long legs kicking the air. It shivered, jerked violently, and fell still.

Tecmassa was sprawled on her belly a few feet from the dead beast. She raised herself with one hand and scrambled for the pines, bellowing, "Cover the gateway!" In seconds Penthesilea readied her bow and an arrow, drew her hand to her cheek, and sent the shaft flying. Behind her, Antiope's bowstring twanged. She sprang onto Tala's back, dug her heels into the horse's flank, and hurtled toward the trees. An arrow whistled past her. The wind made by its flight touched her cheek. She swiveled and shot a second time. A man screamed.

She arrived at the same instant as Antiope did. They dismounted in the cover of the trees. There, Tecmassa lay on her stomach nursing her left hand. She looked up. The three riders exchanged anxious glances, each woman's eyes reflecting the same question. Penthesilea voiced it: "Where was Feodissia?"

"I'd like to know that myself," said Tecmassa. "Something's happened to her, else she'd have warned us." Tecmassa darted her eyes toward the entrance. Worry showed on her face.

Penthesilea pointed to the south-facing cliff. "I saw the remains of a fire there. And somebody bivouacked on that spot."

"Our own women don't come here this season," said Tecmassa. "And it couldn't have been the herders, either, because there aren't any droppings. It was strangers then. But how many?"

"Seven, at the most eight."

"What makes you say that?"

"The size of the ground, the size of the fire."

"How old was it?"

"The ashes were cold but not wet."

Tecmassa wrinkled her brow. "It rained two nights ago. That means they stayed here last night."

"Why would outsiders come back to the same spot?" asked Antiope. "They must know about the Amazon patrols."

"Maybe they don't," said Tecmassa. "Maybe they're from far away." She fell silent and sucked in her lips which parted in a strange smile. "Maybe they left something in here worth coming back for and want to get their hands on it before we do. Why else would they be so hot to get in? Why else would they shoot at us? Once they saw Feodissia they could have just vanished into the hills and waited. We must be blocking their way. They'll have to get rid of us to make sure we don't find whatever it is." Tecmassa rubbed her left wrist. "I thought the damned thing was busted," she muttered, "but it isn't. Still, I can't use it."

"But, Feodissia?" asked Penthesilea.

"If we get out of here we'll find her and take her home, one way or another." Tecmassa's tone was matter-of-fact, but the set of her jaw was not.

A heavy stillness followed. The temperature was dropping; the air was more and more weightless. Rain would fall soon.

Tecmassa scanned the sky. Somber clouds blanketed the valley. "Darkness is less than an hour away," she said. "Maybe it'll come sooner if the rain begins to fall. Whenever it does, we're stuck here. We don't dare go near the entrance. I heard one scream. I suppose you hit him. But how many more are there? Once night falls they'll be able to break in here and rush us. And if there's eight of them like you say, our chances aren't. . . ." Tecmassa's voice trailed off.

"Perhaps there are only seven," said Penthesilea. "Still," answered Tecmassa, "the odds are bad, very bad."

No one spoke after that. Penthesilea bent her head and from that position shot a furtive glance at her companions. Tecmassa focused a stony countenance on the only way out of the defile. Antiope, whose handsome cheeks had paled, darted feverish eyes around the bases of the cliffs.

Penthesilea looked up at the rocky elevations that trapped them there. Was there some spot they had not seen that they could escape through? Were all the hills their enemies? She moved her head slowly; her eyes burned into the eminences, as if her stares could cut a path through one of them to freedom.

Penthesilea shuddered to think what might have happened to Feodissia and what would happen to her and the others if they were taken alive. She realized that she was shaking and hoped Antiope and Tecmassa had not seen her. Then, although she was not aware of it, her eyes stopped moving and focused on the smallest of the elevations.

From a score of paces above its base, boulders and gravel, old avalanches, spilled down and halted a few feet out. Verdant blotches hugged the ground among the fallen rocks and pebbles. Above the old rockslide, a stone escarpment reached vertically to the summit. Tiny crevices, dull black in the slanted light, crisscrossed the upright wall, alternating with twisted fingers of bluish-green scrub pine. The precipice became less breakneck only near the top, where grainy gray scars, some round and deep, some long and shallow, pitted its stony surface. Penthesilea lowered her head again and thought. Yes, they might be able to climb it, to scramble up the bottom, and then there were places to lodge your feet and to pull yourself up. The women would have a chance if they scaled the rock before the rain came and if. . . . Thunder growled in the distance.

"What's on the other side?" blurted Penthesilea without taking her eyes off the cliff. The loudness of her voice surprised her; it startled the others, too, and they followed her gaze.

Tecmassa, who was contemplating the height, did not answer for a moment. She said, finally, "I recall that it's not as steep. Trees grow there—birch, and farther down hornbeam. There's heavy underbrush at the bottom, buckthorn. There's plenty of place to hide; plenty of cover, not like this." She gestured with disgust at the scenery around them.

"We can climb that bluff," said Penthesilea, extending her hand and pointing to the path she had figured out. "It's not far to the top, and we can pull ourselves over the worst spots." Penthesilea glanced affectionately at Tala. "We don't have to worry about the horses. They'll fetch too good a price for the intruders to slaughter them."

Antiope murmured agreement, but Tecmassa did not commit herself. Instead she once more appraised the steep, stared down at her left forearm, and turned her face to the ground. When she looked up, her eyes white in the gray light, Penthesilea could read nothing.

"I can't climb that," said Tecmassa in an even voice. "I can't use this wrist. There's not a way I can hoist myself over the bad stretch. Not a way." She paused before announcing, "You two will go without me."

How could they leave Tecmassa here alone? How could they desert her? It would not be right to sacrifice her. Penthesilea opened her mouth to protest but thought again and pinched her lips together. Tecmassa was right. They must not lose three riders when they could lose only one. And Tecmassa was in charge.

Tecmassa continued, "They'll spot you soon enough and send men over to track you down. But if you work fast, you'll be able to get to the top and halfway over the other side before anyone can reach you. Hide. Slip into the hills and wait. If our patrol isn't back by the day after tomorrow, riders will come out. The men won't chance staying around long if they know that a squad is on its way. It'll still be hard for them to get away—eight men on foot leading animals. And if they take me prisoner," Tecmassa chuckled, "I'll slow them down plenty."

And what if they took no prisoners? If they killed Tecmassa? Sorrow invaded Penthesilea's eyes. She was about to speak, but Tecmassa flashed an angry glare her way, peered up at the dimming sky, and shouted, "Go on, you two! Get out! Hurry!"

Penthesilea blushed as if she had been scolded. She looked at Antiope: her eyes glowed and her lips grinned.

Penthesilea removed her quiver and bow. She drew her knife and slit the thong that held the bow's two arcs of bone together. No one could use it now. She resheathed her blade and jiggled her belt with both hands to make sure that the dagger and labrys were securely seated. "Let's go!" she shouted and ran for the steep. Antiope scrambled on her heels.

Penthesilea paused at the base of the cliff and looked back at Tecmassa, who waved and boomed, "Go on! Go on!"

Penthesilea loped through the stones and gravel that flowed down the side of the cliff. They crunched and slipped from underfoot, and, near the end of her run, her leg slid backward, and she landed on her knee. Pain ripped through her, and she stopped dead but beat down her agony and started scrambling again. Grimacing, she reached the rock face, found a hold, and began to pull herself up. Her arms hefted her skyward where the scrub pine offered help; her feet jimmied her up where fissures welcomed them. She worked her way up the bluff like a crab, now veering right, now twisting left, now scrambling straight. Deep red layered over her face; hot sweat covered her body; her sinews nearly burst her tunic; her arms burned; she gasped. The rock towered above her like a cruel enemy, but she would not let it get the better of her.

She poked her foot into a hole that crumbled away, and her leg slipped out from under her. For a sickening moment she hung suspended from a plant whose roots, by some miracle, held fast. She wrenched herself into a surer position and stopped. Her heart split her chest, and she panted like a winded horse. She wondered dimly if the stones that she had loosed had hit Antiope. Still, she did not look down. She realized that she had stopped crawling and hurled her strength into clambering up the rock face once more. At last she reached the pitted expanse near the summit. The slope leveled off, and she bounded up to the top. Antiope was not far behind. Penthesilea crouched and stretched out her hand. Antiope grabbed hold, and Penthesilea pulled her up. Without pausing, the two hurtled over the crest of ridge and down the other side. Twilight had already overtaken it.

They had bustled down half the distance to the bottom, when Penthesilea stopped short and Antiope plowed into her. Penthesilea lay one hand over her friend's mouth and cupped her ear with the other. Both women held their breath. Irregular noises interrupted the rustling and chirping of the wood. Underbrush crunched. A pair of wings beat frantically; their pulse receded into the forest murmur. Penthesilea moved her palm outward from her shoulder, and the two women tiptoed off in opposite directions, Antiope retracing her steps up the slope and leftward.

Penthesilea slid into a clump of young trees. Chill drops pelted the leaves. They trembled in the wind, which here blew toward the southeast. Soon Penthesilea made out the sound—at first dim but nonetheless unmistakable—of footsteps treading the leafy floor. She drew her blade and crouched low. She wondered if the thumping in her chest would give her away.

The tip of a thrusting spear and an oblong shield of hide loomed into sight, then the figure of the man who held them. He wore a leather cuirasse and greaves—the weaponry of a Hittite infantryman. He walked on cat's feet, turning his face this way and that in search of something. A black beard surrounded bitter lips.   When he passed the spot where Penthesilea lay hidden, she sprang like a snake. Her left arm made a vise around his larynx. The point of her blade found the spot where the pieces of his chestpiece were sewn together. She rammed the dagger in. He gurgled and collapsed backward. She moved out of his way. He crumbled to the ground.

Penthesilea knelt, wrestled his inert form to its side, and retrieved her weapon. She resheathed her dagger. Wet warmth covered the front of her tunic. She stood still and focused her senses on the forest around her.

The acrid smell of sweat and leather and the sweet odor of new blood intruded on the dankness of the woods. The disturbed chattering that had arisen above her head subsided. The rain hit the foliage with a low hiss. Calm had returned to the spot around Penthesilea, and yet, uphill, it seemed—to the left, in the direction Antiope had taken—denizens of the trees twittered out of rhythm.

Penthesilea stopped breathing and strained her ears. The underbrush crackled. She tiptoed toward the spot where the noise was coming from, moving in a half crouch on the balls of her feet, careful to make no sound. A wide patch of steady gray behind the black crisscross of the leaves gave away a clearing. The sound of footsteps froze her in place. She lowered herself onto her stomach and slithered in their direction, making her own movement coincide with the noise of the treading.

She stopped at the edge of the glen and looked out from behind a buckthorn. Its long leaves trembled in the downpour. In the middle of the treeless space, ten yards away, a Hittite soldier, his spear at the ready, his knees flexed, and his head tilted in concentration, moved in a circle around his heels. He had heard something. He turned until he faced Penthesilea's hiding place and stopped. She reached for her labrys. She pulled at it but it did not slide loose readily. Her motion made a noise. The man lowered his weapon and ran toward her. She yanked the axe free and tried to slither sideways without getting caught in the brush. The spear rushed at her, its four-sided head glinting viciously. She hurled her arm at a spot between the man's leg armor and shield. She missed. Her weapon bounced off his protective covering. The soldier bellowed and charged. That she was going to die came to her as clear and cold as ice. Time stopped. Warm liquid trickled down her thighs. Suddenly, the soldier screamed and his knees folded. He pitched forward and landed within inches of her.

She got to her feet. A labrys had ripped open the back of the man's thigh. Waves of blood pulsated from the wound.

Antiope crashed out of the opposite side of the clearing. She had drawn her knife. She neared the prone form, raised her dagger, and made to bend over. Wild glee shone in her eyes.

Penthesilea threw her arms around her to trap her. Antiope struggled against the hold. Penthesilea hissed, "Stop, Antiope, stop! He's already gone." Antiope stared blankly at her, as she might at someone who had addressed her in a strange tongue. Only after a moment did recognition come over Antiope's face. She glanced down at the soldier and relaxed her raised arm. Penthesilea let her go.

"He stalked me for a long time," said Antiope. Her voice sounded loud and high. Penthesilea put her hand over

Antiope's mouth and listened intently. The man at their feet did not stir. No strange sound issued from the forest.

"Listen," whispered Penthesilea, "I also killed one of the men they sent after us. They are Hittite soldiers. I don't understand what they're doing here, unless they're deserters."

Antiope agreed.

"That makes two out of action," said Penthesilea, "perhaps three. Did you hear the scream when I shot at the entrance to the notch?"

"Yes. He flashed into sight as I was taking aim."

"I thought that my arrow. . ." Penthesilea's voice trailed off without her finishing the thought. Her mind was turning. She said, "I'd like to see what the rest of them are up to. Feodissia . . . How much light is left?"

"Not much. Once night falls you won't be able to see a thing."

"We can't leave Tecmassa so easily," said Penthesilea, her voice quavering.

Penthesilea's emotion surprised Antiope, who focused quizzical eyes on her. But Penthesilea did not notice. Her thoughts were still racing. At length she uttered, "We put three of them out of the fight. That leaves five, perhaps four."

"You're right."

"But they don't know that," said Penthesilea. "They most likely think that we were taken care of by the two they sent, or that they're chasing us in the hills right now, or that the night has stopped us in our tracks. They'll never expect an attack."

"An attack?"

"Yes. They'll gather soon to rush Tecmassa. They won't chance sending in just one or two, because she might be waiting for them at the other side of the tunnel. They don't know that she's hurt and can't shoot. So they'll probably rush in all together as soon as the last trace of light leaves the air, and that's soon, very soon. But they've got to go through the mouth of the defile one by one. That's when we can attack, when they're gathering to rush in. But we have to get there fast. We can't let night fall."

"You want to attack?" asked Antiope.

"Yes. There used to be eight of them. Now there are five. And three of us counting Tecmassa. And we have surprise on our side."

"Counting Tecmassa?"

"You don't think for a minute that she'll sit and wait for them to hunt her down? She'll make every bit of trouble she can. Look, Antiope, either we hide in the hills and leave Tecmassa and Feodissia, if she's still alive, to whatever they've got in store for them, or we attack the moment they move into the entrance."

Antiope opened her mouth, closed it, and fixed her eyes on her belt buckle. When she looked up, she had pulled her lips into a cruel grin.

The young women stepped lively down the wooded stretch leading to the trail they had earlier taken on horseback. Unseen roots grabbed at their ankles. Pebbles slid out from under their feet. The rain had all but gobbled up the twilight and turned the ground into hundreds of slippery traps. Penthesilea's foot smote a rock. She lunged forward and fell on the same knee that she had crushed at the beginning of her climb. Flame seared inside her leg; pain slit it lengthwise. She started to shriek but caught herself in time and emitted only a noisy gasp. Antiope stopped, pulled her up, and opened her mouth to ask the obvious question, but Penthesilea clamped her hand over Antiope's lips.

They reached the path leading to the entrance. Penthesilea stopped. Her leg burned and pounded. Antiope drew up to her side. "Go through the thicket," whispered Penthesilea. "Just before we get to the entrance, we'll hide. I don't think they've posted a sentry."

Penthesilea looked at the sky. The remaining shroud of dark purple was dimming to nothing before her eyes. She dove into the thicket near the spruce trees. Antiope did the same. She went forward at a snail's pace. As she progressed, the brush ripped her tunic and clawed at her face and body. Twice she encountered growth so dense that she had to backtrack and try a new way. Once she crashed against the ground. Pain impaled her there for a dull moment. The noise she had made seemed fearful. To calm herself, she put her hands on her belt and felt for her weapons, sliding each one out of its sheath and running her fingers over the metal and wood. As soon as she breathed steadily again, she resumed crawling.

She reached the end of the underbrush and surveyed the space in front of her. There was the entrance. A few paces away from it lay a small boulder. She slithered behind it.

Her head throbbed in rhythm with the wound in her knee and thigh, but she forced herself to look ahead. Four men stood with their backs to her, facing the stone corridor that went into the gap. Each man carried a spear and shield; each wore a leather cuirasse and an ovoid headpiece. The soldiers did not talk, and the sound of the falling rain exaggerated their silence. One of them pivoted slowly in Penthesilea's direction. She ducked. After a while she raised her head, tentatively, cautiously, but the man had turned back to his comrades and was standing still, leaning on his spear. No one was looking her way.

Antiope crawled beside her, and Penthesilea whispered, "Let the first two move in. Get the one nearest you with your labrys. I'll aim at the farthest one. Then we'll get their spears and shields and charge in, screaming as loud as we can."

Antiope nodded without looking at Penthesilea. Penthesilea closed her eyes and asked the Goddess for help, promising to leave rich presents at Her altar if She did. Antiope's lips also moved in silent orison.

Dusk shuddered to its death, and for an instant the sky grew luminous. The knot of men untied, and the first soldier stalked into the vestibule. The others formed up behind him and shuffled as they waited their turns. The second disappeared. Penthesilea and Antiope pulled their labryses from their belts, stood up, and hurled the weapons. The man that Penthesilea had aimed at bellowed and pitched forward. Antiope's target growled in surprise, turned, and charged. But he did not long maintain a straight line; he teetered and fell. Penthesilea broke into a lurching run and reached the man she had lately put out of action. She grabbed his pike and shield. She put her left forearm in the arm strap and, balancing the spear in her right, waited for Antiope to strip her victim and equip herself. Then, howling the Amazon war cry, the riders scrambled for the corridor.

Before they penetrated its entrance, men cried out from inside, hooves thudded. A woman's voice shrieked the Amazon call to blood. A soldier broke in panic from the stone doorway. He carried no weapons. He had cast them down; he was out of the fight. The riders let him pass.

The hoofbeats and screams dinned louder. Then, whinnying wildly, his eyes flashing fire, his ears flattened, his mane shaking and streaming, Antiope's riderless horse hurtled out of the narrow passage and flew past. Blood-curdling screams and a running steed's deafening staccato still roared toward them. Tecmassa, mounted on Tala, burst from the entrance; horse and rider thundered by like dark figures in a dream. Tecmassa made vicious arcs in the air with her axe.

Penthesilea's leg folded, and she sank to the ground.

Penthesilea squirmed and fretted. While Antiope accompanied Tecmassa and Feodissia (whom the intruders had tied and gagged but not hurt) on their northeast rounds, she, Penthesilea, who had never spent a day in bed, much less indoors, had to stay put, in the house, her injured leg confining her first to her sleeping couch and then to the precincts of Thalestris' palace.

After a week, Penthesilea was unable to look with composure on the mural of Shaushka that decorated the sleeping chamber. In it, the smiling divinity, Her eyes shining with pleasure, wrapped Her thighs around the flanks of a dusky mare that leaped through the air in pursuit of a winged leopard whose paws reached for the sky. Nor did the potion that Myrtho had prescribed for Penthesilea's repose comfort her: it made her more restless than if she had not drunk it, for it conveyed her on perfumed water to daydreams of Cletê. Nor did Penthesilea feel at ease exchanging phrases with the members of Celano's staff who brought her meals and bathed her wounded limb. Only Anuphey's conversation lightened her heart, but Anuphey did not much look in on her. As for Thalestris, she visited her once or twice but did not stay long or ask for details about the recent action.

By the morning of the twelfth day, Penthesilea's healing had progressed far enough for Myrtho, who was supervising her care, to declare that she could walk about outdoors. Pity, in addition to medical wisdom, prompted Myrtho to grant Penthesilea permission to leave the house. The young woman fidgeted so while the priestess examined her knee and thigh. Nevertheless, Myrtho lay down strict conditions for Penthesilea's venturing outside. "You must not be on your feet more time than is required to walk to the gate. Not one moment longer. And under no circumstances may you attempt to ride horseback."

Penthesilea agreed with such haste that Myrtho assigned Philippis the task of overseeing the girl and gave the steward the most exact instructions concerning the outing. And something in Myrtho's tone told Philippis that she had better not let her affection interfere with her better judgment.

Within the hour, Penthesilea, followed by Philippis, hobbled out of the courtyard of Themiscyra's principal dwelling.
Penthesilea stopped in front of the wall, leaned on a cane (the
presence of which clashed with her young face and body), and
threw back her head to suck in a chilly breath and whoosh out
the vapor it made. Then she beamed and surveyed the marketplace. A dozen women were bargaining with customers. A score
of onlookers milled around them. Penthesilea gritted her teeth
and halted across the open space, heading for the thoroughfare
that led to the gate. She set a good pace in spite of her injury.
Philippis—her white hair, obese frame, and voluminous
wheezing notwithstanding—scurried beside her.   That
Penthesilea did not hasten her lopsided gait even more must be
credited to Philippis' voluble, short breaths, which rhythmically reminded Penthesilea that she was under surveillance.

Penthesilea and Philippis descended the hill, and soon
faint clanging reached them from the direction of the gate. The
noise grew louder as the women advanced, until, the rider and
her chaperon ducking into a narrow way that ran parallel to
the wall, it split their ears. The women who worked with fire
had their establishments in this lane and in the alleyways and
cul-de-sacs abutting it. The hammering reached its crescendo
when the walkers passed a shack that crowded in on the path.
This building, the smithy, seemed to pulsate with the din that
belted forth from the inside. A stream of blue-gray smoke
plowed up from the structure's roof, bent to the wind, and vanished.

The clamor ebbed as soon as Penthesilea and Philippis
turned into the way known as "the street of the potters." It was
here that the claymakers—and there were almost a dozen of
them, specializing in vessels of diverse shapes and functions—
had their shops. The establishment of Thersandra came into
sight, a squat house made of dun-drab ceramic bricks covered by
a thatched roof. Penthesilea limped more quickly and ducked
into the doorway of the single room that made up the dwelling.
The earthy smell of unbaked clay cooled her head. Tall
storage jars lined the floor, their russet contours glinting in the
light of four oil lamps set up around the potter's wheel.
Thersandra had trundled it from the back courtyard into the
middle of the house for the cold season, during which time a
woolen partition separated the working space from the hearth
set near the rear wall.

Seven persons occupied the little premises—Thersandra, her mother, two of her daughters (a third had been bound over to Oenanthé the arrowmaker, who was daughterless), and three apprentices. The members of Thersandra's household ate and slept and plied their trade in strapped quarters like those of all the city artisans—a closeness encouraging goings-on that peasants and riders described with superficial shock but unmistakable pleasure.

Thersandra looked up. She winked at the sight of Penthesilea. She saw Philippis and closed her eyes for the time it takes to draw a breath. She inclined deeply, straightened up, and whispered to the adolescent who had been turning the wheel. The youngster sprang to her feet and scurried into the curtained precincts behind the hearth.

Thersandra wiped her hands across the stomach of her tunic, leaving ten gray streaks. She flashed a warm smile and stepped toward her callers.

Thersandra had full lips, a hooked nose, and bluish-white skin whose transparence was heightened by perpetually flushed cheeks. Salt-and-pepper hair tied into a single tress hung down her back, and escaping locks framed her face with a halo of powdery wisps. Her waist was slight and her hips and shoulders broad. A mud-caked beige tunic shrouded her from shoulder to knee. She had rolled up the the shirt's sleeves, revealing bony wrists and powerful forearms. Dried earth stained them to the elbows. Only the inside of her hands, whose palms were fleshy and fingers long and graceful, were free of it.

"Well, hello, Penthesilea," said Thersandra in a flutelike voice. "I heard ya had some trouble up north. And welcome to you too, Philippis. The spirits of hospitality were sure nice bringing you this way. Have something to wet your whistles and fill your bellies."

Two clay-caked adolescents appeared from behind the curtain bearing stools. A chestnut-haired girl, just budding into womanhood, followed, carrying a small table. They placed the furniture beside the callers.

"Thank you," said Penthesilea. The chestnut-haired girl lowered her eyes and blushed.

"Be seated, why don't ya," said Thersandra. The visitors complied, Penthesilea sighing with ease to be off her leg. The girl giggled.

A white-haired woman with the same features as the ceramicist's emerged from the back of the shop. She balanced a tray on which stood a decanter, a bowl of dried fruit, and three small cups. She set down the burden on the stand and poured. The potter and her guests made their libation and drank.

Penthesilea sighed with pleasure and sipped. Dizziness crept over her. The drink was far stronger than wine and tasted of a sweet, cloying fruit that she could not name. Philippis put her tumbler down and sniffed, "This is date liquor."

"It comes from Thalestris' household," volunteered Thersandra. "She gave it to me in exchange for a special job I did."

"I see," sibilated Philippis.

Thersandra returned her cup to the stand. "Beggin' your pardon," she said, "I have to finish my job before the clay dries on me."

Thersandra stepped back to her workplace. Her helper was waiting for her.

An unfinished storage jar stood on the wheel. When the vessel was completed it would measure half as tall as a grown woman and wide enough in the middle to put your arms around. Thersandra had started the container by shaping a thick clay disk as its base and placing it on the turning platter. She had then formed earthen ropes and laid them over the plate's perimeter, smoothing each coil against the one she had placed it on. At first, she had made every one longer than its predecessor, so that the belly of the receptacle grew fuller as the handiwork progressed. But once she had completed the fattest part, she had produced ropes that were progressively shorter, so that the pithos' sides now tapered toward its mouth.

The length of clay Thersandra had been working on lay on a table next to the unfinished jar. She picked up the coil and balanced it in both hands to ascertain that its weight was even. She ran her fingers over it to make sure that it was of uniform diameter and that it was not so wet that it would shrink too much in drying and not so dry that it would eventually come apart from the rest. She set it on top of the last roll of clay. She pinched and worked the clay between her thumbs and index fingers, her apprentice hurrying the wheel or slowing it according to the hunching of Thersandra's shoulders and elevation of her forearms. Finally, she shrugged, and the girl stopped. The potter took up a wooden stylus whose end spread into a spatula. Her assistant resumed. Squinting at her work with the suspicion of a trader examining a jewel, she smoothed the pithos' inside and outside surfaces. At length, her brow relaxed, and she straightened up. She put down the spatula, smeared her hands across her tunic, and went back to her visitors.

She poured more liquid. They all drank. Anticipating the questions that first-time callers asked, she said to Philippis, "The body of the jar will take me the rest of today to finish. Then it'll dry inside for a while—four days instead of the two it would need if the sun shone bright. But I can't chance leaving the work in the open this season. It rains a lot. Once it's dried, the girls will carry the greenware to my kiln."

"Greenware? What's that?" asked Philippis."Unfired —."

A puff of outside air chilled Penthesilea. A woman with the long, graceful body and dark good looks of a dancer from the south had pushed aside the curtained door. It was Oenanthé the arrowmaker. She caught sight of Penthesilea, flashed a gleaming smile, and bent in a graceful arc, her eyes never straying from Penthesilea's face. When Oenanthé straightened up, she stared into the rider's eyes for the space of a heartbeat.

A beak-nosed child with rosy cheeks and a wasplike waist followed Oenanthé. The child ran up to Thersandra, threw her arms around her waist, and buried her head in her belly. Thersandra patted the girl's hair and kissed the back of her head, saying, "Well, Oenanthé, have you brought this kid back to her mom because she's plain no good?" Thersandra and the eight-year-old hugged each other tighter.

"Not at all," said Oenanthé in tones that seemed to cling to the air after she had spoken them. "She's doing well enough."

"And when she's not?" asked Thersandra, a teasing light invading her eyes. She was alluding to the cuffs that craftswomen freely dealt to wayward (and innocent) apprentices. Thersandra and Oenanthé burst out laughing; the child's light giggle drifted into their chorus.

The merriment subsiding, Oenanthé approached Penthesilea. "I am truly happy to see you," she whispered, as if sharing a secret. She turned her comely gaze on Penthesilea's leg, and pity wrote itself across her face. She laid gentle hands on Penthesilea's shoulders and brushed her lips against her cheek. Heat rushed into it, at the same time as Penthesilea's nostrils dilated with the fragrance of currants and apple blossoms.

The chestnut-haired girl tittered. Philippis sniffed and raised an eyebrow.

After Philippis escorted Penthesilea home, Anuphey helped her undress. The warm air caressed Penthesilea's skin. She
slid between the blankets. Their soft wool rubbing her skin
made her hum.

Anuphey served her supper, made sure that she drank down
Myrtho's potion, and took her leave.

Penthesilea groaned and tossed about for hours.

It rained the next day and the next. Penthesilea spent all
the time in her sleeping chamber, taking naps out of boredom,
envying Antiope her rounds in the chilly outdoors, recalling
Cletê's softness, remembering a hundred times an hour how
Oenanthé's lips had caressed her cheek.

On the afternoon of the third day, Antiope returned to the
city and looked in on her companion. First, Penthesilea grinned
then she saw that Oenanthé accompanied Antiope.
Penthesilea colored.

"I ran into Antiope near the gate," Oenanthé explained.
Antiope inquired about Penthesilea's health, listened with
half an ear, and left. Oenanthé lingered.

She bent her head over Penthesilea's and made a show of
examining her face. Her eyes caressed Penthesilea's; the odor
of currants and apple blossoms turned Penthesilea's head. Heat
rushed through her. Oenanthé sat down on the bed.
Penthesilea pushed herself up and swung her legs over the side.
She realized that she was naked and, although she would not
have done so any other time, blushed and draped a cover over
her bare skin. Oenanthé gave no sign of having noticed and took
her hand. "I came to visit you," she said, "because I wanted to
say how sorry I am that you're wounded and how happy I am to
see you up and about." Oenanthé's voice had deepened.

Penthesilea lowered her gaze. Oenanthé squeezed her
hand.

Just then, Anuphey burst in, grinning from ear to ear. She
announced that Penthesilea could join the women of the house
for the evening meal in the great hall if she felt well enough.
Penthesilea said that she did, and Oenanthé accompanied her,
offering Penthesilea her arm to help her along.

Thalestris was absent. Her older apprentices sat around
their table—Antiope, Oebala, Marpessa, and Tomiris.
Penthesilea and Oenanthé joined them. After their supper the
women lingered over their wine—trading stories, poking fun at
the absent, repeating rumors. Somehow the talk turned to the
mural in Thalestris' private apartments.

"I have never seen it," said Oenanthé, "although I have heard more than one woman speak of it."

"More than one," repeated Marpessa.

"The painting was done by Amphiara in the early days of Naunamé's reign," said Antiope.

"Amphiara?" said Oebala. "Wasn't she the lover of Glaucê of the deep-sounding voice, you know, the bard that the old Amazons are always raving about?"

"They say that Amphiara was not only the greatest of the painters but also of the lovers," said Antiope.

"She also painted the wall near Penthesilea's bed, didn't she?" Tomiris asked of Oenanthé.

Oenanthé framed her lips in a vague smile and asked, "Is the mural in Thalestris' bedroom as beautiful as they say it is?"

Antiope stood up and declared, "There's one way to find out."

The trespassers tiptoed into the antechamber of Thalestris' bedroom. Caïeta, an aged domestic who had served the noble house for many decades, dozed in an armchair next to a brazier. The intruders spirited past her, drew aside the curtained entrance of Thalestris' private room, and stole in. Their motion disturbed the half-light projected by two brass stanchions holding burning oil, and the wall above the chief's sleeping couch pulsated. On it, brought to life with quick brush strokes, were portrayed Ninatta and Kulitta, handmaidens of Arinna the Sun Goddess. Their likenesses shivered in the flickering radiation like figures underwater, trembled less and less as the air settled, and grew still once it regained its nighttime tranquillity.

The painting showed two scenes from their lives. In the leftmost panel, Ninatta and Kulitta sat naked and cross-legged, their torsos facing the beholder and their happy countenances shown in profile. Each woman's large, almond-shaped eyes stared into the other's. The fair-complexioned Kulitta's were acorn-hued, and the dark-skinned Ninatta's like obsidian set against amber. In front of the women stood a gold goblet full of dark, shimmering liquid and a terra-cotta bowl containing three apples whose layered ruddiness invited the lips. Kulitta's near-translucent digits were wrapped around one of these fruits. The eye followed her pastel-veined hand and forearm to her slight waist, around which hung a girdle of bronze plaques engraved with dozens of tiny spirals.

A string of rubies attached to the belt descended over Kulitta's flesh-pink belly and pointed to her flax-colored fleece. The skin between her legs, which her downy pelt partially hid from view, glistened the incarnadine of the first spring roses, which the painter had lovingly rendered by laying down scores of vermilion lines over an alabaster background. The same flush stained her lips and nipples.

Ninatta's plum-dark hand lay across Kulitta's peach-fair stomach. Ninatta smiled as one blessed of the Goddess, and a faintly perceptible aura, suggested by a whitening of the citrine background against which she was depicted, outlined her head, neck, and chest. The dark, purplish red of her nipples, and her belly the hue of polished leather, seemed to come out of the flat wall; and the flesh between her thighs— which the artist had portrayed with delicious affection— glinted like cherry-meat in the teasing lamplight.

The rightmost panel portrayed the unclothed pair sunk in sleep, their closed eyes suggested by ciliated, indigo arcs. The vibrating daylight that had sharpened the contours of the first scene and deepened its shadows to violet here gave way to lazy halftones that caressed the outlines of the lovers' bodies and cast moon-shade on their peaceful forms. Kulitta slept on her side, facing the onlookers. Her rosy mouth was sketched in a blissful smile, her blonde head cradled in Ninatta's dusky shoulder, her body curled in languid curves that spoke of profound contentment. Although she was not awake, Kulitta's cheeks were more light-giving than before. Her delicate hand was poised on Ninatta's full breast, her burnt-rose thumb and forefinger circled Ninatta's murrey nipple. Ninatta lay on her back, her woolly crown rested on a burnt-orange pillow. Joyful visions pulsed behind her eyelids, and happiness through her lips. She had folded the hand nearest the onlooker under her head, revealing an enticing tuft of the deepest dye; the other hand hugged Kulitta's knees, as if she did not want to let go of her darling, even—or especially—in her sweet dreams. Her limbs mingled with those of her friend, and the bend of her foot hinted at satiety and gratitude.

In front of the supine women lay Kulitta's jeweled belt tangled around itself as if haste had plucked it off and flung it away. Next to it the goblet rested on its side, a thin, plum-colored line dripping from its glittering lips.

Myrtho entered the temple garden. Patches of snow, ghostly masses in the moonlight, still covered the ground. Myrtho wrapped her skirt around her knees and sat down on a bench. She folded her hands in her lap and closed her eyes. She slowly drew in a breath. The atmosphere was less chill than it had been even a week before, and the nights were not so bitter.

Still, how desolate the dark hours felt without Leokadia sleeping by her side. Now that she had gone to the land of the immortals, Myrtho would have to live with this cold eating at her heart until she joined her. How long would that be? How long had it been since she had taken her leave of her? Myrtho counted the months, and her thoughts pulled her downward. But she realized that she was sinking and recoiled from it. In a burst of courage that never entirely deceived her, she repeated to herself that there was no use lamenting, that she had no power over death, that she could not alter such things. They were the Goddess' concern. They were the Goddess' desire. One day perhaps Myrtho would comprehend why.

Myrtho looked at the firmament. In the past week the bee-hive had moved upward from the horizon, the serpent had slithered farther to the right, and the horse, with its brilliant blue wither, had pranced onward. Tomorrow was the day when Arinna rode back across the line that separated the heavens into north and south, the day when the hours of light equaled the hours of darkness, the day when Hebatê struck Texobos dead and the new year began. The priestess Iphinoë would climb up to the parapet and watch for the rays of the new sun to gleam through the crevice at the summit of the southeast mountain. As soon as they touched her feet, she would ring the sacred chimes, and Myrtho would put on her white surplice. All day she would lead prayers and processions. At sunset she would dedicate the young riders to Hebatê and, when night fell, attend the banquet given them in Thalestris' palace. The feast was always a raucous affair, and Myrtho had no taste for such revels. Even less so now. As soon as it was decent to do so, she would pretext fatigue and retire to her apartment. There, at least, the songs and music from the city would be muted. And the new year would begin.

The beginning of the year always depressed her. And this season she was more melancholy than ever. All the nights cast long shadows of grief; more lines scored her brow.

She gazed at the void formed by the triangle of the snake, the horse, and the hive. Just three moons before, at the time of the Longest Night, the same patch of sky had looked as if a generous hand had strewn a ladleful of diamonds across its velvet surface. The huntress dominated the heavens then, and, above her left shoulder, the sacred plow furrowed them. Myrtho remembered her consternation at that time. The temple ceremonies had ended, and the young riders were keeping their vigil, the first of the seven that would finish on the Day of the Year, when they were at last dedicated to the Goddess. All of them had been there, save Penthesilea. Where was she? Why had she taken her place only when the night was half over? It was a grave breach, an insult to the Goddess, who might not forget.

The sound of footsteps, one thumping, one dragging, cut Myrtho's reverie short. That was Iphinoë. Myrtho turned her head.

"Penthesilea is here, as you asked," said Iphinoë. Her voice was calm and deep, as if the act of fetching the young rider had made her thoughtful. Iphinoë withdrew.

Myrtho watched her. "If it is in my power," she thought, "Iphinoë will succeed me when my time comes. She is wise beyond her years."

Penthesilea came up and settled next to Myrtho. Sadness tinged the girl's expression.

Myrtho took her hand. "Look at the heavens," she said. "Tomorrow will be clear. Arinna will shine on you."

Penthesilea looked skyward but frowned.

"Your leg has entirely healed, I see."

Penthesilea made no answer.

"Thalestris is very proud of your exploit, you know. She would have advanced your initiation by one year, were you and Antiope not to be dedicated to the Goddess this very season."

"Yes," allowed Penthesilea in a bitter tone.

"What is the matter?"

Penthesilea drew her lips tight and did not look at her questioner.

Myrtho laid her fingers on the girl's wrist. "But what is the matter, my dear Penthesilea?"

Penthesilea blurted out, "Thalestris is wrong."

"Wrong? What do you mean?"

"Thalestris is wrong when she tells everyone what happened when we were ambushed. Even Antiope tried to stop her at first, but she got angry and ordered Antiope to keep quiet."

"I do not understand," said Myrtho, who had heard Tecmassa recount the episode but not Thalestris.

Penthesilea retold the adventure: how she had seen the way out of the ambush; how she had led the escape up the cliff; how she had led the attack on the Hittite deserters. Penthesilea did not dwell on the danger, or the effort, or the pain.

This girl is valorous and does not seem to be aware of it, thought Myrtho as the recital progressed.

Then Penthesilea described the version that Thalestris rehearsed. In that account, the brave Antiope inspired the deed of derring-do, and Penthesilea had merely acquiesced to her suggestions and followed her bidding.

"Once," Penthesilea said, "I told Thalestris that she had gotten the story wrong. Thalestris told me to keep silent. When I protested, she ordered me to leave."

Penthesilea widened her eyes. "Why, Myrtho? Why? Amazons are supposed to speak the truth and to give every woman her own. Why doesn't Thalestris tell the story right? Why is she unjust?"

"Yes, you deserve to be praised."

"Why is she unjust?"

"Why? That is not difficult to comprehend. She must desire that the greatest part in the affair be attributed to Antiope, because that version coincides with her political designs, because she wants Antiope, and not Melanippe, to become chief of the riders and high judge of the city when she goes to the West. And she is Antiope's mother. A story of Antiope's valor pleases her. Indeed, she may have related it so many times by now that she has forgotten that it is inexact."

"But it is wrong not to speak the straight truth; it is wrong not to give to every woman what is hers. Why does Thalestris not do what is right?"

"There is much injustice in this world."

"But why? Does Hebatê have no power?" Penthesilea's intense eyes questioned Myrtho.

She looked heavenward and sighed. "It is said that once Texobos took Hebatê prisoner and chained her up and dispatched the spirits of disharmony to the land of the mortals. Then the rocks clashed with the sky, the plants revolted against the sun, and the animals attacked their own kind. Humans killed each other for no reason and ate the hearts of the dead. But at length Hebatê broke out of Her chains and restored peace and harmony. That is why the waters now hold their course, the rocks worship the sky, the plants adore Arinna, and the animals live in peace with their own. Still, some of the spirits of disharmony concealed themselves among the mortals, putting on mortal clothing so that Hebatê could not find them. Now they live among us despite Her. It is said that this is the reason why there is injustice among the mortals; it is said that this is the reason why they do injury to one another."

Penthesilea stared straight ahead and wrinkled her brow. How handsome her pouting face was; and how sad she seemed.

After a while Penthesilea asked, "Leokadia was especially devoted to Hebatê, wasn't she?"

"All the riders are dedicated to Her and sworn to protect Her. Still, some offer a special cult to Shaushka, the Giver of Power, others to Arinna, the Giver of Knowledge, and others to Nikilmaté, the Giver of Daughters. But Leokadia was truly devout in her adoration of Hebatê after she discovered you. Leokadia felt that Hebatê had saved you from the Storm God so that she could find you. It was a special grace that the Goddess bestowed upon her. Did Leokadia never tell you that?"

"It isn't true anymore."

"What can you mean?"

"I am no longer pleasing in the Goddess' eyes. I offended Her greatly when I failed to be present at the vigil three months ago."

"The affront was serious indeed."

"I was wrong and have punished myself for it again and again. I have gone for days on end without eating or drinking. I have offered Her all my share of the silver that the Hittite deserters had hidden."

"How like she is to Leokadia," thought Myrtho. To Penthesilea she said, "The piety was great, even exaggerated. But is your heart wiser now? That is the essential."

"My heart?"

"Hebatê loves Her true daughters, those who worship Her more than they worship any mortal pleasure."

Penthesilea shifted her glance away and whispered, "That night I was with Oenanthé the arrowmaker."

Myrtho had already known but said nothing.

"It started," said Penthesilea, "when I was confined to the palace because of my wound. One day she came to me there. She wanted me. She came to my bed. After that, she came into my arms every night. Oenanthé is so beautiful. Oenanthé is so loving. She was. . . . It was . . . like drinking the spiced wine they give us for celebrations of the Goddess. It was like eating the sacred leaves. It was like the story they tell about Ninatta and Kulitta. Like the story they tell about Glaucê and Amphiara. I was like one blessed. I want no other friend to lie down with. I do not know if anyone has ever felt the way I did, the way I do."

Penthesilea's distress was too great for Myrtho to smile at these last words. Instead, she said, "Many women have been infatuated with Oenanthé."

Penthesilea continued without hearing, "All the young riders in Thalestris' house envied me, because Oenanthé is even more beautiful than Antiope or Anuphey. The woman who shares Oenanthé's couch is blessed."

"Philippis says that numerous ones have done so. That Oenanthé has abandoned every one. That leaving them when they still love her delights her more than their love. That to make them cry pleases her above all things."

"I do not believe that. Oenanthé is good."

"What happened on the Longest Night? Why did you not join Antiope and the others to keep watch in the temple?"

"I found Oenanthé in my bed. She said she had been waiting for me, especially on that night, because it was so important to me. She said that we had many hours before I had to purify myself and take my place in the sanctuary. She stretched out her arms to me. My flesh began to ache. I lay down next to her, and she made it joyful. But when I wanted to touch her, she wouldn't let me. She said I was clumsy, that I didn't really care for her. How could she say that? I said that it wasn't true. We talked about it for many hours. Each time she found something wrong with me, I proved that it wasn't so. She said that she forgave me and put her hands and mouth on my body again. I felt pleasure that was like sadness. But when I wanted to touch her, she rolled away and got up. The hour was late, she said. Good-bye, she said. Good-bye. It was long after midnight. I called the women and hurried to the temple. When I got there and saw the others, I knew that I had done wrong. I had offended the Goddess."

"Have you seen Oenanthé since then?"

"Yes. I went to her every day. I wanted to make her understand and come back. But whenever I talked, she laughed. And if I cried, she smiled. That is when my penance and fasting and offerings began. That is when I threw myself at the Goddess' feet and asked for forgiveness. I wanted Her to see how great and pure my devotion was. I did everything for Her. One day She will see that I did. For She is good. My heart is sure of that. "

Mythro wondered whether Penthesilea was talking about Oenanthé or the Goddess?

"Tecmassa tells me that my sadness will go away. That the best cure for an aching heart is a new affair. But Tecmassa doesn't understand. She really doesn't. I don't want to share the couch with anyone except Oenanthé. I am so sad. So sad. No one has ever been this sad."

Penthesilea covered her eyes.

Myrtho caressed the crown of her head. "Your melancholy will diminish. The Goddess will give your heart wisdom and comfort."

The girl tilted her head, then shook it.

Myrtho placed her fingers on the Penthesilea's cheek. "I think I know that heart," she said.

Penthesilea raised her eyes.

"You have profound affection in your temperament. That is why your regrets have been so pervading; that is why your contrition has led you to expiate your affront with such intensity; that is why your remorse at having lost this lover has injured you so greatly. And that, Penthesilea, is why you will have only one great friend."

"Oenanthé?"

"No. I cannot say who she is, because I do not know. But I do know that it is like that with some women. They have only one great friend. That is the manner in which your soul is made. But with some others it is all the contrary."

"You mean Oenanthé, don't you?"

Myrtho laid the index finger of one hand over Penthesilea's mouth. Then she placed the palm of the other on her forehead. It was her benediction.

Penthesilea looked puzzled.

Myrtho smiled. "I am tired, Penthesilea, and I grow chilly. I will retire now. Go back to the sanctuary and beg for understanding. Tomorrow you will take your place among the Amazons. Good night."

Chapter 6

At twilight Thalestris, Antiope, and Penthesilea crossed the field that led to the gate. They bent forward in their saddles. Their horses footed wearily uphill. The women had ridden out before sunrise and dismounted for only a while at midday to eat and rest. Penthesilea's stomach clamored for food. Her head throbbed with thirst. Her backside ached.

Thalestris had chosen that late spring day to head out to the southern steppes, where traders would be spotted any time now. The chief of the riders had lost sleep over these approaches to the land: when the Amazons took up their summer positions, their ranks there would be thin sown, as they would everywhere, and yet rumors of armed strife among the Hittite ruling clan meant that the south might be open to armed incursions in the absence of a united Hittite presence.

Other worries, too, plagued Thalestris. The winter before, the Storm God had visited many deaths upon the city's dwellers.

A fever that carried its victims off in three days had struck when the nights were longest. It had not spared even the most robust women. Fourteen riders had died of it, and a score more—who had been stricken but survived—were still too feeble to take up their springtime duties. As if this were not enough, three more Amazons would not go about on horseback for another month. They had just given birth to babies, two of them girl children. The summer before suitable men—men with fighting blood in their veins—had shown up at the gates, an event the Amazons always exploited. They needed daughters, and now more than ever.

Thalestris and her two followers neared the oak portal that led into the city. The gatekeeper sprang out of her den and waved frantically at Thalestris, who, despite these gestures, did not hasten her horse's gait. She walked the steed to the woman and bent down to hear what she had to say. The gatekeeper whispered in her ear.

Thalestris nodded and urged her pony into motion. Penthesilea and Antiope, who had stopped behind her, did the same.

As soon as the riders emerged from the tunnel practiced in the wall, Thalestris swiveled in the saddle and glared at her two apprentices. Then she set her face in the unruffled mask that Penthesilea knew well and turned away. So there was news awaiting them, and they had better not betray any concern. The two eighteen-year-olds traded glances. Antiope's expression was uneasy.

"What's the matter?" asked Penthesilea. "Do you know what this is about?"

"No. But these days I'd rather sleep away from the house."

Small wonder. Two weeks before, Antiope had kicked Anuphey out of her bed with no warning and for no reason that Penthesilea could figure out. Anuphey had shed many tears and begged to know why. Antiope met her sadness with stony indifference. Now Anuphey had embarked on a campaign of revenge, flirtations that drove Antiope to distraction, although she had no call to be jealous. Two nights before, Antiope had surprised Anuphey in the hayloft (what was Antiope doing there?) with Penthesilea's old comrade, Klymene, who had scaled the stable wall to be with Anuphey. Barefoot and naked, Klymene had to jump down and scramble back to Ariona's. The next morning, Tomiris—who volunteered to do the dirty work—had flung Klymene's sandals and tunic at her feet in front of Ariona and her women. When, snickering, Tomiris later described the look on Klymene's face, Antiope guffawed. Penthesilea did not smile. Klymene would never forgive Antiope for being shamed. That was dangerous.

Anuphey also got even with acts of household sabotage, which she could easily commit as a member of Celano's staff.

"Anuphey lets her older girl play in my sleeping chamber when I am gone from the house," said Antiope. "Two nights ago there was so much grit in my bed that I had trouble sleeping. And my bath—my bath. One day it chills me to the bone and the next burns the skin off me."

Perhaps Antiope deserved it.

In the great hall, Feodissia was seated at the table chatting with Anuphey. When the chief entered, Feodissia bolted up, her huge hands hitting the goblet set before her. It would have toppled over, but Anuphey reached out and deftly righted it. Feodissia grinned. Anuphey tittered. Then, having no more business there, she smiled brightly at Feodissia, pirouetted, and left.

The riders sat down around the table, and a woman brought them goblets and a pitcher of beer. She served and left. The Amazons made their libation and drank. Penthesilea fairly inhaled the prickly liquid.

No one spoke. Feodissia worked her lantern jaw to the left and to the right. Thalestris downed her drink and bid Feodissia deliver the message. Feodissia ran her tongue over her lips and began.

"Tecmassa and I bivouacked last night on the hill where the buckthorn grow. As soon as light showed in the sky, we started toward the border, not in a hurry, mind you. We planned to reconnoiter slowly and rest when the sun got high. We got only as far as the stand of black mulberry trees. We heard someone coming down the trail from the northeast, just people on foot, no horses or pack donkeys."

Thalestris, who had until then listened with an unconcerned expression, raised an eyebrow. It was early in the year for travelers to come in, especially from that quarter.

Feodissia went on. "The footsteps came slowly, very slowly. Our ponies smelled them right away, too. That mount of Tecmassa's threw her ears back when she caught their scent and whinnied. Tecmassa thought it was a party of soldiers, men, and she was right."

"A party of soldiers?" asked Thalestris.

"We moved back out of sight and dismounted. We climbed high to get a good view of the trail. They came round the bend and were not more than a stone's throw away. There were six of them. Tecmassa was right. They were fighting men, not traders. They were hurt. Some in a bad way. Yes, a bad way. They moved at a snail's pace, in threes, the two men on the outside holding up the man in the middle. Even men on the outside had trouble walking. They were a sorry sight."

"Did they have weapons?"

"The ones who could walk had no spears or shields, but it was too far to see if they had knives."

"Bows and arrows?"

"One of the men in the middle had a bow slung across his back; but as for arrows, it was too far to be sure. But no, I don't think so."

"What time of day was it?"

"After sunrise. They must have come into the territory yesterday and spent the night inside the border."

"Where did they come from?"

"I can't say. We did not get close enough to see for sure, still. . . ."

"Still?" prompted Thalestris.

"Tecmassa says they look like Achaeans."

"Achaeans?"

"Yes. They look like Trojans in a way, even though their clothes and hair aren't the same."

"Achaeans? You're sure?"

"Tecmassa says so."

"If they are Achaeans, then they're early," Thalestris said and turned to Antiope. "The Achaean cities lie beyond the warm sea that borders on Troy. The Achaeans have to sail to Troy and then journey overland to get here. But they can sail only around the equinox; then they have to wait in Troy for a month, because the rains are heavy in the early spring, and there's no journeying until the roads dry up. That's why Achaeans usually don't arrive here before the third full moon after the equinox."

"But the equinox was only two months ago," said Antiope.

"We watched them for the better part of the morning," continued Feodissia, "staying ahead of them, and it was slow going. They knew we were there, I think, but that didn't make them stop. They didn't move fast, though. Finally Tecmassa told me to ride back with a message for you. She wants you to bring a party of Amazons tomorrow morning and speak to the fellows, see what they're doing here. I got here about the middle of the afternoon, but you were riding out. Tecmassa says there's no real danger, so I stayed put and didn't rouse any other riders. I waited right here in the house." Pleasure flickered across her face, and her eyes sought the door through which Anuphey had lately disappeared. Antiope did not miss the look.

"I'll go see these strangers myself," said Thalestris. "We'll ride out at first light. Be ready at the gate before dawn."

Women carried in trays of food and set plates in front of the chief and the riders, who were too hungry to talk and polished off their dinner in silence. Thalestris drank a flagon of wine with her repast. At the end of the meal, she took her leave and walked to her apartments with the careful step Penthesilea knew well.

Antiope, Feodissia, and Penthesilea were still at table. Feodissia's appetite showed no sign of relenting as she opened walnuts two at a time by cracking them in her large hands. She chewed them loudly. Antiope rested her chin in her palm and tapped her foot. No one said a word.

A thin-shouldered, gracile form glided into the halo of light made by the oil lamps. It was Anuphey. Warm pink crawled up Feodissia's neck, and she grinned a shy grin full of good nature. Anuphey smiled slightly and seated herself next to her. Feodissia placed her goblet in front of Anuphey, stretched her long arm across the table, and wrapped her huge fingers around the fluted neck of a flagon. She lifted it and poured. Anuphey whispered thanks, lifted the vessel to her lips, and shut her eyes. While she was drinking, she cast a narrowed, sidelong glance at Antiope, who stood up and stalked off.

Anuphey now opened her eyes; satisfied and triumphant, they watched Antiope depart. Feodissia's also followed her. Then Feodissia turned to Anuphey, and the two women gazed at one another.

No one spoke. The oil lamps hissed. A brief burst of laughter from the kitchen disturbed the silence. Then it fell again. Finally, Anuphey broke it by asking in her curious accent, "The Amazon games take place in a little while, don't they?"

"Yes," answered Feodissia, blushing. Somehow, for all her luck in those things, Anuphey made her shy.

"Will you compete?" asked Anuphey.

"I suppose I will," mumbled Feodissia.

"Is it hard to shoot well?"

"Well, yes," stammered Feodissia. "And no."

"Yes and no?"

"I don't think about it much, at least not most of the time." She snapped her jaw shut.

Anuphey widened her almond eyes and said, "But still it must be hard."

"Maybe so."

"Maybe?"

"You've got to have two things."

"Two things?"

"You've got to be strong enough to pull the bowstring back far enough so that the shaft will fly fast and straight. That isn't so easy. Our bows are made of horn and you pull them against their natural curve when you shoot. We like to make our bows of horn—oxen, or mountain rams when we can bag them. We split the horns, or we tie two together, and attach them at the middle with wood and sinew. We use wood, too, for the ears."

Realizing that her words flowed, Feodissia pressed her lips against her teeth.

"The ears?" asked Anuphey, raising her eyebrows in curiosity.

"The end where the notches are so you can string the bow when you're ready to shoot. We use wood for the ears and fasten the whole thing together by braiding wet sinew around its length. When it dries, you've got a strong weapon with a good throw, a cast we call it. You see, the arrow has to take off as fast as a bird chasing prey or else it won't cut through what you're aiming at, especially if it's far enough away. Except it doesn't do much good if your arrow isn't any good; I mean if the wood isn't well seasoned and the grain straight. And the feather has to be cut straight at the rib and glued on proper."

"And tell me," said Anuphey, laying her fingers on Feodissia's shoulder, "How do you aim?"

Bright rose color invaded Feodissia's cheeks. "There are two ways of drawing the arrow," she answered. "You can draw high or you can draw low. Every woman has her own choice, but I like to draw low myself."

"How do you do that?" asked Anuphey, staring at Feodissia like a disciple hungry for enlightenment.

Feodissia jumped to her feet and placed herself in front of Penthesilea. Without changing position, she turned her face and stretched her left arm toward where Thalestris had sat. The archer extended the arm in a straight line from the top of her shoulder and wrapped the four fingers of her left hand around an imaginary bow. She lay the second joint of her left thumb on the second joint of her index finger. She drew her right hand back, its thumb extended and its middle two fingers slightly bent, until it nearly touched her nipple. Her elbow almost touched her waist. She bent slightly from it and sighted down the make-believe arrow, which would have rested on her flexed knuckle.

"Of course," she said without taking her eye off the empty seat or relaxing her arms, "some say that you do better not by drawing low the way I do, but by drawing high like this." Feodissia positioned her right hand, knuckles uppermost, just above where her shoulder joined her upper arm. This gesture lifted her elbow to the height of her middle chest. "They say your aim is truer this way, but I say that it's better to draw low because you can pull your shaft back better and your arm gets less tired."

Anuphey rose to her feet and ran her fingertips along Feodissia's arm. The skin grew incarnadine under their touch. Anuphey turned her back to her and mimicked her stance and gestures.

Feodissia contemplated her form and chuckled, "Well, that's almost it."

"Almost? What do you mean?"

"Here, let me show you how to draw better." She reached over Anuphey's shoulders and took her left hand; she wrapped her right hand around Anuphey's right wrist.

Penthesilea left quietly.

At dawn Penthesilea and Antiope walked their horses out of Themiscyra behind Thalestris, who had also bid Marpessa accompany them. Noble Hippolyta rode at Thalestris' side. Two of her women were also of the party, the gaunt Lysippe, and Ido, the rosy-cheeked gambler. Ariona and her daughter, Charope, a slight, wiry woman with a huge snout, brought up the rear. Feodissia was supposed to join them but had not shown up yet.

Thalestris waved the Amazons forward, and the group crossed the bridge and turned left along Thermodon. At that moment Feodissia caught up, trotted her horse abreast of Penthesilea and Antiope, and said in a voice that bubbled over with good cheer, "Good morning to both of you. And it's a beautiful morning. Beautiful. Tecmassa couldn't have worked very hard keeping track of that lot."

Penthesilea smiled and waved, but Antiope lowered her head and locked her lips.

Thalestris coaxed her mount into a canter. The other riders did the same and ran their horses along Thermodon. After an hour they passed the apple orchard and, after another, the wasteland. Here they turned left and set foot on the northeast trail. They slowed their ponies' gaits, regrouped in twos, and moved forward at an easy pace.

The sun had climbed halfway up the sky when the riders saw a finger of smoke rising above where the men were said to be camped. Soon Tecmassa trotted her horse out from behind a bend in the road. The cortege halted, and Tecmassa drew up to the chief.

"They're where we left them last night," said Tecmassa,"near the black mulberry trees. They set up camp almost within sight of the road and haven't budged from there. They built a big fire before the sun went down. They wouldn't do that unless they knew they'd already been spotted. A redheaded fellow went to snare supper at dusk but stayed away from where I was hiding. Now a hunter, and he is judging by the game he bagged, would have headed my way the first thing. He knew I was watching. There was something in the way he moved, too.

"They didn't even post a guard when they settled in for the night. They just piled more wood on the fire and lay down. One started screaming soon after that. Rot must have set into his wounds and heat taken hold of his spirit. He yelled all night but was quiet at dawn. He must have died because the ones that could walk began gathering wood and laying it in a square pile. I left soon after that but saw smoke rise when I looked back over my shoulder. All we have to do is follow it to where they are."

"You're sure there are only five of them now?" asked Thalestris.

"Yes."

"They've posted no pickets?"

"Not a one."

"They're unarmed?"

"I didn't see any weapons, except a bow without arrows, and three at least have knives. I saw that last night when they flayed and gutted their supper."

"Very good," said Thalestris. "Stay with us for now." Tecmassa drew back a few paces. Feodissia guided her horse through the double line of Amazons and handed her a canteen of beer and half a dozen barley cakes. Tecmassa grabbed the provender and beamed her patched smile. "Thanks, girl," she said. "I haven't had a decent meal for a whole day now. Where'd you get all this?"

Warm pink crawled up Feodissia's neck.

Thalestris called Feodissia to her side and ordered, "Ride back to where those soldiers sit and keep your eye on them." To Antiope, she said, "Go with her. Keep those men in sight and report on everything they do. We'll catch up with you soon enough. It's getting warm and there's no use running the horses if the men don't have any weapons and are on foot." Thalestris looked at the shadows on the ground. "We'll reach them by noon."

Feodissia and Antiope dug their heels into their mounts' sides and disappeared behind the bend. Penthesilea stared at the dust their animals' hooves had raised. She wondered whether Feodissia would again try to strike up a conversation and what Antiope would answer. She suspected that Antiope was a fool but did not say so to herself in words.

Hippolyta, who had listened in silence to Tecmassa's report, now said, "I can't say that I like this very much. They bear no arms but they are soldiers all. They do their best to show us where they are and do not set a man to watch the trail. Their smoke climbs to the sky in broad daylight. They know they will be found." Hippolyta's lips tightened in scorn. "They hope they will be found."

Thalestris showed no interest in these observations. She urged her horse forward, and the others fell in behind her.

The sun was at its zenith when Antiope ran her mount around the curve in front of them and drew up to the head of the column. "They haven't moved from where they spent the night," she said to Thalestris. "They're below a hillside, where there's a stream and wooded cover above. They've cremated the dead one and removed the bones. We can't tell where, though."

Hippolyta glanced skeptically at Thalestris, who did not appear to take notice.

"How far are they from here?" asked Thalestris.

"If you ride hard, as much time as it takes to walk your pony from the bridge to the palace. That's why I came to warn you."

"Very well," said Thalestris. She gestured and the riders drew up around her. She bid Hippolyta post her women along the ridge of the hill overlooking the strangers' encampment. She sent Ariona, Charope, Feodissia, and Marpessa around to the right. They were to follow the goat paths and station themselves on the far side of the foreigners, on the trail leading back to the border. The remaining riders, Antiope, Tecmassa, and Penthesilea, were to accompany Thalestris when she confronted the intruders and guard the way to the city if need be. Once everyone was in place, the men would be surrounded. Thalestris waited in the shade for an hour before moving forward again. Antiope rode at her left. Penthesilea and Tecmassa brought up the rear.

They came into sight of the men's camp. In front of them, a small stream cut down from the tree-covered slope on which Hippolyta stood watching. A smoking heap that suggested a square, the pyre, had been built on the near side of the rivulet. On the far side were the foreigners. The nearest one sat cross-legged, his face turned down, his honey-colored locks matted with mud. A welt as wide as a hand striped his chest from shoulder to waist. Behind him, a wavey-haired fellow, whom the women made out in profile, was seated on the ground, his knees pulled up against his chest and his head buried in his thighs. His trunk shook as if he were weeping. Tattered fabric, whose dirty brown was infused with darker, moist circles, bound his thick upper arms. Uphill of him, in the shade of the first trees, a dark and slender man lay on his back. His forearms covered his eyes, and a length of cloth black with dried blood was wrapped around his rib cage. A broad blue stripe overlaid his hips and groin. He groaned and thrashed. A stocky man knelt by his side and ran a wet rag over his brow.

The man nearest the riders looked up and muttered something. Heads turned and incurious eyes gazed at the newcomers.

Thalestris and her women forded the stream and stopped. The thickset fellow pulled himself to his feet and whistled twice.

A man with red hair came out of the copse. He did not pause to examine the Amazons but sauntered toward them. He favored his left leg. Still, he moved forward with a light, assured tread. He wore no clothes except a loincloth. He had brawny shoulders, a small, well-knit chest, and wiry but powerful arms. Between his tiny nipples hung a gold chain and medal. Two diamonds of reddish fur covered his trunk. The larger one blanketed his breast, the shadow of his pectorals tracing its horizontal axis. The smaller one overspread his belly and groin. The two hairy parallelograms tapered and touched at his waist. His hips were slim, and, as he advanced, an inverted mushroom of pink flesh bobbed in and out of sight behind the cloth covering them. The muscles of his thighs and calves hardened and relaxed with the rhythm of his step. His was a finely balanced body.

"There's a lot of strength in that build," said Tecmassa under her breath, "even if you wouldn't think so at first. He's

quick and light on his feet. And the look in his eyes is fast as
lightning, too."

Antiope, who had been gaping at the newcomer, nodded her
head hypnotically.

The heavyset man fell in by the redhead's side. He was
almost a head shorter; his barrel chest, hairy paunch, and
stomping gait accentuated the thickness of his neck and arms.

"Careful of that one, too," said Tecmassa. "Don't get
within his reach. His weight'll pin you motionless."

He came closer. His eyes were the color of slate and gave
away no feeling, although Penthesilea felt more than she saw
something cagey and cruel behind them. Her face contracted in
dislike. The man saw this and whispered something to the
redhead, who glanced at her briefly without altering his
expression.

The two strangers halted within a pace of Thalestris. The
redhead looked up at her. His straight nose, thin lips, and
dark green eyes radiated the confidence of someone who knows
that his face is pleasing to behold. The fat man's showed
nothing—no fear, no hope. Nothing.

The redhead made a deep, graceful obeisance. He straightened up and looked the chief in the eye. The short fellow surveyed the mounted women with a hard gray gaze.

Thalestris addressed the redheaded man. "Stranger!" she
said in a stern voice, "I am Thalestris, chief of the city of
Themiscyra. You have crossed into these lands without permission. Give a good account of yourself. You may not move from
this ground until you do." Thalestris pointed to the summit of
the hill. The men's heads turned, and their regard followed
Thalestris' outstretched arm. Four mounted fighters looked
back. The stout man's eyes grew colder.

The redheaded man smiled with glittering teeth. "Noble
Thalestris," he said in a melodious baritone, "I am Prince
Theseus of Troezen, a strong city across the western sea, in the
land of the Achaeans. I am the son of King Aegeus of Athens, a
mighty stronghold there, and am especially beloved of the
great god, Poseidon, from whom some say I am also descended."

Antiope raised her brows and looked at Thalestris, who
blinked once without taking her eyes off Theseus. The
heavyset fellow took in the reactions.

"And what is the name of your mother?" asked Thalestris,
whose face and voice had not softened.

"Aegeus got me on Aethra, daughter of Pittheus the Wise, who rules Troezen to this day."

"What goddess does your mother serve?"

"She is devoted to Thetis, the Triple Goddess, who brings men gifts from the sea."

"And of what lineage is Aethra?"

"She is the daughter of . . . Hyperea, Pittheus' legitimate wife, and is descended of Hippodaemea, of noble blood."

The heaviest man, Pirothous, looked at him from under lowered eyelids, but Theseus did not see him, for he was smiling at Antiope as if he were in cahoots with her about something. Antiope stared straight back.

Thalestris pointed to the wounded men and asked, "Who are they?"

"They are my men, or what is left of them. All have been with me for years, except the man at my side, Pirothous. He is my age, and came to Athens when he was fourteen."

"How did you come into the lands belonging to Themiscyra?"

"We came from Troy."

"Troy?"

"We sailed from Athens shortly before the equinox. We stayed in Troy only long enough to buy supplies and outfit pack animals."

"That can't be," affirmed Thalestris. "You can't get through from Troy so early in the year. The paths and trails are turned to mud or they run with water because of the spring rain."

"There's been a drought there. King Laomedon of Troy may have to send for wheat to stave off famine next fall and winter. He told me this himself."

Tecmassa sneered.

"Why haven't traders shown up yet?" asked Thalestris.

"They're waiting for caravans from the north. They will not move until the merchants arrive from the cold sea."

"For what reason did you leave your mother's city and come into these lands?"

"King Aegeus bade me prepare an expedition into the chain of Great Mountains to the east of here that men say are the limits of the world. Travelers have come back from these territories with stones of gold as big as a man's fist. They say the streams run with it and that men take the gold out of the water with sheepskins, although I don't see how."

Penthesilea and Tecmassa exchanged guarded glances. In Themiscyra, too, women panned for gold with sheepskins in certain mountain streams. The grease in the skins trapped tiny particles of the yellow stuff. But the prospectors had all sworn to the Goddess that they would say nothing about the location of these riches.

"But if Pittheus wants gold," said Thalestris, "you could have traded for it at Troy."

Theseus answered almost before Thalestris had finished speaking, "We wanted to try our luck where the gold would be cheaper. Few men have penetrated the great eastern mountains, but they say that gold is everywhere and that you stub your toes on it wading in the streams."

"You say that you wanted to trade," said Thalestris, "but you're soldiers, not merchants."

"Traders don't go to the Great Mountains," replied Theseus without hesitation. "It's dangerous on the way and risky when you get there. That's why there are always middlemen. At Troy, they warned us that we would have to cross dangerous country. They were right, Thalestris. They were right.

"When we set out from Troy six weeks ago, we were twelve in all, seasoned men that I could rely on in any danger. We led four donkeys loaded with goods that Aegeus supplied, amber from the west and plaques of worked gold. Of the eleven men I led, only four are still alive, and they are hurt, and one may die. Nothing is left of our goods, not even our weapons. All we have is our knives to cut meat with and one bow without arrows."

"But fighters never give up their weapons," said Thalestris, "never abandon them, never leave them behind."

"Not far from the entrance to these lands," replied Theseus, "in the recesses of the hills, live savages who do not cook their meat and who paint their faces black and yellow before they go into battle. But *battle* is the wrong word. They never face you like men, but take you unaware. They came at night."

"We know them well," answered Thalestris. "But it is early for the Kaska people to come down from the hills."

"That is what they told me, too, at Troy. But they were wrong. Three nights ago at least twenty of them fell upon us while we slept. In broad daylight, we could have made easy work of them, but that night they crept up and slit the throats of the two we had posted as sentinels—two men instead of one, because we were in dangerous terrain. Luckily, one guard made a noise before he went down. We woke up in time to fight for our lives. Those of us who survived the surprise had all we could do to keep together and fend them off until the dawn came. All of us were wounded. Pirothous and I less badly than the others. One man died of his wounds last night. We just sent him back to his ancestors." Theseus pointed to the still smoking remains of the pyre.

"That still doesn't answer the question," said Tecmassa. "Where are your weapons?"

"And what have you done with the bones?" asked Thalestris.

"We buried them according to our custom. At least we didn't leave the poor fellow behind while he was still alive. But we left everything else in the dark, our spears and shields, our animals, our supplies, the goods we had to trade."

"Count yourself lucky to have escaped alive," said Thalestris. "Few who pass through the Kaska lands come back to talk about it."

"They're like the robbers who infested the hills around my father's city of Athens and the roads along the coast. They lay in wait for you and fell upon you when you least expected it. They showed no mercy. If you were lucky they killed you soon. And if travelers were foolish enough to take women with them...." Theseus did not have to finish. "Attica was not safe, Thalestris, until my father armed an expedition under my command to put an end to the brigandage."

"When was that?"

"Two years ago. It was hill warfare."

"Did you have horses?"

"No. We Achaeans use horses only for chariots. Our horses are not tall enough for men to ride, as yours are. And chariots are useless in those hills. They can't get through. So we went on foot. It took the spring and the better part of the summer. But my men were steady." Theseus glanced at his followers with admiration.

He faced Thalestris again and said, "I made sure that every one of those robbers got what he deserved when we took them alive." Theseus' eyes flashed like a beast's about to rip flesh from still living prey. "They got as good as they had given. "

Tecmassa whistled under her breath. Penthesilea's throat tightened. The Amazons, like their neighbors the Hittites, had no stomach for the screams of those who could not fight back. They hated torture and torturers. So did the Goddess.

Theseus, who had seen the two riders start, glanced sideways at Pirothous, whose lips had thickened and nostrils flared. He turned narrowed eyes on Penthesilea. Waves of hate poured forth from hers like heat from a forge. Seeing this, Pirothous drew his mouth into a cruel grin. Penthesilea met his smirk straight on. Pirothous' expression retracted into lifelessness.

Tecmassa rode forward and glowered down at Theseus and Pirothous. They took her measure in the way that fighters do. The look that came over them, which they tried to disguise, admitted that she would be a fearful match.

Pirothous turned away from her and addressed Thalestris in a voice that had the honeyed hum of a perfume merchant's: "Now that the roads are safe, men can carry their goods and slaves overland to our port. The city of Athens prospers, and Aegeus is a rich man."

Tecmassa rasped, "Ask Theseus why he decided to come into the lands around Themiscyra."

"Your land was the closest by," he said.

"What proof can you offer," said Thalestris, "that your mother is the queen of a strong city, and that you are not a robber who came to no good on the roads and now wants to hide from someone—and perhaps steal things while you're here among the traders?"

Theseus slipped the golden chain from his neck and stretched his hand out to Thalestris. "Pittheus the Wise gave me this medal when I reached manhood and was initiated. It bears the picture of my god, mighty Poseidon, on one side. On the other is the likeness of a coiled serpent, which is the emblem of my father's house in Athens, the Erectheids. The House of the Coiled Serpent has ruled Athens since the day of my father's father, Pandion." Theseus paused the time it takes to close your eyes and open them. "Pandion's queen was the lady Praxithea, on whom he sired four sons and seven daughters. Three of the daughters, Otiona, Protogonia, and Pandora, were priestesses of the Triple Goddess, whom men worshiped in those days—She who gives birth, brings death, and knows all things before they happen.

"Both the chain and the plaque are of gold so pure, so finely drawn and worked, that only a king could have it made for himself and give it away."

Theseus stepped back and looked up at Thalestris. "You could strip this from me by force, for I am surrounded and outnumbered. But I give it to you of my own free will. It is the present made by Prince Theseus of the House of Pandion to the Amazon ruler, Thalestris, of the House of Marpasia. On Poseidon's image and in His presence, I pledge my oath that it is as I have said. If it is not, let the same god punish me with impotence and forsake my house, because I took His name in vain."

Theseus proffered the object, and Thalestris stretched out her palm. He let go of the medal. It fell. The gold dazzled Penthesilea's eyes. Thalestris' hand dropped under the weight. She turned the object around in her fingers, tossed it up once, and closed her fist around it.

"Traders in Troy," said Theseus, "told us that the Amazons, who ride tall horses and brandish iron axes, welcome men and put them at their ease. They say you greet strangers with a hospitality blessed of the gods who preside over men's fortunes. That to all men who come in peace, as we do, you freely give food and drink and send females down to their tents to lie with them. That you desire their company in the fair season because no man may dwell among you when the winter comes. That from the season when the days grow longest until the equinox four months later, men may come into your kingdom and sire babies on your women. That the only tribute you exact from the men is their seed. Strangers, they say, are welcome here. That is why Theseus of the Erectheids begs the hospitality of Thalestris of the Marpasians."

Penthesilea and Tecmassa traded glances again. If Theseus had really been heading for the Great Mountains, would he have taken the trouble to learn the name of Themiscyra's ruling clan?

Out of the corner of her eye, Penthesilea caught a glimpse of Antiope. No such question troubled her handsome eyes, which were riveted on Theseus.

Pirothous gazed up at Thalestris with a demeanor that pleaded and cajoled at the same time. "Noble Thalestris," he said in a caressing tone, "you are a fighter yourself. Look at us and tell me what harm we can do you. We come without weapons. We have only knives to cut our meat with. We have no spears, no shields, no helmets. Look at these men. How far can they run? How straight can they throw? I am sure that you will not turn us out. Prince Theseus of the lineage of Pandion requests this favor of the Amazon ruler, Thalestris of the lineage of Marpasia. Will you deny his plea, mighty lady?"

Penthesilea stared at Pirothous with narrowed eyes; he was a hateful fellow, not to be trusted. His glance flickered her way; he seemed to take in her loathing and suspicion. She met his gaze and set her mouth. His lips hinted at a sneer, and he turned again to Thalestris.

Thalestris told Theseus that the men could wait where they were. Before the sun set on the next day, a messenger would be sent to tell them if she would allow them to approach Themiscyra. Until then the Achaeans were not to move camp. These orders given, she wheeled her mount around and prodded it into a nimble run. Her followers executed a brisk turn and ran their horses behind her. Tecmassa, who brought up the rear, swiveled in the saddle once and stared with ice in her eye at Theseus and then at Pirothous.

Once they were out of the men's sight, the Amazons slowed their horses. Antiope did not take her usual place at the right of Penthesilea but instead, with the trail widening almost immediately, moved into position by Thalestris' side. Penthesilea rode a few paces behind, and following her was Tecmassa.

Antiope and Thalestris leaned toward one another and talked rapidly. Penthesilea heard the rise and fall of words, but could not make them out. Once, Antiope turned in the saddle and pointed in the direction of the men they had just seen for the first time. Once Thalestris nodded her head. At length, Antiope stopped her pony, Thalestris outdistanced her, and Penthesilea came abreast. Antiope's mount fell into step with Penthesilea's.

Antiope said with no other preamble, "What do you think of Theseus?"

"Think of Theseus?" answered Penthesilea, who knew that Antiope would not like her opinion. "I don't."

"Really, woman. I have to know."

"I can't say." She could, but Antiope was prone to sulk when anyone contradicted her.

"Please. I need to know."

Penthesilea could not stop herself from saying what she thought. "Something's not right; that's what I think. His words came too easily. He has repeated them before. As for the fat man who is his lieutenant, you can tell by looking at him that he hasn't got an honest bone in his body. And they're torturers. Torturers! You know how bad that is. You know what the Goddess thinks of torturers."

"Hasn't an honest bone? Words came too easily? Come, come, Penthesilea. They're foreigners, that's all.

"Thalestris told me that the Achaeans come from beyond Troy, and to get there must cross waters as wide as the steppes. They fight on foot with thrusting spears and round hide shields that cover them from shoulder to ankle, and sometimes they fight with javelins. You have to move on them from their right, and strike before they turn, because they hold the shield in their left hand. They live in strong cities, behind walls made of stones so big that only giants could have built them. They get their wealth from crossing the seas to trade, and field hundreds of men at a time.

"As for Theseus, he must be the child of a mighty queen and king among the Achaeans. You can tell by the way he carries himself and the way he addressed Thalestris. He is no ordinary soldier out for booty. You can tell, too, by the way his men look at him. He is a prince. Thalestris showed me the chain and medal he gave her. I have never held such fine gold in my hands, or set my eyes on such beautiful work. It is a jewel of great price, and only a ruler could commission a goldsmith to fashion it."

That was all well and good, thought Penthesilea, but something was still not right.

Antiope went on. "Theseus' house, the Erectheids, can only be a great one; you can tell by the way that Theseus bears himself that he is of high birth. The noblest Amazon may look on him without shame."

Penthesilea kept still until she realized that Antiope's eyes were seeking hers out. Antiope repeated, "Theseus is a great noble, and a brave fighter, don't you agree?"

The question was direct. "Maybe it's the way you think it is," opined Penthesilea. "But maybe it isn't. I'm not sure that he's the son of a queen and king. The medal and the chain could have been the gift of his father, as Theseus says. But they could just as well have been his share of the booty from a raid."

"But the story Theseus told is true. To go from Troy to the Great Mountains you have to cross Kaska country. And if you do, you invite a raid. Don't you see how badly hurt his men are? One of them may never get up from his wounds and another died of them last night. Isn't that what Tecmassa said?"

The bridle of Tecmassa's horse jingled and its hoofbeats grew louder. She caught up with Antiope and Penthesilea.

Antiope continued. "That is why Thalestris has accepted the gold medal and chain as a guest-gift. She wants to say yes to Theseus and his request for hospitality. She'll call the Amazons together tonight and bid them approve her decision. After all, he and his men fought the Kaska folk, who are our enemies and have been since the days of Marpasia. It would be shameful for Thalestris, the chief of the riders and high judge of the city, to turn Theseus down. Her name and the reputation of the house of Marpasia would be dishonored. But if she bids him stay and honors him as the prince of a mighty city, then Marpasia's race and Theseus' will henceforth be allied against all enemies."

Penthesilea tried to keep her misgivings out of her eyes but had no luck.

Antiope said in her most self-assured tone:, "The Goddess commands Her daughters to welcome strangers and treat them well and commands that our welcome be the best when the man who visits us is a fighter whom an Amazon may call on in his tent. And Theseus is of high enough rank so that even the highest-born Amazon may not blush at sharing her couch with him."

"But, still," said Penthesilea, "man strangers like that have to wish the Goddess well, and they don't. I can tell."

"Why do you think that Theseus doesn't? Didn't he say that his mother, Aethra, daughter of Pittheus the Wise of Troezen, worshiped the Triple Goddess, and that three of his father's sisters were Her priestesses?"

Tecmassa edged between the younger women. Sleeplessness weighed down her jowls and eyes. "Theseus and his men are bandits," she declared. "No one else would be out so early in the season. And there's no believing their story about the drought to the north and the Kaska men to the east. And they're a torturing lot, too. You heard that fellow, that so-called prince. The Goddess doesn't like that one bit, and we Amazons hate it."

Antiope shot an annoyed glance at Tecmassa. "They are soldiers," said Antiope. "They are under the command of Prince Theseus."

"Look," Tecmassa said, "soldiers or bandits, if we invite them to stay before the gates, the badly hurt one will be dead or whole in a month. By that time there'll be at least two-dozen tents and three score men in front of Themiscyra. Four, maybe five, trained fighters—and Achaeans to boot—in among them would mean trouble, do you understand? They'll drink and when the drink's in them, they'll brawl. They like to shed blood. It gives them a thrill. Didn't the redhead boast about torturing his prisoners? Didn't you see the look on his face when he did? Those fellows will be nothing but trouble. The garrison in town is shorthanded as it is. You know that. The other patrols are, too. They couldn't spare a single rider if there's mischief down in the tents. And we have to watch the southern steppes like hawks. Let's send those guys packing."

"Theseus is our enemies' enemy," replied Antiope. "He is descended from a race of chiefs. He knows the laws of welcome."

"Chief? Laws of welcome?" said Tecmassa. "Those are fine words, my girl, but don't rely on them to stop that gang. We've got enough work cut out for us this season."

"Theseus is the son of powerful rulers, didn't you see?"

"Anyone can make up a story about her fine family when she's months away from home. And anyone can pass off a gold chain she's stolen—or looted—as the gift of a great king. It's all been done before. As for me, I think Theseus and his men are a gang of bandits plain and simple. They set off early so they could work the road to Troy, but met another gang and got the worst of it."

"It would be shameful," said Antiope, "for the House of Marpasia to fail to welcome a fighter who has been attacked by the Kaska enemy. And they have been attacked. There is no reason to think that Theseus' story is not true."

Tecmassa stared at her in disbelief. "What about their weapons, girl? You don't believe their story about their weapons?"

"They lost them in a raid."

"Where's your common sense? They didn't throw down their spears and shields. No trained fighter would do that if she were attacked by Kaska men—even if she had to dismount and run away on foot. I'll bet my bow they found out that we disarm all visitors to Themiscyra so they stashed their weapons somewhere near, to get them if they need to. They must have asked about us. How else would soldiers from so far away know the name of Thalestris' clan? They're no fools."

"But you see they passed through Kaska country."

"That's where they say they came in from. I don't believe them."

"One of them died in the raid."

"That's another thing. What happened to the bones? I never heard of a god who wants a fighter's bones left in a strange land. They belong to her kin. What are they worried about? Do they think we'll try to lay our hands on the bones and hold them for ransom? Do they think we're their enemy?"

Antiope hurled a defiant pout at Tecmassa, who raised her eyes to the heavens, closed them, and wagged her head wearily. It would have been the same had the young rider— the worse for wine she could not hold—flung taunts and threats at all who came into sight.

A thought crossed Tecmassa's face. She opened her eyes and stared in pity at Antiope. "Listen," said Tecmassa, "don't believe a word that Theseus says. Not a word, hear. When I first spotted those fellows yesterday morning, Theseus had on a chestpiece, something like what the Trojan soldiers wear, and a leather kilt. He wore them this morning, too, when I left to join you all. But when we rode to meet him not too much later, he was naked as a babe, except for that little cloth you could see the tip of his prick behind.

"Do you know why he took his clothes off? He's heard about the Amazons' land. He knew I'd watched him all the night before. He saw me leave and figured that a party of women would come to meet him that morning. He must know that we don't see men for months on end. He told himself that by this time we'd be pretty hungry. And some are. Some are. He wanted the girls to lay their eyes on his snake. Once we did, he figured, we'd fight over getting him to the couch."

Tecmassa's long lashes came together. She broke into a grin and snorted, then opened her eyes again. They glinted with merriment. "You can tell that the redhead believes the women will run after him," she said to Antiope. "He walks like he thinks his ass is a honey cake. So don't trust him. Don't believe a word he says. Listen to your head, woman, and not any other part of you." Tecmassa's eyes shifted to where Antiope's thighs wrapped around her sheepskin saddle.

Crimson spread over Antiope's cheeks. She opened her mouth to object, but Tecmassa didn't let her get in a word.

"Trust your head, my girl," said the scout, "and not your itching flesh." Tecmassa still stared at Antiope's haunches.

Antiope raised her nose and sneered with such haughtiness that Penthesilea wondered why Tecmassa didn't take the back of her hand to her. Tecmassa, however, burst into ear-splitting guffaws, her broad frame shaking so hard that she looked as if she were sitting a running horse. Thalestris swiveled in the saddle to see what was going on, at the same time as Antiope dug her heels into her mount and rejoined Thalestris.

Penthesilea and Tecmassa stared at Antiope's back.

"She hasn't got the sense to get in out of the rain," said Tecmassa.

Penthesilea, too, saw that Antiope had taken leave of her senses, but did not unbutton her lips to say so. Her duty was to stand by Antiope no matter what.

Tecmassa went on, "This Theseus says he's the son of a queen and king. Antiope likes that, she does. It goes with her highfalutin' ways. Theseus is nothing more than a highwayman. He's the chief of that gang, and for some reason they have to talk fast. Antiope can't see that. She's got the itch in her belly."

Penthesilea thought the same but kept her counsel.

"Do you remember the old saying?" asked Tecmassa.

"Which one?"

"About the itch and the twitch. They turn a woman's mind into a donkey's—dumb and stubborn."

Leokadia had said it many times, and it fitted here. Still, Penthesilea stuck up for her friend. "Antiope wants us to welcome Theseus because she thinks that he told Thalestris what really happened."

"He didn't."

"Antiope thinks the men are our friends because they fought the Kaska enemy. With friends, her generosity is great. She says it goes with her rank. And I also think that these are the ways the Goddess has given her. I can't count the times Antiope's offered me presents I didn't ask for."

Tecmassa's eyes alighted on the silver and leather band that wound around Penthesilea's arm. Antiope had thrust it on her merely because she had mentioned one day that it was handsome.

"Antiope is brave, too," added Penthesilea. "She's a good Amazon. She saved my life." So saying, Penthesilea lowered her head. She once more saw the spear tip coming close and wondered what the pain would have been like. But when it all happened, she had only seen the man fall suddenly forward and Antiope spring out from the bushes behind him.

Still, there were things about Antiope that Penthesilea did not like to see. Antiope loved living in the greatest house and being waited on by a dozen women. Her eyes would light up whenever her approach made other young riders stop their talking and wait for her to speak. Her lips would curl in satisfaction when she took off her clothes in front of the other women to plunge into Thermodon or lower herself into her bath. Penthesilea once again saw Antiope fix burning eyes on Tecmassa while the veteran Amazon was delivering her judgment of Theseus' nakedness. Then, Anuphey's picture tumbled up, and the long face she had worn since Antiope announced that she no longer desired to share her couch. And yet Anuphey had been Antiope's faithful friend for years.

Penthesilea's expression mirrored these silent likes and dislikes, and Tecmassa reached across, grasped her shoulder, and murmured, "I see. I see."

A thud of hooves that had first sounded dimly from behind caught up with them. Hippolyta came abreast of Tecmassa, and Penthesilea retreated a length.

Hippolyta asked what had gone on while she was standing guard. Tecmassa related what she had seen and heard. She told of her suspicions and what brought them on. She spoke of Thalestris' intentions with regard to the interlopers.

"As for Antiope," Tecmassa said, "the girl has lost her wits. Her head's been turned by her liking for Theseus' naked body and his story about his fine family and mighty cities on the far side of Troy. She can't see beyond her itching flesh and taste for being better than the rest of us."

Tecmassa said no more. Hippolyta turned the news over in her head. Finally she pronounced, "I do not like this, not at all. Five soldiers in the midst of scores of traders will mean trouble when Arinna shines the hottest. We cannot spare a single rider to watch over them. We must patrol the southern steppes with special vigilance this season. No. No. It would be folly to invite them in, and all the more because they are Achaeans. Thalestris must know that they are."

"She does."

"The Hittites have no use for the Achaeans. Achaean chiefs rule five cities on the warm sea to the west; their territories border on the Hittite lands. When the Hittites do not quarter a large army in those parts, Achaean bands invade. They rob the silver and enslave the people. Nor do the Trojans I have spoken to care much for these Achaeans. They say you never know when they'll sail in with goods or slaves to sell and when they'll come as raiders in the dark of night."

Tecmassa repeated how Theseus had started bragging about laying cruel hands on his prisoners.

"If Thalestris is inclined to welcome him and do him honor," said Hippolyta, "there is but one construction we can put upon her thoughts. She wants to make good use of him. She thinks that doing so will strengthen the dynastic claims of the usurper."

"How's that?"

"Of course Thalestris wants to welcome him. She wants to welcome this supposed prince to help Antiope's claim to be the ruler of the city on the day when she is dead. Don't you understand? His name and rank impress Antiope, and she looks twice upon his nakedness."

"Antiope is five kinds of an idiot. I'd love to thrash some sense into her."

"Thalestris will convince the riders that she's right, that Theseus bears in his veins the bravery that suits a mighty race, the mettle of a god. She'll greet this so-called prince as her firm friend and bid him take his ease before the gates. And," Hippolyta growled, "send him to the girl whom she would have usurp the throne."

"Is that what's gotten into her?"

"Can you have any doubt of it, Tecmassa? Thalestris will make sure that Theseus is well treated by Antiope, who'll perfume her breasts and lay caressing fingers on his snake. He'll want to share her couch, all right. She's pretty. He's surrounded and no fool. He'll embrace her well and often. And there's no woman who could raise her voice against the coupling. Antiope is of the proper age. She's shown her worth in fighting, killed her man. There's nothing we could say."

"Melanippe, not Antiope, should invite Theseus to the couch," said Tecmassa.

"Thalestris has done everything she can to frustrate Melanippe of her rights. She won't stop now. If from this alliance there should come a child—and there's no reason to believe there won't—Antiope gains greater rights to govern Themiscyra one day. For henceforth she is allied by her blood to mighty warriors, or so Thalestris will not fail to claim. And if there comes a daughter of this wrestling match, it will enhance the upstart's claim to rule us when Thalestris is gone. Antiope will have birthed a rider of the noblest strain—or so they'll say. That's why Thalestris wants to welcome him—and that's why she will call the Amazons together right away."

"And Melanippe?"

"Melanippe patrols the farthest reaches of the steppes. She's ridden out this very morning to have an early look."

Hippolyta covered her eyes and peeked at the sun through her fingers. "It will be of no use to send a messenger to call her back. To send a woman out for her would take two days. But if Thalestris gets her way, the damage will be done by then."

Tecmassa nodded but said nothing.

Hippolyta went on, "Still, Melanippe's cause counts many friends, and many Amazons won't like the presence of these fighting men before the gates this summer. Thalestris cannot do her will without the riders' approbation. So, we shall see the outcome of her schemes. You know the proverb that's repeated at a time like this."

"Which one is that?"

"The Amazons may ride, but the Goddess will decide."

The women went the rest of the way in silence.

Chapter 7

Tecmassa rode through the gate of the temple grounds. She jumped down from her horse and rocked as if she were going to drop to her knees. Black lines scored her face. Myrtho met her. "I want to speak to you," she whispered.

Myrtho conducted Tecmassa to her apartments. The Amazon collapsed into a chair. Myrtho sent for Philippis, who came back bearing a tray of food and drink. Fetching and carrying were not her habit, but she had caught Tecmassa's tone and wanted to hear what had brought her. The priestess did not object, and the intendant seated herself in a corner and folded her hands in her lap.

When the hunger and thirst had gone from Tecmassa, she reported on the events of the past two days—how she had spotted the intruders and summoned Thalestris, what Thalestris asked the foreigner and what he had replied, how Antiope behaved, and the opinion Tecmassa herself had of it all. She finished by saying, "Those guys mean trouble. That's why I came here right away. Thalestris wants to let them stay here for the summer. It suits her fine, and Antiope, too. Thalestris is a damned fool, and Antiope's not any better. You've gotta talk sense into Thalestris, Myrtho. I'm just a plain rider and no good with words, even if she'd listen to me."

Philippis exhaled sibilantly.

Myrtho asked, "They are Achaeans, of that you are sure?"

"That's what they said, and that's what I think, too."

Myrtho sat up straighter and glanced at Philippis. "This is news of the least propitious sort," said the priestess. "All the people who live by the warm sea have a close acquaintance with the Achaeans, who speak a language like ours and that of the ten peoples to the east of Troy. Still, many affirm that these Achaeans are not of the same descendance. Certainly, their gods are not the same."

"Have you ever heard of this Poseidon of theirs," asked Tecmassa, "the one their redheaded captain says he comes down from?"

"Poseidon?"

"That's right."

"The Achaeans claim that Poseidon's ancestor was She who created all living things. But I give no credence to this story, because Poseidon and his worshipers violate Her ways. The Achaeans say that among the Great Mother's offspring was a man child called Uranus. Uranus, it seems, violated his mother."

"What? Raped his own mother?"

"Yes. And from this mother-rape a giant was begotten, whose name was Cronus. Cronus, according to the Achaeans' priests, castrated his father, Uranus, and then did away with him."

"What? Gelded and slaughtered his own sire?"

"Yes. The Achaeans recount, too—but I am not at all certain of its veracity—that Cronus' sister was the goddess to whom the oak tree is sacred and whom we hold in great reverence both here and in the cities on the warm sea to the west. Just as Uranus forced his mother, so Cronus violated his sister. And Poseidon, the god of these foreigners, came of this sister-rape."

"What!"

"The Achaeans relate as well that Cronus liked to eat his own children but that She to whom the oak tree is sacred, blessed be Her name, hid one of them, who killed Cronus when he grew big and freed his brother Poseidon. As a result of this parricide..."

"Parricide?"

"Father-killing. As a result of this father-killing, Poseidon gained dominion over the sea to the west of here, the vast salt waters that separate the cities in the west from the land of the Achaeans."

"Well," declared Tecmassa, "let Theseus go back there and take his god with him. I'll offer cloth and incense to the Mare Goddess and ask her to chase them out."

"That will be better than you think," said Myrtho. "Their presence cannot be pleasing to Shaushka. No doubt Theseus will ask for a foal to sacrifice on the eighth day of the next month."

"A foal? They'd sacrifice a foal? They're worse than the Kaska folk. Even they don't kill horses. What kind of a god is that, who likes blood on his altar?"

"According to their teachings," said Myrtho, "Poseidon himself has stopped at no violent act. Many are the lands and islands on the western sea to which this god has laid waste, and many are the women—goddesses and mortals—whom he has kidnaped and raped.

"And his followers, too, have done all that they can to overpower the goddesses who rule the cities and islands to the west. These pirates have defiled the sanctuaries of many worshipful deities—of Cybele, of Rhea, of Britomartis, Dictynna, Euphoria, and Eleuthera. They have beaten, imprisoned, and killed the holy priestesses. They have ravished some. They have striven by fair means and foul to make them surrender the double-headed axe given to us by the Great Mother, which she has endowed with numerous powers."

Tecmassa put her hand on her labrys.

"The Achaeans steal the treasure and then put the cities to the torch. They kill the men or sell them into slavery. They rape and enslave the young women and sell them or carry them back to their own countries. And when the Achaeans do not devastate the towns that they raid, they place their own princes on the throne (they know not of woman rulers).

"And everywhere that they have prevailed by force of arms, they have populated the temples of the goddesses with eunuchs and with women constrained to perpetual virginity. It is a desecration that She will one day chastise."

"You've got to talk sense to Thalestris," repeated Tecmassa. "I don't care how much she wants to breed Antiope with Theseus. I don't care how high and mighty Theseus says his family is, this 'House of the Coiled Snake,' he called them."

The color drained from Myrtho's face.

Tecmassa's tired eyes interrogated hers.

"Achaeans belonging to this clan," answered Myrtho, "devastated the city where I come from, Apasas, which lies in the path of the winter sun as she retreats into the warm sea."

"I've never heard that name."

"Apasas was a great and rich port, to which two trade routes led—one from the hinterlands and one from the empire of the Hittites. The Triple Goddess, She who watches over the roads and harbors, ruled Apasas and made it prosper; may Her name be held in reverence for all generations. At Apasas, the sea herself worshiped at the Goddess's feet, for Her temple stood on the shore and the waters of the harbor bathed its foundations. The dwelling was constructed of pink stones from hills far away. In the long afternoons, it glowed with a radiance that it seemed to hold in its heart. You could see its rosy warmth from the sea until the last bit of day was gone from the sky. It was the Goddess's beacon to all who would come to Her city. And many were the rich traders who bestowed luxurious gifts on Her as thanks for successful journeys.

"At the center of Her dwelling was a courtyard in which grew a tall oak tree. Around it stood three statues of the Goddess—as a girl, a beautiful woman, and an old one with a wise smile and cruel eyes."

Myrtho's voice and expression had warmed.

"I was the older daughter of the high priestess, Delphica—Delphica of the gentle white brow and warm arms. I was destined to take her place one day. I had a younger sister, too, Eripha, of the wide smile and plump cheeks. She, too, had been consecrated to the Goddess and was destined to serve Her. Delphica ruled a large establishment, thirty-six votaries and a numerous household, for the Goddess possessed much wealth—chests of gold, silver, gems, granaries, fields, slaves.

"The temple grounds occupied the base of a hill at least as high as the slope on which Themiscyra is constructed and even more precipitous. The citadel of Apasas—with its thick walls hewn out of the stone hillside—overlooked the Goddess's dwelling. The road leading up to the fortifications and city twisted and turned so many times that even Philippis, who is five years my senior and who knew how to count long before I could, had trouble tallying the number. Philippis is the daughter of my mother's steward, Amaltheia; may the Goddess smile on her in the West.

"Numerous soldiers occupied the fortress on the summit. From the top of its walls you could see the plain to the northeast and the rivers that flowed through it, Marnas and Selinoüs, which emptied into the bay. You could also see the port below, with its timbered ships, and the harbor, which opened into a vast stretch of radiant blue.

"The soldiers always kept watch over the land and the sea—always, night and day, even when the winds and rain drove all others inside."

This military detail made Tecmassa sit up straight.

Philippis explained, "We feared both pirates from the sea and bands of armed men from the land—robbers or soldiers; I don't see the difference."

Myrtho continued. "I never learned by what mortal my mother got me. In those days, the people—free and slaves—ran amok on Midsummer's Night, when the oak branch burns the brightest and the sacred drink warms their breasts. The priestesses must not tell by whom they get the babies that are to be born after the day of the year. Only the Goddess knows.

"From my tenderest age, Delphica taught me the attributes of the Divinity and the days on which to celebrate each aspect of Her being. And when Eripha, my dear little sister, was big enough, she, too, learned the knowledge that Her holy women hug to their hearts. My mother sang to us of the mysteries of the oak tree, which the Triple Goddess holds dear, and the sacred hunt, for which She grasps a silver bow the shape of the new moon in Her left hand and sun-gold arrows in Her right. The bow is to destroy the city of unjust men; for the circle, like the moon, will come full again."

Tecmassa nodded in understanding.

"When I was old enough, they gave me the sacred cup and led me to the innermost part of the temple to dance the dance of ecstasy. Here it was that I first set my eyes on the thick oak statue around which, in the time of our mothers, they had built the first temple. A golden robe draped the trunk. Forty insets repeated Her mysteries—saffron-robed bees, and red hinds such as She harnesses to her golden chariot to pursue the north, and women with babies emerging from between their legs, again and again. The Goddess Herself had seven breasts, and a turret crown ornamented Her head. Her eyes were deep-set glowing jewels, Her smile was enigmatic, and She leaned on two twisted pillars, one of red on which a hundred yellow suns had been painted and one of blue-black on which twenty-eight sickle-moons had been inscribed in silver.

"Next to the presence of oak stood a statue of the Goddess carved out of a shining black rock that had fallen from the sky. The Amazon queen Myrinne had presented it to our ruler, the lady Caÿster, when she constructed the great stone temple in the time of my grandmother.

"The ruler of Apasas was Idas. I remember him as a short, plump, affable man. He was very rich and very generous to the Goddess. It seems that in his old age, She had given him a child, although he had been barren all the years before that.

"To help administer his ships and harbor, Idas had appointed one Medus by name to be his steward."

Philippis aspirated disapproval.

"Years before, Medus had escaped ship, a Cretan galley to which he had been condemned—for what crime I do not know. He said that the charges were contrived and that he had been an intendant in his own land. I remember him as a tall, gaunt man who was exceedingly polite to my mother."

"He was a swindler," said Philippis. "I don't remember a single time that he questioned the accounts that my mother kept. That's why she didn't trust him at all. 'There's something wrong,' she used to tell me, 'with an intendant who doesn't haggle and snoop and fight you all the way.'"

"I do not think," said Myrtho, "that the high priestess, Delphica, had much faith in him either. Perhaps she was biding her time. But it is too late to speculate now."

Philippis sighed. It was more like a hiss.

"I remember," continued Myrtho, "the midsummer celebrations that year, for it was the first time that my mother—who had watched me ripen with pleasure—permitted me to sip the holy wine and taste the sacred leaves. At the end of the summer I was pregnant, and the high priestess was content to let me lead the dance of the autumn rites, when the long-necked cranes intersect the sky above the Goddess's head as they flee the bear.

"I looked forward to that. I was happy. I felt that I had grown up. And I knew that the young man would be watching the sacred dance, pleased to see my belly beginning to ripen. He made my heart smile, and my senses—all of them—for he revered the Goddess and studied what made Her women happy. Often, on the path to the port or on the trail to the citadel, I would find flowers strewn where my feet were about to touch—hyacinths bursting with gold they had taken from the sun and irises of blue captured from the firmament, flowers that he had ranged far to gather at the break of day."

Myrtho lowered her lids and confided, "I still miss the smell of the sea air and the sound of the triple-reed calling us to adore the Goddess. I miss my mother's warm smile and, for years, I missed him, too."

Tecmassa's brow wrinkled with an unspoken question.

"Yes," answered Myrtho, "once I told Leokadia, and we agreed never to speak of it again. It had all occurred so many long years before. I still marvel that so much of my life has gone by since that day.

"Day? No, night. It happened at night. On the eve of the autumn rites, to be exact. Clouds covered the moon, and Idas had   dispatched a numerous troop inland two days before. It seems that news of armed hordes approaching the city had reached his ears."

"Armed gangs, indeed!" sniffed Philippis. "That traitor, Medus, no doubt made the rumor larger than life."

Myrtho continued. "On the night before the autumn rites, I had difficulty falling asleep. I was nervous about leading the sacred steps for the first time, although I had repeated them so many times that even today, I am sure, I could dance the ceremony without missing a single gesture. But it seems now that my uneasiness came from farther off, that it was greater than the occasion merited, that I apprehended something else, although I did not know what it was. Whatever the truth, I could not sleep, and for a long time lay awake listening to the breathing of Eripha, who occupied a bed beside mine. My darling little sister's respiration was deep and slow and must finally have lulled me to sleep. Yes, I must have been in slumber, because when the claps of thunder ripped me from my repose, I believed that I had been torn from a bad dream, from some fearful vision that the Goddess had sent me—to warn me of what? But by the lamp that burned in our room I saw Eripha sitting bolt upright, her face distorted with fear. I knew then that it was not a nightmare that had startled me.

"The deafening noise began again. Monstrous thumps echoed from the direction of the temple entrance. I realized that someone was battering the great oaken door. Then a crash louder than the others shattered my ears and almost stopped my heart. The bars that secured the portal must have given way. Then I heard nothing. Silence. Then a woman's shrieks.

"At first I did not have a clear idea of what was going on. This had never happened. Then more screams sounded and I comprehended. 'Pirates!' I shouted, and Eripha and I fled toward the courtyard thinking to run uphill and take shelter in the citadel.

"But strange light illuminated what we thought would be our refuge, a trembling glow, yellow and silver.

"'Look at the hill!' said Eripha.

"Flames were leaping out from behind the fortress walls. Someone had put it to the torch. Someone had stormed the citadel and overwhelmed the garrison. All along, in the back of my mind, I had been certain that Idas and his soldiers would come down from the fortress and drive out the marauders. Now I knew that our soldiers would never arrive. And *he* was among them. We were at the mercy of the raiders. My legs almost gave out from under me.

"Philippis told me later, when the madness finally abandoned my spirit, that Medus had betrayed the citadel."

"The week before," said Philippis, "Achaeans had sailed in to trade, or so they claimed. They had really come to spy on us, and Medus sold them the secret of the small door in the wall on the steepest part of the hill. They even sent swimmers around the point to get a good look at it. They transacted some business, sailed away, and waited. When they were sure that the moon would not shine, they returned with two other ships. They scaled the acropolis and took the citadel by surprise in the dead of night. That same day, three other Achaean ships had arrived in the harbor—to trade, they said. They also said there were goods in their holds. There weren't. There were soldiers. It was they who took the port and the temple. I learned all this while I was hiding in a storage jar in the kitchen and overheard two of the Achaean curs talking about it. I also learned that those beasts had paid Medus by knifing him."

Myrtho went on. "Heavy, shod feet came from outside, and three Achaean soldiers burst into the courtyard. One held a torch. They all stopped to take their bearings, then saw us, two young women in scant gowns, and ran for us. We fled in panic. Eripha fell. I stopped to help her to her feet. One of the Achaeans caught me and lifted me away. Another pinned her to the ground. She bit his upper arm. He barked like a dog and plunged his blade into her. She opened her mouth to scream, but black death cut short her cry.

"Then, as if she were leading a procession, my mother stepped out of the temple. She had been keeping vigil there. Behind her walked two soldiers, one carrying a torch and one pointing his sword at her back. The saffron robe and the tiara of silver oak leaves covered her body and the white clay her face.

"She saw Eripha lying dead on the ground, and her countenance ignited into a mask of fury that glowed white like the Goddess' wrath. The Achaeans facing her took a step back. She drilled her eyes into the one whom she saw was their leader, for all the other men's faces were turned toward his. She said in a commanding voice, 'I am high priestess here. By spilling blood in the Goddess's temple you have desecrated it, and by killing a holy woman you have called down the worst of her punishments—death in flames that you yourself have ignited.'

"The Achaean captain took a step backward; but, then, he glanced at his followers and swaggered up to Delphica. 'Lady, where have you buried the double-headed axe? I have orders to take it back with me, and if I don't, I'll take you back instead.'

"Delphica stood up straighter and glared back with such intense ire, that confusion overcame him, and he began to tremble. But the beast who held me said to him, 'Why don't you ram the slut with the tip of your sword? That'll make her talk.'

"The soldier who was holding the torch exclaimed, 'Don't say that! The Goddess will hear you. That is Her priestess.'

"The brute who had murdered Eripha sneered. He went up to Delphica and wrapped his hands around her throat. She stiffened but did not budge. The torchbearer shouted, 'Don't!' and I screamed 'Mother!'

"The beast who held her exclaimed, 'We've got her now!' He let her go and took me by the hair. He pulled it up and lay the blade of his sword across my throat. I saw the coiled snake engraved on the weapon.

"Delphica's voice resounded. 'She, too, is consecrated to the Goddess. Beware!'

"The cur laughed.

"Delphica raised her arms to the heavens; cruelty made a razor line of her mouth. In a voice that echoed everywhere she chanted, 'Oh holiest of the immortals, oh You of greater power than all their gods, hear me now. Bring Your curse down on them all for they filthy the fair seas and the skies and the forests.'

"'She is cursing us!' said the torchbearer. He put his arm, sword and all, in front of his face.

"The Achaean who held me by the hair pulled it tighter and drew his blade across my throat. I felt warm liquid on my skin; the urine fled down my legs.

"Lightning flashed from Delphica's eyes. She raised her arms. 'Oh You who bring the gift of spring to the mortals and the plagues of winter, listen to my prayer. May their own violence turn against them. May their own greed destroy them. May their own cruelty burn their cities and cut down all their people.'

"'Stop that!' shouted the captain.

"But she did not stop. She drew her mouth into a murderous smile and pronounced, 'May you and all your sons meet so painful a death that you curse all the immortals. And may your sons curse the ground you walk on and the shadow you cast, because you infuriated the Goddess.' The captain put his palms over his eyes to protect them from the wrath that seared out of Delphica's.

"She turned the gaze that scorched his insolent face on the Achaean who had killed Eripha and who now threatened me. 'And you, the Goddess has reserved special punishment for you. She, who loves and gives life, will curse you with painful fire in your snake for the rest of your days. And your eyes will go blind, for they have been blind to your blasphemy and crimes.'

"He let me go and advanced on her with his sword. 'Stop cursing me or I'll kill you!' he said.

"Delphica's eyes narrowed; blue flames of hatred burst from them. 'Remember Achaean,' she intoned, 'that as the sky turns full circle over your head, so will your crimes turn back on you.'

"'Stop it, I say!'

"'Oh Goddess, make all creatures run from him for his foulness.'

"The Achaean plunged his sword into her chest. She screamed and fell. My world went black, and I sank to the ground.

"I do not know how long I lay there, but when I finally surrendered to the pain of being conscious and opened my eyes—it was like a knife in my breast—the sky above had turned gray. Heavy steps—they were those of a shod man—had awakened me. They approached. I closed my eyes rapidly. The footfalls were strangely out of rhythm. They grew louder, passed me by, and stopped not far away. I heard the sound of an animal urinating. Then the same creature belched. The steps staggered off. I opened my eyes and raised my head, timidly. In the feeble light, I distinguished a soldier lurching away from the statue of the goddess as a young woman. I could see that it was plain white, except where urine had sullied it. The jewels and golden garment had been stripped from it. I looked at the other statues. The raiders had not only bereft them of all the riches that adorned them but had also ripped the jeweled tiles from the mosaics at their pedestals.

"Obscene, raucous men's laughter and panicked cries of a higher pitch reached my ears from the direction of the sanctuary. The Achaeans must have gotten into the wine. The women's screams told the rest. Would my turn come soon? Rage and fear drained the blood from my face and the will and strength from my body.

"I heard a faint shuffle coming from the living quarters. The sound augmented. I recognized the tread of bare feet. They stopped over my head. I did not—could not—move. I heard my name. It was Philippis. I opened my eyes. She reached down and pulled me up. I started to blurt out her name, but she clapped her hand over my mouth. She pointed to where she had just come from and beckoned me to follow her there.

"I did not budge but looked around me at the ground. I saw neither Delphica's body nor Eripha's, only dark stains. I felt the vomit rise in me and my knees weaken. Philippis yanked at my arm and pulled me toward the living quarters.

"She guided me into the steward's apartment and from there pushed me toward a small door and down a stairway that led to the cellars and tunnels beneath the temple buildings. What little light there was disappeared when we descended the steps. We made our way to the basement of the temple. How Philippis found anything in the dark, I did not stop to think. But it seems she had played there since she was a little girl.

"My bare feet recoiled when they touched the cellar floor. It was below water level, cold and wet. I felt small stones and heard rats scurrying. I stopped. My teeth began to chatter. I could not move. Philippis put her arms about me and held me for a while. Then she nudged me along.

"She found her way to a tiny door that led to the water. It had once been a boat landing. She lifted the bar and tugged at it with all her might. At length it creaked open. The light dazzled my eyes. The dawn sky was vivid gray with yellow brightness behind it, and the water shimmered black, silver, and gold.

"'Jump and swim,' commanded Philippis. I hesitated. She wrapped her arms around my middle, lifted me off my feet, and threw me in. The water was frigid. I sank and bobbed up. I coughed violently but kept myself afloat. I saw Philippis jump, and there was a resounding splash. A wave submerged me. Water flooded my insides, but I surfaced and retched most of it out. Philippis put her hand on my shoulder and pointed to a spot on the mainland far from where the Achaean boats were beached. She began to swim that way. I followed her. We crossed the water to safety and left the filthy snake-pirates behind."

Tecmassa had spent two days in the saddle without sleep. She struggled to keep her eyes from shutting and her chin from dropping. Myrtho left her to the ministrations of Philippis and crossed the marketplace on her way to the palace. The sun had set, and the last of the sellers were packing up. To those who said hello, Myrtho inclined her head graciously without seeing them. Her thoughts were elsewhere. She took no pleasure in going to speak with Thalestris, who—despite the service Myrtho had rendered three years before in favoring her election to the throne—was now rarely happy to see her. The priestess frequently contradicted Thalestris' sentiments, a point doubtless dwelt upon by Celano. And on the subject of Theseus' admittance to Themiscyra, Thalestris would like Myrtho's statements even less than usual, for they sought to frustrate her dynastic ambitions. Even supposing that Myrtho's words by some miracle had a good effect, the blandishments of Celano might neutralize them as soon as she had a few minutes alone with the ruler.

The attendant at the door bowed low when Myrtho entered and conducted her to the great hall. Celano scurried forward to meet her. She affected a pleasant countenance and made a profound obeisance. Her cheeks and lips appeared more bloodless than usual.

"Pray inform Thalestris that I wish to speak with her," said Myrtho.

Celano hesitated for a heartbeat before bending from the waist and turning away.

After a time not quite long enough to be deemed discourteous, Celano escorted Myrtho to the ruler's apartments. They passed the old Caïeta, who sat dozing near the entrance. They walked through the sleeping chamber, with its love-painting. (Myrtho took but fleeting notice of it.) They entered Thalestris' bath chamber. A full-bosomed serving woman was helping her out of a tiled recess in the floor.

Thalestris was a tall woman, a fine figure in her long-skirted tunic, and now her presence was made more imposing by her nakedness—her long legs and wide hips, her small breasts and graceful arms, her pale skin and rose-hued nipples, and the thick, blue-black hair under her arms and over her belly. Even the furrow across her thigh that drew ripples of flesh toward it added to the strength of her body, made muscular and erect by long days in the saddle. And yet a roundness in her belly, grayish rings under her eyes, and a hint of uncertainty in the set of her lips—all the result of her immoderate love of drink—detracted from the power of her form.

She spared Myrtho a glance. The servant threw a blanket over her and rubbed her vigorously. After the woman finished, Thalestris walked past Myrtho into the sleeping chamber. Myrtho followed. Still wrapped in her towel, Thalestris seated herself in an oaken armchair. A small table on which stood two goblets and a pitcher of wine had been set next to it.

She recited the customary words of welcome, and Myrtho the response. She offered Myrtho drink, and Myrtho refused. She filled her own cup, made her libation, and imbibed. At last she nodded to signify that she was listening.

Myrtho asked if it were true that five Achaeans, who claimed to have been ambushed by the Kaska folk, sought asylum in Themiscyra, which Thalestris was inclined to grant, and that she had convoked the riders to announce her wish and ask for approval.

"It is true," replied Thalestris, "that I will ask the riders to welcome these men and to put them at their ease before the gates. They have fighting blood in their veins, and it is my duty to offer them shelter and send young riders to them to share the couch and get new Amazons.

"But," said Thalestris, rotating her cup by the stem, "why does it concern you? These are the ways of the Amazons and have been since the time of Marpasia." Thalestris put her lips to the drinking vessel.

Myrtho repeated what was commonly known about the Achaeans, their treachery and marauding ways, and how she herself had seen them take Apasas by ruse and lies, rob its treasure, and put it to the torch. "That is why we must suspect that the men who entered the lands yesterday lied about their motives for seeking refuge here. They are not to be trusted. Your decision must be reconsidered."

"Don't you think I know their reputation?" said Thalestris, smiling like a grown-up reasoning with a child who fears unreal visions. "But their presence in front of our gates does not worry me. They are only five, and," Thalestris grinned, "we have other things we want them to do. Since the beginning, we've bred man soldiers to our young Amazons. It makes sense. When you want fillies with high spirits and good legs, you have to make sure that the sire, not just the dame, has it in him. We can't let them leave the land without their first leaving tribute inside five riders. There aren't enough Amazons as it is. What will it be in twenty years, unless we do all we can right now? I tell you, Myrtho, it's a boon."

"We do not know where they have come from at such an unusual time of year. Nor do we entertain any certainty that the story they tell is true. They may be contriving some perfidy against us."

Thalestris took a sip of wine, rolled it around her mouth, and swallowed. "It's a risk I'm willing to take," she said, "and all the more because the Achaeans are a mighty people, and we should not pass up the chance to make new allies. That would be a mistake in view of the unrest among the Hittites. You know about the civil war there. You read me the dispatch yourself. That is why we need these Achaeans' alliance, and I will welcome Prince Theseus."

"I care little," said Myrtho, "for alliance with a people whose stronghold and armies are so far away."

"Strategic matters do not concern the temple."

"I care little for alliance with a people who do not worship goddesses like ours and do not wish to trade goods so much as to steal them. Their word cannot be trusted. We worship the womb of living things, the earth, and the moon that turns full circle around her, and the sun that gives warmth and movement to all that is born and grows. They worship the thunder that shatters all that breathes, and the sea whose rages no one can predict, and the underworld, a cold dark land of death. And they do not love to plant and harvest, giving back in offerings what they take from the earth's body for the next full circle. No. They rip goods from her bosom and give her nothing in return. They're murderers and thieves. They're torturers, too. What kind of reverence is that? Who knows whether such confederates would send soldiers to aid Themiscyra in her hour of need or bandits to take advantage of her weakness and plunder her?".

"Matters of alliance do not concern the temple. You say that Tecmassa came to you with the news as soon as we all got back?"

"Yes," said Myrtho, wondering where the change of topic would lead.

"Tecmassa, you know, rode all the way home with Hippolyta. Hippolyta wants nothing more than to send those fellows packing."

"I have not come here to participate in the rivalries and disagreements that exist among the riders about the succession.

The Goddess has not yet pronounced Herself on this matter, and I, who am but Her servant, will not act on it until She commands me to."

"My dear Myrtho, the Goddess has indeed pronounced herself. She has sent a strong man of high birth into these domains, and he pleases Antiope's eyes."

There was no proof whatsoever that Theseus was of high birth, but Myrtho knew better than to argue with Thalestris on this point. It would only make her more stubborn. And if it were true, as Thalestris claimed, that the Goddess had sent Theseus into Themiscyra to breed with a high born rider, then it might as well be with Melanippe as with Antiope. It did not matter much whose eyes he pleased. Myrtho did not allude to this inconsistency either, although Celano, whose expression Myrtho caught out of the corner of her eye, needed no prompting to see it.

Myrtho said instead, "I do not think that what you say is entirely true. The Goddess will not be pleased with your decision to welcome these men. Their god, Poseidon, the immortal from whom their chief claims descendance, has sworn to conquer and humiliate our Goddess and craves nothing so much as to reduce Her to thralldom, rip Her magic from Her, and sell Her women into slavery. This is common knowledge among the priestesses."

Myrtho told of Poseidon's origins in rape, castration, and parricide, of his crimes against mortal women and goddesses, and of his laying greedy hands on their sanctuaries and lands. "And Poseidon's followers share this hatred."

"Is that what concerns you?" smiled Thalestris. "Are you worried for your lands and treasures?"

Myrtho narrowed her eyes. "Do not degrade the cares of the Goddess to worldly concerns."

Thalestris turned her head down.

"Do not endanger Her, Her priestesses, and Her worshipers."

Thalestris drummed on the table.

"Her memory is long, and Her wrath will not forget."

Thalestris lifted her goblet to her mouth. She sipped, put her cup down on the table with a decided gesture, and pronounced, "The Amazons, and the Amazons alone, decide in matters of security."

Sounds of riders gathering in the great hall filtered into the apartment. Perhaps they would prevail upon their leader to change her mind. Perhaps they would not. As for Myrtho, there was no use in her pursuing the matter. She inclined her brow and turned to depart. She caught a glimpse of Celano's face. Humility tightened the steward's lips, but satisfaction suffused her glance.

Myrtho swept past the Amazons, now dozens strong, who had found their way to the palace to hear what their chief had to say and to approve or disapprove. Tomiris, who was among them, smirked when Myrtho walked by and nudged Oebala, who grinned knowingly. Penthesilea and Antiope joined them at this moment.

Amazons slowly filled the room, their tunics of cherry red and azure blue, belts and armbands of mahogany brown, and gilded pins and argent buckles transmuting the hall, already bright with the light of scores of torches, into a gaudy rainbow whose single pigments shrunk, shifted, and burst open again as women took themselves from group to group. As newcomers entered, the exuberant chatter would chime to a crescendo and drop off to a hush before once more churning up into a deafening hubbub.

During one such voluminous wave, Hippolyta made her entrance. The clamor ebbed. She was magnificently attired in royal blue and glittering gold, and a varicolored cortege of Amazons followed her—Melanippe in madder yellow that accentuated her swarthiness; at her side the fair-skinned Perseia, attired in silver gray; after her skinny Ido, whose rosy cheeks and dull gray tunic made her black leather waistband, with its little sack of gambling bones, stand out; and on her heels the dreamy-eyed Andromache, a willowy woman clothed in the color of rowan berries, with bay-colored hair and walnut eyes that always focused elsewhere.

The din once more overwhelmed the room. Members of Hippolyta's suite smiled to one another when they sidled past the group in which Penthesilea was standing. Tomiris whispered in Antiope's ear, Antiope's handsome lips pursed in amusement, and Oebala placed her hands on her hips and chuckled. Marpessa, who, together with her comrades, had just arrived, looked at the ceiling and shrugged, "The show does not amuse me." Penthesilea agreed. Individuals of Hippolyta's suite singled out clusters of women already huddled in conversation and joined them.

Ariona arrived during the interplay, in the company of her huge-nosed daughter, Charope. Following them were the tight-sinewed, reckless Klymene, Amynome, a slight woman who nervously fingered three small wooden balls, and the big-jawed Feodissia, whose head towered above those of her cohorts. Penthesilea expected to see Tecmassa next, but instead the valorous Omaïa, dean of the riders, clad in raven black that set off the pink of her wrinkled face, hobbled into the hall. The hoary-haired Amazon, her spine twisted by years of archery, grasped a sturdy cane in her left hand. Her forearm, thick from gripping and pulling the bow all those decades, slammed the walking stick on the floor before her feet. She stomped toward the front of the hall. As riders bowed and stepped out of her way, her progress reminded Penthesilea of that of a boat's prow cutting through waters glittering like jewels.

But where had Tecmassa gone? She had veered off in the direction of the temple when the party reached home earlier that day. Why? Was it on account of her that Myrtho, who disliked visiting the palace, had walked out of Thalestris' apartments a little while before?

Penthesilea was still lost in speculation when Thalestris strode out of her quarters. A saffron tunic of soft wool set off her light skin and black hair. She stepped front and center. Antiope's friends moved in close.

Thalestris raised her arms. The talk and laughter trailed off. Thalestris spoke.

"I have called you together to take counsel with you and ask you to confirm a decision I have made. Yesterday, a party of foreigners—men, six of them—crossed into our territory from the northeast. It is early in the year for strangers to come here, and I rode out to have a look at them. I took a small squadron with me. The newcomers were all hurt. One is hurt badly and may not get up from his wounds. Another of them died last night. They are Achaeans, who live in strong cities across the warm sea, beyond Troy. The man who leads them is Prince Theseus of Troezen.

"When the Achaeans started out, they were twelve in all. Their mission to this part of the world was to barter for gold in the mountains of iron, near where the sun rises. To do this, they crossed the sea between their own country and the Troad at the equinox. Once they reached Troy, they set out right away.

There's been little rain there this winter and they didn't have to wait for the roads to dry out.

"To get to the mountains of iron, you've got to cross through Kaska country."

Oebala hissed.

"And because the Achaeans carried many goods, they armed themselves heavily, as soldiers must to cross enemy territory. They reached the Kaska country after six weeks' march. There, one night, although the Achaeans had posted pickets, the marauders fell on them as they slept."

Tomiris jeered.

"Theseus and his men fought back like lionesses, with knives and with their bare hands."

"Right!" said Antiope.

"It was dark and desperate. Six of Theseus' men died combating the Kaska bandits. He and the other five got away, wounded every one of them, but alive. But in the dark, they had to leave everything behind—their weapons, their supplies, the goods they had brought to trade, everything."

"They're lucky to have escaped at all!" rang the Amazon Lysippe's voice from the back of the room. This tiny, gaunt woman had arrived late, as she always did.

"The men who did battle with the Kaska folk made their way to our borders after a week's march. Their chief, Prince Theseus, has asked me to let him and his men stay here during the fair season. They have heard about the Amazons and our land. They know that we are sworn to destroy the savages and that we count as friends those who also go into battle against them."

"And we also like the boys around," said Marpessa.

"Civil war has broken out among the Hittites," said Thalestris in clipped words. "While King Tudhaliyas led his army to the west to put down a revolt in Arzawa, his own brother tried to capture the throne. Now Hittite armies march against each other and do not watch for invaders. Perhaps some among them welcome them. Our borders to the south are no longer secure. The Achaeans have great military strength, and we need that. A detachment of them asks for refuge. If we say yes, we gain Achaean allies against other enemies. Not just Theseus and his four remaining men, but their kinsmen and friends. The Achaeans have a great fighting reputation, and Prince Theseus comes from a powerful family. Let us count ourselves lucky that chance, or something better, brought them here.

"That is why I will extend the right hand of friendship to them.

"And I will also receive them with open arms because they are fighting men with fighting blood in their veins and because they know well what we ask of them in return. They know that it is the Amazon way to give a warm reception to warriors from whom young riders may receive the tribute of girl children. And now more than ever we need strong daughters, for the fever has taken many of us, and who will ride in their place when the time comes?"

Thalestris folded her arms to signal that she was done speaking.

Thalestris' women cheered; Hippolyta's followers muttered; Ariona's kept silent.

The valorous Omaïa halted forward. She was the oldest of the riders and had the right to speak after the chief. She leaned forward on her staff. "Thalestris is right," she said. "Ever since I can remember, we've counted as friends those who raise their weapons against the Kaska enemy. And it's been true at least since I was young, that when man visitors are fighters, we put them at their ease before the gates and ask young Amazons to couple with them if they care to, because we need brave daughters."

"Aye," said Marpessa, "there's a redheaded one among them who doesn't look too bad."

Omaïa beamed with flawless teeth that gave the lie to her age and said, "But we must bid them stay, only if they come with peaceful intentions, only if they've told the truth and not some lying words to get our guard down."

"Omaïa's right," said Ido. "Maybe they've got some mean trick hidden in their waistbands."

"No!"

"Yes!"

"Silence!" bid Thalestris.

Hippolyta sauntered to the front of the hall, smiled benevolently on the crowd, and said, "Thalestris speaks the truth. Those who fight against the Kaska folk can be our allies. And we greet men who give us vigorous daughters with gladness in our hearts."

"That isn't the only thing we greet them with," observed Marpessa.

Hippolyta dropped her grin. "But is it really as it seems to be? Are Theseus and his men the soldiers that they claim they are? And did they really wish to barter peacefully in the great mountains? And were they really set upon by Kaska men who came at night to rob their lives and steal their goods?

"Their story need not be believed so readily, my friends. All that we have to tell the truth by is the word this foreigner has offered as an explanation of his presence. But are we to believe him? He's an Achaean, and Achaeans are a lying, brawling lot, whom we don't care to see around the city."

"That they are!" bellowed Miminousa, one of Thalestris' followers, who was standing near the front. She was a small, red-faced, heavyset woman with huge fists. She led the squadron that kept the peace when the foreigners camped near the city. She could lay most men flat with one blow. "We've seen them come in now and again, those Achaeans," she boomed. "They talk smooth with the riders but pick fights with the other men the minute they've got some wine in their bellies. And I've heard that they're none too honest in trading either, if they can get away with it. I can't say that we women would be happy with them here, being shorthanded and all. Five soldiers in among the buyers and sellers, and plenty of drink and women around, I can't say it's a good idea."

Perseia shouted "Aye!" and clapped her hands.

Thalestris flashed an impatient glare at Miminousa, then changed her expression and said, in a teasing voice, "And what's a woman like you afraid of? The Achaeans are unarmed, and one look at your muscles would make anyone think twice about doing something foolish."

Antiope, Oebala, and Tomiris burst out laughing.

Hippolyta did not. She put on a pleasant expression and waited for the mirth to die down. Once it had, she changed her face and, with a serious air, said, "Hear me, women, and tell yourselves the truth as it is, and not what Theseus would have us believe. I say this fellow's story is fraudulent. He says he journeyed overland from Troy a month before the travelers start their march. He says the roads are dry because there has been a drought. But if that is so, where are the others from that part of the world? We've not spotted a one of them. Why have they not come down already?"

"The merchants travel in caravans," said Thalestris. "They're waiting for travelers and ships from the northeast and won't set out until enough of them for a caravan have reached Troy."

"Is that what Theseus told you?" asked Hippolyta in an amused tone. "Well, who among us would believe a stranger right away?"

Thalestris crossed her arms.

A woman shouted, "Ask Thalestris about the weapons."

Others added their agreement.

"You tell us," said Hippolyta to Thalestris, "that these Achaeans went as soldiers, because their expedition was so risky. If that's the truth, then why, Thalestris, do these soldiers not have weapons?"

"They had to flee the Kaska men by night," answered the chief.

Hippolyta pursed her lips. "Come, come, Thalestris," she said. "I've never heard of trained fighters throwing down their weapons, unless they want to beg the mercy of the enemy; and in a night attack there is no mercy. And among the Kaska folk there is no mercy, as even foreigners must comprehend. No. No. These Achaeans hid their weapons somewhere in the hills, and there is no other thing that you can think."

Thalestris' riders raised their voices in boos and hoots. Hippolyta's friends started cheering. Ariona's women did the same and the newly united factions overpowered Thalestris' loyalists.

Thalestris waited until the shouts died down and then spoke again. Her posture was regal and her tone assured. "Theseus and his men have no weapons and can do no harm. Ask the women who kept watch over them."

"I was there, and Thalestris is right," volunteered Antiope.

Thalestris smiled.

Feodissia stalked to the front of the hall. Omaïa granted her permission to speak.

Feodissia worked her tongue inside her jowls, then said, "I kept an eye on them, too, these outsiders, when they first came into the territory yesterday morning. They're hurt bad and have no weapons to speak of, not a one. Still. . . ."

Feodissia stroked her jaw. No one said a word. Finally she uttered, "Still, they could just as well be a band of robbers. You see, there's nothing in what they say to show otherwise— except what they told Thalestris. I mean maybe they're a band of highwaymen who got licked proper when they ran into another gang out early to have a look at the road. It just doesn't make sense that they threw down all their weapons. At least not to me. Maybe they hid them, because they knew we'd take them away when they got here." Feodissia paused and ran her hand over her chin. "That's what Tecmassa thinks, too," she said.

Displeasure flickered across Thalestris' eyes.

"Where is Tecmassa?" asked Omaïa. "She's ridden many years and knows about these things. I'd trust her judgment."

Tecmassa's name resounded. Penthesilea scanned the room. Other heads swiveled and other eyes searched for Tecmassa. But in vain.

Feodissia went on, "Tecmassa's also wary about the bones."

"The bones?" yelled someone from among Hippolyta's followers.

Hippolyta raised her eyebrows in amusement. "And well Tecmassa might be," she said. "Here is the straight truth. One of these men got hurt so badly that he died last night. They cremated him this morning, on the other side of the black mulberry trees. We saw the smoke when we rode out. When we reached them, the pyre on which they cremated the fellow still smoked, but his bones were nowhere to be found. Where were they? Why had they taken them away so hastily?"

"They buried them, as is their custom," said Thalestris.

Hippolyta puckered her lips as if she had tasted something sour. "A fighter's bones," she said, "are never buried in a foreign land but go back to her kin. There is no god or goddess who would teach us something else. Do the Achaeans fear that we will steal the dead man's bones and hold them prisoner until the fighter's family sends a ransom? How did that notion ever come to cross their thoughts? Of what are these intruders so afraid? Do they think that we are just like them? Why do they lie? I ask you all, why do they lie?"

Perseia and Klymene grumbled the same question.

"Their story is true," affirmed Thalestris. "Theseus need not fear that we would rob a dead man's solid bones."

"These strangers have not spoken the truth," said Hippolyta. "They are a danger here. We should not count them as our friends."

"Theseus' house," said Thalestris, "is a powerful one among the Achaeans. He is a prince of his city. This I know from what Trojans have told me."

Thalestris reached inside her shirt and produced the chain and medal Theseus had given her. "This piece of gold," she said, "bears the emblem of Theseus' house, a coiled snake. On the other side is the image of his god, who is also his ancestor. It is such a fine piece—of gold so pure and work so fine—that none but a mighty chief could have commissioned it. And Theseus swore his oath upon it, in sight of his god and ours, that he told no lies about himself and his men."

Thalestris tossed the object to Omaïa, who turned it around in her fingers and held it up for all to see before passing it to Hippolyta. Hippolyta looked at it carefully and broke into a tolerant grin, as if a little child had just uttered foolish words. "Thalestris claims that Theseus is a great prince among the Achaeans," she said. "She tells us that his family is a great one in their lands. But all she has to prove it by is this." Hippolyta dangled the precious object from the tips of her fingers so that it trembled in the light.

"He could just as well have stolen it," said Miminousa, to Thalestris' displeasure.

"Or won it in a gambling game," said Ido.

"Great family indeed!" sneered Hippolyta, flipping the golden object back to Thalestris. "Thalestris tells us that his people live in mighty cities on the other side of Troy. Well, even if they do, I can't see how alliance with them helps the Amazons. Who would ever march here from the western limits of the world? Especially when they can set sail here only at the equinox."

"Yeah!"

"You tell her!"

"Theseus comes from a powerful family," said Thalestris, "a strong city whose alliance we must welcome. And if we offer him our hospitality, then we can call upon his house's allies, too, in time of need. There are some that live closer by, among the ten peoples to the east of Troy. And times of danger may be near at hand."

"Times of danger may indeed be near at hand, Thalestris," said Hippolyta in ringing tones. "But what real proof can you show us that he's not a robber to be run out of these lands before he causes trouble? And ask Tecmassa, too, if Theseus is not a cruel man, who loves to torture prisoners when they're taken. He told you what he did to those he captured. How are we to trust a man like that within our borders?"

Bodeful murmurs swept the hall like moans of rising wind. Torturers were a cursed, dangerous lot.

"That's what Tecmassa told me," said Hippolyta, "and that's what I believe of him, this barbarous man you want to make your honored guest."

"Tecmassa isn't here," said Omaïa, "but surely the other women in the party heard this talk of torture."

Thalestris spoke. Her voice was calm and even. "Theseus told us of an expedition that he led into the hills around his father's city. Bandits infested them, torturing their victims after they had taken their goods. And raping the women. No traveler to that city, no merchant was safe. People would not go there to trade, and the city grew poor until Theseus and his men hunted the robbers down. That's all the talk of torture there was."

Penthesilea felt her stomach sink. It was wrong not to speak the straight truth, above all to other Amazons, women sworn to die at your side.

Omaïa asked Thalestris, "Who rode with you when you spoke to this man?"

"Beside Tecmassa, Antiope and her companion stayed with me when I met Prince Theseus." Thalestris's glance, full of unspoken threats, darted briefly in Penthesilea's direction.

Omaïa turned to Antiope. "Did Theseus say anything more?" she asked.

Antiope did not move her lips but stared directly at Omaïa as if to signify that there was nothing to report. Shame for Antiope made Penthesilea's cheeks grow hot.

Omaïa turned to Penthesilea and questioned her with a clear gaze that went deep into her. Penthesilea lowered her eyes. All the riders must be staring at her, and Thalestris, too. If Penthesilea spoke the truth, especially after Antiope's silence, Thalestris' wrath would fall upon her. Antiope wouldn't like it either, and who knew what hidden punishments Celano would find.

"Did he say anything more?" asked Omaïa.

"Yes," whispered Penthesilea.Her gaze was still downcast.

"Yes?" prompted Omaïa.

"He said more."

"What did he say?"

Penthesilea looked up at her questioner. "He said that the bandits tortured all the travelers who were taken alive and raped all the women. He said that when he and his men caught the robbers, they got as good as they had given."

"He tortured them?" asked Omaïa.

"He said, 'The robbers got as good as they had given.'" Penthesilea inclined her head once more. She heard far off rumbling, like thunder, and thought it was the blood coursing through her cheeks. But when she looked up, she saw women muttering darkly to one another. Their imprecations growled like wrathful winds.

Hippolyta curled her lips in satisfaction.

Anger burned in Thalestris' eyes. She crossed her arms and stared grimly at the riders. There was something else in her glance, too, some warning, some vision of peril, that made the Amazons grow still, albeit slowly, unevenly.

Thalestris spoke.

"Yes, the Achaeans' story sounds suspicious, although I am convinced that Theseus told the truth to me. But even if his story is a lie, even if he is a robber and his men are what is left of his gang, we cannot turn them out. If we do, there will be four, maybe five, trained fighters somewhere on the roads that come into our territory. If they decide to linger there, they'll be free to fall on traders traveling into our land, and that's not good."

No one replied.

"And they'll be glad to cause us woe," continued Thalestris, "because we turned them out when they were in need. And if they've hidden weapons in the hills, then they'll be even more of a danger to the traders and to us."

The riders had grown still.

"It'll take a dozen Amazons to track them down," said Thalestris. "If we can spare that many riders. We've got to keep them right under our eyes."

"That makes sense," said Miminousa.

"No it doesn't," shouted Ido. "Why don't we just ride out and kill them on the spot?"

Some riders mumbled agreement.

Thalestris continued, "We don't need those Achaeans wandering about the approaches to our territory. We don't need to spread our forces even thinner, especially if the Achaeans get to work in the northeast, on the road from Troy. But we do need the traders for the goods they bring and for the daughters they leave and for the boy children they take off our hands."

Thalestris paused, but no one, not even Hippolyta, spoke against her. The silence was complete.

Thalestris went on. "But Theseus is a noble. His family is a powerful one among his people, and one day soon we may need help from every quarter. And the daughters we get from these soldiers will have fighting blood in their veins. We must give thanks to the Goddess for bringing them here."

Antiope clapped her hands. Tomiris and Oebala gave a cheer. Whoops and shouts burst the meeting apart the way the wind breaks open a bank of fog that vanishes in all directions. Women turned away from the speakers and began to chatter among themselves; Amynome started juggling the three wooden balls she had carried in; Feodissia stationed herself near the door leading downstairs to catch a glimpse of Anuphey; Ido circulated among the betting women to lay wagers on which Amazons Thalestris would chose to couple with the Achaean soldiers. A line of attendants entered carrying trays of goblets and pitchers of wine. Thalestris reached for a drink.

Hippolyta's lips etched a bloodless smile.

Chapter 8

A week after the Achaeans arrived, the Amazons staged their games. They did so every year, when the summer corn had sprouted from the earth, the guardian star of the bear shone its brightest in the sky, and the ground was dry enough for the riders to race their horses. The contests of skill and daring took place on the gently sloped pasture that lay a short walk from the city walls. This year, the games also overlooked the tents of the strangers, and it was the first time in many women's memory that foreigners, and men at that, would witness the contests.

The day was a holiday in honor of Kaïta, goddess of grain, to whom the events were offered in supplication of a good growing season and plentiful harvest. On this occasion, the women put aside their labors to recline, banquet, and drink, to watch riders vie with one another, wager on the outcome of their competitions, and cheer their favorites on.

Those who dwelt in the temple precincts had begun the celebration the evening before. They had carried Kaïta's image, along with great skinfuls of beer, to the site of the games and had rung in the feast day with revels that the profane were forbidden to attend. That night, women in the city (where raucous songs and frenetic music also rang out) heard cymbals clash beyond the walls, drums throb, and voices wail. The carousal clamored ever more deliriously as the stars swept from east to west and died out only when the first pale fingers of the day reached upward from behind the hills.

An hour after that, when luminous blue infused the sky, bands of happy women and the exuberant children who skipped alongside them or swayed on their backs, poured out of the city—effervescent, dancing, chattering groups that would break apart and knit together again to strike up fresh songs and tell other jokes. And once the merrymakers reached the site of the games, they found cakes and cheese waiting for them, and dried fruits and sweets, and drink enough to drown them. The chief of the riders and the high priestess had supplied it all from their own stores.

Penthesilea rode down behind a gang of holidaymakers. But her mood was as black as theirs was sunny; for, since the Achaeans had arrived, she had been left to her own misery. Her imagination did the rest.

Thalestris had flouted long tradition by not asking her, Antiope's chosen companion, the very comrade that Thalestris had named to ride beside her daughter, to accompany Antiope on her dynastic duty. In Penthesilea's eyes, the neglect sullied her honor, and she stung from it. The chief might as well have slapped her in the face. (Penthesilea did not realize that most women put Thalestris' deed down to spite: Penthesilea had almost crossed her schemes.) Nor was Penthesilea consoled by the thought that Theseus' henchman, Pirothous, would have fallen to her lot had she been granted what was hers. Marpessa got him instead.

Thalestris had compounded the punishment by ceasing to invite Penthesilea along on her duties, as she had always done before. Indeed, whenever the young rider was in her presence, she kept a chilly silence and looked through her. Nor did household attendants dare speak to Penthesilea, save to wait on her body. Celano had threatened to punish any woman who did, and they all dreaded Celano's anger. Only Anuphey took the risk of addressing Penthesilea, for she already lived under a cloud of displeasure—Antiope's jealousy of Feodissia had seen to that. Still, Anuphey's visits were rare, and Penthesilea suffered from the isolation.

Thalestris had shown less rancor when she selected two other young Amazons to mate with the foreign soldiers. Doubtless in consultation with Celano, she had chosen Adrasta and Charope. Adrasta was Hippolyta's niece, and summoning her prevented the old noble from finding fault and insult; Charope was Ariona's daughter, and Ariona was not to be slighted either, although she was less powerful than Hippolyta.

Antiope had disappeared with Theseus as soon as he and his men took up residence in the tents and had not sent word to Penthesilea since then. And when Penthesilea occasionally called at the pavilion reserved for their mating, Antiope would take her time coming out, pronounce meaningless greetings, and vanish inside. Indeed, sometimes, Antiope would not emerge at all. The scorn burned Penthesilea.

Penthesilea arrived at the pasture where the games were to take place. Numerous women had already gathered. Myrtho was there, standing in the center of a knot of blue-robed temple attendants. She turned at the sound of hoofbeats, saw who the rider was, and, smiling, extended her arms. Penthesilea jumped down and took Myrtho's hands. The high priestess said nothing, but closed her eyes. When she opened them, they hinted at sadness. Penthesilea's own heaviness of heart took comfort from Myrtho's, and they stood with fingers locked for a while.

The four Achaeans and the Amazons who accompanied them arrived and settled on the ground nearby. Crowns of lilacs ornamented their heads. Antiope sat cross-legged. Theseus sprawled beside her. His golden-haired breast, which was bare, glowed like a god's in the morning sun. A linen waistcloth of the same color as the flowers he wore was draped around his middle. He rested on his right elbow and hip and drew back his left leg so that it pulled at his garment, whose tightness revealed the outline of his penis. He kept rolling the ends of his beard between the fingers of his left hand.

The remaining women and men of Antiope's party formed a loose arc behind her. The three Amazons made up one sector; the three Achaeans the other. Only Marpessa and Pirothous sat side by side.

Antiope leaned over and whispered in Theseus' ear, and he stared at Myrtho. Pirothous, who sat in back of his captain, also riveted his eyes on her; although, once he saw that Penthesilea was watching him, he dropped his face into a lifeless mask.

A cortege on horseback, Thalestris, Hippolyta, and Ariona leading it, arrived and dismounted. Myrtho composed her face, then unraveled her fingers from Penthesilea's, and caressed her cheek. The priestess swept up her long skirt and promenaded to the altar.

The chief of the riders dismounted, handed the reins of her steed to an attendant, and joined Myrtho. The talk around died to nothing. Thalestris bowed to Myrtho and, in unison with her, kneeled and placed her palms and forehead on the earth. Myrtho intoned a prayer and Thalestris the responses. Both rose. Myrtho laid grains of einkorn, emmer wheat, and barley on the altar, arranging them in patterns that only the Goddess and Her chief worshiper knew how to read. The two celebrants faced the assembly. Myrtho stretched her arms toward the sky and turned her palms and brow upward. "Oh Kaïta," she intoned, "goddess of the grain, who gives us the fruits of the earth, we thank You for Your bounteous goodness and beseech You, continue, oh continue, to smile on us, for we laud and worship You."

Thalestris raised her hands and brow to the heavens. Her voice rang out. "Oh Kaïta, goddess of grain, who gives us the fruits of the earth, may You bestow upon Your adoring servants a good growing season and a fine harvest. To pray for them we offer these games to You. May they please You and may You smile on us." Thalestris paused longer than she needed to before mouthing, "Let the games begin."

Hundreds began to speak and laugh again, and the throng spread out into a ragged ellipse, many women settling on the ground, the riders seating themselves close to a wooden stand set up near the starting line. Antiope beckoned to Penthesilea to join her party. Surprised, Penthesilea did so, taking her place on the opposite side of Antiope from Theseus.

"The first event," announced Thalestris, "is the horse race. Let the prizes for it be shown." Someone handed her a large electrum brooch, and she held up the glittering object: the rays of the morning sun ricocheted around it.

"I offer this to the woman who finishes first. It is from my own treasure."

Onlookers hummed in admiration.

"And to the woman who comes in second, I offer this." An attendant stepped forth, her arms stretched over her head. She showed off a fluted cup resting on four slim, horselike, legs. The vessel shone blinding white in the sunshine.

Women praised it out loud.

"And to the third rider, I'll award this armband of hammered bronze." Another servant brandished the prize for all to see. The bracelet, which shimmered hyacinth in the morning brightness, gave off uneven reflections. "There's a picture engraved on the inset," said Thalestris. "It's a charm; it makes you lucky in love."

Laughter rippled through the crowd. Theseus whispered in Antiope's ear. Antiope closed her eyes; her handsome lips sketched a smile.

"Let the riders who wish to race come before me on their mounts," said Thalestris.

Antiope jumped up. An attendant brought her leather belt; her labrys and dagger hung from it. Antiope fastened it around her and slid the weapons up and down in their sheaths. The woman gave Antiope her bow and a quiver containing one arrow. Antiope checked the bowstring and the true of the shaft and slung the sheath and weapon across her back. An hostler led Melanthus, her nervous-footed black stallion, to her. She sprang up on the horse's back, took the reins so that they extended over her forefingers and through her grip, and adjusted their length. Her shoulders square over her hips, her waist set forward so that her back made an arc at the midpoint, she touched her mount with her heels and walked him to the spot that Thalestris had indicated. When Antiope reined the animal in, he pawed the ground.

Melanippe rode forward. Her brooding eyes looked neither left nor right but took in everything. She was similarly equipped as Antiope and sat a short, restless, piebald mare, which pranced from side to side. Antiope puckered her lips. The mole over Melanippe's right lip started pulsating.

"Who's the new rider?" asked Pirothous. He and Marpessa lounged in back of Penthesilea.

"That's Melanippe," answered Marpessa. "She's a high born woman; her mother was Thalestris' sister, who ruled before she did. One day Melanippe and Antiope will vie for the throne. Melanippe is Antiope's rival in this race as she is in everything else."

Antiope's stallion whinnied at Melanippe's mare, which bucked with all her might. Melanippe bent her trunk back until the mare stood on all fours again. Melanippe kneed her, and the mare sidled away from Antiope's mount.

Perseia rode a young gray mare into the lineup. Antiope sneered; Melanippe raised her eyebrows in pleasure.

"That's Melanippe's loving friend, Perseia," remarked Marpessa. "She rides for Hippolyta, too."

Perseia's horse jerked her head back, but Perseia moved effortlessly with the thrashing, her long fingers on the reins drawing the horse's mouth down so that she stopped misbehaving.

Klymene walked her roan stallion into the starting circle. Antiope turned her horse around so that his croup and her back greeted the newcomer. Melanippe laughed and bid her hello.

"That's Klymene. She follows Ariona. She hates Antiope, too. It's a grudge match for her. And she's reckless, so who knows."

Klymene's horse attempted to bite Antiope's. Antiope pulled away, but not in time to prevent her mount from kicking at Klymene's, who reined back her beast with a flick of her wrist and chuckled.

Tomiris, who sat a speckled gelding with small, shiny eyes, moved forward out of the sidelines, from where she had been observing the others.

"There's Tomiris. She rides for Thalestris. She's Antiope's comrade."

Tomiris stationed herself at Klymene's side. Satisfaction lit up Antiope's eyes; Melanippe raised her nose to the left in scorn.

Klymene's mount, having had no luck with Antiope's horse, lowered his head and bared his teeth to bite Tomiris'. Tomiris showed no sign of having seen the beast. But when his muzzle approached her, she punched his nose, and he leapt back and unbalanced Klymene, who began to slide off but grabbed his mane and shot a furious glance at Tomiris, who beamed in all innocence.

"That's Tomiris all right—malice on two feet. You never know what she's turning over in that devious mind of hers. She probably has some dirty trick up her sleeve for the race. Tomiris will ride interference for Antiope."

"Interference?"

"Klymene and Perseia are set to harass Antiope as soon as they're out of sight of the judges. They'll pull every trick they know to slow Antiope down so that Melanippe can ride ahead and get as much of a lead as she can. She has to take it early and get far, because, on the flat, Antiope's horse flies like the wind. But Antiope's friends Tomiris and Oebala are going to protect her until the final stretch. I can't for the life of me tell where Oebala is, though.

"What they're up to is against the rules, though, and it means disqualification for two years."

"Does Thalestris let it go on anyway?" asked Pirothous.

"She'll exercise her authority only if someone's caught in the act. And she'll fly into a rage if it's any of Melanippe's friends. If not—especially if Antiope wins—she'll not know a thing about it. There's much bad blood mixed in with the race."

No more competitors rode into view. Antiope swiveled in the saddle, turning her eyes this way and that.

The spectators, who had hushed up when the Amazons rode into the starting lineup, began to babble among themselves. A few stood up and moved from seated group to seated group. Others, who had been on their feet all along, huddled in twos and threes. Ido, who loved to gamble, walked among the riders, slapping the hands of some to seal bargains.

"The betting's begun," said Marpessa.

"Who's the favorite?" asked Pirothous.

"It's a great question, and half our riders will answer Melanippe and the other half Antiope. It's a rough course those girls have to cover, none of your chariot races on level ground, the way they're said to do it in Troy. Here racers sit their mounts, with tricky obstacles to get around—a stream to ford, a rock to jump in the middle of treacherous ground, and close set flags to weave through without touching them, lest you be disqualified. And when the racers near the finish, they've got to hit two targets on the dead run—one with the arrow and the other with the axe. It's a rare Amazon who misses.

"Melanippe's favored by some because she's got the clear advantage in this kind of course. She rides like the Mare Goddess, and her pony fairly flies over barriers and boundaries, hedges and ditches, rocks and water. Still, Antiope sits the fastest mount and knows how to make him run swifter than white water. And Tomiris and Oebala will be there to protect her from Perseia and Klymene.

"But I wonder what's become of Oebala. She's late. They'll be starting soon."

The same thing was on Antiope's mind. She frowned and darted anxious glances among the Amazons surrounding the competitors. She did not find what she was looking for and fixed a puzzled gaze on Marpessa, who asked Penthesilea, "Where's Oebala?"

"I haven't seen her since yesterday afternoon."

"Now that's strange, very strange," said Marpessa. "She was supposed to ride. Without her, it's three to two against Antiope, and she's sure to lose."

Omaïa hobbled up to Thalestris, and Miminousa and Amynome, on horseback, joined them. The four consulted. Then Thalestris turned her attention to the racers; Omaïa made her way to the platform and the woman who was to act as her crier hoisted her up and joined her there; Miminousa and Amynome walked their mounts to the perimeter of the crowd and then ran them uphill.

"Miminousa is to keep an eye on the goings on up the hill," Marpessa told Pirothous. "And Amynome is to observe the flags the women have to twist through. Omaïa is to watch the finish. But where is Oebala? She is supposed to make a third for Antiope."

Antiope's face was contracted in worry, and her horse, which had caught her nervousness, shrugged and trembled. Antiope broke out of the lineup and approached Penthesilea and Marpessa, who got to their feet. Antiope wrinkled her brow in a question.

"I don't know where Oebala is, nor does Penthesilea," answered Marpessa.

"Let the riders get on their marks!" boomed the crier.

"One of you must ride with me," said Antiope.

"My horse isn't here," said Marpessa.

Antiope looked down at Penthesilea. "Then you will ride." Antiope's low staccato commanded rather than asked. Without further word, she turned and rode back to the starting place.

"Let the riders get on their marks!" insisted the same voice.

Penthesilea did not move.

"What makes her hesitate?" asked Pirothous. "Can't she do it? Is she afraid?"

Penthesilea stared at him in disbelief. "Can't do it?" she snapped. "Afraid?" She turned to the attendant and shouted, "Bring my horse!" As soon as she had, she vaulted onto Tala's back so abruptly that the mare reared. Penthesilea threw her trunk forward and grabbed the mare's mane. The animal settled down and Penthesilea walked her into the midst of the other riders.

Buzzing rose from the spectators. Women hurried around again. The Amazon Ido, who had seated herself on the grass, jumped to her feet. The odds had changed.

Feodissia, who was there to shoot in the archery contest, ran forward and handed Penthesilea her own belt, bow, and quiver. Penthesilea thanked her in haste, attached the weapons around herself, and reined up next to Antiope, whose lips pressed hard against one another and whose eyes flickered from Penthesilea to Tomiris.

Penthesilea looked over her shoulder. Pirothous was on his feet, exchanging merry glances with Theseus.

"Begin!" exclaimed the herald.

One by one the Amazons walked their horses through the seated onlookers, clucking their mounts into a canter only after they had reached clear ground. When Tomiris' turn came, she bowed in the saddle and graciously beckoned Penthesilea to go before her. Penthesilea giddapped Tala into motion, passed among the spectators, and then gave her the heel. Tala began to lope uphill.

The women and horses moved forward in a loose string, no one trying to surge ahead so early in the race. The hard work and dirty tricks would start only when the competitors were no longer in sight of the crowd and not yet in view of Miminousa. Melanippe led the racers. Antiope had faded behind her, and Melanippe was slowly increasing her lead. Perseia rode behind Antiope, and Klymene behind Perseia. Penthesilea followed her. Tomiris took up the rear.

Penthesilea gazed at Antiope, once more heard her bark the order to race with her, and furrowed her brow in distress. Then Penthesilea saw Pirothous' face again. He had made a fool of her in everyone's eyes. Still, she had let him bait her into racing. She had let the hot blood get the better of her. She dressed herself down for it with more vigor than Tecmassa would have done, or Leokadia, if she were alive.

Melanippe reached a stand of birch trees that stood halfway up the slope. The racers were to turn here, and Melanippe's piebald footed smartly left. Penthesilea and Tomiris had to make their move now: to pass Klymene and Perseia and wedge themselves between them and Antiope. Otherwise, they would would begin harassing her once they all had disappeared behind the trees. Penthesilea glanced back: Tomiris waved at her. Penthesilea gestured in return and looked ahead. She relaxed Tala's reins, leaned over her neck, and whistled. Tala lowered her head and lengthened her stride. Penthesilea raced past Klymene, who grinned as they flew by, and began to catch up with Perseia. Behind Penthesilea, the thudding of Tomiris' horse's hooves grew louder and blended with that of Klymene's.

Perseia saw that she was being chased. She bent over her gray's neck and gave her the heel. The beast leaped ahead. Penthesilea prodded Tala. Her hooves beat faster. The tail of Perseia's mount began to sweep Tala's nose. At the same time, the staccato that was pursuing Penthesilea sounded close behind and to the left. Penthesilea moved Tala right. The noise closed in. Tomiris drew abreast, stuck her mouth in

Penthesilea's ear, and bellowed, "Watch out!" She waved a
bright red cloth in Tala's eyes.

Tala flung herself away from the sight. Penthesilea felt
herself stiffen but stopped herself from pulling back on Tala's
mouth. Instead, the rider bent forward, locked her legs around
her mount's girth, and, letting the reins slack, clutched her
mane. Tala lurched to the right and lost her footing, but clambered upright and bolted. She scrambled away from the race.
Penthesilea let Tala have her head until her panic was spent.
Then Penthesilea pulled gingerly at the straps and coaxed Tala
into a wide half-circle, so that she was again making her way
toward the spot they had just come from.

No other rider was in sight. The others had already vanished behind the birches. After a while, Penthesilea passed
into their shadow. It chilled her cheeks and made her lungs
tingle. The thud of Tala's hooves grew quieter as they beat
against the ground. Leaves and branches streamed toward
Tala's ears. Penthesilea had time to think. Why had Tomiris
tried to unhorse her? Did Tomiris, too, want Perseia to harass
Antiope? Why? And Klymene, was she in on it? She had
smiled when Penthesilea passed her. Had they all struck up a
secret bargain? Did they all dislike Antiope that much?

Penthesilea broke out of the copse. A short distance downhill, a twelve-foot-wide ribbon of water rushed from the direction of the iron hills toward Thermodon. Marks cut the soil on
its near bank, and the grasses were trampled. Clouds of brown
particles hovered over the water. On the other bank,
hoofprints and footmarks sank into the mud. Dark swathes
among the reeds there led to a birch-covered ridge.
Penthesilea saw no one.

She jumped down. The earth gave slightly under the balls
of her feet. She tied Tala's reins around the animal's neck,
slipped the bow and quiver off her back, and held them over
her shoulder with her left hand. With her right she grasped
the side strap of Tala's bridle, led the still skittish animal
into the stream, and waded across. The water numbed
Penthesilea's legs and hips. The current tried to push her over.
She struggled against it and slogged toward the other side.
Once she reached it, she slung her bow and quiver across her
back again, vaulted onto Tala's back, and walked the mare
through the wetland. The mud squeaked and puckered under
Tala's hooves.

Horse and rider reached the ridge and trotted up. A notch no longer than a short arrow's flight and no wider than a stone's throw opened up in front of them. No riders were in sight. The defile's north slope was so steep that a goat could not negotiate it. Horizontal veins of black and red showed through dark shrubs on its side. Stones and pebbles cluttered the margin running along the base and choked the notch's floor. The southern steep was less breakneck, but a thorny brambles covered its side, and no woman in her right mind would set foot in them, much less ride her horse there. A shallow stream meandered through the low ground separating the two hills. The rivulet pushed this way and that, taking new turns every time the rains fell and the snows melted. Horses' tracks, crushed grasses, and bushes whose branches were newly broken followed a winding course along the valley floor.

Keeping a sharp eye out for unseen stones and stumps, Penthesilea walked Tala quickly along the same track. Near the middle, thick hedges grew around a large, flat rock. There was no circling it. Gouges in the earth in front showed where the riders had pulled back to jump their horses over it. Penthesilea came close and saw the water on the other side. Suspended murk made it opaque; animals landing there had stirred up the silt.

Penthesilea turned Tala back and took what distance she could. She set Tala into a run. Then she tightened her fists slightly around the reins so that Tala slowed. Horse and rider neared the hedges. Penthesilea opened her hands, locked her thighs around Tala's girth, and pressed. The mare's legs bent; she launched herself over the bushes and stone and landed with a smack. Dirty water slapped against Penthesilea's face. She let Tala continue her run, which followed the other horses' prints, emerged from the the pass, and immediately faced a rugged little steep. Tala clambered up; Penthesilea inclined her trunk well forward; Tala scrambled down; Penthesilea straightened up.

On the right, a thick woman on a squat mount—Miminousa—was rushing toward the wood that began there. On the left, stretched the slope leading back downhill. Penthesilea turned her mare and gave Tala her head. The mare widened her gait. Penthesilea saw no horses and riders in front of her. The others had doubtless finished and only she, whom Tomiris had driven from the course, remained.

Before Penthesilea had time to speculate further, ten poles planted in the ground at nine, six, five, four, and three feet from one another, loomed up. The pairs formed a swiftly changing diagonal. A cherry red banner waved from the top of each stake. Amynome sat her mount on the far side of them. Under this referee's eyes, Penthesilea worked Tala's head and forelegs and dipped left and right as the mare swerved and twisted between banners.   To negotiate the last two, Penthesilea leaned over and guided Tala into a about-face. Once Penthesilea had gotten through, she looked back. No flag fluttered out of rhythm with the others. Amynome waved to show that all had gone well.

The targets that the racers had to hit rushed toward Penthesilea—thick stakes planted in the ground on either side of the course. The second was twenty-four feet farther along. She slackened Tala's reins and draped them over her left elbow. She slid the bow off her back and strung it. She took an arrow from the quiver and, fixing it in position, pulled. It was hard to draw the cord to her cheek. It was Feodissia's bow, made for her, and Feodissia's arms were longer than her own. As Tala hurtled by the pole, Penthesilea loosed the shaft and heard the bowstring twang. Without looking back, she grabbed the labrys suspended from her belt. The axe, too, was heavier than the one she was used to. Tala swept past the second stake. Penthesilea heaved the weapon with all her might and heard a thunk.

She took the reins into her hands again. Here was the homestretch. Bending low over Tala's neck, she whipped her withers with the ends of the reins. Tala quickened her stride; her belly nearly touched the ground. Penthesilea hurtled toward the onlookers. She heard them shouting. She made out Anuphey and Marpessa jumping up and down. Other women leaped to their feet as Penthesilea goaded Tala toward them. Was someone behind her, trying to catch up? She looked back under her arm. No one chased her. She was within a stone's throw of the crowd. She shot through it. Bodies streaming across her vision made her dizzy. Screams made her deaf. She rushed by the platform as if a giant hand had flung her. She struggled to slow Tala and reined her in.   She collapsed forward. It hurt to breathe. Her heart's pounding split her chest. Tala was panting; sweat glistened on her neck; foam dripped from her mouth.

Anuphey, her face flushed, hastened to Penthesilea's side, reached up, and threw her arms around her waist with such abandon that she started to topple over sideways and had to right herself. Marpessa ran up to her and pounded her on the backside. What had gotten them so excited?

Penthesilea jumped down, and Marpessa led Tala away. Penthesilea looked around. Antiope was nowhere to be seen. Hippolyta and Melanippe stood in the shadow of the platform. Hippolyta smiled triumphantly. The mole over Melanippe's lip trembled with satisfaction. On the platform, Thalestris, who stood at Omaïa's side, stared at Penthesilea from under stormy brows.

"Where's Antiope?" asked Penthesilea.

"Have you taken leave of your senses, girl?" asked Marpessa. Anuphey laughed and pointed uphill. Halfway along the slope, two riders, who had just negotiated the poles, were hastening toward the onlookers. The one in the lead crouched over a long-limbed black horse. That was Antiope. The other gripped a roan horse between her thighs and beat its sides with her heels. That was Klymene. Antiope was quickly outdistancing her. Antiope shot her bow and hurled her axe. Her horse stretched out into a dead run. The thudding of its hooves grew louder. It flew through the onlookers and past the judge. Antiope reined in.

The race was over. Women who were not standing bolted to their feet and flocked around the winners. Most spectators shouted at the top of their lungs. Many clapped their hands over their heads. Ido flung her arms around Penthesilea and danced up and down. Penthesilea extricated herself just as Antiope dismounted. Purple welts stained her left arm and leg. Dried blood striped her cheek. Her comely face was pale under her tan. Fury flashed in her eyes.

Thalestris jumped down to her side.

"Klymene played a dirty trick on me," gasped Antiope. "A dirty trick. She unhorsed me with her treachery. Up until then, I rode second. I would have come in first, but for her. You saw me let Melanippe take the lead from the start. I was going to let her ride first. I was going to follow her until the downhill turn. Then I was going to outrun her." Antiope riveted her eyes on Melanippe. "But, just before the downhill turn, when we came out of the notch, Klymene came on me from my right and Perseia drew up behind me. I swear I don't know how. They drove me into the forest and followed me, both of them. Klymene flung herself in my path. She waved something in my stallion's eyes. He reared. I saw what was coming. I threw myself away from him. I landed on clear ground. And luckily for Klymene—and for whomever put her up to this," Antiope turned a hate-filled glance on Melanippe— "my horse wasn't lamed. Then they rode off. I mounted and caught up with Klymene, and passed her." Antiope gasped for breath again and glowered at Melanippe. "The first place in this race is mine. They ganged up on me. Someone will pay, mark my words."

Tomiris had played the very same trick on Penthesilea, and Penthesilea was going to speak up when a woman screamed, "Look!" and a thousand eyes turned in the direction of the homestretch. Halfway uphill, a stocky Amazon on a short-legged pony was making for them in great haste.

"Miminousa!" sounded a ragged array.

Miminousa thundered in and reined up in front of the platform. Dust caked her face, except where lines of sweat uncovered flushed skin.

"There's been foul play!" she shouted to Omaïa. The women looked at one another as if they had known so all along.

Miminousa took no notice. Her sides heaving noisily, she made her report to Omaïa. "I was at my station in the tree at the far end of the pass, when the first of the racers came out of the gap and crossed uphill of me. Melanippe, on that piebald of hers, was well in the lead. Well in the lead. You couldn't see the second racer yet, although she came along soon enough. That was Antiope, on her black horse. Four lengths behind her were Perseia and Klymene. Those two rode in such close formation that I didn't like it. So I got down from the tree and mounted. From the saddle I saw them stampede Antiope into the woods. I followed them. But before I got in there, the two of them came back my way, riding like the Storm God himself was on their heels. I headed in a little further and spotted Antiope standing by her horse, inspecting his legs and hooves. Judging by the way she looked, she'd been thrown. I didn't have a chance to ask what happened, because she jumped back on and headed out as fast as her horse could go. I turned back myself, so I could get here and tell you. On the way I passed Tomiris, on foot, leading that speckled gelding of hers. The poor creature's hobbling around."

Women started to chatter all at once.

"Silence!" boomed the herald.

Antiope addressed Omaïa. "The first prize is mine. Those two ganged up on me. If they hadn't, I would have come in first, not Melanippe. I would have beat her by at least a dozen lengths—everybody knows it."

Some Amazons huzzahed; others booed.

"Silence!"

Thalestris looked from Miminousa to Omaïa and said, "Antiope claims her right. She wants the first prize. I want to see that justice is done."

Ido hooted. Hippolyta drew her lips into a sarcastic line. She gazed at Omaïa and pronounced, "I grant you that Antiope was dealt an unfair blow. But Miminousa's word is also to be reckoned with. She said that Melanippe outpaced all the others when they crossed before her station. 'Well in the lead,' said Miminousa. 'Well in the lead.' Those are her very words. Weigh Miminousa's observation against Antiope's claim, weigh what one saw against the other's wish, and you will see that Melanippe wins the race without a doubt."

Ido shouted, "Hear. Hear!" Thalestris gazed at her with half-closed serpent's eyes.

By this time Miminousa had dismounted and hefted her frame onto the platform. She huddled and consulted with Omaïa. Buzzing arose from the ranks of the Amazons. Some smirked; others frowned. Still other spectators prattled to one another. Thalestris folded her arms and glowered. Hippolyta put her hands behind her back and surveyed the onlookers. Omaïa finished conferring with Miminousa. Miminousa pulled at her ear and poised her knuckles on her hips. Omaïa, who was leaning on her cane, stared for a long time at its base. At length, she raised her head and focused sourly on Hippolyta and Melanippe, then on Thalestris and Antiope. Omaïa raised her palm, and everyone grew still. "Antiope has met with foul play all right," she said. "and I call a foul. It's sure and certain that Antiope would have finished much sooner if someone hadn't played a dirty trick on her. She rides a fast horse, kept second all along, and had a clear shot at taking the race."

Thalestris' brow lightened; Hippolyta tapped a foot. "But still," said Omaïa, "Miminousa has just told us that Melanippe led Antiope handsomely when they passed the oak tree. And Melanippe came in long before anyone else, even Penthesilea here. So I judge that Melanippe gets the first prize."

Whoops and catcalls filled the air.

"Silence!" roared the crier.

"Silence!"

"And as for second," continued Omaïa, "Penthesilea finished in that position, but rode in well after Melanippe. But Antiope kept close behind Melanippe all along, until they ganged up on her. So—barring any objection from the parties to the dispute—I'll award second place to Antiope here and third to Penthesilea." Omaïa turned to her. "You have the right to object, my girl. What have you to say for yourself?"

Penthesilea had turned her head down. Women stared mutely at her. Omaïa's stentor did not have to call for quiet.

She wanted to say no to Omaïa, to snatch the prize from Antiope and smirk at Pirothous the next time she had to look at his face. And she wanted to embarrass Thalestris. And she was tired of their hatred and rivalries. And she had ridden well: she had passed all the racers except Melanippe, despite Tomiris' trying to stampede her out of the race. Not that she intended to cry foul. There had been no witnesses, and women might imagine that she had made up the story only to get what she wanted.

Still, if she said that second prize was hers, Antiope would do her best to get even. So would Thalestris and Celano. What else could they think of to make her miserable? They would try to shame her again. They would say that Penthesilea, the daughter of a rider unknown except as Myrtho's lover, lacked gratitude to Thalestris, who had raised her up from obscurity, to be the companion of an Amazon who might one day rule the city and lead the riders.

"Say what's on your mind, my girl," said Miminousa. "There are ways of settling disagreements."

Yes, there were, thought Penthesilea without raising her head. If she asked for second prize, Antiope would challenge it, and the two would race again to settle the matter. Antiope's horse could outrun Tala, and Antiope would beat Penthesilea by many lengths.

But at least then no one could say that Penthesilea's heart and mind belonged to both Thalestris and Antiope or that she had no will of her own.

For that is what many women would think if Penthesilea accepted third place without a word. They would repeat that she had no backbone, that she could be turned this way and that like the weather vane on top of the temple granary. Hippolyta would make sure of that. She would give it as proof that Antiope's companion, Thalestris' choice, could not be counted on to stand up for what was right. But how could she when she was the child of forebears no one knew? And Pirothous would remark to Theseus that Penthesilea had no guts to stick up for herself, either. And Theseus would repeat it to Antiope, who would perhaps believe it, because Penthesilea had not protested.

Penthesilea's head pounded. She wanted to blurt out that second place was hers. But this anger did not ring pure, the way a blade sings on the whetstone when you have sharpened it to its keenest. If Tomiris had not played dirty with Penthesilea, she might have protected Antiope from harm, and Antiope would have ridden in first and Melanippe second. But not Penthesilea. To this she could not blind herself.

"Say what you think," repeated Miminousa. "Claim what's yours if you see you've got it coming to you."

"That's right," shouted Ido. "Don't let anyone cheat you." Penthesilea looked evenly at Omaïa. "I rode past all the others except Melanippe. It is not my doing that Antiope met with foul play, although I would have done my best to stop it if I'd been there. So I can claim second place as my due."

Penthesilea paused, but no one spoke. Some riders shaded their eyes and interrogated hers. Omaïa and Miminousa traded puzzled looks. Thalestris folded her arms. Hippolyta stared.

"But whatever claim I have," continued Penthesilea, "I do not elect to quarrel with Antiope over this matter. Antiope has lavished gifts of great price on me, and I do not choose to vie with her for this one.

"And I have no desire that women say of me, of Penthesilea, Leokadia's daughter, that my ways lack politeness and my heart thankfulness. And I do not want to forget what I owe to Thalestris. I ride with her Amazons and eat at her table. And I will not allow myself to forget what I owe to Thalestris' daughter, to Antiope, the woman I ride with, the woman who has saved my life. I do not care to stand in her way and so will not."

Voices clashed, and the throng swirled apart. Hippolyta, however, did not move. She stood scrutinizing Penthesilea through narrowed eyes. Thalestris, also motionless, stroked her lips. Antiope turned her back and walked toward Theseus. Myrtho came up to Penthesilea and took her hands. Penthesilea raised Myrtho's fingers to her lips.

At dawn the next morning, Penthesilea came out of the gate and halted Tala a short way from the battlements. In front of her stood the tents, their canvas walls flapping in the fitful breeze. Beyond them, streaks of shimmering alabaster—reflections of the sky that brightened even as you looked at it—traversed the raven black ribbon of Thermodon, from which a few traces of fog curled upward and vanished. Across the river, rows of green wheat pulsed back and forth. In squares of earth that lay fallow, women were shoveling over the burnt straw and manure that had rested there for a year. The sun was gobbling up broad shadows on the hillsides, and from their summits fat clouds rolled across the sky to the northeast hills, whose tops were aflame with the new day. Penthesilea was going to head in that direction with Feodissia, join Tecmassa, and spend the next days far from the city. No one would care about her staying away. Antiope would not miss her, and Thalestris would turn her back on her absence now that the icy wall of the past week had melted.

Penthesilea took a deep breath. The morning air, which smelled of earth and grasses, chilled her chest like water from a mountain stream. She exhaled slowly, deliberately.

Footsteps came from behind. Two stragglers passed on their way to the fields, one pronouncing her name and wishing her a good morning, the other waving. Penthesilea returned their hello with a grin and a gesture of her hand.

Hoofbeats echoed in the tunnel; Feodissia emerged. A bulging gourd and a full sack swayed on her horse's croup. Still dreamy-eyed, she drew abreast and nodded. Penthesilea grinned and clucked at Tala. The Amazons walked their horses toward the riverbank, giving a wide berth to the tents. They reached the path along Thermodon and raised their heels to goad their mounts into a run.

"Wait! Wait!" sounded Marpessa's voice from behind. The riders relaxed. Her flame-colored hair bouncing around her shoulders, Marpessa strode toward them from where the Amazons entertained the Achaeans.

"Antiope saw you and woke me," she said when she came up. "She's to give a feast this evening for the riders who went with her to the tents, and for her dearest darling Theseus. She wants you to be there, Penthesilea. They'll lay the banquet under the trees when the shadows begin to fall on the slopes. By the looks of the weather, it'll be a fine night."

Penthesilea could not refuse and grumbled acceptance.

Marpessa laughed. "I wish it were a farewell feast, myself," she said, "and wish I could go with you two wherever you're riding. The whole thing is wearing on my patience. Pirothous knows no way to talk to a woman except crooked. And he bores me silly when we share the couch. I'm sure I'll get a boy. And I'm not the only one who is having second thoughts, you know. Adrasta and Charope are none too happy with those fellows. But Antiope's having a fine time, so there's no talking to her about it.

"Oebala's lucky she didn't get called to the tents. We finally found out what happened to her, by the way. She spent the night celebrating with friends in the city—in the artisans' quarter (although she won't say where). Neither will Arne the sandalmaker, who told me about it, nor Scarphe the perfumer who said so, too. Oebala fell asleep at the party and didn't wake up until late in the day, with a raging headache. She swears someone drugged her wine. Antiope is certain that Melanippe is behind the misdeed, and Melanippe is bound to swear Antiope made the story up to hide something else."

Penthesilea and Feodissia took their leave and set their horses running along Thermodon. Penthesilea resigned herself to heading back that afternoon.

The Amazons and Achaeans took their places around a table that should have buckled under the weight of wheels of snow-white cheese, marigold and umber pyramids of dried fruit, and heaps of gold-crusted bread. The perfume of meat sizzling on nearby cooking fires made the banqueters dizzy with anticipation. A flute player and a harpist were charming sweet sounds out of their instruments. Half a dozen women from the palace staff—Anuphey not among them—bustled around the table. Celano herself directed the servants.

Antiope sat at the head of the board. A tunic of ivory white linen that left her throwing arm bare adorned her lithe figure. Her thick tresses, set free from their Amazon braid, cascaded over her shoulders. Theseus occupied the place of honor on her right. A tight-bodiced, emerald chiton set off his good looks. Its collar, which was embroidered with threads of saffron yellow, scooped low enough to expose the oiled squares of his breasts. Between them, suspended from his neck and dangling below his larynx, he wore a fine gold chain. It had been one of Antiope's favorite adornments.

Antiope seated Penthesilea on her left, opposite Theseus. The Achaean Soloön, the one they had carried in on a sledge, occupied the seat next to hers. His head was turned down. His hair shone the color of volcanic glass. He looked up only when Penthesilea sat. His beard, a jet black triangle standing on its point, called attention to cheeks and lips still pallid from his loss of blood. He riveted his eyes on Penthesilea. They burned as if the fever ruled them.

She averted her gaze to the table in front of her. A small iron knife with a curved, red oak handle lay there. A tongue of gold was set into one side of the blade. The outlines of three horses were etched into it—one rearing, one pawing the ground, and one stretched out in a run. Next to the carving implement, a shallow cup of delicate gray clay rested on a stem shaped like a diving bird's long and supple neck. A jade green stalk inlaid with viridian diagonals climbed up the stand until it reached the goblet and burst into three curves that rippled like tree leaves submerged in the water. Between the knife and the cup lay a russet-grained trencher of cherry wood.

Theseus was also scrutinizing the knife set before him. He picked it up and turned it slowly, inspecting its least details. He balanced it in his palm to measure its weight. He glanced at Antiope, saw that she was gazing at him, and pointed the instrument at the drinking vessel set before him.

"Our Achaean potters make these cups," he said, smiling. "My father's ships carry them to all corners of the world. So my kingdom is not unknown here. But, tell me, where does this blade come from? It is as fine as any King Aegeus himself would set before him."

"From Themiscyra," answered Antiope.

"And the smith who wrought it, where did you get her?"

"She's a freeborn woman and comes from Themiscyra. Her name is Telkhinia. She's the chief of the artisans."

"And the first as well to stroll down to the tents when the traders begin to arrive," volunteered Marpessa, who sat across from Penthesilea, at Theseus' right. "Many's the man who has taken a fancy to her; so be prepared, my brave boys."

Pirothous, who was sitting at Marpessa's side, ignored her and asked Antiope, "These daggers, do you make any except for your own use?"

"We do not trade them. It would not please the Goddess."

"And the gold set in the iron, where do you get it?" asked Theseus.

Antiope paused, then said, "We get it from traders."

Theseus's face did not change, but his pupils contracted.

A line of attendants shuffled to the table bearing pitchers of wine spilling mauve foam over their spouts, sides of pork marinated in strong drink made of plums, racks of lamb steaming with the oil and herbs in which they had soaked a night and a day, and ducks from the river—a dozen of them—crackling with the honey and wine that the embers had baked into their skin. The flesh's fragrance trailed it as it advanced, as the odor of incense follows a processional march. Attendants poured. The revelers made their libation and drank. Penthesilea emptied her cup.

When the first hunger had gone from the guests, they began to talk again, all at once, except Soloön, who lowered his eyes and kept a moody silence. Penthesilea, thankful for his reticence, fixed hers on the table and paid no mind to the chattering around her, until, from far to her left, she heard one of the Achaeans assert, "But Theseus' father is a rich man."

The fellow who spoke, Chalcodon, had honey-colored hair, a craggy face, satisfied eyes, and fleshy lips. Bits of food and rivulets of wine stained his beard, which was also the color of honey. His torso under his tunic hinted at corpulence. While he talked, he waved a half-eaten duck in front of him. Grease from the ragged carcass dribbled down his wrist. "The old man owns so much iron, gold, silver, jewels, cloth, and slaves, that he keeps a household guard in his pay to watch over it, four-dozen picked men."

"How does Aegeus come by so much wealth?" asked Hippolyta's niece, Adrasta, a hulky girl who sat on Soloön's left, facing Pirothous. She spoke through a jawful of food that made her round cheeks even more swollen than they usually were. "Does he have as many lands as the emperor at Hattushas?"

"I am told," murmured Pirothous in his perfume merchant's tones, "that Attica's lands do not stretch as far as the Hittite king's and that its earth does not hold as many grains and metals. Indeed, in lean years, we have to send to Troy for barley and wheat. And we always need copper and tin from other places to forge bronze and make weapons and armor, and tools."

"But whatever we need, we have plenty of gold to buy it with," said Chalcodon. "Plenty of gold."

"We are mighty and wealthy, Princess Antiope," said Pirothous, "because what Attica doesn't hold in its bowels, our sailors and traders get from across the sea. Aegeus' land borders on it, and his fortress of Athens is a short journey from his seaport."

"And if Aegeus' ships can't buy what we want," volunteered Chalcodon, "we take it anyway."

Pirothous, who was tossing down a cup of wine, lowered it and shot an angry glance at Chalcodon.

Theseus hastily asked Antiope, "Have you ever looked on the sea?"

"I have heard about it, but have never seen it."

Penthesilea felt Soloön shift position. She glanced sideways. He had riveted his wild gaze on Antiope. He dropped it as soon as he saw Penthesilea's focused on him.

"It's as if saltwater is," said Theseus, "unfit for any man or beast to drink, covered the valley of Themiscyra and the lands around it, and the plains to the south of it; and only the mountain peaks showed above them."

"You can get over the sea," said Pirothous, "only in ships as big as a dozen boats that carry scores of men and tons of goods. Athens offers a safe harbor for ships to anchor. Princess Antiope, there is no other port in the land like Aegeus' for the number of trading ships that come to rest there, and there is no city in our lands as large and mighty as his Athens."

Soloön raised his dark head, stared blankly at Pirothous, then turned his face down again.

Pirothous continued, "I remember my first view of it, I remember it well. I was still a boy, sent there by my father from my native city of Marathon, and first saw Aegeus' stronghold at dawn in the distance. The citadel and palace sit on top of a hill far higher and steeper than Themiscyra's. Walls three times the perimeter of the walls of your Amazon city surround them. No force on earth has ever shattered those defenses. A roadway wide enough for eight armed men to march side by side leads upward from the foot of the hill to the great gate. Aegeus' palace is so large that the throne room occupies as much ground as my father Ixion's entire palace. The queen's apartments alone are as grand as my father's hall."

"And the imperial latrine is as spacious as our marketplace," interjected Marpessa. Everyone burst out laughing, except Pirothous, whose face became a bland mask.

"The queen's apartments," said Antiope to Theseus. "Didn't you tell me that your mother lived with her father, King Pittheus, in Troezen?"

"Of course she does, my dear," said Theseus, waving his drinking vessel in the air so that a servant would fill it. "And that's where Pittheus brought me up. But when I reached manhood, he sent me to Athens to claim my birthright from my father, King Aegeus."

"And it was not so easy to do," said Pirothous, "for at that time Lady Medea occupied the Queen's apartments. She was Aegeus' concubine."

"Gongubine?" asked Adrasta, through packed cheeks. "What's that?"

"She shared Aegeus' couch," answered Pirothous, "as you women of Themiscyra say. He even got a son on her, Polyxenus. But she wasn't Aegeus' legitimate wife, and so the son had no right to inherit Athens and its riches."

"Legitimate?"

"Given by her father, brothers, and uncles," replied Pirothous, "along with treasure and promises of military help sworn before the gods ... and goddesses. Finally, though, Aegeus bred a son on a legitimate wife. That was Theseus."

"Finally? Finally?" said Marpessa. "You mean that there were wives before?"

"Yes. A woman called Chalciope, who didn't give him any sons, and one called Melite, who couldn't have children at all. So he sent both back."

"Do you mean to say that daughters are no good?" nasalized the wiry Charope. She sat between Pirothous and the Achaean who occupied the far end of the table, facing Chalcodon.

"And are you telling us that only sons can inherit land and rank?" pouted Antiope over the cup poised at her lips.

"Yes," said Theseus, staring into her eyes. "That is why we marry only women of rank and power. No one else will do. No one. My mother, Aethra, was such a woman. Her father, Pittheus the Wise, King of Troezen, gave her to Aegeus, and I was born to them within the year. Aegeus had to sail back to Athens before I saw the light of day, though. One of his younger brothers, Pallas, was stirring up trouble. Aegeus left my mother his sword so that later he could recognize his son. It has the coiled snake of the Erechtheid house on it. I still use it in ceremonies."

"When Theseus arrived at Athens," said Pirothous, "Medea tried to murder him. She wanted the throne for her son, Polyxenus, and did everything in her power to get it."

"Medea was a witch and a bitch," said Brimus, a square thick-armed man with wavy hair and eyebrows like a wicked spirit's. When this Achaean walked, he limped slightly and his gigantic fists punched the air in front of him. "She was in cahoots with the Snake Goddess."

"The Snake Goddess is Poseidon's enemy," said Theseus, "and the enemy of my clan, the Erectheids. She gave Medea hidden powers over men.   Her magic was so great that Aegeus obeyed her out of the god-given order of things, as if she were...."

"As if she were the king and he the subject," said Pirothous, lowering his goblet from his mouth.

"She had Aegeus under her thumb," continued Theseus, "until I put things right, until I sailed to Athens to claim the throne and get rid of Pallas."

"Pallas?" said Marpessa.   "I thought his name was Polyxenus."

"Medea's goddess," continued Theseus, "must have told her why I had come there. So she tried to poison me. She told Aegeus, who'd never set eyes on me, that I was an assassin sent by his brother. She put wolfsbane in the cup of hospitality that Aegeus offered me. When I raised it to my lips, Aegeus saw the coiled serpent carved on my sword hilt and knocked the cup from my hands."

"What happened to Medea?" asked Antiope.

Chalcodon and Brimus gurgled.   Soloön snickered. Pirothous hastened to remark, "She disappeared, and her child, too. Her goddess carried them to safety."

"Do you wonder where that was?" asked Marpessa of no one in particular.

Penthesilea's look sought Antiope's, but Antiope turned hers away as she put her goblet to her lips and tilted her head back. Her cheeks were flushed. Penthesilea contemplated the dark liquid in her own cup, raised it, and drank deeply.

"Medea could never be Aegeus' legitimate queen," said Pirothous. "She had came from Corinth as an exile, a refugee, and brought no alliance with her."

"Alliances with likely women," said Theseus, gazing into Antiope's eyes, "are very important to my family and always have been."

"That's how Theseus' grandfather, Aegeus' father, Pandion, got to lord it over so many lands and armies," said Pirothous. "Before him, Attica was divided into eleven cities— Eleusis, Perati, Marathon, Laurion, Megara, Brauron, Avios, Kosmos, Menidi, Thorikus, and Athens. The eleven fought among themselves all the time, raided each other whenever there was anything worth carrying off. Several of them them would band together to plunder the others until one ally looked like he was stronger than the rest. Then they would attack the one that had grown mighty. My own Marathon sometimes joined with Athens and sometimes raided it. Nothing was safe, land, cattle, slaves, women, nothing. The only time the towns in Attica didn't fight each other was when they all joined to make war on the cities across the narrow seas—Mycenae, Tiryns, Argos—or when these cities made war on them.

"But Pandion made all the cities unite once and for all. He had twenty children and married them all to his advantage."

"Twenty children?" said Marpessa. "Not all by the same woman?"

"By his legitimate wife, Lady Pylia, and by others," said Theseus. "When he'd overcome a town, he'd take women from the ruling family to his bed to have chiefs that belonged to him."

"Did he ask them what they thought about it?" questioned Marpessa.

"What Pandion's sword started, his prick finished," said Brimus. His huge fist raised his goblet to his face; his upper lip shone with sweat and grease.

Pirothous continued, "Sometimes he'd make his legitimate sons—there were four—lords of the towns his sword or ruses had gotten the best of. Sometimes he'd marry off his legitimate daughters to princes who didn't dare take him on. Sometimes he'd use his bastards."

"His what?" asked Adrasta between bites.

"Bastards. Not the children he got on his legitimate wife but on other women."

"I don't understand."

Pirothous drained his goblet and went on, "One way or the other, the territories came into his hands. That is why Theseus will come into so many lands and soldiers. But at the time, he had not done away with all his rivals for the throne."

"Aegeus's brother, Pallas," said Theseus, "also had it out for me. But I soon took care of that. He was no match for me."

"Aegeus," explained Pirothous, whose words had begun to slur, "was the oldest of four brothers and so claimed the best part of the lands and treasures their father, Pandion, left."

"You mean that the oldest child gets a bigger share than the others?" asked Antiope.

"Of course, girl, of course," said Chalcodon, lifting his goblet to his thick lips.

"I'm thirsty, too," said Brimus, waving his cup above his head. An attendant rushed to his side and poured.

"Pallas," said Pirothous, "was the next in line for the succession to Athens after Aegeus. When their father died, Pallas got a tract of land southeast of Athens, but no seaport worth its name, certainly not like Aegeus', with all the goods and slaves and gold that come pouring in. Pallas wanted Athens and the seaport. But he hadn't a big enough army to take it outright. So he went about corrupting Athens, bribing men who had a grudge against Aegeus.

"He bought the loyalty of the commander of Aegeus' guard, Leos. He even spread the rumor that Aegeus was not entitled to the throne because he was a bastard."

"There you go again," said Marpessa.

"One day Pallas was forced to make his move. That was when Aegeus told everyone that, on the next, he was going to take Theseus to Poseidon's temple, declare Theseus his son and heir, and sacrifice three horses."

"Horses? Horses?" said Charope.

"Pallas' undercover men planned to ambush Theseus and Aegeus on their way to the temple. Then Pallas was going to march on the citadel with his soldiers."

"But Leos couldn't keep the secret," said Theseus. "He got drunk with us the night before and started bragging about a slave girl he had just bought for his bed. I asked him where he had gotten the price. He said he had won it gambling, but his story didn't sound right. Pirothous and I convinced Leos to come clean."

Soloön snorted; an obscene chuckle rose in Brimus' throat. Marpessa's look crossed Penthesilea's. Penthesilea shook her head and raised her drinking vessel to her lips.

"Pallas was no match for me," said Theseus, "and I set things straight. Not a one of the ambushers got away."

"Even those who threw down their weapons?" asked Marpessa. "What happened to Pallas?" asked Antiope.

Soloön cackled.

Annoyance fleeted through Pirothous' eyes. Then he said, "Aegeus exiled Pallas for the rest of his days. He will never return. Aegeus didn't take revenge on any of Pallas' soldiers, though. He needed their fighting power. He made them take an oath to obey him, and put Theseus in command."

"It was a good thing, too," said Theseus, "because bandits from the mountains north of Attica were attacking our traders, and I had to mount an expedition. Not that travelers passing near the border were ever safe."

"Don't you keep patrols there?" asked Marpessa, "or are you too busy at each others' throats?"

Penthesilea, Marpessa, and Adrasta laughed. Antiope glared at them.

"I taught them what was what," said Theseus.

"On the Day of the Year," said Pirothous, "these mountain folk sacrifice a stranger. Most of the time it's a prisoner they've taken and fattened for the ceremony, a man they marry to the Moon Goddess."

"When the Kaska raiders take prisoners from us," nasalized Charope, "it's to have women to live among them."

"I can understand why," said Theseus, flashing a pearly smile at Antiope.

"These guys want men," said Brimus, "and not to have fun with, neither."

"They whip the fellow raw," said Theseus, "especially around his prick so that his blood and sperm fertilize the few fields they plant. Then they chop his head and manhood off and spread the rest of him out on a tree."

"When they've got no prisoner to sacrifice," said Pirothous, "they ambush a traveler, often a trader from one of our cities."

"Traders complained to Aegeus," said Theseus, "and said they wouldn't carry his goods there any more. So he sent me and the boys. It was hard. You can't fight in the mountains with thrusting spears and body shields, because they're too heavy to run with in broken terrain. And you can't throw up a shield wall against your enemy because they don't come at you from the front. They wait in hiding and hit your men and run before you know it. You've got to use your bows a lot. But my boys got used to hill warfare soon enough."

"Those who lived through it did, anyway," said Chalcodon.

The other Achaeans chortled.

"The men and women mate among themselves as they please," said Brimus.

"No one knows who his sons are," added Chalcodon.

"The gods have not taught them the right ways," said Theseus.

"The booty's not as good as around here," said Chalcodon.

"You only find out if you've fought a man or woman when you strip the bodies," said Brimus.

"But it's better to take them alive," said Chalcodon. "That way you can sell them as slaves. Slaves fetch the most gold. But the Achaeans only do business in young women and strong young men."

A hiccup interrupted his recital.

"Slaves are the hardest cargo to transport," he went on. "We took three shipfuls home last year, when Theseus led us to Miletus. We helped the Hittites push out the Achaeans who ruled the place. The Hittites paid us in slaves. We took the craftsmen—there was even a smith among them—and the virgins. At least they were until we got our hands on them."

Brimus slammed down his cup and bellowed.

"The men we carried off made plenty of trouble on the ship," continued Chalcodon. "But we showed them who was boss, even though we couldn't murder them or cut off their hands."

Merriment shook the shoulders of Soloön, whose head was downturned.

"You're slavers then," said Penthesilea, thinking of her words more quickly than she could pronounce them. "And bandits. And torturers. And you turn your weapons on other Achaeans for a price. I wouldn't want your alliance, wouldn't trust it. It's a good thing they took your weapons away."

Adrasta cheered. Marpessa said, "Hear, hear!" Charope, whose head now rested on the table next to her goblet, raised her face and flashed a toothy smile. Antiope glowered.

"Listen baby," Brimus said to Penthesilea, "they say that Poseidon rules the sea. That's a load of crap. The strongest ships do, and everything is for the taking."

"And slaves are what you get if you fight and win," said Chalcodon. "And Hittite gold shines just a bright as anyone else's. And fighting's how you get it." He tossed down his wine.

"You think so," nasalized Charope, not bothering to raise her face this time.

Penthesilea filled her third cup and drank. The talk began to slip past her; the outlines of servants carrying pitcher after pitcher drifted in front of her eyes like the shadows of ghosts moving in and out of the torchlight.

At last Antiope, her cheeks and eyes aglow, pushed herself to her feet and lifted her goblet. The others fell silent and raised theirs. It was the farewell toast.

"Prince Theseus," she pronounced, "worthy visitors and noble Amazons, let us lift our cups, our voices, and our thanks to the Goddess, who. . . ."

Pirothous staggered to his feet. "Noble Antiope," he uttered in a slushy baritone, "I want to say something first."

His interruption trampled on good manners. Antiope was the host. He was the guest. It was her moment. Penthesilea smirked at his boorishness. But Antiope paid it no mind and nodded permission.

"Princess Antiope," Pirothous intoned, "gracious and powerful lady, how can we toast your immortal, when we have not celebrated our mortal? I raise my cup to Penthesilea here," he said, elevating his goblet, "To Penthesilea, who jumped into the horse race at your bidding yesterday. Of course, she hesitated at first. But she got over her fear and obeyed your wishes. No servant, no slave, could have been more obedient. It must be in her blood to obey like that. For her meekness she deserves the third—and last—prize, the little armband that, I am told, is charmed. Since it is full of magic, it will make her lucky in love. Isn't that right, Soloön?"

Soloön looked up, bared his teeth, and coughed out a laugh like death's rattle. Chalcodon guffawed, spraying a mouthful of wine over Brimus, who barked out a deep-throated roar. Self-satisfaction spread over Pirothous' face, and, his brow flushed with it, he turned to Theseus. Theseus grinned and winked at Antiope. Antiope threw back her head and laughed.

Penthesilea bolted to her feet and sprang across the table at Pirothous. At the same time, he picked up a carving knife and pointed it at her. Marpessa grabbed his elbow and jerked his forearm sideways, while Adrasta tackled Penthesilea and wrestled her to the ground. Clay cups, bronze trays, sticky liquid, heels of bread, lumps of cheese, and shreds of meat dripping sauce crashed down and littered the grass on which Penthesilea lay pinned under Adrasta's weight.

Chapter 9

Penthesilea got up long past sunrise. Her skull and neck throbbed. Her eyes ached. A glum veil separated her from the world. It hurt her head to piece together the events of the night before. The Achaeans—they cared only for gold and blood; Pirothous—he had shamed Penthesilea in front of the other Amazons; Antiope—she, too, had mocked her. Adrasta had helped Penthesilea stumble home, and Anuphey had put her to bed, although she remembered this last detail only after she swallowed the draft that Anuphey gave her. Soon the pounding in Penthesilea's head ebbed away, and she pulled herself out of bed and walked to the bridge, to stare at the valley, to suck in great lungfuls of air, and to brood.

She wanted to strike Pirothous dead and, among the Achaeans, could have done so without disgrace, for this barbarous folk shed blood to pay for mockery. But that was not the way among the riders of Themiscyra, although the fellow was bent on humiliating Penthesilea. But why? Because . . . because she despised him but did not fear him, and he hated that. And he could get away with jeering at her: he was Antiope's guest, and Thalestris', and could hide behind their hospitality for as long as they tolerated him.

As for Antiope, she had more than tolerated him; she had laughed when he had ridiculed Penthesilea; she had enjoyed the joke at Penthesilea's expense. Why had she turned her back on Penthesilea, who had never done her wrong? Penthesilea stung from it, fretted, and raged—and ever more savagely as the morning wore on. Only the sight of a rider cantering a gray horse along the opposite bank snatched her from her gloom. It was Perseia, Melanippe's friend, who must have hastened back to her station at the beginning of the steppes once the race was over.

Perseia crossed the bridge and, although she had never shown such deference before, reined in, inclined her head, and bid Penthesilea a good morning. "It's the first caravan of the year," Perseia announced, "Fivescore pack donkeys and two-dozen traders. They're up from the Hittite royal road. They'll cross into the valley before sunset." She bowed once more and dug her heels into her mount. She would take herself straight to the palace. There, the chief of the riders would doubtless listen with an unmoved face before giving her orders. Celano would listen, too. But in private she would rub her hands together. Merchants calling at Themiscyra learned quickly to offer her gifts in exchange for her goodwill. It was common knowledge that, although the city's queen and high priestess asked no fee of the merchants, the palace steward allowed them to give her presents and granted the gift-givers permission to buy and sell right away. She showed no such haste for those who were not so generous.

Penthesilea rode out later that day to have a look at the new-comers. Chill wind and dark clouds pursued her as she headed upstream. She reached the far edge of the farmland. Thunder growled like wrath in hiding behind the clouds. The air fell away, the heavens opened, and icy water battered her. She took shelter in the clump of plane trees that separated the farmland from heath. She dismounted. Rain hammered on the trees. Their thick tops shook in the howling wind. Jagged shafts of light pierced the murk scudding over the valley. Crashes shattered the skies and snuffed out the hissing surrounding the copse. Penthesilea stared in the direction of Themiscyra but saw only a sheet of gray lines. The city, its lands, and dwellers, might as well be gone forever, leaving her alone to gaze at nothing and shudder. But then the sky lightened, and the flashes and thunderclaps swept toward the south. The drumming of the drops grew faint and died away. From the branch of a tree, a bird chirped; another answered it; still another joined them. Soon small high voices whistled and chattered all around.

Penthesilea mounted and rode toward the steppes. She arrived at the ledge above Thermodon where traders coming up from Hattushas entered the valley. The rays of the afternoon sun pierced the mists like golden arrows flying over the river-bank. Penthesilea stationed herself where the exposed shelf ended and the road to the city began. The dreamy-eyed Andromache soon led a line of traders and donkeys toward the city.

They began to file by Penthesilea. The beasts, their nappy pink muzzles pierced by huge oval nostrils, lurched forward in hiccup cadence, their bellies swaying as they did. Some merchants, on foot, led two or three animals, and others only one. Still others rode donkeys themselves and held the lead ropes of pack-bearing beasts. The legs of the riders were bare except for thick-soled sandals on their feet. These nearly touched the ground, and the merchants' knees jerked so close to their chests that Penthesilea wondered if they would strike them. White robes whose skirts were ample enough for the voyagers to sit their mounts in comfort swathed the men's trunks and limbs and left their right shoulders bare. Each rider had a short rod attached to his left wrist and would wield the instrument to goad the single-mindedness out of his donkeys or to quicken their amble.

Cloth bundles were perched on the backs of the beasts of burden, above two panniers that rested against their ribs. These baskets held tin to make bronze with. The traders would carry that to Troy. The Amazons had little use for it: they knew the secret of forging iron for their weapons and tools. But what was wrapped in the packs above the panniers fascinated the women. No one could tell what they concealed until they were untied—perhaps ingots of dark blue glass, perhaps fine oils with dizzying scents, or sweet spicy powders, or delicate weightless cloth, or minuscule clay statues . . . or things that Penthesilea had never seen, smelt, or touched before.

A short, stocky man holding the lead rope of a long-eared animal trudged by Penthesilea. Then a woman toting a baby in a sling on her back led a dark brown donkey past. Penthesilea started. She had rarely seen a woman in the caravans, much less a woman carrying a child. She stared at the stranger, whose face was turned toward the ground and whose legs not so much trod it as pushed it out behind her. Penthesilea urged Tala into motion and trailed the newcomer. The way widened. The woman came abreast of the man. Penthesilea moved near them. Tala fell in step with the donkeys. The one that the woman handled flattened its ears and brayed. The child, who had been slumbering, stiffened, wailed once, but fell back to sleep as suddenly as it had awakened.

The woman turned her head and looked up. Dark, close-cropped hair framed a small, sloping forehead and thick eyebrows, one of which was raised in annoyance. Her skin, despite its tan, revealed handsome yellow undertones, and her eyes— black, set deep, drawn up slightly at the edges—flashed in irritation. Her small, well-sculpted mouth surrounded by cheeks as full as a healthy babe's tensed as if they were holding back sharp words. Then her glance met Penthesilea's frank and melancholy one and lingered there. The tight line dropped away from the woman's mouth. She closed her eyes. When she opened them, a kind glow had spread through them, although something less happy tinged their gentleness. She broke into a dimpled smile and raised her eyebrows—both of them this time.

The ache that had gripped Penthesilea's temples since morning vanished, and the corners of her lips began to tingle.

The fellow who walked at the woman's side uttered words in a strange, guttural language. Penthesilea looked at him. He was not much older than the woman, and his features resembled hers, except for his forehead, which was wider and higher. His eyebrows formed an upside-down V, and his jet black beard covered a fleshy lip and heavy jowls.

The woman chuckled. Her eyes invited Penthesilea to share the mirth. "That is my brother," said the stranger in a low voice and singing accent. She listened to her words as she spoke. "He says that he told me the truth, that there is a land of women, and an army of women riders. I saw your riders first—Amazons, you call them—when they met the caravan three days ago."

"Yes," said Penthesilea. "This land is called Themiscyra. My name is Penthesilea. I bid you welcome." She inclined her head.

The stranger nodded gracefully. "Thank you," she said. "My name is Abba-Bashti. My brother is called Artatama."

Artatama touched his forehead and swept his hand outward. Penthesilea bowed again. Then she focused on the child that the woman toted on her back.

"That is my son, Tushratta."

"A boy. I see. Where are you from?"

"We come from the city of Harran, in the land of Mitanni. Our river is the Balis."

Penthesilea's face showed a question.

"Harran is five days' journey from the city of Carchemish, which overlooks the Euphrates."

Penthesilea had heard the last name once. Her brow cleared. "We have been journeying for almost three months now. We left Harran when the farmers put the seeds in the earth and made their sacrifice to Nisaba to ensure a good harvest. We reached Carchemish after a week. It took another week to get to Kanesh. Scores of merchants stop there to get the tin carried in from the mountains. We left Kanesh with this caravan soon after we arrived."

The man voiced strange consonants again, and his sister explained: "My brother says it is a good thing that we left when we did. The army of Assur was about to lay siege to our city of Harran. The men of Assur want to take the land of Mitanni away from the king and have been making war on us ever since I can remember."

The sadness in the back of Abba-Bashti's eyes now spread through them, and she said, "On our way to Carchemish my brother and I went through a village that the Assyrians had sacked the year before. The house of my brother's great friend, Murashu, once stood there, and we had come to see him on our way north. But when we got there, we learned that the Assyrians had burned it to the ground. They had carried off Murashu and his two sons. They had killed his father. You see, when the Assyrians took the town, they carried off the men who could work their lands or they sold them. The ones who were too young to work for them, or too old, they killed. They lined up the old men and cut them down in front of the rest. They murdered the boys who were too young to be taken away. They ripped babies from their mothers' arms and knifed them before their eyes." Abba-Bashti tugged at the straps of the sling holding Tushratta.

Rage reddened Penthesilea's cheeks.

Artatama now spoke in the language that Penthesilea knew. "They made so many men slaves," he said in a thick accent, "that only their king's scribes know how to say the number. That is why they make war: to have slaves to sell, or to build their palaces and temples and canals and to work the king's fields in the hot sun. They took out each prisoner's right eye. So he can work for them but never again use weapons. They do this in the name of their god, Assur, and their goddess, Anat."

"Make no mistake, Artatama," said his sister, "the men of Mitanni would do the same for the their own god, Isturu."

"That is not our way here," said Penthesilea. "Blood and tears do not please the goddess of our city. They are impure. The Amazons take no pleasure in wounding those who have already lain their weapons down."

Abba-Bashti's glance lighted on the knife and axe at Penthesilea's side. Puzzled, she turned her face upward. Penthesilea's softened. Then Abba-Bashti's did.

Abba-Bashti slowed her step until her brother, who continued at the same pace, was out of earshot. Then, her cheeks and lips growing pale, she said softly, "Only one of Murashu's kin, his young sister, Nana-Dirat, a girl of thirteen, was still alive. Her belly was big with the baby of a soldier she was given to as a prize of war. You see, when the Assyrian soldiers had finished taking out the eyes of all the prisoners, they carried the virgins to their camp. One tried to fight back. They beat her to death in front of all the other girls. No one else fought back after that. After two weeks the soldiers marched on. Nana-Dirat was left behind, with a rape-baby in her. She has not been able to get rid of the hate-child with herbs and potions, and her belly grows so large that she can no longer try. For if the Assyrians come back and find out that she did, they will drive a stake up through her body to kill her because they say for a woman to rid herself of an unborn child is a crime against the gods and their laws."

Penthesilea winced.

"And they would not let her be buried with prayers and gifts but would throw her body to the dogs, so that even in death she would not rest."

"We have no such laws in Themiscyra! The Goddess would not allow it. Never. A child, especially a girl, is a great blessing that She sends a woman. But it does not please Her when a woman gives birth to a baby she will hate. That is an evil omen for the woman and the child."

"Still," said Abba-Bashti, "the same priests and soldiers say that once a baby is born its father can throw it to the dogs if he does not want it to live. For then, he is like a god over it."

Penthesilea puckered her mouth.

Abba-Bashti said, "They tell me that no man is allowed to live here. Is that really so?"

"The Goddess commands it."

"What Artatama said is true, then: that you welcome traders by sending women to them; that you ask no fee of them to do business here other than their seed?"

Penthesilea nodded agreement.

"What do you do with the boy children?"

"We exchange them for girls when they are weaned. The people from the lands around us bring us healthy girl babies to trade. If we did not take them, their parents would abandon them to the beasts and the weather. Sometimes the baby boys' own fathers buy them back. Sometimes traders adopt them."

"To sell them on the slave market in Troy," said Artatama, who had stopped to let the others catch up with him.

Penthesilea made no reply.

"Who is this Goddess of yours?" asked Abba-Bashti.

"Hebatê is the earth in whose womb all things are born and grow. She is the sister of Arinna, the sun, and Nikalmaté, the moon."

"Do you know only goddesses and not gods?"

"Hebatê's consort is the Storm God, Texobos. He takes Her prisoner every year and casts a spell of death over the valley of Themiscyra and the world beyond. He imprisons them in cold snows and whips them with icy winds."

"Snow? What is snow?"

"Cold white down that falls from the clouds. But when it touches a breathing person or animal, or fire, or the earth warmed by the sun, it turns into the water of life."

"Your goddess's sister is the moon?"

"Yes."

"The city that I come from, Harran, has a great temple, of the moon. But it is not the house of a goddess; it is the house of a god. His name is Sinn. Many people come to Harran to sacrifice to Him. But many others say that Sinn stole the throne from the Moon Goddess Nanaï; that She and not Sinn made the moon from the angry waters of the beginning and gave it a name. It was Nanaï that my mother prayed to, not Sinn. All the women of my family always have. We had a statue of Nanaï in my mother's room, and I carry Her likeness with me wherever I go."

Abba-Bashti slipped her hand into her shirt and pulled out a clay figurine. She gave it to Penthesilea, who laid it in the palm of her hand and bent her head over it. A naked woman with full breasts and thighs, her knees bent slightly forward, smiled benevolently. She wore a semi circle crown and stood on an orb. Her right hand held the likeness of a sickle, and her left a feather-shaped branch with dozens of slender leaves reaching upward from its stalk. Penthesilea puzzled over this detail, and Abba-Bashti spoke up, "That is the frond of the date palm. It is the tree of life and sacred to our goddess. It grows in all our orchards. It gives us sweet fruit to eat and strong wine to drink. We mix the mud of the river with its fiber to make the bricks for our houses. Its wood and leaves make the roofs over our heads."

They rounded the clump of trees in which Penthesilea had taken shelter a few hours before. Thermodon's valley came into sight, its contours soft and shadows elongated in the late afternoon light.

Abba-Bashti stopped. Her gaze followed the river's glittering waters to the white cloud far in the distance where the apple trees bloomed, traced its way back to the hill where the city stood, its stone walls glowing beige, its summit shining black, moved to the emerald green pastures on the same side of the river, crossed it, and took in the farmland in front of her: squares of earth, some clay red and fallow, some pale green with newly sprouted corn. Then she raised her eyes to the terraced, white-blossomed vines that crowded up the hills embracing the fertile fields. "Your goddess is good to you," she said in hushed syllables.

"Our land is flat and dry, our rivers and canals brown and slow. Our fields burn in the sun, or the flying beasts take their fruit, and we are often hungry."

"Yes," said Penthesilea, after a pause, for she had always taken the land for granted. "Yes. Our Goddess is good to us."

Abba-Basthi knitted her forehead, drew her lips tight, and resumed walking. Penthesilea clucked Tala into a walk and bent her head. She heard the blood rushing through her ears and, above that, donkeys' hooves beating their syncopated cadence against the horse's. Once, she stole a glance at Abba-Basthi, who looked straight back at her. Penthesilea blushed and lowered her face.

The traders reached Thermodon, crossed the bridge, and filed through a double line of women who had come down to run an eye over them. Some inhabitants put their hands on their hips and gawked without shame; others, pretending to chat with their neighbors, examined the bearded newcomers from under lowered lids. A few men blushed in reply; many broke into brazen smiles; some pretended not to notice. But Penthesilea paid no heed to these goings-on. She stared ahead without seeing and heard only the buzzing in her head. Then, women's voices chattered and babbled and moved in. Tala nudged within a hand of Abba-Bashti's donkey. The brown beast's ears slammed down. It brayed and sank its teeth into Tala's foreleg. The mare reared. Penthesilea sprawled through the air, slammed against the ground, and saw stars. She came to in the midst of titters and tehee's—Anuphey's.

Penthesilea lowered herself into the bath. She groaned when the water touched the welts and scratches covering her backside. She reclined, gingerly, rested her head on the side of the tub, and breathed deeply. Aromatic vapor from two cauldrons sputtering over hardwood fires filled her lungs. Warmth radiated from her center into her hips and shoulders. Her limbs loosened. She pushed out the warm air with a hiss and sank farther back. Waves of heat from braziers made the sweat break out on her brow. She closed her eyes, and her lids drew the two halves of an orange dome over them. It glimmered darker and lighter with the flames of the lamps; its brightest hue was the same color as the undertone of Abba-Basthi's skin.

The curtain swished; footsteps brushed the ground.

"What shall we do with the baby?" That was Abba-Basthi's voice. Penthesilea straightened up, winced as she did, and looked over her shoulder. Abba-Basthi's glance was waiting to meet hers.

"Let's put the baby there," said Anuphey, "so he will see you when you bathe."

Anuphey called for help; she and another woman lifted a cauldron and poured water into the bath that faced Penthesilea's. Anuphey brushed by, mischief twinkling in her eyes. She averted them the moment she saw Penthesilea looking at her.

Abba-Basthi came from behind. She had removed her sandals and robe. The skin of her chest and shoulders scooped around her walnut-tanned neck like an ivory collar. Her breasts were full and ripe. Large puckered brown circles surrounded nipples that glistened with a redder, deeper tone. Ribs that showed under her skin tapered into a tiny waist, which flared into broad, pale hips that embraced a spare belly, deep in the middle of which was set a black, cruciform navel. A thin line of curly hair descended from it to a triangle of fleece of such deep dye that it made her hips look paler than her trunk. Dark down began at her pelt and covered the inside of her thighs. These were as solid as a horsewoman's and planted on equally muscled calves, which tapered to slight ankles. She stepped into the scented liquid and gasped with pleasure.

Anuphey offered her a jar containing pink paste. Her face lit up, and she reached for the vessel. She raised it to her nose and inhaled three times, each time holding her breath longer. She plunged her fingers into the stuff and pressed it between them. She smiled ecstatically. The cannikin held a glimmering pink pulp that Scarphe the perfumer boiled out of the ashes of the beech tree and the orange-red berries of a flat-leaved plant that grew near the orchard. "I have not seen or touched or smelled this for a long time," said Abba-Bashti, "since before my brother and I left Harran. The woman I waited on put it on her body for her bath."

"The woman you waited on?" asked Penthesilea.

"I was a slave there."

"I did not know."

"Yes. I was born free. But when I was fourteen, I went with my brother to be a slave."

Penthesilea wrinkled her brow.

"I am free again, if that is what you are worrying about. You have not welcomed a runaway slave."

"What do you mean?"

"That is a great crime in Harran, to take in a runaway. For it is a great theft. And they kill you for it."

"We have no such law in Themiscyra. Any woman who runs from bondage and reaches the Goddess's temple here is free."

Abba-Bashti looked puzzled, then nodded her head.

"How did you get free?"

Abba-Bashti said nothing at first. The torch flames hissed, and the bubbles snapped free of the cauldrons. Finally she spoke. "You know that my brother and I come from the city of Harran," she said. "My father's name was Adad-Duri and my mother's Belit-Selim. They were free people. They were not rich but not poor. They had a small orchard of date palms outside of the city walls—five acres, and a canal watered it. Adad-Duri cared for the trees, as did my brother and I when we were old enough. There were six times sixty of them, and father never let the number grow smaller, for it is blessed of the gods. And so, for years they were good to Adad-Duri. He always said that the gods gave him his lucky days when they gave him Belit-Selim and took them away when they took her. "She was a small woman with a nose like a falcon's and large eyes that never stopped moving. Her right leg was shorter than her left. But my father was a poor man and took her for little."

"Took her for little? What do you mean."

"They did not have to pay a large dowry, because she limped."

"Dowry? What is that?"

"Goods—cloth and house goods that the woman's father gives to the father of the man who marries her."

"She buys her husband like a slave, then?"

"No. Her father pays her husband's father, and she is her husband's from that day on."

"She is his slave, then?"

"No, she is his wife."

Penthesilea furrowed her brow, and Abba-Bashti smiled at her dismay. Then she continued.

"The gods gave Adad-Duri and Belit-Selim five children, but evil spirits took three. Only Artatama and I lived.

"Mother was a good woman. She kept the house and went to the market herself to trade the dates my father grew and the drink he made from them, for grain or cloth or clay. As long as she was alive, we never lacked anything—food to eat, clothes to wear, a house to sleep in, land to feed us.

"I often went with her when she bought or sold. She would drape the veil over her hair and walk to the market as soon as the sun rose. Sometimes she carried a basket of new dates with her, sometimes a jar of dried dates, sometimes a jug of the liquor. I was happy to go with her. Everyone knew her; everyone wished her a good day—on the street of the weavers, on the street of the tanners, on the street of the potters, in the square where farmers came to sell grain and cheese. We spent half the morning walking to the market, although it is not far, for we had to say hello to everyone. Still, she always took my hand and walked fast past a little house near the trading streets. Outside of it sat women who wore no covering on their heads and shouted words I did not understand to the men who walked by. The women were prostitutes and the building was an alehouse. They belonged to the innkeeper."

"I have heard that in the strangers' lands there are women who take gifts from the men who share their couches," said Penthesilea. "But it should be the other way around."

Abba-Basthi raised her eyebrows in surprise.

"These women use the men to get babies, and babies who live are arms to work the land. The women should give gifts to the men for it. That is what many do here."

"Perhaps," laughed Abba-Bashti. Then she reflected on something and repeated, in a more subdued tone, "Perhaps."

She continued, "Belit-Selim ate the bread and drank the water of death when the fifth child was born. The demons that attack a woman on the bed of childbirth took her from us. They took the new baby, too. I was not yet a maiden. Artatama was almost a man. I cried for days. My father did not speak or eat for weeks. He was thin and grew thinner every day.

"He did not want to marry again and so bought a serving woman to take care of my brother and me and his house. The woman, Batteia, had been a slave since she was young herself. The price was small, because she came from a large landowner and could no longer have children for him. So they kept the ones she had already made and sold her. She came from the north. She spoke your language, and I was with her all day for years.

"Still, after my mother left us, we became poor. For we ate less, more bread and less cheese, more water and less beer. And the presents my father carried to the gods in the temple were smaller than they had been. And we wore old clothes, that Batteia sewed so many times the other children called us beggars. Once I fought a boy my age who had said that. He pulled my hair until my nose bled.

"That was also the year I got my first moon's blood. After that, Batteia did not want me go to the market with her. I did not like that.

"One day long after that Batteia came home with nothing. My father came home after dark. He never spoke many words and now spoke none at all. He did not look at us, and we went to bed hungry. When the sun came up, he sent my brother and me to the orchard but did not go with us. He took my mother's statue of Nanaï and went to town.

"Soon he came to the orchard with bread and beer, and we ate. But I was afraid. He had sold Nanaï. I knew that She would not be pleased with us. How could She be?"

Abba-Bashti heaved a sigh.

"Date palms grow high," she said, "very high—as high as your Themiscyra's walls. My brother and I took ropes and climbed them all the time to work among the flowers and fruit. From the top of the trees, you could see over the wall of the orchard to the road that goes from Harran to the north.

"That same morning, I climbed up and saw two men coming from the city. They were funny to look at walking side by side.

One man was short and fat and tiptoed fast to walk next to the other man, who was tall and thin and took long steps but did not look like he was moving. He helped himself walk with a black stick. They came closer. The fat man wore a robe of blue with a dark red sash that made his belly look like that of a woman about to lay on the bed of childbirth. He looked as old as my father, and I could not see hair under his cap. The tall man, who was even older, wore a white tunic with a black sash and no jewels or pins. He, too, had no hair, and a thin beard. His clothes were so plain that I thought that he was a slave or a man of nothing. I was wrong: the tall, thin man was Tehip-Tilla, the richest man in Harran. He had more silver, land, and slaves than the king's governor himself. He sent out caravans. Men far away obeyed him as a god. The fat man was his slave, Kaptia the scribe.

"The men came to my father's orchard, and my father ran to the gate. They came in without asking if they could, and my father put his hand in front of his mouth, the way a man goes before a god and a slave before a master. They walked past him and stopped. Kaptia the scribe took out a string of counting beads. My father bowed again and began to take him around the orchard and point to each tree. Tehip-Tilla leaned on his stick in the shade. His head did not move, but his eyes followed every step my father and Kaptia took. When they came to the tree where I was sitting, the fat scribe turned to me. He did not look away for a long time: I was not a little girl anymore but a young woman, and so I looked down. Finally, I heard him walk away.

"My father and the fat scribe finished looking at the trees and came back to the entrance. Father stood back while Kaptia and Tehip-Tilla put their heads close and talked. Then, Kaptia told my father to come near, and he did, his head low and his arms crossed over his stomach, the way you go to the altar of a mighty god. Tehip-Tilla showed him the orchard with his hand and said something. My father stepped back and shook his head. He opened his hands in front of him and said something to Tehip-Tilla, who folded his arms and turned his head. Then Adad-Duri spoke to Kaptia, who looked away. Adad-Duri got on his knees. Tehip-Tilla and Kaptia turned their backs on him and walked out of the orchard. Adad-Duri did not get up right away. Then he looked up—first at my brother and then at me. Then he ran out the gate. Tehip-Tilla and Kaptia did not even slow down when Adad-Duri got to them. He pulled the sleeve of Kaptia's robe, and Kaptia stopped. Tehip-Tilla did not. Adad-Duri spoke. Kaptia nodded and walked away again. Adad-Duri stood watching them go back to the city. Then he returned to the orchard. He hung his head and walked slowly, like a prisoner just taken in war. When he came in the gate, he ran his forearm over his eyes.

"That night, we could eat all we wanted, and Batteia got money to buy cloth for new clothes. But at dawn, when all in our house said good morning and kissed, I could see the sadness in my father's eyes. Yes, after that he was not the same.

"Artatama told me what Adad-Duri had done. 'Father has borrowed money from Tehip-Tilla and promised the orchard in return. If the season is good, father will pay it back.'

"'And if the season is not good?' I asked. 'After all, father has sold the statue of Nanaï, and She does not like to be forgotten.'

"And the season was very bad. For no rain fell in the months when the days are shortest. None. And when they grew longer, Shamash, the Sun God, who chases the evil spirits that haunt the night and makes the birds sing when He appears, changed into Nergal, who burns the crops at high noon and strikes people on the head so that they become mad and fall down. When the time came to climb the trees and cut down the fruit with our curved blades, there were not many dates, and these were small. Adad-Duri said nothing during all the time we gathered the fruit. I heard him crying that night."

Abba-Bashti wrinkled her brow and closed her eyes. "They came to collect the next year in the same season. I was sitting in a tree when they did. This time Tehip-Tilla did not come, but Kaptia the scribe came, and someone who was even shorter than he, but in fine clothes. It was Tehip-Tilla's son, Gubarnu. The scribe began to measure the land and count the date palms. When he came to the tree where I was sitting, he turned his eyes to me, and the blood came to his cheeks. Then he turned away fast.

"As for Gubarnu, he put his hands behind his back and walked around the orchard. His hair and beard were curled so much that a barber must have spent hours on them. He wore a white tunic with gold on the edges of the cloth. He came close to where I was. He looked up and smiled the way men smile at the women who sit outside of the alehouse. And it was true that the prostitutes and the ale-sellers knew him well. When he looked at me that way, I grew angry and ashamed. So Gubarnu laughed the way men do when they have hurt you and like that.

"The scribe finished counting. He told my father to come to him and spoke to him, and Adad-Duri pulled at his beard but said nothing. Then he and Gubarnu left. But Gubarnu turned once, and looked at me, and laughed the way someone laughs who is not your friend.

"The next day my brother told me, 'The orchard belongs to Tehip-Tilla now. Father will work in it for him and pay most of the fruit as rent. Father is a man of nothing now for we have no land anymore. What does it mean to be born free and have nothing? And to feed us until the next harvest, and to pay all the people he owes goods to, father has borrowed money from Tehip-Tilla again.'

"'What has he promised if he cannot pay?' I asked.

"'You and me,' answered Artatama."

Penthesilea looked puzzled.

"It is according to our law," explained Abba-Bashti. "The father of a family may pledge his wife or children or himself to the man who lends him money. If he does not pay, that man owns them."

"We have no such laws here! The Goddess would not allow them."

"I see," pronounced Abba-Bashti, lowering her head, "I see." She continued, "My father had borrowed one-hundred talents of lead, the same price they would pay for us on the market: sixty talents for a young man my brother's age and forty for a virgin who is old enough to have children. I was afraid of what would happen and I prayed to Nanaï to talk to the god of the harvest, Nigizzida, to ask Him to be good to us.

"And the next season the rains fell, and the water in the canal was high, and the dates grew fat, and there were many of them on each tree. We were sure that Adad-Duri would pay everything he owed and have plenty after that. I promised Nanaï that I would buy a little statue of Her after the harvest to hold close to my heart. Yes, I thought that Nigizzida was giving back what He had kept from us the year before.

"But you can never tell the ways of the gods. Never. What is good in our eyes is bad in theirs, and we do not know it. And what they see as good one day, they see as evil the next, and we do not know it. And they punish us.

"One evening, the night before we were to take the knives and cut the fruit, I climbed a tree to see the sun before it went away. Around me were the fields thick with barley ready for the harvest. They moved in the airs as the land grew cool. I looked toward the setting sun, which drops from the sky after it reaches the desert. It had gotten there and began to hide from the stars. A gray cloud stood over it and settled on the land. The cloud was not big. When I put my hand out, it covered it. Then night came, and I climbed down. I did not think of the cloud.

"The next morning we went to the orchard. The sky was light and the sun came fast into the sky from where they say there are high mountains. I put the rope around a tall tree and took myself to the top. I looked around. People walked into the fields with bronze scythes that threw back the light like laughing. I looked toward where the sun sets. A gray cloud was there again, larger than it had been, lower and flatter than it had been. When I looked again later, it had grown wider and moved toward us. I turned my eyes to the next bunch of dates. Then I knew what it was.

"'Locusts!' I shouted at the same time as my brother."

"Locusts?" asked Penthesilea.

"Flying creatures, green flying creatures, as long as the tip of your arrows, with long wings that you can see through. They are sent by the evil spirits. They are sent to destroy us. Your arrows kill beasts and men; locusts kill beasts and men, too, by eating the grains and fruits. They eat until there is nothing left. Nothing. And then we starve. They make the land naked and kill the people better than the king's soldiers. They fly during the day and settle when the sun sets. When they fly again the next morning, nothing is left—not an ear of barley, not the leaf of a palm tree, not one fruit.

"A big cloud of them, a cloud as wide as the hill your city sits on, came toward Harran. All of the people ran out of the city—every child, every woman. We all tried to frighten them away. We built fires around the orchard. We waved cloths. We screamed until we could not speak. But when the sun went down, they came to rest in our fields and orchards. They ate everything—every ear of barley, every leaf, every fruit. By dawn the next day, not a palm frond remained, not a date. They went away when the sun began to heat the earth. They made my brother and me into slaves. Tehip-Tilla would send someone to get us."

Abba-Basthi covered her eyes with one hand and pushed the other flat in front of her like someone chasing a bad spirit. Penthesilea reached across and touched Abba-Bashti's forearm.

She drew her hand away from her brow. Her moist eyes stared into Penthesilea's. Penthesilea opened her mouth to speak, but could not.

Anuphey's voice chimed through the silence, "I have set out food and drink for you."

Penthesilea and Abba-Bashti ate their meal in a corner of the kitchen. While they were at table, Tushratta awoke and began to wail. Abba-Bashti stopped, took him in her arms, and lovingly spooned porridge in his mouth. Then she put him to her breast and, her lips growing full, gazed at him with adoration as he sucked and gurgled. When he slept again, she finished her dinner and followed Penthesilea to Themiscyra's wall. The women climbed the steps to the parapet in silence.

The tents, light-colored phantoms in billowing robes, rippled in the restless airs. The cooking fires had shrunk to glowing orange-red spots, from which tongues of yellow would flare and stab the darkness and die as soon as they had burst. Beyond the encampment, the river, a strip of deep blue trembling with countless specks of light moved from right to left and stood still at the same time. On the opposite bank, a blanket of grasses that stirred in the warm breezes stretched away and reached up to gentle, deep-dyed eminences, which the night's magic transfigured into friendly spirits guarding the valley. A silver disk that blinded onlookers with its radiance traced a stately arc across the firmament, drawing behind it a diaphanous train of white and yellow pinpoints.

Abba-Bashti stared at the moon for a long time. Then her voice came out of the stillness. "The Queen of Heaven loves the earth. She holds her close and warms herself by her. She loves the earth and her children."

"And the earth loves the moon," said Penthesilea. She noticed the back of her hand, which rested on the cool stone beside Abba-Basthi's.

"Tell me the rest," said Penthesilea.

Abba-Bashti put her chin to her chest and thought. Then she said, "The next day, Kaptia the scribe came to take me to Tehip-Tilla's house. They had sent for me but not my brother. He could stay and work in the orchard as their slave, but I could not, although I knew how to care for date palms. That was because Gubarnu wanted me. There could be no other reason. So I could not stay with my family.

"My father did not speak when he said good-bye. His face had no color and his eyes had no life. He kissed me and turned away. But I, too, did not speak. He was my father and so he was as a god over me. But he had sold me into slavery, and in my heart I was angry at him, although that is a sin in the eyes of the gods. But I could not help it.

"My brother felt the same anger. Adad-Duri had made him a slave, too. Artatama put his arms around me, and I around him, and we kissed with tears in our eyes. I was sad for him and for myself; he was sad for me and for himself. We would miss one another. He was my friend; we had not spent one day apart, not one, since the gods—or demons—put me into this world.

"Batteia was crying, too. She took my face in her hands. She looked at me for a long time and then shook her head. She kissed me and, I felt her tears on my face. She said, 'So you, too, will never wear the veil on your head when you walk about.'"

"You have spoken of the veil two times," said Penthesilea. "Why?"

"Only free women may cover their heads with the veil when they walk in the streets of the city. If a slave girl does, they cut her ears off. And if a prostitute does, they pour hot pitch over her head."

"What? The Goddess would never permit it!"

Abba-Bashti pursed her lips. Then she caressed the figurine of Nanaï suspended between her breasts and said, "Batteia put this little statue into my hands, and I have had it ever since.

"I followed Kaptia through the city. I did not know it then, but he had asked Tehip-Tilla if he could go and find me. Most of the time, a less important slave would have come for me. But Kaptia had asked to do this.

"Inside of me I was crying and afraid. Gubarnu could do anything he wanted.

"Kaptia did not look at me at first, but finally he said, 'Remember, you are in your masters' power now. Obey them as you obey the gods.'

"'Even Gubarnu?' I asked.

"'Do not be so rude!' Kaptia answered. I turned my face to the ground, and we walked some more. But once I looked up, quickly; Kaptia's face was unhappy, and his lips were white.

"When we got to the door of Tehip-Tilla's house, a slave woman was waiting for me. The woman—her name was Tashmetum—was older than I; she was taller and had curly hair and eyes that never stopped moving. Kaptia said to her, 'This new girl will be a body servant of Gubarnu's wife, Nihtesaru.' Tashmetum led me to wash and put on clean clothes.

"Later that day, they led me to Nihtesaru's apartment. Another woman stood at the door holding a little baby in her arms. That was Nihtesaru's wet nurse, and the baby was her little boy. Nihtesaru did not turn her head to look at me when I walked in, but I saw her eyes move. She was sitting naked in an armchair next to a table. On it were many little pots and many little jars, full of creams and oils and colors for her face and body.

"Nihtesaru was beautiful, beautiful, as beautiful as Ishtar."

"Ishtar?" asked Penthesilea.

"The goddess of love and war," said Abba-Basthi.

"The same goddess?"

"Yes. Nihtesaru was beautiful. Like Ishtar, her hair went down to her waist.

"The woman slave Tashmetum was combing Nihtesaru's hair. It was as black as the night without stars or moon, but the ends were colored red, like the hawk with black feathers and a red tail. And like the hawk, too, she was much bigger than her husband, for Gubarnu was very short.

"I waited a long time. Tashmetum finished combing Nihtesaru's hair and tied it in two piles on her head and put pins with jewels in them. Then she draped a robe of linen with flowers sewn on it over Nihtesaru and tied its ends and fastened it with jeweled pins. She stood back. Nihtesaru looked at herself in the mirror. Tashmetum pressed her hands to her chest and waited. She did not take her eyes from Nihtesaru's face. At last, Nihtesaru said, 'Yes, that will do,' and put the mirror down. Tashmetum breathed loud like someone who was freed from pain and stepped back.

"Then Nihtesaru noticed the wet nurse and the infant and said to the woman, 'I have no time today,' and the woman took her child out of her sight.

"Then Nihtesaru looked at me. 'Come here, new girl,' she said. I did. She took my hand and pulled me to a small window on the garden, the way you pull a donkey by the halter. She put her hand on my face and looked at it the way a buyer looks at a bunch of dates in the market.

"I hated what she was doing and looked down, and my cheeks grew red. Nihtesaru thought it was the way a maiden's face grows red when the young men look at her. She said, 'Good, good. I like young serving maids around me, for I am young, too. But I do not like them to be brazen. You are modest. I am sure you will be, too, after Gubarnu gets his hands on you. That's why he sent for you, isn't it?' I felt more heat in my face and pulled it away from her hands. She took my shoulders and shook me. 'Well isn't it?'

"Fear and hate rose in my throat, I felt tears in my eyes. But I said, 'Yes.'

"She let me go and turned from me and took up her mirror to look at her face. I was no longer there for her. I left her apartment with Tashmetum.

"Gubarnu was waiting outside. 'You,' he said to Tashmetum, 'go away.' It was like she had seen the demon Puzazu: She put her hands in front of her mouth and ran fast.

"'You,' Gubarnu said pointing at me, 'come with me.'

"I did not move. Gubarnu grabbed my hair and pulled me into a storeroom. He pushed me against the wall. I screamed, but he opened his hand and crushed my mouth, and I tasted blood and began to cry. He laughed and pushed me to the earth and threw himself on top of me. My breath went away. I hit his shoulders. He punched me in the stomach. I screamed, but he put his hand over my mouth and ripped my skirt from me. I tried to fight back but he held me there and stabbed his snake inside of me. It was like burning me with a stick from the flames. I screamed again, but his hand was over my mouth. He moved his rod in and out of my dry flesh and I hurt, and bled, outside and in. He breathed faster and faster and pushed his snake in me harder and harder, and it burned me more and more, and I howled from my throat, but his hand was over my mouth. When he finally pulled his body off me, he put his foot on my belly and smiled like some men do when they are whipping their donkeys. 'I'll be waiting for you tomorrow,' he said. He left.

"I lay there and cried like my baby does when he is hungry and I do not come to him. I thought of running from them but

knew I could not. Who would take me in? Who would hide me?
I remembered that once, when I was still a girl, in the streets of
the city I had seen a slave woman who had tried to run from
the governor's house. They caught her and left her in the sun,
without clothing or water, for two days. So the spirits of
madness took her mind away. Then they shaved her head and
sold her to a slaver from a foreign land. She would never see
her children again—her children. I saw her chained in a line
of poor folk who were marching away forever. She looked into
our faces but saw nothing. Then a shadow flew across her eyes.
She stopped and began to laugh like a barking dog. The man
behind her bumped into her, and the foreman came with the
whip and made her move.

"And so I sobbed and sobbed. I could not get up from there. I
cried for my pain. A hot iron inside me could not have burned
more. I cried for my shame. I cried for my mother's, too, who
was watching me from the land of the dead. Were the demons
that had taken my mother still walking in the land of the mortals? I held Nanaï's statue in my hands and wiped my tears on
it so she would pity me and help me.

"Then someone came into the storeroom holding a lamp. It
was Kaptia. He got down on his knees next to me. He looked
into my face. I was sobbing, my lips were bleeding, and there
was blood on my skirt. He patted my hair and then stood up
again. I remember hearing him breathe hard because he had
trouble getting to his feet. But when he did, he pulled me up. I
wrapped my skirt around me. He led me to the woman slaves'
room and called Tashmetum to wash the blood from me and
give me herbs and powders. Then he went to Tehip-Tilla and
asked him if he could have me for his concubine. Tehip-Tilla
said yes, for he trusted Kaptia more than his own son and was
glad to do him this favor. And now Gubarnu would not touch me,
because he would displease his father if he did.

"Kaptia told me this and left the house to go to his
master's granary. I did not go to Nihtesaru that day and
waited for Kaptia. At least he was not Gubarnu. But I did not
see Kaptia soon. He went away that evening and did not come
back for a year. It seems that Gubarnu went to the alehouse
after he had raped me and got very drunk and killed a free
man. He did not even remember doing it, but a friend of the man
did. The man's father and brothers wanted Gubarnu's life, to
spill his blood over the dead man's grave. That evening the
king's agent came to Tehip-Tilla, who is the owner of Gubarnu's

blood, and told him what they wanted, and Tehip-Tilla offered a gift of atonement to the father of the dead man, but the father said no. So Tehip-Tilla sent Gubarnu away with Kaptia and told them not to come back until he sent for them."

Abba-Basthi sighed. "The planting season came, and Gubarnu was not in Harran, and I served Nihtesaru and learned the secrets of that house.

"Nihtesaru's father was a rich man like Tehip-Tilla, and Tehip-Tilla married his son to Nihtesaru because her dowry was so great and because he wanted a hostage in his house; and Nihtesaru's father said yes so that he could have a spy in Tehip-Tilla's.

"Nihtesaru hated Gubarnu. She called him 'half-pint' and treated him like a stray dog on the street. Most of all she hated to lie with him, and I see why. But she had to. She preferred to lie with Ibbi-Shamash, who climbed the garden wall when she sent for him. She gave him cloth and jewels for it. Tashmetum said that the baby boy was Ibbi-Shamash's. But Gubarnu did nothing about it; though he could have killed them both for adultery."

"Adultery?" asked Penthesilea.

"It is a crime when a wife lies with someone who is not her husband."

"And a husband with someone who is not his wife?" asked Penthesilea.

"That is not the same. It is not a crime for him unless the woman is the wife of another man. Then it is a crime against her husband, because she is part of what he owns. And he can kill them for it."

Penthesilea lay her fingers over her mouth.

"But Gubarnu did not punish them. For in my land the husband can punish the man only if he punishes his wife. And Gubarnu did not dare touch Nihtesaru, and Nihtesaru knew it. Tehip-Tilla was afraid that she would leave and take her dowry back. So he let her do what she wanted.

"Gubarnu hated Nihtesaru as much as she hated him and did not spend one night in a dozen in her bed; instead he lay with the slave girls in the alehouse and those who lived under his father's roof. None of them could say no, no matter what he did to them, no matter what he made them do to him.

"I could have pitied Nihtesaru, but I did not, because she thought that I was another animal to bear her burden, and she loved only her face in the mirror.

"While Kaptia was away, my father ate the bread and drank the water of death. I cried, but when I ask my heart, I do not know how much salt my tears had. He was my father, but I was a slave because of him.

"During that time, too, Artatama came to see me whenever he had to carry something to Tehip-Tilla's house. He would wait for me in the kitchen. We would talk and laugh until my mistress called for me or until Artatama had to go back. One day we were sitting there, smiling and holding hands, when a short, fat old man came into the kitchen. It was Kaptia. He and Gubarnu had returned, for the murdered man's father had died and his brothers had agreed to the price Tehip-Tilla had offered for his blood.

"Kaptia looked at Artatama with a strange look, and I saw that he thought Artatama was my lover and not my brother. So I told him who it was. Kaptia still did not seem happy, but never ordered me not to see my brother when he visited the house. For this reason and for others, I can speak only good of Kaptia. May the gentle spirits look after him in the land of the Dead. He was a kind man. He never beat me.

"And soon after he came back, Tehip-Tilla ordered him to go away again—this time on a caravan to the north. He had to lead Tehip-Tilla's men and animals north to join a man called Murashu, who was Tehip-Tilla's agent. Kaptia asked for Artatama to come with them. Kaptia did this to please me; but I also think he did it to keep Artatama away from me. When Artatama went away, Batteia came to Tehip-Tilla's. They could not sell her, she was too old, and so kept her. But she soon joined my mother in the land of the dead.

"I remember once, after Kaptia and Artatama had gone away, I was leaving Nihtesaru's room one morning, and Gubarnu was coming in. I gasped in surprise, and he saw my fear and smiled as if he was going to do something bad to me.

"My belly was growing big then, too, for my Tushratta was in me. Soon my time came, and I knew that Kaptia would be pleased with me when he returned and learned the news. For I had given birth to a boy child; Kaptia would thank the gods for blessing his old age and going on with his life—for Kaptia wanted his oldest son to be a scribe like him if Tehip-Tilla let that be."

"Let that be?"

"Yes. Tushratta belonged to Tehip-Tilla, for he owned Kaptia and me.

"I loved my baby. I was like a god over him. Without me he could not live. And the way he needed me for everything reminded me of how I was a slave and how my life and death were in my master's hands. And he was my body; he came out of my body; and when he put his lips around my breast to drink, and when he smiled, I smiled, too.

"But once, I remember holding my baby to my tit and singing to him and being happy and thinking that we were alone. But when I looked up, Gubarnu was standing in the door looking at us with that smile of his; I felt that he had hit me again. But I knew that Kaptia would come back and that Tehip-Tilla did not want Gubarnu to lie with Kaptia's woman.

"But Kaptia never came back. For after the seasons had turned and it was time to harvest the fruit and grain again, we learned from a trader who came from there that Kaptia had died before the caravan reached Kanesh. I cried for Kaptia, for he had been good to me. And I was alone now, with my little Tushratta, and we were both slaves. I was afraid again: I knew that Gubarnu was there and that Tehip-Tilla was very old and very sick.

"Then Tehip-Tilla died. Gubarnu was the master now. I knew that soon Gubarnu would think of me again and send for me or find me and rape me. And if I said no, he would beat me or sell me. And he would rip my baby out of my arms and sell him, so that I would never see him again."

Tears brimmed over Abba-Bashti's eyelids.

"Tashmetum saw my pain and said to do all that Gubarnu wanted, that there was no other thing that I could do. And when she learned that Gubarnu had sent for me, she gave me perfumed oil to smear on his prick so he would not hurt me and told me to do whatever he wanted. When I walked into Gubarnu's room he bid me stand before him. He was sitting naked in his chair. "I hear you have a baby," he said. The blood went away from my face, and his prick rose.

"And I," whispered Abba-Bashti, "I did whatever he wanted." She shuddered. "I wanted to take a stone and break Gubarnu's head. I wanted to shove hot coals into his mouth. I wanted to take a stick with snake poison in it and push it into his ass, and hear him scream. But I knew what would happen to me—and to Tushratta—if I did. I prayed to Nanaï that Gubarnu would grow tired of me, and I prayed to Her not to let a hate-baby grow inside of me before Gubarnu forgot that I was in his house. And Tashmetum gave me herbs to drink. I did what was pleasing in his eyes and vomit rose in me each time but I fought against puking. I thought of throwing myself into the canal near the city so that my tears and pain would end and I could see my mother and Batteia again.

"But how could I?" sobbed Abba-Bashti, "Tushratta needed me. What else was there to do?"

Penthesilea's throat tightened. She raised Abba-Bashti's hand to her lips, kissed it, and let it go. But Abba-Bashti did not drop her arm to her side right away. Penthesilea's cheeks grew hot, and she turned to look out over the parapet again. "What happened after that?" she said, amazed at her rough, low voice.

"I had never stopped praying to Nanaï, even though I wondered if the demon Lamashtu had taken Her prisoner the way your Storm God does your goddess. Maybe I should pray to Lamashtu, I even thought. But I never did. And it was a good thing. For my brother came back. He had pleased Tehip-Tilla's agent, Murashu, who had lent him tin to trade. And he had bought and sold wisely and had enough to buy back his freedom. And he also carried Kaptia's wishes, inscribed on a tablet of clay.

"Tehip-Tilla sometimes gave Kaptia small gifts, coins and spices, and Kaptia had also bought and sold with them, and the pictures on the clay told where he had hidden all that he gathered. This was Tushratta's now and was enough to buy his freedom and mine.

"Artatama wanted to join another caravan, but he had enough only to buy one pack donkey and nothing to trade. So I told Artatama to adopt the boy and take the coins that were left to him: there were enough of them to buy goods and even a second donkey. Artatama was happy to do this. I begged him to take me and his son along with him, for Tushratta is still at my breast. Artatama did not want to: such a life is not for a woman, he said, such a life is not for a small child.

"Then I told Artatama that there was nothing in Harran for me but sadness and anger. Mother was dead. Batteia was dead. And I wanted to leave that place and find something I did not know, something I could not see. I wanted to leave so much that only my Goddess could have put this feeling in me. Artatama could not make up his mind.

"Then I sold my long hair to a man who makes wigs and bought some small statues of clay and one of ivory and told Artatama that he could trade them, too, if he took us along.

And he said yes at last. That was four full moons ago. Now I am here and in two moons I will be in Troy."

Penthesilea and Abba-Basthi came down from the parapet. Themiscyra's gate had long since been barred, and Penthesilea led Abba-Bashti to a sleeping chamber on the lower story of the palace. She intended to give Abba-Bashti its one bed and stretch out on a skin on the floor. But someone—Anuphey no doubt—had set a cot down near the sleeping couch. Penthesilea would take her rest there.

Abba-Bashti sighed with pleasure when she laid her eyes on the sleeping couch offered to her. She placed Tushratta on it and pulled the garment that she wore over her head. The motion of her arms made the flame of the lamp on the nearby table tremble, and the deep circle of her navel and jet triangle of her fleece grew larger and smaller in the nervous light. Penthesilea fancied that some goddess dwelt in those dark places, and she longed to bury her mouth in them and celebrate their mysteries with lazy kisses and whispered prayers. But she said nothing, slipped off her tunic, and slid under the coverings. She smiled wearily at Abba-Bashti, who nodded a silent good night and stretched her body out on her bed. She turned and patted Tushratta's belly. Then she lay on her back and closed her eyes. She groaned softly. Soon, peace spread out from the corners of her eyes to her brow and mouth, and she began to breathe slowly and deeply.

But not for long. Her face contracted in the way a child's does before it screams with fear. She thrashed about and babbled frantic words in her strange language. Penthesilea got up, sat on the edge of Abba-Bashti's bed, and stroked her temples. "It's all right," Penthesilea whispered. "It's all right. You are safe." She paused, then added, "Tushratta is safe. It's all right." She lay her lips on Abba-Bashti's naked shoulder, and Abba-Bashti, her eyes still closed, sat up, kissed Penthesilea on the mouth, and fell back to sleep.

Penthesilea lay down on her bed. Her mouth tingled; her thoughts swirled in her head. The beams above her shuddered fitfully in the lamplight. The vein in her neck fluttered. Abba-Bashti's breathing, now grown easy, hummed steadily against her blood's unpredictable coursing, for Abba-Bashti had once more wafted down to the world that mortals sometimes share with the goddesses and gods.

Penthesilea longed to join Abba-Bashti there, and when the divinities finally beckoned her, Abba-Bashti was waiting. Mist surrounded her, but as Penthesilea came closer—no, slipped closer, because she did not have the sensation of moving—the haze dissolved, and Abba-Basthi, naked and radiant, stepped out of it like the dawn from the fog. Her arms outstretched, she stood in the shimmering shade of a willow whose roots bathed in clear water. Her pelt was a triangle of night blue flecked with snow white diamonds, and her lips and nipples the moist, sweet meat of cherries picked in the fresh of morning. Her flesh gave off the smell of cherry blossoms, too, and their perfume twined around Penthesilea's nostrils and dizzied her.

Abba-Bashti waded backward into the water. Her steps made the sound of a sacred dance, and small fishes swam in silver circles around her ankles. Penthesilea splashed in after her. Abba-Bashti drew one foot in back of the other, her footfalls tinkling like tiny cymbals. The crystal liquid reached up and embraced her. Her calves, thighs, hips, breasts, shoulders, neck, and face were transmuted into undulating alabaster. Penthesilea plunged forward to reach her; only then did she understand that she, too, was naked. Secret waves carried her to Abba-Bashti's side, and the women drifted underwater, parallel to one another, not needing to breathe. For a time without measure they glided through the shimmering luminescence, and, although they did not speak, longings passed between them like limpid currents.

Chapter 10

Penthesilea strode downhill. She grinned and waved at the women who greeted her by name. The morning sky dazzled her like the flowers that sparkled in the wheat fields. The dawn's rays made her think of Abba-Bashti, who had left at first light. The sweetness Penthesilea felt at this remembrance dissolved the gall that had flooded her when, unbid and unwelcome, Antiope's snickers and Pirothous' smirks had invaded her heart.

Penthesilea turned into the street of the artificers. Once she was done with her errand there, she would find Abba-Bashti and ask her.

Hammer blows assaulted Penthesilea's ears as she made her way through winding ways and narrow alleys to the smithy, a large hut whose unfired clay walls were made of crazy patterns of brown and beige earth that the heat from the forge within had baked dry in unpredictable places. The sky above the roof trembled, but no pounding rang from inside. Penthesilea entered. Heat slammed against her face and arms. In the middle of the room, which a wall of clay separated from the living quarters, a circle of stones pulsated with the glowing coals that it held. Blue fingers now grasped at the embers and now let them go. The heat made the air shiver upward through an opening in the ceiling and cast trembling daylight on the crucible below.

A grown girl squatted next to the forge, pumping a leather bellows whose tube penetrated a small hole in the base of the hearth. She was singing to mark the rhythm of her labor. Near her, on a flat rock that a woman could just reach around, stood the anvil, a slab of iron seated on a hollow iron base. Years of hammering had made the flat piece harder than any stone or metal. In back of the anvil, against the wall, leaned the blacksmith's tongs, thin metal arms ending in claws to grip the iron so that it did not escape the hammer blows that battered it. This tool, a tapered black fist set in an oak handle, stood beside strips of iron, which the artificer would forge together into a knife, a saw-toothed sickle, which she had to reattach to its handle, and a labrys, whose chipped blade she would repair and shape anew. It was this weapon that Penthesilea had come to fetch.

Another, younger child came out of the back. It was Athaia, the smith's middle daughter. She wore her flaxen hair tied back in a club; wisps of it escaped and made a blonde halo around her head. Her powerful arms carried a scuttle of charcoal. She put it down at the other girl's side and flashed a half-bold, half-embarrassed smile at the visitor. "Mother will be right here," she said. The girl by the forge, Aella, the smith's oldest child, straightened up and said hello. She measured a head taller than her junior but had the same frizzy blonde hair fastened behind her ears and the same broad shoulders. She ran her forearm across her brow, kneeled, and began to work the bellows again.

Telkhinia the smith, her flax-colored locks streaming over powerful shoulders, sauntered in. She held the hand of Dirce, a straw-haired girl child who came up to her thighs. Dirce's golden tresses flowed over thick upper arms, and her steps, although still uneven, took possession of the ground, in the same way that Telkhinia's did. Telkhinia let go of her hand, and she scampered to the back of the shop.

Telkhinia addressed the visitor. "Hello, Penthesilea. You've come for the axe, I bet. Not ready but won't take long." Telkhinia ambled to where it leaned against the wall, snatched it up, and plunged it in the coals. "Have some bread and beer with me while the axe heats."

Telkhinia seated her guest and herself on stools near the doorway. The middle girl fetched food and drink, and Telkhinia talked and chewed, uttering a stream of gossip between mouthfuls that Penthesilea listened to with care, for Telkhinia knew about most goings-on before news of them reached even Anuphey.

"I'm hungry. I haven't eaten since yesterday evening. I couldn't. Wasn't allowed to. I had to go to the temple before dawn. They had to purify me and say prayers over my head, because I'm going to make a furnace later. Aella, my oldest, is going to take some ore from the mountain later. There's enough wind to smelt it. So the bloom can be born."

Bloom was the spongy white stuff that Telkhinia brought forth from red and yellow pebbles she dug out of the iron mountains. She then transfigured it into iron to forge tools and weapons. She changed stones into bloom in an oven that stood by the mouth of a cave on the opposite slope of Themiscyra's hill.

Women were forbidden to look upon Telkhinia's magic—her taking the unborn metal from the Goddess's belly and hastening its gestation: the sight of it could harm the uninitiated. Nevertheless, years before, Penthesilea had stumbled on the smeltery when the blacksmith was making bloom and, in the delight of doing something prohibited, concealed herself behind a bush and spied on Telkhinia. Just below the mouth of the cavern, at the point where the slope evened out, the smith was kneeling beside a shallow, stone-lined hole as big around as one of the jars women stored grain in. She had already laid a bed of kindling and charcoal on the bottom and was layering ore and more fuel on them and chanting a spell. Once she had done, she fetched wet clay from the darkness of the tunnel and, with deft hands, fashioned a beehive-shaped dome that covered the hollow she had just filled. She raised her arms and whispered strange words. She picked up a small clay vessel, blew into it, and lighted thin strips of wood from the hot coals it held. She crammed the matches into a chink in the base of the oven, faced the wind, and got down on her knees. Repeatedly touching her brow to the ground, she mouthed rising and falling syllables. The winds that rushed through the cavern's entrance penetrated the furnace and quickened the fire inside it. White smoke snaked upward from a small opening in the roof of the kiln. The air above it began to shiver. Telkhinia intoned one more prayer, found shade, and stretched out. Soon her snores shook the branches overhead.

Penthesilea had made sure to return to the site the next day. This time, the smith, who was munching an apple, sat cross-legged beside where the clay beehive had once been. But now its sides had been smashed down, and brown sherds and gray ashes lay on the ground around it. In the center of this heap, on a bed of half-consumed coals, lay the bloom.

Telkhinia's voice cut into Penthesilea's recollection.

"I can't say that Myrtho was happy to see me. She's still riled up at me because of what went on the last time the men came around."

"Last summer?"

"Yup. But it wasn't my fault. No it wasn't." Telkhinia shook her head vigorously. "When the boys got here last year, I went down to the tents like I always do, to have a look. There was a blonde fellow from way up north who took my fancy. I like blondes; that way I get blonde children. He wasn't bad looking, neither, with blue eyes, and a mouth full of the whitest, prettiest teeth I ever saw. Goddess, he smiled pretty. It was like the sunshine, I tell you."

Telkhinia closed her eyes and grinned.

"I never found out what they call the place he came from, because he didn't speak but a few words of our language. But those things don't draw much water—he was a nice enough fellow.

"Well, one evening I went down there and I brought him a skin of our wine. Cleothera the winemaker had traded me some that day. She always has some to trade for when the boys come around. Well, me and blondie drank and ate until the moon rose." Telkhinia blinked, grinned, and took another swig.

"So he cuddled up to me and pinched my cheek, and I did the same."

Penthesilea wondered, had Telkhinia left a black and blue mark on his jowl? She was the strongest woman in Themiscyra.

"Then he twisted the tip of my nose—playful like, mind you—and playful like I did the same."

Penthesilea winced.

"Then—just for laughs—he patted me on the cheek, and I did the same—just for laughs."

Penthesilea shuddered.

"I mean it was all in fun. But this fellow just went and started bleeding from the mouth. He took a while to figure it out, too, but finally saw it on the front of his tunic. Then, like he didn't believe what he was doing, he spit out two teeth—one from the front and the pointed one just behind it. When he saw them lying on the ground he got mad, babbled in that lingo of his, and started to take a punch. I just put one arm up to cover myself and pushed his face away with the other. He fell to the ground, but hollered as he went down. Then he just lay there, quiet, like he was asleep. A friend of his came out of his tent, took one look, and started yammering something I couldn't make out. So the other blonde fellows ran out to see what was wrong. When they saw my little blondie there out cold at my feet, they all went for me at the same time—howling I don't know what at the top of their lungs. I thought I was in for it; it was five against one. So I gave the Amazon war whoop. . . . "

Telkhinia raised her head and shrieked. Her two big girls hurtled out of the back of the shop. They stopped short and gawked about. But nothing was wrong, and they returned.

"Anyway," continued their mother, "some women came out of the same tents as these fellows. They'd also been into the wine. They took one look, started screaming their heads off, and jumped in to even things up. Then other guys ran out of other tents and joined the fight, hollering all sorts of strange words. Then some more women ran out to help us."

Telkhinia laughed. "I'll tell you one thing, Cleothera had visited them all. They all came out swinging. Some of them were as naked as the day they were born. Everyone was red in the face and howling up a storm. They all set at one another, the boys against the girls—punching and pulling hair and trying to take hold and no one was winning.

"The blonde guys were especially out to get me, because I had laid their friend flat. One of them came swinging and I caught his wrist and decked him. Another jumped on my back to hold my arms while a friend of his smashed me. I shook the first one off, but the other guy walloped me so hard he closed one of my eyes; it was black for days. I punched him back, in the chest, and broke two of his ribs. So we were even.

"All of a sudden Miminousa and her riders swooped down out of nowhere and tried to stop the fight, but couldn't. Then more Amazons rode down from the city and started to pull us apart, throwing the girls on one side and the boys on the other, and things quieted down.

"Well, the next day those fellows complained to Thalestris and weren't good sports about it, neither. They said they were our guests and that, to show their respect, they'd forked over nice gifts to Celano before pitching their tents in front of the walls. And look what they had got in return. That it wasn't their fault. That I had started it.

"I told Thalestris I hadn't, that it was all good clean fun, but she wasn't hearing any of it. My black eye didn't look too good, neither.

"So the men counted up the bruises and broken bones. My friend, you know, blondie, he was all worked up about losing his two teeth. Well the list of damages was long—missing teeth and smashed ribs, and welts and bruises and black and blue marks. Most of these fellows were free men, too, so Thalestris and Myrtho had to pay plenty—metal and cloth and wood and the likes—to make up for what we did, because they want to see them back again. Celano was riled up; you know how she hates to give anything away. Thalestris hasn't sent me any wine or beer since then, either, and Myrtho—the water they bathed me in this morning was awfully cold. And that after a whole year.

"Now, begging your pardon, I'll go to work."

Telkhinia tied her hair back and donned a leather apron. She took up her tongs and plunged them into the coals. Sparks flew; tongues of blue flame flickered upward. Her face flashed orange in the glare. The sockets of her eyes were black cavities from out of which danced reflections of the flames. It was the look of the Goddess shaping the world at the very beginning.

Telkhinia fished the red-hot axehead from the coals and, turning it this way and that, scrutinized every inch before laying it on the anvil. She tightened her left hand around the end of the tongs, picked up her hammer with her right, raised the tool shoulder high, and dealt the hot iron so mighty a blow that the walls trembled and Penthesilea's hearing nearly burst inside her skull. Telkhinia slammed the hammer up and down, up and down.

The blows blared and blasted.

Telkhinia plunged the red-hot labrys into a nearby bucket of water. The liquid shrilled. She ran her forearm across her brow and waited for the screaming to die down. When it did, she placed the axehead in the coals and worked the bellows until it once more shone bright orange.

Again and again she hammered it, quenched it, and reheated it, all the while keeping up her talk.

"I went down to have a look at the traders who came in yesterday evening. They look all right to me. I mean there's a tall fellow who came with them who isn't bad. But, I don't know, he's got black hair. They always do when they come from that direction. I think I'll wait for some blondies to get here. Anyway, I'm smack between two moon's bloods, and you know what they say."

It was said that a woman had to share her couch with the same man starting right after her moon's blood so that, the next month, there would be a girl in her belly. That if she shared her couch with a man in between moon's bloods, she would get a boy, and no one wanted boys.

"I saw you ride in with the caravan yesterday. Now that's not your patrol. You've always ridden with Antiope. But she's mighty busy these days with that redhead of hers—so I guess you don't ride out much these days. Of course, everyone says that by rights you should have gone to the tents, too, along with Antiope, to get new Amazons. They say Thalestris did you wrong. That she tried to shame you because she was riled up at you for what you said about not letting those fellows in in the first place."

Penthesilea raised her brows in surprise.

"Yup," said Telkhinia, "word got out."

Word always got out, and Telkhinia never hesitated to speak her mind no matter who her words irritated: Thalestris balked at angering the woman who made weapons for her and Myrtho hesitated to chastise a magician of the race that changed the earth with the flames.

"Well, Thalestris didn't shame you," continued Telkhinia, "because nobody around here thinks you did wrong. Instead she shamed herself, mark my word. Not the fairest ruler we ever had anyway, all the women say so. And the day before yesterday, at the race—you won, you rode in second. We all saw that. But Thalestris wouldn't hear any of it, because of that Antiope of hers. If she were my girl, I'd take the back of my hand to her until she stopped being so spoiled. Not that Melanippe's much better."

Telkhinia smote the weapon with her hammer.

"Still, you did right taking third place. A lot of betting women didn't like it. But you did right. There's no use arguing with fools. Better just to show them up.

"And I heard tell, too, about what happened at Antiope's party the same evening—that fat little stinker saying scurvy things to you. If he'd have done the same with me, I'd have broken him in two, just to show him. All the women say that Antiope should have let you have a go at him, to teach him some manners. But he's Thalestris' guest. That's what Antiope says. I never heard a guest insult anyone like that. And considering that we took them fellows in when they were in a bad way. . . ."

Telkhinia stabbed her red-hot weapon into the water; it yelped back at her.

"Anyway, I saw you ride in with the traders yesterday next to that woman with the baby. I can't say I've seen many women going around with caravans. They say that Anuphey took her to the palace last night. Is she running away? Does she want to stay? Of course, if that's a boy baby she's got, she'll have to give him up as soon as he's weaned."

Penthesilea lowered her eyes.

"Not that you missed anything, not going down to the tents to share the couch with them Achaean fellows. I been down there a couple of times to have a look. Like some of the others. Not that we can touch. No. They're only for the riders. But we aren't sure we'd want them.

"I got a good look at that redhead Antiope's so crazy about. He's a little skinny for my taste, and I guess Antiope keeps him thin. He trots around like he thinks his prick's a magic wand. He smiles a lot, too. Most likely because he's got a mouth full of pretty teeth and wants Antiope to see them. Ha! I never seen someone smile so much. But only at Antiope and her friends. Not at the rest of the women. No. He looks at the one's who aren't riders like we were riffraff.

"The only time he talked to me was yesterday. Then he said hello. I was walking round the hill and came on him just standing staring up at the wall. He turned quick when he heard me and said hello like he was happy."

Telkhinia walloped the glowing labrys.

"Then there's that fat little henchman of his, the stinker. That one never looks anyone straight in the eye; at least he didn't me until he found out that I make iron. Then he turned all honey. Every time I come down there he sidles up to me—all smiles—and chats me up. He makes eyes at me, too. And Marpessa, why she doesn't mind at all. She'd just as soon he was making babies with someone else; she wants one quick so she can be out of there. Trouble is, that guy's gray eyes wouldn't warm an icicle.

"Not much to look at, neither. But he's not as bad as that scarecrow, you know, the one with the black hair and beard, and the strange eyes. The wounded one."

Soloön.

"Now who would want to go near him, I ask you? Not a bit of meat on his bones, and he walks around all the time with a face so long you'd think he'd trip over it. And he's got dead eyes, I swear. Except when Antiope's around. I saw that once. She walked by, and this fellow's eyes took to burning so bright you'd think they'd go clear through to the back of his skull. But when he saw I was looking at him, he turned away fast. Not that Antiope notices anything. She only has eyes for that stuck-up redhead. Goddess, how can she be such a fool?"

Whack!

"Then there's that wavy-haired fellow with the eyes like a demon, the one who limps."

Brimus.

"He stares at all the women who pass by with this sly smile on his face. Just yesterday, me and Aella were walking by. He grabbed his breechcloth around his prick and shook it at us. We laughed. She's not quite ready and I'm not interested."

"Of course, there's one who isn't bad. You know, the fellow with the hair and beard the color of honey."

Chalcodon.

"He sure looks strong, maybe as strong as me, but I doubt it. Not that I'll ever know: I'm not allowed to get anywhere near him. I saw him naked a couple of days ago, too. He ain't bad to look at. He was in the water, under the bridge, with the red-head. But you gotta be crazy to do that. The current will toss you down to the first elbow in the river. I guess they were hanging on to the piles. The water's still chilly this time of year, too.

"Well, he may be pretty and all that, but I don't care for the Achaeans much. Neither do the other women. Did you ever see the way one of them looks at one of us when he thinks she's not watching? Like the Amazons look over the young horses the breeder trots out for them. And when two of them guys are together and a woman walks by them and they like the way she looks, they laugh funny. Not so much a laugh as a threat. Now the trading fellows don't do that when we welcome them every year.

"Those guys are strange, I tell you. Of course, Thalestris doesn't know it, and Antiope isn't telling. But Antiope's a damned fool, and Thalestris's is no better."

Telkhinia clobbered the axe with her mighty tool. Penthesilea's ears still rang when she made her way toward the tents.

They undulated like snake dancers in the morning breeze. White-robed traders walked among them or stood at their entrances: women from Themiscyra, many dressed in the purplish-red robes they wore on feast days, strolled amidst the visitors. That night no merchant's couch would be empty, and, when the men took their leave, the lucky ones among them—the ones who had pleased the women who chose them—would carry away the crimson attire worn on that first day. By the same season next year, the babies would already have been born.

Abba-Basthi was not among the crowd, but Tecmassa stood near a small cloth dwelling on the far edge of the encampment. Penthesilea headed that way but stopped when she heard hooves thudding over the bridge. Adrasta, Marpessa, and Charope were running their mounts across the wooden span—Adrasta's stocky figure balancing easily on her mount's back, Marpessa's orange hair flapping like a flame as her horse sprang forward, and Charope's slight hips surging in unison with her pony's motion. The Amazons spotted Penthesilea and reined in around her.

Marpessa's eyes twinkled. "Well, well, here's the woman whose fault it all is. And how are you this fine day, Penthesilea?"

"Hello to you, too. I don't understand the joke."

"The joke is this," said Marpessa, "except it isn't a joke. We've had our fill of those Achaean lads. The banquet was the end of it, and we'll have no more to do with them. If we're pregnant, then we've done our duties and need do no more."

"And if we're not," said Charope through her large nose, "we'll sneak down to the traders, get pregnant with them, and say it was the soldiers. What do you say, girls?"

"That we'll surely do," said Marpessa. "Pirothous' insulting you was not right, and his taking a knife in hand. Mind you, I've never cared for him, but now I think I should have broken his arm. That's what I told Antiope. And do you know what she said to me in return? She said it was all your fault."

"What?"

"Precisely what I think," said Marpessa.

"I hope I didn't hurt you," said Adrasta.

"No. Don't give it a second thought."

"Not that we've seen much of those fine specimens since the banquet," said Marpessa.

"And it's a good thing, too," drawled Adrasta, her full cheeks becoming rounder and pinker. "I'd have strangled Chalcodon while he slept. He's terrible. He worships the Belly God, I swear. He wants nothing more than to fill his gut with wine and meat and poke his prick into me—but only after he's eaten and drunk. And the way he talks to me—like I was some kind of robber—makes my fists itch. But the Goddess punishes a host who doesn't treat her guest well, so I can't."

"Your gold's not safe around him, either. Chalcodon tried to talk me out of the buckle I wear. When I wouldn't give it to him as a present, he stole it while he thought I was asleep. I took it back when he had passed out from the wine."

"That lad's as dumb as he is pretty," said Marpessa. "Who did he imagine you'd suspect?"

"Not that Brimus is better," nasalized Charope. "He never talks to me except to tell me to lie down so he can lie on top of me. He does that two or three times a day. But he doesn't care what I like. He just pokes and grunts and gets up smiling when he's had enough. They never said that to get new Amazons I'd have to put up with the likes of him. Do you think the Goddess is punishing me for a sin I don't remember?

"And his breath stinks. I told him once, so he made me turn over and tried to poke his prick into my butt. I got away from him and told him what I thought of it. I swear he didn't understand. Do you know what he said? That the Achaean soldiers bugger each other all the time, even when there are women around. That they bugger the new ones as part of their initiation. That it makes them all brothers. That it makes them all fight better. That he was doing me a favor since I was only a woman. Only! I heard that and slammed him up against the tent pole and told him what I'd do to him the next time he tried that on me." Malicious pleasure vibrated through her snout. "I know you're not supposed to threaten your guest, but there's no other way with those fellows."

"Still," said Marpessa, "we didn't lay eyes on them from the night of the banquet till yesterday evening. After Antiope sent you home, the Achaeans disappeared. All except Antiope and Theseus, who hurried to their tent and didn't come out before yesterday noon. But the other Achaeans, why as soon as the banquet was done, they grabbed a wineskin and torches and staggered off into the night. They didn't come back until the next morning and were still drunk. At least that's what the serving women told us. We had retreated to plan our strategy."

Marpessa turned her eyes toward the city.

"We'll not spend another night with them, and if there are women who want to, bring them on, it's fine with me. We've told Antiope so and we'll speak to Thalestris as soon as she'll see us."

The three rode off, and Penthesilea made her way to Abba-Bashti's tent.

Tecmassa stood with her fists on her hips, huddling with Abba-Bashti's brother, who held a tiny clay figure, a black-and ochre-glazed lioness' head. When Penthesilea neared her, she beamed, her glittering white teeth setting off the empty jet-colored rectangle in their midst. Artatama bowed low and retreated into the tent. The two Amazons embraced one another.

"Feodissia told me about the race," said Tecmassa, thumping Penthesilea on the shoulder. "You did right, my girl, you did right. There's no arguing with the likes of Thalestris when she gets a damned fool idea into her head."

"Antiope," Penthesilea explained, "I've sworn to the Goddess to be Antiope's companion."

"I know what you mean, girl. I would have done anything for Leokadia. Anything. She never let me down."

"Have you spotted any traders from Troy?" asked Penthesilea, eager to talk about something else.

"Not a one, my girl. Not a single one. And there hasn't been any. . . ."

The tent entrance flapped. Abba-Bashti stepped into the daylight, blinked until her eyes became accustomed to it, and stared at Penthesilea. Penthesilea gazed back. Her heart stabbed against her ribs and her cheeks burned. She heard Tecmassa ask "Who's that?" but could not move her lips.

A low, singing syllable escaped from Tecmassa's throat. Penthesilea jerked her head around. Tecmassa grinned, bowed to Abba-Bashti, and said, "Tell the man I'll be back." She turned on her heels and strode off in the direction of the city.

Artatama emerged from the tent holding another figurine, saw that Tecmassa had left, and ran after her.

Abba-Bashti disappeared inside, and Penthesilea followed. It took a moment for her eyes to get used to the dark. Abba-Bashti stood a few feet away. Penthesilea approached but stopped at arm's length and looked into Abba-Bashti's eyes. Deep fire glowed in them.

Penthesilea wanted to tell Abba-Bashti, but her tongue was heavy, and she knit her brows. Abba-Bashti raised her fingertips to her mouth. Penthesilea stretched out her hands. Abba-Bashti stepped up to her and wrapped warm arms around her. Penthesilea clasped Abba-Bashti tight, and they rocked back and forth to the same cadence. They kissed deeply, breathing only when they could no longer stand the stabbing in their lungs and the trembling in their legs. Then, weakened, chastened, they stepped back from one another and narrowed their eyes. It was as if the two had rained blows on one another and now, surprised to be out of pain, stared at one another with suspicion and fear. Of what? Of the other's treachery? Of her own body's?

Penthesilea moved forward, stretched her arms over Abba-Bashti's shoulders, and bent her head. Abba-Basthi put her arms around Penthesilea's neck and drew her even closer.

Penthesilea pressed her lips against Abba-Bashti's; Abba-Bashti's tongue flicked over them; Penthesilea's chest nearly burst. She pulled her face back and focused on Abba-Bashti's. "Stay," she pleaded. "Stay. There is no slavery here. You are my. . . ." Abba-Bashti leaned her hips against Penthesilea's, and the pulse in Abba-Bashti's belly throbbed against them. Penthesilea's mouth once more lighted on Abba-Bashti's, which opened and sucked in her tongue. Heat rushed through Penthesilea's flesh.

Then, of a sudden, as if she had touched a live coal, Abba-Bashti jumped away. Her eyes had focused behind Penthesilea, who turned and saw a cradle suspended from the tent post.

"I cannot," sobbed Abba-Bashti.

Penthesilea's skull began to throb.

"Don't you see?" whispered Abba-Bashti.

"Don't I see?"

"I cannot stay in Themiscyra. For soon they would take my Tushratta from me, and I would never stop crying because of it. Do not ask me again, I beg you. I cannot!"

Abba-Bashti did a violent about-face.

The tent walls whirled around Penthesilea's head, and she staggered outside but stopped at the entrance and stood there, breathing deeply, her forehead turned toward the heavens, begging them for . . . what? Tears began to tumble down her cheeks.

Abba-Bashti came to her and stood next to her, the sleeve of her robe touching Penthesilea's flesh and making her shiver. Still, Penthesilea did not turn her gaze from the heavens. Abba-Bashti wrapped her fingers around her wrist. "I am sorry," she said.

Penthesilea yanked her arm free and, still weeping, her head downturned, stamped away. She did not see Artatama, who was on his way back to the tent. He took in Penthesilea's posture and his sister's face and composed his own.

Penthesilea paced uphill, drowning in her dark mood, until yelling, cursing voices—some of them men's—ripped her from her pain.

Miminousa and two of her riders sat their horses in the middle of three white-robed, black-bearded, traders and at least a dozen women. Each of the men was expostulating at the top of his lungs. The man nearest Miminousa was shaking his fist and spitting out a stream of guttural complaints with such violence that Miminousa's horse shied. Miminousa reined the beast back. Her barrel chest expanded and her thick neck grew purple. She bellowed at the throng, "Shut up! For Goddess' sake, shut up! I can't hear anything!"

Miminousa barked this order four times before the protests ebbed into ragged exclamations. A merchant whose white beard shone pale blue in the sunlight made his way toward the mounted women. The other men parted respectfully.

Someone edged up to Penthesilea. It was Cleothera the winemaker, a small, broad-built woman with a wide brow, narrow lips, and a fleshy nose crisscrossed by scores of fine veins. Full gourds hung in bandoleers from her shoulders. "That guy in the middle, is worked up," she said, pointing to the trader who had been protesting. "Seems that someone stole a gold bracelet from his tent while his back was turned. He's sure it was one of the women. A lot of us don't like that, though. Women from Themiscyra don't steal. Not our way. We don't want more from those guys but their thick milk. The Goddess and the priestesses don't like stealing."

"Tell me who you think did it," roared Miminousa.

The trader whose goods had disappeared examined the faces around him one by one. Nobody spoke while he did. His glance lighted on a young woman with plump cheeks and powerful arms, Thalia the farmer.

"Come into town like the rest of them to check out the merchandise," chuckled Cleothera.

Thalia looked to left and right. She realized that the man had singled her out and widened her eyes.

"Do you say it was she, then?" roared Miminousa.

All faces turned toward the merchant, who said, "She was the last one I saw."

The white-bearded man was whispering something to Miminousa. Once he finished, she spoke under her breath to two of her followers. They dismounted and planted themselves on either side of the farmer.

The purple rose from Miminousa's neck to her face.

"Miminousa don't like this one bit," said Cleothera.

Miminousa shouted to the accused woman, "They'll take you into the tent and search you."

The riders grabbed Thalia's arms, but she jerked free and, putting her hands on her hips, sidled up to the man who had pointed the finger at her. She stuck her face in his. "If you want to search me," she proclaimed, "do it in broad daylight. All that I have the Goddess gave me. "

A few women giggled.

Her gaze still fixed on the merchant's, she deftly undid the sash that tied her red robe around her, saying, "The Goddess gives us all we need, and we don't want what we don't need 'cause there's plenty to go around." The waistband slid to the ground. The folds of the garment cascaded down the woman's body, billowed around her feet, and shuddered still. The young woman, now in glimmering nakedness, shook her jet-colored mane until it spread around her shoulders and chest. She stepped out of the dress, and, placing her arms akimbo again, planted her feet defiantly.

Her ivory shoulders were as sturdy as the hills; her deeply tanned arms as thick and supple as the alder bough; her fleshy breasts as firm as full gourds of cider, her belly as smooth and rich as the grains of ripe wheat. Her muscled legs reminded Penthesilea of the piles that held up the bridge over Thermodon and her fine ankles of a young mare's.

Thalia bent down, her breasts and buttocks shimmering as she did, and scooped up the robe. "Themiscyra's women don't steal!" she said, flinging the garment at the head of the man who had maligned her. He yanked it away and sputtered guttural words as he groped its every fold. He found nothing, and a stain of the same red as her dress spread over his cheeks and neck.

Their incarnadine grew deeper as Thalia twisted slowly around him, her hands on her hips, agitating her long black tresses, dipping her shoulders this way and that. She completed a circle, stopped in front of him, and poked her nose into his. "Is there any other place you want to peek into?" she asked.

A woman behind Penthesilea tittered. The white-bearded merchant's mustache trembled. One of Miminousa's Amazons covered her mouth. Cleothera gagged. A woman burst out laughing. Then another exploded. Then laughter pealed to the firmament, and a v-shaped flock of barn swallows surging above crumbled into blurs and materialized as another open triangle pointing the other way.

The din died down when the naked woman, who now clutched her robe against her, raised an arm toward the tents where the Achaeans lodged. All eyes turned that way. Chalcodon stood in front of his tent, his arms crossed, facing the merrymakers.

"Why don't you search the blonde fellow, too?" asked the woman. "He was visiting that man the same time I was."

"Is that so?" said Miminousa.

"Yes," answered the accuser.

Miminousa furrowed her brow and turned her head in the direction of the pavilion where Thalestris' daughter entertained her foreign captain. When Miminousa looked ahead of her again, the plum color had spread from her cheeks to her brow.

No one laughed any more; no one spoke.

Miminousa peered at the white-bearded merchant, whose clear gaze fixed hers. Miminousa took in the face of the naked woman, who smiled in triumph. Miminousa surveyed the crowd around her. "What about that guy?" muttered a woman. Cries of "Yeah!" percussed from all quarters, and Miminousa furrowed her brow. She spoke brief words to her Amazons and guided her horse toward Antiope's tent.

Penthesilea continued toward the city.

Tecmassa made her way toward the palace. Once, she was obliged to duck quickly into an alley while someone whom she did not want to see her passed by. She took up her step again and set foot in the large dwelling at the same moment as Marpessa stormed out. Marpessa's tresses shook like an orange banner, and her eyes were narrowed in emerald fury. Adrasta and Charope stomped behind. Adrasta's cheeks shone waxen white instead of healthy pink; Charope's huge nostrils throbbed like an angry cat's.

An attendant escorted Tecmassa to the great hall. Thalestris was seated in her tall chair, her left leg propped on a footstool. A low table that supported a grayware decanter and four wine goblets, one half empty, stood next to the throne's right arm.

Tecmassa planted herself before Thalestris, who offered her wine. The scout refused. It was not her way to say no, and Thalestris' impassive eyes scrutinized Tecmassa's. The scout gazed straight back. Thalestris signaled that she was listening.

Tecmassa spoke: "While Feodissia was in town for the games, I rode out of the territory a little way. Up the road, I came on goatherds driving their beasties to the grazing lands south of here. They say that there's been plenty of rain up there, just like there always is. So that redhead you've set loose in Antiope's corral lied when he said he came here from Troy. He couldn't have, unless he had wings. The road's still soft."

Thalestris did not move a muscle.

"The Achaeans didn't tell the truth, Thalestris. They lied. Did you ever think why?"

Thalestris did not budge.

"Don't you see? The Achaeans are up to something." Thalestris made a fist and stared at her knuckles. "You heard them yourself," she said. "They came here because the Kaska men gave them trouble."

"I didn't believe them then and sure don't believe them now."

Thalestris raised her face and pursed her lips in irony.

"Has Hippolyta put you up to this?"

"What's the matter with you, Thalestris? They lied on purpose and they're up to something bad."

"What of it?"

"What of it? What of it? Those guys are a bunch of robbers, or spies, or both."

"So what? Even if they lied to us, it's better to have them here in front of Miminousa than making trouble in the approaches to the land during the trading season."

"The Amazons know how to handle troublemakers like that."

"The Amazons are shorthanded."

"Those strangers are here for some bad reason."

"I told the riders why I intended to welcome them as my guests," said Thalestris. "They agreed. These men will stay as long as I see fit. I had good reason to do what I did."

"Good reason? Good reason?"

"Yes. Very good. You may not understand that."

Tecmassa stared at the wine decanter. "It's you who've let your guard down," she said, "because you want to breed Theseus to Antiope. Everyone knows that."

Annoyance fleeted across Thalestris' brow, and she drilled her eyes into Tecmassa's.

Undaunted, Tecmassa went on, "Listen, Thalestris, what do you reckon the Amazons will say after I tell them what Feodissia and I just learned?"

Thalestris crossed her arms. "I have heard your report," she said. "You can go."

Tecmassa did not budge. "There's one more thing you maybe haven't thought of," she said. "Because of how those fellows lied in the first place, I wouldn't count on anyone believing that Theseus is the son of a chief. He may be mounting Antiope, and she may have a filly inside her. But there's no saying it's got anything but bad blood in it."

Thalestris looked away and began to drum her fingers on the arms of her chair. "I have heard your report," she repeated. But Tecmassa was already striding toward the entrance. Here, she crossed paths with Miminousa, who was scowling more than usual. Miminousa muttered hello. Then she took on the look of a swimmer about to plunge into icy waters and stepped into Thalestris' presence.

Iphinoë ushered Tecmassa into Myrtho's apartments, and Tecmassa recounted what she and Feodissia had learned on their ride out of the territory. Myrtho immediately sent Philippis to beg the attendance of Ariona and Hippolyta. Philippis no sooner disappeared, than Miminousa was shown in. Ariona and Hippolyta quickly joined them.

Tecmassa retold what she had reported to Thalestris and ended by saying, "Thalestris doesn't care at all that those Achaeans are up to something. It doesn't make a bit of difference to her. Where's her sense flown to?"

"Those guests are nothing but trouble," said Miminousa. She then told of the missing bracelet and of whom they suspected and why. "I went to speak to Chalcodon's captain. He was in the tent and took a long time to come out, and Antiope with him.

"I told him what I supposed. He said it wasn't true and dismissed me—like he was giving orders. My riders didn't like that, and the traders kept looking from my face to Theseus' to see who was in charge. And the girl they'd blamed first, Thalia the farmer, said that if she found the bracelet in Chalcodon's tent, she'd wrap it around his prick and tighten it. Women started laughing and moved in close. Antiope finally spoke up, to tell me to go about my business."

Hippolyta raised an eyebrow.

Miminousa continued. "I told Antiope that it was my business and that the traders didn't want me to leave until I searched Chalcodon's tent. Then Thalia the farmer said she was going to see for herself. She ran to it, and a lot of women followed her, and Chalcodon took off. They found the stolen bracelet right away. The old man who leads the caravan was angry. He told me they'd be out of here by dawn, if Thalestris couldn't promise there'd be no more thieving. I went to the palace and told her everything. And for my trouble, she got mad at me."

Ariona, who had listened in silence, her sinewy arms folded across her chest, now let them fall to her sides. "They're a no-good lot," she said. "That's what my daughter Charope says. She, Adrasta, and Marpessa will have nothing more to do with them. She also told me that the fat man. . . ."

"Pirothous?" asked Miminousa.

"Yes. That, at the banquet Antiope gave her guests, he insulted Penthesilea on purpose, taunted her to get her angry, and, when she went for him, he drew a knife."

Tecmassa's hand slid down her scabbard, and Myrtho's pupils contracted to a pinpoint.

"Marpessa disarmed him," said Ariona.

"And did they also tell you," asked Hippolyta, "what her companion did and said in all of this?"

"Antiope?" replied Ariona. "When the Achaeans laughed at Penthesilea, Antiope joined them."

"You're kidding," said Tecmassa.

Ariona shook her head no.

Hippolyta smiled sourly. "This is the girl Thalestris wants to lead us when she's gone. This is the girl Thalestris wants to usurp Melanippe's place."

"Why are those men here?" asked Ariona.

"They're bandits or spies," Tecmassa answered, "and most likely the two together."

"Espionage?" came Myrtho's melodious intonation. "Perhaps that is the key to the enigma. For such tactics are customary among the Achaeans." Myrtho's eyes darted from face to face, as she told how Achaeans disguised as traders spied out the weak points of her city's defenses, sailed in by night, and plundered it.

Miminousa let out a low whistle. "I see now. Every morning, Theseus takes a long walk—mostly around the walls—and doesn't come back until the tents cast shadows on the ground. Most likely he's going over the defenses stone by stone. And the day before yesterday, one of my riders spotted him and the thief in the water under the bridge. We wondered what they were doing in the cold currents, not swimming but hanging on to the piles that hold it up."

"They must have been checking them out," said Tecmassa.

"They're spies all right," said Ariona.

"If they are spies," said Hippolyta, "then they have been here long enough."

"I'll report this to Thalestris," said Miminousa.

"I'll go with you," said Ariona. "Two are better than one in this. Maybe she'll have the sense to do something." But as Ariona pronounced these words, her fox's eyes began to twinkle and she uttered, "But then again maybe Thalestris won't."

"Won't what?" asked Miminousa.

"Have the wits to do what's called for. There's no telling what she'll say, with her head full of bad ideas and good wine."

Ariona and Miminousa took their leave.

Hippolyta watched them depart and then said, "They'll waste their words. And now's the time when words are not what's needed."

Myrtho nodded her head in connivance. Hippolyta bowed and stalked out.

Tecmassa was going to do the same, but Myrtho placed her hand, which was cold, on Tecmassa's arm. Tecmassa's look quizzed hers.

"Take Penthesilea away with you," answered Myrtho. "She is Antiope's companion and might try to defend Antiope to her own harm."

"Penthesilea won't like going," answered Tecmassa. "She's still Antiope's friend, she's still loyal, though I can't figure out why. I mean, Antiope's nothing like Leokadia. And then there is a woman Penthesilea won't like leaving."

Myrtho shut her lids at the last words, but opened them right away and said, in tones that commanded and pleaded all at once, "Tell Penthesilea that the Goddess desires her to seek exile. Keep Penthesilea away until I summon you."

The sun had descended halfway down the sky. Tecmassa guided her horse toward the gate. The Amazon's saddlebags bulged with the food and drink that Anuphey had pressed on her when she had called at the back door of the palace and asked for Penthesilea, who had sharpened her weapons and saddled her mare right away. Penthesilea now followed Tecmassa into the tunnel that led to the portal.

Without looking over her shoulder, Tecmassa asked, "Do you want to say good-bye to the trader woman?"

"No," sounded a flat reply that echoed against the stonewalls like ten sad spirits. Puzzled, Tecmassa wrinkled her brow. Then she smiled.

Tecmassa and Penthesilea crossed into the daylight. Shouts reached them from downhill, where, a short arrow's flight away, a score of crimson-robed women pressed against seven mounted riders, who composed an arc separating them from the Achaeans' tents. Men in white robes looked on. Without breaking formation, the Amazons moved slowly forward, and the crowd fanned out. Then, someone broke from it and bolted around the Amazons' flank. One of these goaded her mount sideways and herded the trespasser back. The throng shrunk into a compact mass and started advancing on the patrol.

Tecmassa and Penthesilea ran their horses to the spot and joined their comrades. Women were yelling and shaking their fists. Telkhinia stood at the forefront of the press, facing Miminousa, who sat her horse in the middle of the line of riders.

"Let me at them or I'll kill you, too!" bellowed Telkhinia. She swung a sickle around her head; it flashed near the eyes of Miminousa's beast, which jumped out of the way. Miminousa threw her trunk forward and clutched at her horse's neck. Telkhinia advanced, brandishing the curved blade. Miminousa was defenseless. Tecmassa dug her heels into her mount and wedged herself between attacker and the victim, pushing the former away.

Miminousa regained her seat. She, Penthesilea, and Tecmassa, began to circle Telkhinia, who, pivoted and slashed the air with the tool to keep them away. The throng grew quiet. Once, when Telkhinia's back was turned, Tecmassa lunged. The smith sidestepped and lifted the instrument to strike her. Tecmassa drew her labrys, but too late. Penthesilea hurled herself from the saddle and toppled Telkhinia. The tool rolled from her hand, and Tecmassa jumped down and snatched it up. She tossed it to Miminousa and hoisted herself back onto her piebald.

Penthesilea sprang to her feet; Telkhinia pushed herself up. Still facing the earth, she clenched her knuckles and pulled them back to her shoulder. Penthesilea put her guard up. Not that it would do much good against that enormous fist. Telkhinia raised her glance and, blinking like a woman just roused from sleep, stared at the riders and at the onlookers. She let her arm fall.

She glanced over her shoulder at the tents where the Achaeans stayed. "By rights I could kill them," she boomed.

"What's this? What's this?" asked Tecmassa.

"My girl. My oldest girl, Aella. She was coming down from the iron mountains with a sack full of ore. Two of them jumped her. Two of them. The skinny pale guy and the one who walks with a limp."

"Soloön and Brimus," said Penthesilea.

"Aella, fought back. She's big and strong. She kicked the limping guy in the balls and tried to run for it. He got mad and ran after her. Then she fell, and they caught up. The skinny guy held her down, and the limping one put her own knife to her throat and raped her. Then the other guy did. Then she wrestled free and ran off, bleeding and knocked black and blue. She wants to kill them. But I'll kill them for her. Their lives are mine, do you hear. Their lives are mine."

A chorus of "yeahs!" rose to the heavens.

Miminousa wrinkled her brow. "I can't let you touch them," she said. "You're right about the law. If they raped her, they're yours to do with what you want. But those men are also Thalestris' guests, and guests' heads are sacred, too. She's gotta decide."

Hoots, boos, jeers, and catcalls answered Miminousa, whose face turned the color of ripe plums.

"Whose side are you on?" someone screamed.

"Come on, girls!" bellowed Telkhinia.

The Amazons tightened their formation. "Hold on!" Tecmassa yelled. "Hold on!" Telkhinia stopped.

"Bring Antiope here fast!" said Tecmassa to Penthesilea. Penthesilea walked quickly to Antiope's tent and called her.

She came out. Penthesilea spoke, pointing to the crowd. Theseus emerged from the shelter. Penthesilea talked and gestured again. Pirothous came out of his quarters. The four strode silently toward the waiting women, crossed the line of riders, and faced them. Penthesilea mounted Tala and took her place at Tecmassa's side.

Without looking Miminousa in the eye, Antiope asked her, "Why have you summoned me?"

"You know damned well why," said Tecmassa.

Antiope glanced angrily at her.

"Where're Brimus and Soloön?" asked Miminousa.

Antiope turned to Theseus, who nodded slightly. Antiope looked at Miminousa, directly this time, and scowled. "What business do you have asking where these men are? They are Thalestris' guests."

"Where's Brimus and Soloön?" bellowed Telkhinia.

Antiope stiffened, and Theseus began to balance on the balls of his feet.

"We have not seen them since yesterday," said Theseus to Miminousa. "They were not here this morning and have not returned."

"I'm looking for them," shouted Telkhinia. "Their lives are mine, d'ya hear?" Telkhinia gestured over her shoulder, "Right, girls?"

"Right!" came the deafening answer.

Theseus waited for the shouting to die down and growled, "We are Thalestris' guests. If we are hurt, you'll answer to her sword and to our gods, who hold hospitality sacred."

"I don't care whose guests you are," raged Telkhinia. stabbing the air with her finger. "If Thalestris don't like the way you're treated she can take it an' shove it. And as for yer' people's gods, you can shove them, too."

Someone behind gasped at the blasphemy. Theseus reached for his knife but grasped only air; still, he moved on Telkhinia. Tecmassa and Penthesilea unsheathed their axes. Pirothous gripped Theseus' arm and yanked him back.

Telkhinia put her hands on her hips. "What's the matter?" she bellowed. "You guys scared?"

Deafening laughter made Theseus' face grow pale. Pirothous, who had not taken his hands off him, spoke to him in low, urgent tones. Still livid, Theseus stepped back and crossed his arms over his chest.

Pirothous came forward—not glancing at Telkhinia, although she stood two arm lengths away—and addressed Miminousa.

"Surely," Pirothous intoned, "you do not think that because we are Thalestris' guests, we will not pay for the injury you claim our men have done?"

"Payment? Are you serious?" said Telkhinia.

"Is this girl of marriageable years?" asked Pirothous.

"There's no marriage here," answered Miminousa.

"Is she of childbearing years, then?"

"That doesn't make any difference," growled Tecmassa.

Pirothous stroked his fleshy jowls. "Still," he opined, she is no longer a virgin."

A rider sniggered. Penthesilea wrinkled her brow. Tecmassa shrugged her shoulders.

"Surely we can settle on some price," said Theseus.

"Price?" boomed Telkhinia. "We have a price all right— their balls at the end of a stake!"

Pirothous paled.

"It will be as Prince Theseus says," affirmed Antiope. "If the men are guilty, we shall settle."

"Whose side are you on?" asked a woman in the crowd. A score of voices echoed her question.

"Settle?" repeated Penthesilea in disbelief. "You know that they can't pay gold or goods to make up for the attack. The rapists' lives belong to Telkhinia. That is the Goddess' law."

"You are bound to protect us," said Pirothous. "We are Thalestris' guests."

"Guests who've gone against her Goddess," said Penthesilea.

"We are Thalestris' guests," insisted Pirothous. "The gods hold guests' heads sacred."

"What kind of gods do you Achaeans worship?" answered Penthesilea, "Gods who lie and thieve and rape just like yourselves?"

"She's right!" yelled a voice.

"You tell them, girl!" shouted another.

Yeahs shattered the air.

Antiope stared grimly at Penthesilea. Loathing burst like flames across Pirothous' eyes.

"Gods just like themselves, I bet," shouted Telkhinia, clenching her huge fists and stamping forward. Women behind her started jostling. Theseus, Pirothous, and Antiope slipped behind the line of riders, who pushed back against the rioters. But Miminousa's squad was outnumbered, and their line began to break.

The thud of hooves sounded from the direction of Themiscyra's gate. Thalestris was running her white steed toward them, six riders following her in a strict double line. The newcomers hurtled through the assembled women, some of whom had to throw themselves out of the path of the speeding horses. Thalestris reined in next to Antiope, and Theseus hoisted her onto the croup of her mother's animal. Thalestris paraded her mount between the arc of riders, whose number was now almost doubled, and the crowd. Antiope was frantically whispering in her ear.

Silence fell. The chief of the riders stopped close to Miminousa and conferred with her. Dark color invaded Miminousa's neck and arms. She replied to Thalestris' brief words with longer ones.

Thalestris looked down at Telkhinia. "I will hear your complaint tomorrow," she said, in a tone that brooked no answer.

"Not if we find those guys first," answered Telkhinia.

"Not if we find them first," yelled a ragged chorus.

"You will not touch them," threatened Thalestris. "They are my guests. Disperse, all of you."

Telkhinia planted her feet and folded her arms over her chest. No one behind her moved. "Go about your business at once!" snapped Thalestris.

Not one woman budged.

"Miminousa!" called Thalestris in an angry staccato. "They will not obey me. Disperse them."

Miminousa sat still.

"Take your riders and break up this mob, I say."

"Find someone else," answered Miminousa.

"Disperse these women!" rasped Thalestris directly at Miminousa's riders.

Not a one of them stirred.

"Come on girls!" shouted Telkhinia. The crowd pushed ahead. Thalestris shouted to her women to charge. Telkhinia reached for the bridle of her mount. Thalestris struck Telkhinia in the jaw. The smith reeled and the mob hesitated. Thalestris' riders shoved against it.

The rest would be a brawl.

"Let's get out of here," yelled Tecmassa.

Penthesilea did not stir. She sat gaping at the spot from which the traders had witnessed the scene. All had disappeared except the trader woman, who stared back at her.

"Come on! Come on!" rasped Tecmassa.

Penthesilea woke up from her trance and urged Tala forward. The riders passed Pirothous and Theseus. Pirothous glanced at Penthesilea and then at where she had been staring. He laughed obscenely. Penthesilea turned to look at him. Cruel mirth hiccuped in his throat again. Theseus, who stood at his side, sneered and hooked his thumbs into the waist of his kilt so that his fingers pointed down in a rigid line.

Penthesilea's fists tightened around the reins. Tala shuddered. Tecmassa put a hand on Penthesilea's arm. "Don't let them take your temper prisoner," she said.

Penthesilea focused on Tecmassa's fingers and then swiveled her head to take in the men who had mocked her. When she turned back, her eyes sparkled with contempt. Tecmassa grinned, revealing the pearly smile from which one tooth was absent. Penthesilea laughed, wheeled Tala around, and dug her heels into her mount's sides. Tecmassa did the same. The two women ran their horses away from Themiscyra.

Chapter 11

Miminousa and her followers watched while Thalestris' six riders pushed into the crowd and sent women about their business. Cleothera shook her fists at Thalestris, and Thersandra put her hands on her hips and spat on the ground at Theseus' feet. He pretended not to notice, as did Thalestris, who said to him, "Produce Brimus and Soloön by tomorrow, so I can judge the matter. And don't try to escape before that. Swear on the Goddess and on your god that you'll do as I say."

"I swear," answered Theseus.

"All right, then. Go back to your tents."

The men obeyed.

"You're making a big mistake, Thalestris," said Miminousa, watching them go. "You should post guards around the Achaeans' camp and put a price on the rapists' heads. There's no trusting any of them, even if they did take an oath."

"Silence!" barked Thalestris. She steered her horse toward Themiscyra. Antiope still sat behind her.

Telkhinia lay on the ground. She rolled her head and groaned. She rubbed her jaw where Thalestris had punched her. She blinked her eyes and raised herself to her knees. Miminousa dismounted and put her gourd of beer in front of Telkhinia's face. Telkhinia widened her eyes, snatched up the canteen, and sucked down its contents without taking a breath. She focused on her surroundings—on Miminousa, on her riders, on the Achaeans' tents, on the city wall. She got to her feet, ran her hand over her chin, and growled out a lengthy roster of curse words.

She concluded, "I am not going back. I promise, I am not going back. I am not makin' another blade or axe for Thalestris, no ma'am. Tell my girls to let the fire in my forge die out. Tell my Aella to come and find me at the stopping place uphill. She knows where. You can also say to her to tell the women of the tool that I've gone into hiding. There's some who'll join me, especially after today."

Miminousa nodded at one of her riders, who turned her horse and ran it toward the city.

Telkhinia cocked her head at Miminousa, "You're in trouble, too," she said. "There's no telling what Thalestris will do to you if you stick around. So, you'd better come along."

"She's right," said one Amazon. The others agreed.

Miminousa followed Telkhinia to a hut at the edge of the forest near the base of the iron hills. The sun had set when the women turned in for the night; but the moon, which was just past full, cast brilliant silver light on the meadow and the wood. The sleepers bolted awake when Miminousa's horse snorted and pawed the ground. They stepped outside. In moonlight almost as bright as day, not more than an arrow's flight, a woman on horseback and five men on foot were heading fast for the forest. It could only be Antiope and the Achaeans.

"Let's get those criminals!" said Telkhinia, picking up a timber that lay near the door. The two women ran for the fugitives who, seeing that they were being pursued, lengthened their strides, and disappeared into the shadows.

Miminousa grabbed Telkhinia's arm and stopped her. "They're traveling too fast," she said. "And two against six aren't very good odds when we can't surprise them."

"Damn!" said Telkhinia, heaving her weapon against the earth. "They'll get clean away?"

"No, they won't. There's only one way out of the land without climbing those hills—the track that cuts from the pasture land to the northeast trail and from there to the road to Troy. Antiope knows that, and she's leading them. But we know that, too. I'll ride in and tell Thalestris."

"Thalestris? Are you kidding? She would have helped them. Myrtho's better. She's got friends who'll ride out once they hear."

Miminousa ran her horse back to Themiscyra. When she neared the tents, the Goddess's crown of stars was shining above the southern hills: it was past midnight. Miminousa thumped at the gate. The gatekeeper opened it right away, as if she had been waiting up. A strange, bitter smile on her lips, she let Miminousa pass. Miminousa wondered, was she about to ride into a trap?

As soon as she was out of hearing, she dismounted, hitched her horse, and headed on foot for the holy precinct by the most roundabout way through the sleeping city she could think of. She was inching along a street near the marketplace, when steps

sounded behind her. Shod feet. They could only be those of a
rider or a votary. Miminousa froze. The steps stopped. She
moved. The steps resumed. She pivoted and saw someone in an
Amazon cloak. The stranger laughed and threw off her hood. A
mop of light hair cascaded down around her shoulders. It was
Marpessa.

"What are you doing walking around past midnight?" asked
Miminousa.

"And yourself?"

Miminousa told her.

"Escaped? I'll go with you to Myrtho's, then."

The women reached the marketplace. They intended to
spirit around its borders until they reached the temple wall,
then climb it. But the sanctuary gate was open, and, when they
approached the palace door, Iphinoë pulled it wide, bowed, and
immediately showed them to Myrtho's apartments. It looked as
if she had been waiting for them.

The torches were burning bright. Myrtho was seated in her
big chair. Ariona and Charope faced her. She noticed the newcomers and raised an eyebrow. Ariona and Charope turned and
gawked.

"I beg your pardon for bursting in like this," said Miminousa,
"but I've got news." She reported what she'd seen: Antiope and
the Achaeans running away, and their only possible destination.

Myrtho listened without changing her expression and at the
end of Mimousa's recital said, "We already knew that Antiope
and the Achaeans had taken flight. Thanks to you, we now
know in which direction they are traveling. As for your supposi-
tion that they march toward Troy, it is a sound one: for in that
city the Achaeans can find passage back to their own land."

"Or allies to raise an army and come back," said Ariona.

"But . . . but . . . how did you find out?" said Miminousa.

"My rider Klymene," said Ariona. . . .

"The small, reckless one on that roan stallion who makes so
much trouble?" asked Miminousa.

"The very one," said Ariona. "She brought word of it a little while ago. She'd ridden in to tell Thalestris that they'd
spotted another Hittite soldier floating downriver. That's the
second corpse since the new moon. She was running her horse
past the Achaean tents when something struck her as funny.
The fires in front of them were dead. Not a coal was glowing.
And one of the tent flaps waved in the breeze: someone had neglected to peg it down. She circled a couple of times and called

out for Antiope and others. No one answered. So, Klymene rode into each tent. Everyone had disappeared—all the Achaeans and all the Amazons.

"She ran to the palace, roused Thalestris, and made her report. Then she brought me the news. I got my daughter Charope out of bed (she'd given up sleeping with that Achaean), and we carried the news to Myrtho, who. . . ."

Iphinoë rushed in cutting short Ariona's words, and announcing Hippolyta, who tore in with Adrasta. "The Achaeans have spirited out of the city in the dead of night," proclaimed Hippolyta.

"We know," said Ariona.

"What?"

"And you, how did you find out?"

Hippolyta said nothing, but Adrasta volunteered, "A few of Hippolyta's riders called at the tents a little while ago. We had business there—but found no one."

Adrasta's listeners looked at each other knowingly.

"Even their fire was cold," said Adrasta.

"Antiope's gone off with them, too," said Miminousa, explaining what she and Telkhinia had seen earlier that night. Hippolyta crossed her arms and turned the news around in her head. She broke into a supercilious smile.

"Obviously you're pleased that Antiope's out of the way," said Ariona. "She's left the field to Melanippe. But the trouble is that Antiope could lead her newfound friends back to Themiscyra with reinforcements. And they've been spying. Goddess only knows what they've got planned for us."

"What gives you the liberty to. . . ."

Hippolyta could not finish her question, because Thalestris rushed in like a summer storm, her face haggard from too little sleep and too much wine. She stopped short when she saw who was taking counsel with Myrtho. She crossed her arms over her chest and narrowed her eyes.

"We know what has brought you here," said Myrtho. "We were discussing the news ourselves. Ariona brought it to me, and Miminousa. Hippolyta was keeping vigil in the sanctuary, and I saw fit to summon her."

Thalestris smiled without showing her teeth.

"Antiope, too," said Myrtho, "has taken flight along with the Achaeans. They will seek refuge in Troy."

Thalestris took a step backward. "That cannot be true!" she said.

"It is," said Miminousa, repeating her story for the fourth time.

"Are you sure? Then they have taken Antiope with them against her will. You say she was leading them, but you saw them at night and at a distance. You must be mistaken."

"There can't be any mistake," said Miminousa. "Antiope is showing them the way, how else would they know about the shortcut? The moon is just past full, and they passed not an arrow's shot away. They're getting out while the getting is good."

"Didn't Antiope know they were spying?" said Ariona.

"I never told her of this unproven suspicion," said Thalestris.

Hippolyta raised her nose in the air and smirked. "This girl whom you would have as high judge when you're gone, has contrived to let her paramour, the would-be prince, and his unsavory followers evade their rightful punishment."

Thalestris turned away from her.

"The Achaeans," said Ariona to Thalestris, "have had a half moon's time to reconnoiter our terrain and defenses. They'll come back."

Thalestris faced Myrtho.

"The Achaeans," said Myrtho, "are pirates on the land and on the sea. By just such a subterfuge—by spying and returning later—they raided and conquered the city where I was born. If the Amazons do not prevent them from reaching Troy, they will return to Themiscyra as well."

"We cannot let them get away from here," said Hippolyta. "They know too much about this place, and there are many secrets they might sell or use. We've got to ambush them and make sure none escapes."

Dismayed, Thalestris looked from one woman to the next like a cornered animal. "And Antiope? she asked. "What if she is killed or wounded?"

"If Antiope's caught in the middle of an ambush," answered Hippolyta, "few will grieve for her. For is she not a traitor?"

"That's not proven!" said Thalestris.

"You must protect the Goddess's city from the Achaeans," said Myrtho.

"If you do not," said Hippolyta, "your name will disgrace that of Marpasia. If you do not, the long ages will repeat that the chief who lost the city was the very sister of Naunamé the Just, whose blood and lineage she betrayed."

The color fled from Thalestris' lips. Hippolyta shook her head righteously. Thalestris folded her arms in front of her chest.

"Have you quite finished?" said Myrtho.

Thalestris blinked her eyes again and again.

Silence fell.

Ariona broke it after a while. "We've got to act now," she said. "We've got to start right away. If we don't, they'll get too far for us to catch them easily. If we don't, they'll get to their stash of weapons before we find them. Then it'll be harder to make sure no one escapes."

"Weapons?" said Thalestris.

"Of course, woman," said Ariona. "Of course."

"Pshaw!" said Hippolyta, triumphantly. "Did I not tell you that. . ."

Ariona interrupted, "Some other time, will you? Listen, Thalestris, we need at least a dozen Amazons to be sure that the job is done properly."

"Properly?" Thalestris asked.

"You cannot be allowed to let those men escape," said Hippolyta, "in your effort to protect Antiope from harm."

"I'll take four of my riders," said Ariona, "Thalestris, you take four, and Hippolyta, you take four. That will leave enough in the city."

"I'm the chief of the riders!" said Thalestris. "I'll decide who goes where."

Ariona spread her hands out and raised them to the ceiling. Myrtho folded hers in her lap and closed her eyes. Hippolyta put hers on her hips and stuck her chin out like someone who was about to trade nasty words with her neighbor.

Miminousa, Marpessa, Adrasta, and Charope, who had observed the conversation in silence, looked at each other impatiently. The three nobles' haggling would take time, even if they ended up by deciding on the action that Ariona had suggested in the first place. And then they'd need still more to rouse their women and get them to horse. But Miminousa and the young Amazons were ready to ride.

"There's no time to waste on this," muttered Miminousa under her breath. She did an about-face and left the room. Thalestris, Hippolyta, and Ariona did not notice her depart. Nor did they see Marpessa, Adrasta, and Charope sneak out on her heels. Only Myrtho saw the woman leave, but she gave no sign that she had.

They rode out hours before the others.

That night Penthesilea and Tecmassa bivouacked in a stand of white poplar not far from the entrance of the passes. The moon splashed silver triangles on the ground, triangles that danced and shivered with the swaying of the treetops in the night airs. Tecmassa breached the gourd of beer that she had carried with her, raised it to her lips, and sucked down a draft. She handed the container to Penthesilea, who only wet her tongue. Tecmassa ran her forearm over her mouth, and from out of her saddlebag, fished barley cakes that Anuphey had sent along. Tecmassa gave Penthesilea her share and bit into her own, clucking her thanks to the Goddess and to Anuphey, as she chewed with the painstaking deliberation that food always inspired in her. But as carefully as Tecmassa ingested her meal, Penthesilea swallowed hers even more slowly, keeping her eyes down, forcing herself to take food because her body must be hungry. Once, she looked up at Tecmassa, whose face the flames made into polished leather and whose eyes they transmuted into amber circles from the dark centers of which pinpoints of light drilled into Penthesilea's glance. Penthesilea turned away.

She fell into a cold sleep that fatigued more than rested her. She started awake when a voice in the branches trilled a string of nervous notes to announce the end of darkness. The uneasy somnolence still dragged at her as she saddled up, swung onto Tala's back, and started down the path beside Tecmassa.

As the riders moved forward, the pink fingers of dawn reached up through the night's indigo waters. They turned luminous blue and dissolved the moon into a transparent reminder of her nighttime rule over heaven and earth. Soon the dusk's seas all but engulfed her, and her tilted face surveyed the land from under the misty ripples of a new morning.

Her quiet melancholy made Penthesilea's own more bitter. Antiope had made fun of her, laughed at her, wounded her. Abba-Bashti had turned away from her, injured her, grieved her. The sadness was enough to split Penthesilea's chest apart, and. . . .

Tala lurched. Penthesilea slid sideways, but caught herself in time and did not fall. Her cheeks began to burn. She had not seen a rock square in front of her pony. How could she have not? Even little girls did not make that mistake. She alighted from her mount, inspected her ankles and hooves, which were unhurt, and swung herself into the saddle again.

Penthesilea came abreast of Tecmassa, who had stopped. Tecmassa now urged her horse into motion, and the two Amazons rode side by side, their knees sometimes touching. Penthesilea fixed her eyes ahead and kept silent. At length she heard Tecmassa say, "Look at me, girl." Penthesilea forced herself to focus on her friend's face. Tecmassa was frowning. "You're on patrol," she growled. "You can't see ahead of you for your day-dreaming. You're blind eyes and a dead hand to the woman riding with you, or worse than that, you're one more thing to worry about. That's bad. Forget about that trader woman. She'll be long gone by the time you're back in the city."

Penthesilea opened her mouth to speak but Tecmassa waved her hand. "Forget about Antiope, too. What's sworn before the Goddess can be unsworn if the other doesn't keep her oath."

"But I owe Antiope my life," protested Penthesilea. Tecmassa scowled but nodded in agreement.

Feodissia met Penthesilea and Tecmassa after the sun had reached its zenith. They headed for a camp the patrolling Amazons maintained three hours from the border. While they rode, Tecmassa told Feodissia about the rape of Telkhinia's daughter, how Antiope and Thalestris had sided with the Achaeans, and the furious scene that followed.

"There's a lot of Amazons," said Tecmassa, "even women who ride for her, who've had their fill of Thalestris. It's not only that she gets falling down drunk and that Celano's a swindler. She's put us in danger, inviting those Achaeans to stay. Everybody knows that she's done it for Antiope, so she can get a baby girl and be our chief one day, instead of Melanippe. And those guests of hers have been spying on us right under our noses."

"Spying?" asked Penthesilea and Feodissia at the same time.

"Yes."

When the shadows had grown long, the riders came to the cross-roads of the northeast trail and a hunter's track that led there from the foot of the iron hills. The Amazons stopped as one woman. Pieces of earth darker than the rest indented the ground where people had trodden, and a horse's hooves, too, had up-turned pebbles and soil. The women traded puzzled glances. Tecmassa pointed down the high road. Penthesilea and

Feodissia urged their ponies in that direction. Penthesilea
halted where the paths joined, and she dismounted. Feodissia
rode on. Penthesilea examined the meeting of the trails. Five
men in sandals and one horse with a rider had stepped onto the
larger way from the smaller one. Five men? There could be no
doubt who that was: There were five Achaeans. The horse and
rider could be only Antiope on her stallion. Penthesilea had
cupped her hands around her mouth to call out, when the sound
of small wings fluttering and a chorus of "Quek! Quek! Quek!"
reached her from down the road.

"Ho! Ho!" shouted Feodissia. Penthesilea hastened toward her friend, who was kneeling over a string of horse droppings. "It's had time to cool," said Feodissia. "And the birds
haven't gotten much of it yet. Yup. *They* passed here not too
long ago." There was no need to ask who Feodissia was referring
to.

"That means they left Themiscyra in the dark of night and
traveled since then," said Feodissia.

Tecmassa joined them. The other riders did not have to tell
her, either, who had crossed the path on the way out of the
land. Feodissia said, "In the middle of afternoon. Not before."
She stroked her lantern jaw. "What do you suppose Antiope was
doing with them?" she asked.

"No idea, girl. No idea," answered Tecmassa, before looking
at the western sky. The sun had just set. "No use riding after
them," she said. "They've been going all night and day so
they've got to stop soon. And so will we. We'll rest and feed the
horses and ourselves while we've got a chance to. The night
will fall before we come near them, and by that time they'll
have hidden and posted a guard. We'll get them tomorrow.
They're on foot and we're on horse, so we'll catch up soon enough.
Maybe we'll even be able to surprise them."

"Why go after them at all?" asked Feodissia. "Not many
women will care that Antiope's left."

A protest formed and dissolved in Penthesilea's throat.

"I know," answered Tecmassa. "By all rights she's free to
leave. But Thalestris would want our blood if we let Antiope go
without a fight. And even if we let her go—and a lot of women
would say good riddance to her—we'd be crazy to let the
Achaeans get away." A thought crossed Tecmassa's face. "Of
course," she said, "by the time we catch up with them, they'll
have left our territory and gotten their hands on their weapons
again."

No one spoke after that, and the Amazons rode back to where they intended to spend the night. They settled in and ate their evening meal. Then they began to sharpen their knives and axes. They were not long at it, when a faint staccato cut into the whirring of flint on iron. Dull thuds reached the women from the trail below. Three—no four—horses were running toward them from the direction of Themiscyra. Penthesilea hoisted herself into a tree. The brilliant moon cast bright light on the trail. Four riders, whose silver forms were like those of spirits from the other world, ran their horses in single file: a squat silhouette with thick shoulders; a pale outline with a banner of hair streaming behind; a small body, who seemed welded to her mount; and a stocky profile whose full frame the silver waters of the night transmuted into a weightless doll floating on a toy horse.

"Hello!" shouted Penthesilea.

Miminousa, Marpessa, Charope, and Adrasta slowed their ponies and guided them to the camp. Penthesilea and Feodissia took care of the newcomers' horses. Tecmassa threw more wood on the fire and cooked more cakes.

While the newly arrived women ate and drank, Tecmassa told them how she and her friends had discovered the tracks of the escaping Achaeans and how they intended going after them.

"That's what we're doing, too," said Miminousa, reporting what had happened. "We'll ride with you. And a bigger party's coming."

Tecmassa stirred the fire. "Ambushing them without hurting Antiope will be hard," she muttered.

No one spoke after that. All were lost in their thoughts, until Marpessa said, "Have you brave girls ever thought of this: what if they get away despite our vigilance and hold Antiope for ransom?"

"That could happen, too," said Miminousa.

"Only the Goddess knows the future," said Tecmassa.

The women lay down to sleep under a serene sky.

At that moment, Antiope and the Achaeans were settling down away from the road. They had trekked over the northeast trail, interrupting their flight only to retrieve the bones of the man whom Theseus and his friends had cremated weeks before, and arrived within half a day's march of the hill that overlooked the river Lycus. This waterway, traversed by a wooden bridge, marked the limit of the Amazon territory. Once they crossed the span, they would have only a short hike to the Trojan road.

Antiope saw to her horse and joined the men, who had dropped to the ground and were sharing bread in boneweary silence. Once they had swallowed their rations, they stretched out to sleep under the calm skies. Theseus stood up to keep the first watch. He turned away without sparing a glance for Antiope, but Antiope, in her weariness, did not notice.

The Achaeans were on the move again at first light, and the rising sun saw them at the mouth of the cave in which they had hidden their arms one month before. The men filed inside. When they emerged, they were fully equipped. Each one's armor and weapons had transformed him from a target of flesh into a threat of death. A dark leather helmet covered every soldier's head. From the top of the headpiece, two horns pointed forward and a horsetail streamed behind. The protective gear's elongated cheekpieces drew each man's face out into a pitiless triangle, and the brow of the helmet, which tapered and descended to the top of his nose, cast such darkness over his eyes that they were fused into pits without soul. Breastplates, also of deeply tanned hide but studded with bronze plaques, circular shields that screened a fighter from shoulder to knee, and tough leather greaves, gave little place for an arrow or blade to penetrate. All the men except Theseus carried thrusting spears taller than they were; the weapons' shafts ended in deadly, metal polyhedrons. Pirothous and Chalcodon were also armed with slings that hung from their waistbands and Brimus and Soloön with bows and quivers that were slung across their backs. The arcs were shorter than the Amazons', and the arrows were tipped with obsidian. As for the soldiers' chief, he bore a long sword in a hilt suspended from a strap around his left shoulder.

Antiope sized up the Achaeans. The bolts they loosed would not fly as far or cut as deep as Amazon arrows. Nor would the stones the men hurled cover as great a stretch without losing speed. But the bronze and leather that guarded them made them hard to strike without pulling within range of their missiles or spears. Still, mounted archers could always get the better of foot soldiers, if they moved correctly—if they surprised and harassed them.

Theseus, who had been running a professional eye over his men, strode toward Antiope. With every step he took, the horns on his helmet stabbed the air and his sword beat against his side. In his right hand he balanced a length of knotted cord, which swayed back and forth as he progressed. Antiope stood up.

"I want your weapons," rasped Theseus; scorn poisoned his tone. "Undo your belt and quiver."

She sought his eyes in disbelief but saw only fathomless sockets. She opened her mouth to protest. Theseus swung the rope. It slashed into her biceps. The breath fled from her. She lost her balance but caught herself in time and crouched to spring on Theseus, who drew his sword, pointed it at her and sneered. She dropped her arms to her side. Her flesh stung; her chest pounded.

"You are my prisoner," said Theseus in a voice that threatened violence. "Your horse and weapons are also my prize. From now on, you will go on foot like everyone else."

"And spread your legs for everyone else," said Brimus, jabbing his hand between her buttocks to grab her lips. He had come up behind her to take her weapons and mount.

"No," said Theseus, not taking his eyes off the Amazon. "I want to be sure that everybody knows any baby in her belly is mine. Even if I sell her, the brat stays with me. I've got plans for it."

Soloön snickered.

Trembling with pain and rage, Antiope said, "Do you think the Amazons will let you escape?"

"We'll escape all right," said Theseus, "because you're going to lead us to safety. You'll do it because you have no choice. Even if you weren't my slave, you'd have no choice. You can't go back to Themiscyra. You've helped us run away. You've betrayed your Amazons. So you'll lead us to the seashore north of here. It can't be more than a day's march away. From there we'll get to the port. They're waiting for us there."

Antiope gaped in disbelief. "Amisos?"

Theseus' eyes twinkled. "That's what I said, bitch."

Theseus wanted to trick his pursuers. He had asked Antiope to guide the Achaeans to the river Lycus, so that the Amazons would read his tracks and think that he had taken the way to Troy. But now he was going to double back over the northeast trail and head for the cold sea, while the riders hurried along the Trojan road, in the wrong direction. And once he got through one of the gorges that led to the littoral, he would be out of danger, even if the Amazons finally saw through his ruse and gave him chase. They would hesitate to trespass onto the coastal plain: It belonged to their enemy, to Amisos, whose ruler,

Otreus, would send out armed men right away and use a border incident as a pretext for a strike inside their territory. Theseus laughed at Antiope's dismay.

"In Amisos there's a ship's captain waiting to take us to Troy. If we get there, you'll have your life as your reward. After all, I got a baby on you, and I want to see it live."

"Do you imagine the riders will stop before they've hunted you down?" said Antiope.

Theseus lifted his sword until its point pressed into her left breast. "If the Amazons catch up with us, you'll die before I do. Let's start."

The fugitives crossed the trail again without being discovered and began their march through the rough hinterland toward the sea.

Miles away, the party with which Penthesilea rode reached the hill overlooking the river Lycus and the Trojan road. The women had ridden single-mindedly since before sunrise, passing over the section of the northeast trail that the Achaeans and their prisoner would cross one hour later. The Amazons followed a serpentine path up the hill and halted their mounts on a sandy flat that faced southwest. An arrow's shot below, at the foot of the slope, a glimmering ribbon of water coursed from left to right. A dirt track snaked around the base from the opposite quarter, followed the river's edge for a few hundred feet to a narrow wooden bridge above shallows, and crossed over them. Then the way wound back in the direction it had just taken, curved west around a tiny hill, and went straight through the dale that ended a half mile farther on at the beginning of a chain of peaks that stretched toward the sunset. The way to Troy twisted through these elevations. The runaways would have had enough time to step onto it but not to have traveled far.

"Look!" exclaimed Charope. She raised her arm and indicated a scattering of dark blotches that flecked the road. Was someone moving along the route? And in which direction? If the specks were the fugitives, it wouldn't be long before they caught sight of their pursuers, if they hadn't already, and melted into the hills. If they were traders and their animals—it was the season for merchants to begin showing up from the west—they would move toward the Amazons. The women urged their mounts down the path to the bridge, traversed it, and began to rush toward the minute blurs, which grew bigger and more distinct, until the riders made out a merchant caravan.

Feodissia groaned in disappointment.

"Still,"said Tecmassa, "they may have seen the band of them."

The riders reined up.

Four men led ten donkeys. The travelers came from Troy. No, they had not seen any group of the description the riders were looking for; they had not set eyes on a horse since they left the plains near the city they came from. But a larger caravan, sent by King Laomedon, would probably be along in a few days. The women could ask them if they'd seen anything. Marpessa mumbled, "It would have been too fine a thing to pray to the Goddess for."

"Just because these traders haven't set eyes on the runaways," said Tecmassa, "doesn't prove they aren't there. They could have spotted the pack train and taken cover."

The Amazons continued down the Trojan road, among heights thickly covered by low-lying mountain pine, pendulous-fingered spruces, and sky-reaching fir. This rough blanket of verdance rippled with the breathing life inside the slopes and the moving airs around them. Slate-colored streaks, where the rocks had tried to flee toward their birthplace, gouged vertical scars on the flanks of many steeps. Troughs of deep shadow furrowed up and down their sides. Small streams, first hinted at by thin, dark lines among the treetops, then exploding into blinding rainbows, rushed down and shimmered alongside the road, sometimes crossing it to hurry to the sea. The smell of pine sap and of moist forest turned the riders' heads. The branches and foliage hissed and rattled with the uneven rhythm of the winds, which sang and danced through the dales and ricocheted among the elevations.

The Amazons progressed slowly through this splendid country, for each time that a break in the cover signaled a path up the mountainside, Tecmassa dispatched one of the younger riders to follow the trail on foot and look for signs of the runaways. But there was none, and after two hours' searching, disappointment weighed the riders down, although they did not speak a word of it to one another.

From the slope on the right, perhaps halfway to the top, came a flat clap, wood hitting wood. The Amazons stopped as one woman. Was that a goat's rattle? A short bleat confirmed that it was. Tecmassa nodded to Feodissia, who dismounted and handed the reins of her horse to Charope. Feodissia's large feet pushed her uphill.

Feodissia scrambled down a while later. Her face wore a sour look. She ran her tongue along the inside of her cheek, and her long fingers stroked her jaw. "Nothing and nobody," she intoned, as if she were announcing a death. "Those goatherds have seen nothing and nobody. And they've been all around here since the day before yesterday. They only picked up camp and began to move their flock around midday. Lucky for us, we heard the stragglers. Or unlucky, maybe, because if the goatherds haven't seen them, then they haven't come through."

"They say they've been around here since the day before yesterday?" asked Tecmassa.

"Yes. Day before yesterday."

The riders traded glum looks: two days before, the Achaeans had not yet sneaked out of Themiscyra.

Penthesilea pressed her lips together and stared at her hands. Thoughts surged into her head. Heat flooded her cheeks. When at last she looked up, she said, "They're not going to come this way. They're not going to chance the Trojan road. Theseus didn't intend to pass here in the first place."

"What's this? What's this?" asked Tecmassa.

"If the fugitives haven't yet filtered into these parts, either they're still somewhere between the Lycus and Themiscyra, lying low, waiting for the Amazons to give up looking for them, or they've set out for somewhere else. Now they haven't done the first. They're not hiding somewhere between here and our city. Theseus knows better than to take a chance like that. He knows we'll search every inch of our territory and catch them."

"Then where did he intend to go?" asked Charope.

"He won't chance heading south to the Hittite lands, either," said Penthesilea. "That's also too risky for him: to get there, he'd have to make a long detour around our valley, and someone would catch sight of him. That leaves the direction of the rising sun or the sea."

"The direction of the rising sun?" asked Tecmassa in disbelief. "The Kaska lands? They're not going to do that. He knows they'll get cut down the first night."

"So he can be headed only for the sea north of Themiscyra," said Penthesilea. "That's the single safe place for him. Once he crosses the ridge before the sea, he'll be in territory belonging to the chief at Amisos. And if we ride into there, we chance running into soldiers who'd just as soon cut us down as see us smile.

The Achaeans must have doubled back over the road right before, or right after, we rode that way. If they got across safely, they'll cover a lot of ground. By sunset, maybe even before, they'll reach one of the defiles that leads to the lowland by the cold sea."

"Aren't there four of those passes?" asked Tecmassa.

"Yup," intoned Feodissia, "and each one's a good hour's ride from the next."

"Let's hope Thalestris and the others have reached the river by now," said Miminousa, "so we can cover every one of them."

"We've wasted half a day," said Charope.

"And we won't waste any more time," said Penthesilea.

The six Amazons hastened back to the bridge; Thalestris and her reinforcements had just crossed it.

"The Achaeans are not going that way," said Penthesilea, reining up next to her. "They're making for the cold sea, for Amisos."

"How do you know?" asked the chief of the riders.

Penthesilea explained and went on, "We'll have to split into four groups to cover the gorges. The earlier we catch them the better."

Thalestris opened her mouth to scold the young rider for presuming to give orders. Ariona interrupted, "The woman's right. That's the only tactic that'll work. Don't waste our time quibbling, will you."

Annoyed, Thalestris turned to unleash her displeasure on Ariona, but Hippolyta intervened. "That is what we ought to do. But I am also of a mind to send a party back along the Trojan road on the slim chance they've given us the slip."

"Very well," replied Thalestris. "You take some women and do that."

Hippolyta pulled up her head in indignation.

Penthesilea, Feodissia, and Miminousa hurried their mounts toward the easternmost defile. They halted at midday, to eat and drink and give their horses rest.

At midday, too, the Achaeans found shade and halted to ingest the last of the bread that they carried with them. In the distance, a strip of gray whose contours shimmered in the humid airs marked the ridge running east to west that separated them from the coastal plain. Theseus wanted to reconnoiter the terrain before moving on. He and Brimus took off in one direction, and Pirothous and Chalcodon another. Antiope, her hands tied behind her, was left to Soloön, who had volunteered to stand guard over her and her horse.

Antiope was sitting on the ground under a tree. Soloön removed his bow and quiver and placed himself, cross-legged, a few feet in front of Antiope. He stared at her at the same time as he seemed not to see her. A crazed fire burned in his eyes. Antiope lowered hers.

"Yes, look at the ground," whispered Soloön. "Humble yourself. I'm in charge now. If Theseus hadn't forbidden it, I'd jig you till you bled. Now you're Theseus' prisoner, his slave. You don't tell us what to do anymore. Theseus will give the orders and you'll obey. You'll do what he wants when he wants, and if you don't, he'll beat you. And when he's tired of you, he'll sell you, or give you away as a gift. And if you complain, he'll beat you harder. You got a taste of whipping earlier." Antiope's back contracted, and Soloön gurgled in amusement. "Theseus told us that he promised to marry you, that he promised to take you to Athens and told you that that one day you'd be Queen there."

A soft bark exploded through Soloön's nose. "Theseus only said that so you'd lead us out of Themiscyra before the women got their hands on me and Brimus. Take you back to Athens? Theseus can't go back himself. And even if he could, he's no more the prince of Attica than I'm Poseidon. He's the son of a soldier and a slave. A slave just like yourself. Theseus joined Aegeus' palace guard when his father cast him out after a row they had. Then, to get even, he bedded his father's favorite woman slave, who wanted some of this."

Soloön inched nearer Antiope, squeezed her nose between the thumb and fingers of one hand, and yanked her face up. He lifted his kilt with the other hand and pulled his penis out of his breach cloth. She closed her eyes. He snickered.

"Finally Theseus' father found them while he was slamming this into the slave girl. Theseus killed his old man right there and took it on the lam with Pirothous, who was a guard, too, and who got caught shaking down some farmers. They can't ever go back. Theseus isn't even his real name. He met me and the others on the road here and there."

Antiope shuddered. Theseus had lied when he said the men were his childhood friends—lied when he said he was a prince—lied. . . .

"But even if Theseus could marry you, do you think he'd take you? Your Amazon friends could never give you a dowry that weighed as much as the three casks of gold powder we found in Themiscyra."

Antiope opened her eyes and stared at Soloön in disbelief.

"Yes. Don't pretend you don't know about them. We found where they were hidden while we were going over Themiscyra's defenses. That's why we came to your little fort in the first place—to see if there was treasure worth raiding and, if there was, to go over every stone and find the weak points so we could come back. You never saw because you were busy with this. This is all you saw." Soloön pressed her nose with such violence that she dared not shut her lids. He started to caress his snake, which had grown red and thick. His nostrils flared, as if he had sipped delicious wine.

"We spotted the cave when we were looking around where Telkhinia makes iron from pebbles. The night of your banquet, Theseus ordered us to go back and have a look inside. The other brood mares had left, and Theseus knew how to keep you interested so you wouldn't notice we were gone."

Antiope raised her eyes and stared at Soloön with hatred. Another rapturous gurgle erupted from his chest. He ringed his finger and thumb around his prick and jerked them up and down. "We went off to have a closer look. We took torches. We got to the cave. We followed the shaft to a little room. We figured we were under some building, maybe the temple. We were thirsty. We had run out of the wine we took along. There were three barrels in the room. Chalcodon opened a spigot and put his cup under it. What came out wasn't wine, it was gold powder! There was gold powder in the other two casks, too. More gold than any king has ever had. We're gonna go back to take it. We know how to get in before you hags sound the alarm! And when we're finished splitting up the treasure, we'll divide up the women and take the ones we want, not just the ones you bitches say we can—slaves for our beds just like you."

Soloön snorted with delight, crept closer to Antiope, and grabbed her by the hair. She did not move. He yanked her forward. She had no way of counterbalancing and fell toward him. Pebbles seared her cheek. He laughed and rasped, "On your knees, slave girl." She remained motionless, her face against the ground. He pulled her tresses up until she was raised on her knees. Her head was now above his groin. "Lower your face, slave girl, bend your head, make yourself humble." He tried to shove her mouth toward his erect flesh; she stiffened. "Bend your head I say! Lower your face!" He jerked her locks again and again. Her nose bled. Her head was splitting. Still, she did not yield. He unsheathed his dagger with his free hand and lay the blade's edge across her cheek. "You know what to do, slave girl. Theseus said he trained you well." Soloön pressed the edge of the blade tighter against her skin. Antiope opened her lips and surrounded his flesh. He gasped.

"It was all for this," he hissed. "It was all because Theseus rammed this into you. Bedded you so you'd moan with pleasure. Plowed you so you wouldn't see us leave. Shagged you so you'd lead us out." Soloön moaned. "So we can raise an army. So we can go back. To the gold. Now that we know. I'll get my share. I'll buy you for my bed." Soloön gasped convulsively. "Slave girl, bend your head. Oh. Bend your head. Oh! Oh!" Soloön squealed and sprawled backward. Antiope jabbed her head away and spat.

He edged farther from her and lay with his eyes closed, grinning, breathing throatily, scratching his member, which was shrunken and limp. She curled her lips and sneered at his prostrate form; she knew what she would do to him if she ever took him alive. But the image dissolved when she tried to move her hands and felt the thongs around her wrists. She raised her head to the sky and begged for help. Blue silence answered her. Then her gaze traveled south, in the direction of Themiscyra. Could she return there anymore? She moved her eyes west, toward Troy, where she did not want to go.

Feodissia, Miminousa, and Penthesilea hastened past hills and valleys fragrant with bursting flowers and grasses until, when the shadows began to lengthen, the riders reached the easternmost cleft through the ridge. At the defile's lowest place, swift water fled seaward over shining rocks. A strip of pebbled ground wide enough for two persons to walk over side by side followed the left bank of the stream and ended where it became shallow and spread out for a few yards. The path began again on the opposite side.

The Amazons traded knowing glances after they had laid their eyes on the ford. The fugitives would have to cross it to get any farther. To do so, they would have to surrender their attention to it and turn their backs on one of the hillsides. The riders would ambush them at the crossing. "We'll even up the odds before we ride down on them," said Penthesilea, "confuse them about where we're coming from and how many we are." The others murmured assent. Penthesilea pointed to the places at which the Amazons were to station themselves. They would shoot two arrows each, Penthesilea aiming for the man in the lead, Feodissia for the one nearest the horse, and Miminousa for the man guarding the rear. Then the women would charge.

Penthesilea walked Tala twenty paces up the east-facing slope and hid behind heavy hedges. Feodissia, who had ridden with Penthesilea, dismounted, gave her the reins of her horse, and climbed up until she could see the approaching path. Miminousa ascended the facing hillside and took cover.

The riders waited. The water splashed the same sound over and over again; birds warbled and twittered in rhythmic fits; insects buzzed and chirped without interruption. The sun sank farther to the west. The shadows stretched out more and more. The winds hissing through the treetops began to die. Nothing. Where were the fugitives? Would no one find them? Had they already slipped through the Amazons' vigilance? Were they laughing at them, having already reached safety?

Feodissia trilled twice. Miminousa's palm flashed white from behind branches. Feodissia slipped down to where her mount stood, took its reins, and hoisted herself on its back. She moved ten paces to Penthesilea's left. The two women removed their bows from their backs, drew arrows from their quivers, and, resting their half-drawn weapons on their thighs, stared at the trail in silence. The thumping of Penthesilea's heart was like thunder crashing in her ears. A fly buzzed around Tala's head. Tala's ears twitched.

The first man came into view. The sunlight bouncing off the hilt of his sword blinded Penthesilea, who had to blink. She opened her eyes again. That was Theseus. Antiope followed him. On foot. But why? Where was her horse? Brimus trailed her, leading the beast. Pirothous and Chalcodon came into sight. Better not give them time to wield their weapons. Soloön marched last, swiveling his head, frequently looking behind him.

Theseus stopped at the water's edge. The party halted for a moment. Theseus said some words over his shoulder, turned, and stepped into the shallows. Penthesilea drew her bow. He splashed quickly across. Penthesilea shot. Theseus yelped, pivoted, and fell. Soloön turned to see from where the arrow had come. At the same instant, Miminousa loosed two bolts in quick succession, and Feodissia took aim and let a shaft fly.

Soloön screamed. Brimus collapsed in his tracks. The horse he was leading reared and ran away. Penthesilea shot again but did not see her arrow land. Feodissia's second shaft whistled straight at Pirothous and dinned against his shield, its force jerking the armor from his hand, spinning him around, and throwing him to the ground. Soloön splashed frantically across the stream and clambered up the slope where Miminousa was hidden. Chalcodon's feet flew in the same direction. Feodissia dug her heels into her mount and gave chase, waving her axe and shrieking the Amazon cry as her horse plunged downhill.

Penthesilea urged Tala toward Pirothous who, facing upstream, was raising himself up on his hands and knees. She howled the war whoop and brandished her labrys over her head. She charged him and hurled the weapon at the small of his back. He threw himself flat. The arm skimmed over his cuirass and clattered to the ground. Penthesilea, whose horse had hurtled past him, turned it instantly and bore down on him again, hoping to trample him. Pirothous had already gotten to his feet. He threw something in Tala's face. The mare swerved and lost her footing on the wet pebbles. Penthesilea flung herself from the saddle, sprang up, and unsheathed her knife. Pirothous drew his.

They leaned forward and eyed each other with hate. From the slope where the others had run, a woman screeched.

"I can tell you're not as good at fighting as you are at obeying," sneered Pirothous. "This time I'll finish the job, you ugly cunt."

Penthesilea looked at him evenly. The smile dropped from his face; his lips came together in a grim line.

She took his measure. He was not tall, but his bones were wide and square, his flesh and muscles thick. He was half again as heavy as she was. That made him dangerous. Still, his weight would also slow him down and make him easier to topple. She sized up the terrain. The stream was two paces behind him, the wooded hillside five paces behind her. She stood uphill of him. She had the advantage of position. It would be the first thing he would try to reverse.

Pirothous stepped forward diagonally, staying out of her reach, focusing his gaze on her. The same murderous choreography dictated that she pirouette to keep facing him, but that she not stray from the spot she occupied. Would he try to maneuver uphill of her? He lunged. She put up her arm to block the stab. He shifted. He had tricked her. Her neck was now in the way of his blade. His right arm struck. Her left hand grasped its wrist and pushed the stab away. He had thrown his body behind the blow and could not stop from lurching forward. She revolved neatly, and his mass carried him to the ground. His weapon flew from his grasp. But he had taken hold of the hem of Penthesilea's tunic and dragged her down with him. The fall knocked the breath from her. The next thing she knew, he was crashing uphill. His footsteps seemed to shake the earth.

She jumped up and sprinted for him. He disappeared behind the same hedges that had given Penthesilea cover before the ambush. She stopped a few feet away and listened so hard that she heard the blood coursing through her head. A branch shook in front. She flexed, expecting an attack from that quarter. Mighty forearms seized her from behind and pressed her middle until she choked and saw black. But the sound of her fallen knife on the rocks below brought her wits back. Lightning-quick she seized Pirothous' left wrist and joined her hands below his reach. She tilted from the hips, and his fingers loosened. She wheeled nimbly around and wrenched his arm. He grunted with pain and sank to the ground, clutching at her knee as he went down. His heft dragged at her, and she lost her balance. He butted a shoulder against her. She stumbled backward but caught herself in time not to fall.

He dove for the knife. She kicked it away.

She waited for him to get up. He raised himself carefully, so as not to sacrifice balance to speed. Nevertheless, just as he straightened his legs to stand, Penthesilea thrust herself at him, locked his arm, and began to press. But he folded and pitched forward. She fell, and he got free. They stood up again. Sweat blinded Penthesilea. Her throat pounded and tightened. Before she knew what happened, Pirothous tore off her headpiece and wrapped his fingers around her braid. He tugged with every bit of strength he could muster. She gasped. His left hand went for her throat. She clenched the wrist that was twisting her locks and whipped around, forcing his arm back. The fingers that sought her windpipe clasped air; his clutch relaxed. She planted her feet and bent her body to the rear. His heaviness dragged him down. His fall wrenched his shoulder out of place. He screamed. Still she did not let his arm free but folded it behind him and knelt. He thrashed to get loose; she tightened her hold until he lay motionless. She put her thumb behind his ear, on the killing spot. He whimpered. She pressed. . . .

Eriboea's field in the fall. Penthesilea is lying on her back between rows of stubble, cut wheat; the women have brought the harvest in. The skies are the sparkling blue of autumn. The sweet perfume of newly cut stalks, the bitter smell of melted pitch. A man screams.

"I know that voice."

Where is Eriboea? She has gone far away. Penthesilea tries to raise herself up and follow her, but her body does not move. She cannot. She sinks back. Leokadia is near. Leokadia will lift her into the saddle and transport her there. Leokadia runs her horse toward her.

Its hooves move so fast that they blur; but they make no sound as they rush toward Penthesilea's prone form. The beast looms above her head and dissolves into gray silence, flat silence, silence with bright orange pinpoints, silence with a transparent pink wall and jagged lines of red.

"Abba-Bashti has a baby boy," says Anuphey in guttural tones.

"She cannot come with you."

Penthesilea wails out her despair but can hardly hear herself. She shrieks once more but no noise comes from her lips. Tecmassa rides in on her big-bellied piebald. Feodissia halts her bay behind her. "We'll rescue them. We'll outsmart them." Fog engulfs the riders and pushes them back into the mist. The smoke curls around where they have disappeared, and from the same place Antiope's mocking laughter clangs in Penthesilea's ears.

Pirothous' voice. Pirothous' voice in the darkness,"That bitch Antiope got away."

"Too bad, the boys had plans for her."

Who is that man? He talks like an Achaean.

Theseus: "Don't worry, we'll get even with this one while we're waiting for the ransom. We'll make the bitch sorry. She's almost as good. The high priestess will pay plenty to have her back. We'll ask for the gold powder. All of it. All three kegs. And we'll sell the horses to King Laomedon."

Myrtho says from behind the curtain of mist: "The Goddess watches over her. The Goddess will prevail."

Theseus: "The captain says seven days if there is no storm."

A man's voice, a rough voice, "Get that horse up the gangplank. Hit him! Make him do it!"

Wild neighs. Whinnies of fright. Penthesilea struggles but cannot move. Ropes hold her to a board. It is lifted and sways. She is carried somewhere.

"Cast off! Cast off!"

Her bed plunges and rolls. Her stomach heaves, but only hot stabs shake her gullet. Her head pounds. She opens her eyes. The sky is the same color as an iron knife. She closes her eyes. Cold air wails and makes her shudder. Thunder roars and deafens her. The wind slices her. The earth gives way under her. She pitches backward. Icy water pounds on her neck and breasts. Her ears ring, the chill cuts her. She tries to raise herself but thongs hold her fast. The bed she is tied to falls down, down, down, into a black pit. Her insides convulse; her guts wrack her. She cries out but hears no sound.

Chapter 12

Penthesilea could not remember the passage as separate days or acts, although she knew in the racking darkness of her mind that the Achaeans had taken her prisoner and were carrying her to slavery and grief.

Sometimes, when the shadows of clouds scudded across her lids, beloved faces, longed-for faces took shape and disappeared before she could reach out—Tecmassa's dark leather visage, Myrtho's tight mouth and gray hairs, Leokadia's sturdy, bronzed countenance, and, in the dimness, Abba-Bashti's face—with her burning deep brown eyes and small red lips that bitterness and amusement fought over. Sometimes Themiscyra's fertile green valley and rich blue mountains formed out of the dark mists of Penthesilea's mind. But the knowledge that always lurked there like an unspoken threat would wrench her thoughts back from these pictures, just as pain jerks a hand away from the wound it has touched.

She awoke late one afternoon when the gulls following the ship squealed and flapped in panic. Thongs no longer held her to her pallet. She looked up. A large bird was diving toward the vessel's wake. The gulls hurried out of the way. The big creature plummeted into the water like a well-aimed arrow and emerged holding slapping silver in its beak. It soared high, wheeled north, and hastened toward the shore with easy flaps of its wide wings. Penthesilea watched the short black lines that it traced in the sky grow fainter and dissolve; she thought of the eagles that glided over Themiscyra, floating on the airs, diving and banking in lazy majesty, swooping in and out of view whenever it was their pleasure.

She moved her eyes down to the shining swell that stretched back as far as she could see and rose to touch the white tatters of cloud shooting up from it. The sea's deep violet blue, which was like none she had ever seen, tilted first over her left shoulder and then over her right, offering a treacherous hold to the vessel that crashed through it, dropping away from under her feet or pushing up on them. She did not trust these waters—

where no solid earth met her step and no mountains protected her from the heavens. She turned and looked toward the bow. The ship was plunging toward narrows between two rocky promontories that crushed the sea into wild currents. The craft sped through the passage into straits that stretched to the setting sun's orange disk. Once the vessel entered the narrows, the sailors took in the sail and rowed for the shore. Men wielded knotted ropes and bellowed to drive the horses over the side into the shallow water. Once the craft had been lightened of their weight, the sailors dragged the vessel up until its prow rested beyond the waterline.

Penthesilea carefully lowered herself onto the strand. When her feet touched the ground, she sprawled forward. Pebbles cut the heels of her hands and ripped the flesh on her knees. She groaned. Someone behind her snickered. She turned her head. Pirothous stood over her. He brandished a length of cord in his right hand. She determined not to spare him another glance nor think of the scourge he held. She raised herself up slowly. Her temples pounded with the effort. Her legs would have folded under her had she not commanded them to bear her weight. She shuffled like a sick woman to the grassy stretch on which the newly landed animals stood grazing. She blew in Tala's nostrils. Tala exhaled in contentment. Penthesilea whispered gentle words to her and stroked her muzzle. Antiope's stallion, Melanthus, nosed in. Penthesilea patted his long neck and spoke to him, as well. She knelt—it took all she could do not to lurch forward with the spinning of her head—and inspected the beasts' hooves. They were intact. The bones and muscles of the animal's legs were, too. But the horses' ribs showed through their fur, which was matted and hardened with dried brine. The hide underneath the salt was swollen in places. One of Tala's fetlocks oozed blood; someone had raised a long welt on the stallion's croup. Penthesilea drew her lips tight and looked toward the beach. Pirothous, who had followed her, stood two paces away. He growled at her to return to the encampment.

A fire had been started. Food was cooking. Six men lounged around the blaze—Theseus, Chalcodon, and four sailors. Penthesilea seated herself on the outskirts of their group. She did not look up, even when Pirothous tossed bread at her before he joined the other men. They filled their bellies. Penthesilea heard one of the men belch and stand. Someone kicked the food from her hands and pulled her to her feet by the front of her tunic. It was Pirothous. Penthesilea struggled free and threw herself at him. But she was weak. He snorted with delight and pushed her away. Chalcodon came from behind, knocked her down, and pinned her. Pirothous threw his heft on her, knocking the breath from her lungs, ripped the skirt of her tunic from its waist, and raped her. Then, at his urging, the others took turns tearing into her. She held back screams. She passed out from pain and anger.

The next day the Achaeans tied her to a rowing bench before they sailed. That evening they did not let her approach the horses. After feeding themselves, the men went for her again. She fought back with every trick her feeble forces knew. Pirothous gurgled in delight as he knocked her senseless. She awoke on deck the next morning. It burned her chest to breathe. Strips of fire laced her back and neck. She raised her head: the stabbing in her brow made her gasp. Her flesh seared where the men had rammed their pricks into her while she lay unconscious. She looked down at her legs. Brown streaks, coagulated blood, caked her thighs. She wondered how long she could stand the cruelty. She swore she would get away from the Achaeans. She promised the Goddess that she would kill Pirothous when she got free of them. She fell into numbness again.

Rowers shouting, the vessel lurching to rest, and horses whinnying, jolted her awake. The ship had landed again. What would the men do to her this time? A woman giggled. It sounded like the rising notes of a lyre, like the delight of a naughty child. Spirits from the sea were playing tricks on Penthesilea. The joyous sound rang out again. She raised herself up, slowly, painfully, tentatively. She focused on the beach. Scores of vessels with elongated prows and sterns lay on their flanks at the waterline. Farther along, well away from it, clusters of bales and woman-sized jars surrounded the blackened remains of cooking fires. Dozens of men, many in costumes like those of her captors, stared at the craft that was being guided onshore. A few women, dressed in soft robes of hyacinth or spring green, also gaped at the vessel. One green-garbed woman, who stood a few paces uphill of the others, held her hands on her hips and her head back. Was it she who had laughed? She formed a semicircle with two men. One man, who wore a bronze helmet that glittered so brightly its reflections hurt Penthesilea's eyes, held the bridles of two horses, a black and a gray. Even in her groggy state, Penthesilea wondered at the animals' small stature. A single shaft attached them to what must be a chariot, not more than a wooden basket set on two wheels taller than it was. The other man, a slender blonde, rested his knuckles on his hips.

Chalcodon waved his arms at the horses to make them leap into the shallows. Pirothous screamed threats and smashed the end of his knotted rope against the deck. Tala neighed in protest but launched herself over the side. Melanthus stood still, his mane and tail twitching. Pirothous laid the whip into the animal's wither with a sickening snap. The stallion bellowed and jumped onto the beach. Pirothous leaped after him, grabbed his halter, and jerked it down abruptly. The beast flattened his ears, curled his lips, and sank his teeth into his tormentor's biceps. Pirothous yelped like a dog; a bloody arc sprang up on his arm. He yanked Melanthus's cheekpiece and swung the lash. It landed with a crack. The stallion tried to rear. Pirothous hung on. Chalcodon came running and lay his own rope into the horse's testicles. The animal screamed and shook his head from side to side but could not free himself. Penthesilea threw herself over the side. She landed on her belly and pulled herself up. She lurched toward Pirothous.

"Stop, in the name of the king!" shouted a high-pitched but stern voice. The helmeted young man had guided his chariot down to the ship.

"Stop!" bellowed Theseus.

Pirothous' arm dropped to his side.

"I am Priam," said the man, whose commanding bearing belied his short stature. "I am son of Laomedon, king of Troy. I see that you are these men's chief. They had better not abuse those horses anymore, or you will all be sorry. Understand?"

Theseus nodded.

"As soon as you have pulled your ship onto the sand, report to the palace with those horses." He ordered the blonde man to conduct the newcomers to the city, cracked his whip to set his team in motion, and disappeared over the hill that came down to the shore.

The Achaeans and their horses and prisoner fell in behind the blonde man. Penthesilea trudged on doggedly, bent on keeping pace although her head was splitting and her legs faltering. The journeyers plodded up the height and paused at the top. Stiff winds began to blow at them even as the noonday heat made them sweat. Before them, pastel green squares of plowed land and fields of emerald and ochre grasses stretched toward a distant plateau whose top glittered in the sun. The party climbed down the ridge and wended their way among the flat-lands until they reached the river that the Trojans called the Skamander. A wooden bridge stretched over its waters. The man who was guiding them crossed onto it; so did Penthesilea. Their footsteps echoed against the planks. A horse stepped onto them; it whinnied in panic. That was Tala. Chalcodon belched out foul words. He was yanking the mare by the bridle, trying to make her negotiate the span, but she had planted her legs and was tugging back like a donkey. Melanthus, too, had stopped in his tracks.

"Can't you get those fucking nags over here?" shouted Theseus. Pirothous came up behind Tala. He held a knotted cord. He raised his arm.

"Stop him!" said the blonde young man beside Penthesilea. Pirothous heard and fell back. Penthesilea retraced her steps, laid her fingers on the mare's cheek strap, and cajoled her across. Once Tala's hooves smacked against solid ground, Chalcodon grabbed her lead rope.

The blonde fellow paused until Penthesilea came abreast then set to walking next to her. Penthesilea kept her eyes on the road lest he see them and take pleasure in their rage and suffering, in the way that strangers did.

After stepping on silently for many minutes, the guide finally said, "My name is Jason. I serve the young man in the chariot. His name is Priam. He is king Laomedon's oldest son."

Jason's tones were those of someone who knew how to talk to skittish horses. Penthesilea turned her head and looked up. He smiled with genuine pleasure. He was more than a head taller than she. His hair was the color of ripe wheat. His eyes, which were of the same hue as the late afternoon firmament, held no spite. They were set in a long, oval face with full lips and a strong jaw whose beard was closely trimmed. A downy tunic of the same dye as his gaze and embroidered with animals that looked like wide-eyed, fleshy helmets draped his lithe body. His legs and arms glowed with clear oil. His long hands ended in uncallused fingers and clean, carefully cut nails. His clear gaze searched hers.

"Who are you?" he asked softly. "Who do you belong to?"

Penthesilea flinched.

"So you were just taken," he said. "Where did they capture you? Who are you?"

"I am Penthesilea the rider. I come from Themiscyra. I was captured in battle by the fat man who likes to beat horses."

Jason glanced over his shoulder, his face growing expressionless as he did. He turned back to Penthesilea and raised his eyebrows. "You were an Amazon, then?" he asked.

"Yes. I am a freeborn rider. The mare I just led over the bridge is my horse."

"And whose was the stallion?"

"He belongs to the woman I ride with." It was the first time since Penthesilea had opened her eyes that she thought of Antiope.

"Was she killed?"

Penthesilea's neck ached as she labored to recall the details of the ambush. Antiope had vanished as soon as the first arrows were loosed. There had been a woman's scream, but it had come from the hill where Miminousa was hiding and Feodissia had disappeared. Penthesilea said, "I do not think she was killed, but I don't know where she is now."

The road snaked left. The travelers negotiated the turn and then stopped as one person to gape: The track led uphill past mud-brick huts to the massive oak gate of the city. A stream of people and animals poured in and out of the entrance. A rock-gray keep towered over it. On either side loomed huge, thick stone walls whose light-colored brilliance in the midday sun made Penthesilea's eyes burn. She strained her head back. It hurt to look up. Immense upright projections formed the ramparts. On top of them, two moving, metallic glitters revealed where helmeted men patrolled the parapet. Penthesilea's eyes swept right and left. The under half of the immense western bastion was longer and less steep than that of the others and of a darker hue. At its foot, a narrow strip of soil gave life to six fig trees.

Jason, who had been peering at the face of the Amazon as she contemplated Troy's great bulwark, now spoke. "Some say that the walls of Troy are the highest in the world, and the largest, for all of king Laomedon's city lies within them." Jason pointed to the rampart east of the gate. "When I was carried here as a little boy," he said, "they were building that section again. An earthquake had thrown it down. Poseidon often shakes the ground here. They say that he is jealous of the Trojans' wealth and of the goddess Idaea, who lives in the mountain behind us."

Penthesilea looked back. In the distance, a slate black peak rose against the luminous sky.

Jason continued. "That is why the city's walls, as huge as they are, rest on packed earth and not on smaller stones —to keep the earth's shudders from pushing them over." Sadness roughened Jason's smooth voice. "They sent slaves to dig the earth up from the swamp north of the hill. My father got the shaking fever there and died. Many do. The spirits of sickness lie in wait for men in those marshes. That is why the Trojans built the city up there, on the top of the hill, above the sickness. The winds summoned here by Idaea drive it away."

A still mask fell over Jason's face, and his lips pressed against each other in bitterness. The Achaeans, too, had stopped talking. Only the regular thuds of the horses' hooves marked the party's slow progress.

Then, as if he had come to the end of a chain of recollections, Jason said, "Is your captor holding you for ransom?"

Penthesilea did not remember the Achaeans' saying so but was somehow certain that they would try to exchange her life for a great treasure. And so she answered yes.

"Then they do not dare harm you."

Penthesilea's pupils grew tiny from the pain she recalled. Jason laid a soft hand on her forearm. She drew her mouth into a stubborn line. "And what if no ransom comes?" she asked.

Jason sighed.

Sadness engulfed Penthesilea. What terrible wounds would Pirothous inflict on her if no treasure came to buy her back? If no treasure came in time? She had seen women, once slaves, arrive at Themiscyra with missing ears and eyes and fingers, and had heard of even worse amputations. Penthesilea shuddered. If no one bought her back, she must run away from the Achaeans. She must. But the horses—the captured horses; she did not want to leave them behind. Still, she must escape even if she had to do so without Tala and Melanthus.

The party crossed into Troy. Movement, brightness, and clamor broke up Penthesilea's speculations. Shouting men toting bales of raw wool, singing women bearing baskets of yarn, braying donkeys supporting clinking panniers and glistening oil jars— crowded the courtyard inside the walls. Bearded, gesticulating, expostulating merchants in rich robes bustled about with an air of importance. Two soldiers, whose spear tips glittered above the people's heads, moved to and fro among the press. People chattered and laughed and hawked wares. Still, as Pirothous and Chalcodon led the horses through the cacophony, the beasts pulled a train of silence behind them.

The newcomers turned up a paved street. Penthesilea's steps hit the stones in the same rhythm as her head throbbed. Her legs weakened, and she pulled herself up.

The thoroughfare she stumped along was wide enough for four mounted women to negotiate without difficulty. It ran straight, past alabaster stone houses arranged in ascending rings, to the flat height of Troy's hill. Here, a vast, L-shaped edifice constructed of limestone, which Jason indicated was the palace, dominated the city from the top of a terrace buttressed by high walls. Pear, plum and cherry trees decorated the edges of this elevation, their emerald leaves and gray-brown bark setting off the seafoam brilliance of the royal building. Penthesilea could not look directly at it for long; its brightness was like a blade cutting into her skull. Not far behind this structure, the upper reaches of a watchtower made of massive gray stones forced itself into the sky. Even in her black state, Penthesilea realized how rich and powerful this city was, how wealthy and grand those who dwelled at its summit. Themiscyra was a village in comparison, its fortifications playthings, and its ruler a chief of no account.

A ramp led diagonally up the rise and ended in front of a garishly ornamented portal practiced in the longer wing of the palace. Two men watched the newcomers approach: one, a small fellow with thick gray hair, a beak face, and one shoulder higher than the next; the other, a stripling of a lad with the same sharp nose and jaw. The Trojans unceremoniously took the horses' leads from the hands of Pirothous and Chalcodon. The older fellow gave both leads to the younger one and halted around the animals, his right side tilting over his foot. The man ran his eye over the blood, welts, and angry hide that roughened the horses' coats. From under lowered lids, he flashed a furious glance at the Achaeans; he softened it to look at the Amazon and shook his head: these crude soldiers had abused the steeds. She nodded.

Jason conducted the party through a columned vestibule into a large hall and bid them stop near the door. The cool and shade made Penthesilea dizzy. She had to settle her senses. When her eyes focused again, she saw a floor of sea-green and sky-blue tiles. She raised her head. A profusion of gaudy circles and jumbled triangles decorated the room's walls. A few paces in front, four pillars of azure-painted wood with night-black and sunset-orange bands surrounded a circular hearth (fireless in this season) that was practiced in the floor and set slightly back from the middle of the room. To the right, an elevated chair of carved oak faced the fireplace. A large-nosed man with sparse hair and a jet black beard sat in this seat. That must be Laomedon, king of Troy. The young charioteer, Priam, held himself at his side; on the other was stationed a tall, fat, balding fellow dressed in the leather skirt and studded cuirass of a soldier. Opposite the king's throne, on the far side of the posts, stood a smaller, similarly worked chair of state. A lady with hair the color of polished steel occupied this place. She wore a sky-blue gown and dangled elegantly draped wrists over the chair's arms. Penthesilea learned later that she was Laomedon's wife, Glaucia. Someone old enough to be her mother crouched on a stool at her feet. Three spear-carrying guards leaned against the wall near the throne. A bald man was tiptoeing out of the room with a diffident tread.

The king looked in the direction of the Achaeans. Theseus advanced and made a deep obeisance. The king nodded curtly and spoke abrupt, staccato words. Theseus hooked his thumbs behind his back and shifted from foot to foot. Pirothous handled his belt near his dagger. Chalcodon ran his fingers over the scabbard of his own knife. The soldier at Laomedon's side crossed his arms. The guards straightened up.

Laomedon grew silent. The fighting man next to him pronounced a brief question. Theseus replied at length, turning once to point at Pirothous and Chalcodon and once to designate Penthesilea. The king glanced at her; Glaucia, who had also been examining her, rose, joined the king, and said something in his ear. He bid Penthesilea come forward. She began to drag her feet across the hall. She braced herself and set her mind on not missing a step. She had covered half the distance, when she heard stirring and low voices behind her. She stopped. A black-haired young lady had just entered and was making her way toward the throne. An alabaster robe decorated with tiers of cherry red parallelograms accentuated her tiny waist and broad hips. As she glided past, she glanced at Penthesilea's face, but Penthesilea did not allow herself to take notice. The newcomer reached the throne, settled at the king's feet, and wrapped her hem around her ankles. Penthesilea set in motion again and faced Laomedon, who was absentmindedly stroking the seated woman's hair as he scrutinized the prisoner from Themiscyra. Penthesilea met his gaze with level eyes and a set mouth. The queen smiled and raised her eyebrows in distracted interest. Still, a fire inside her pupils tried to penetrate Penthesilea's—to no avail. The young lady at the King's feet gasped. She was staring at Penthesilea's blood-streaked thighs and tattered skirt. She raised her head and examined Penthesilea's face. Penthesilea tightened her lips. The young woman's softened with pity, and her look pierced Penthesilea's like the first ray of springtime sun penetrates a dank cave. Still, Penthesilea did not change her expression.

The young woman tugged at Laomedon's sleeve. He bent forward, and she whispered to him. He straightened up and asked Theseus who the slave belonged to. Theseus flashed his flawless smile at the young lady and said, "Sire, the horses are for sale, but the slave is not. I cannot part with her. She does not belong to me but to my companion, Pirothous." Theseus again pointed to him. "But even Pirothous cannot let her go, for he is waiting for ransom to arrive and has given his word that nothing will happen to her while we are waiting."

"He has given his word," said Laomedon in a high-pitched but self-assured voice. It was the same as that in which Priam had addressed Theseus earlier that day.

"Is she highborn then?" continued the king.

"She is the daughter of Themiscyra's high priestess and a cousin of the royal house there."

Penthesilea took a while to realize that Theseus' words were false. She gathered her strength and uttered, "That is not so."

Laomedon looked at Penthesilea blankly. He had not heard what she had said.

Penthesilea contracted her body in order to speak loud enough to be heard. "That is not so," she repeated. "Theseus is lying. Theseus is a liar. He lied to the ruler of Themiscyra, and he will lie to you. I swear this before the Goddess."

"You dare say that, slave!" blurted Theseus. He raised his hand to strike her. Penthesilea crouched into the fighting position. A jumble of blackness buzzed around her, and she sank to the ground.

Her senses returned when the back of her nostrils tingled with the perfume of a woman's flesh—flesh, breath that smelled of roses, and newly washed wool. The warmth radiating from someone's body caressed hers. She opened her eyes. The young lady who had been sitting at Laomedon's feet was kneeling over her. Brows that swept up into a coal-black arc and large eyes of the same intense hue dominated her face. Its pale-skinned cheeks and small chin formed a long triangle whose sharpness was exaggerated by a thin, blossom-pink mouth. The mouth was pursed in worry; the eyes glowed with pity; the brows were raised in curiosity.

King Laomedon watched his daughter Hesione fuss over the Amazon. He turned to the portly soldier, who bent down to hear his confidence. "So Hesione likes her," whispered Laomedon. "What softies those bitches are. By all rights the Achaean should whip the prisoner until she's broken, calling him a liar. But I'm not going to let him. I need her too much. She's a mounted archer. And I've just gotten my hands on two horses tall enough to ride, not just to pull war chariots, but to ride. And a mare and a stallion, at that."

The soldier blinked. Laomedon fingered the wart on his left nostril. "A cavalry!" he continued. "Mounted archers! A handful of them can pin down a hundred foot soldiers. A squadron of them can bring an army to a standstill." In his mind he saw a white-walled citadel on top of a high hill. "The first one I'll sell on the slave market—as a eunuch, I'll make sure—is that Achaean warlord who took Pergamon, and the tribute, away from my uncle. Yes, all those pirates are finished; no more eating away at Troy's empire, my empire. No, the reconquest will begin."

Hesione had approached Laomedon while he was talking; she tugged on his sleeve. He broke off his private conversation and beamed, "What is it, sweetheart?" he asked.

"Sweet father," she cooed, "I want that Amazon to live in our palace until her family buys her back. Those dreadful Achaeans. . . ."

"Yes, my darling. Anything you want."

Hesione threw her arms around him and kissed him. He stroked her shoulder and slid his hand down over her buttock. He felt someone staring at him and glanced up: Glaucia's steely eyes met his.

Hesione ordered one of her slaves, Aegista, to attend the captive for the duration of her stay. Aegista was a short, plump woman, with honey-colored hair. Her hazel eyes and thick, pale lips were perpetually drawn in a pleasant expression. Still, had any member of Glaucia's family thought to look closer, she might have made out hardness in the back of the slave's pupils and resignation in the set of her mouth.

Aegista led the captive by the hand to a tiled room in which a sunken tub full of steaming, perfumed water awaited her. She pulled her tunic over her head. The prisoner was a woman, but instead of a round, soft body, she had a slim and wiry one. Even so, her woman's flesh was not as the men snickered and said that the Amazons' was. Welts and bruises striped her from head to foot, and dried blood and black-and-blue marks mottled her pelvis and thighs. Aegista hummed in commiseration. Her arms encircled the rider, and she lowered her into the bath. As she did, the captive's guarded and pained gaze melted into a look of thanks. Aegista's heart warmed; but no sooner had it done so, than she darted her eyes around her to make sure that no one else was there.

Penthesilea groaned once her skin touched the hot water. Aegista kneeled and began gingerly to wash her wounds. Penthesilea sighed, relaxed, drowsed. When Aegista reached between her legs, the Amazon sat bolt upright and stared at her in alarm until she recognized her. Then, her lips sketched a feeble smile, and she sank back.

After the blood and filth had been soaked and rubbed away, Aegista pulled Penthesilea upright, helped her step out of the water, and daubed her dry with hot cloths. She spread unguent over the contusions that covered her. She put tiny spade-shaped leaves into her vagina. She clothed her in a long robe dyed the pale orange of the clouds at sunset. So attired, Penthesilea took a few groggy steps, stopped in her tracks, and whispered that the skirt beat around her ankles like chains. Aegista's voice bubbled up to a giggle. Penthesilea grinned weakly.

Aegista led her to a sleeping chamber. Meat and wine were set out for her there. Penthesilea gobbled them down. When she was done, Aegista made her swallow a bitter herb draft so that no hate-baby would come of the men's brutality. The drink soon made Penthesilea's eyelids heavy. Aegista undressed her and tucked her into a bed whose sheets had been warmed by heated stones. Aegista stretched out on a cot that had been set up near it and listened to the Amazon's breathing, which slowed, then grew sibilant like a dying person's. Penthesilea sobbed once before she fell asleep. But even so, her fists were clenched, and she did not murmur or stir the way people do when they dream.

Not long after that, she cried out and sat up suddenly, her eyes wide, her mouth pinched. Aegista came to her side. Penthesilea saw who it was, heaved a sigh, and sank back. She closed her eyes. Her respiration slowed and deepened. As soon as Aegista was sure that Penthesilea had dozed off, she lifted the blankets. Blood flowed down, moon's blood. The potion had worked. Aegista stroked Penthesilea's hair. Penthesilea whimpered and turned over.

The days stole by. Penthesilea slept, ate, drank. At night, Aegista lay on the small bed next to hers; during the day she carried her meals to her and gave her wine heavy with strength. Penthesilea spent fewer and fewer hours lying down; the deep blue stripes across her ribs became green. Alert fire returned to her eyes. Something else returned—a quiet rage that the slave Aegista knew well—burned in their depths.

Hesione looked in every day. Soon Hesione and Aegista accompanied Penthesilea to the palace garden. At first they sat in silence on the bench in the shade of the the tall laurel tree. Then Penthesilea began to talk, or rather to answer the questions that Hesione put to her in a level voice that hid her fascination from everyone but Aegista.

Where did Penthesilea come from? From Themiscyra, from Thermodon's valley, which lay near the rising sun, a land blessed with plentiful crops and sleek herds, a domain ruled by women. What had her life there been like? Eriboea and the womb of the earth; Leokadia and Tecmassa and the fighters' ways; Myrtho and the Goddess. How had Penthesilea been taken? Theseus' flight, the ambush, the fight with Pirothous; Penthesilea's capture, the men's savagery. Was it true that Themiscyra's daughters lay with men only to clear the path for the souls that dwelt within their wombs, but that for their joy the women lay down with one another? Penthesilea told of the men's yearly stays, of the baby-trading, of the foundlings, and of the happiness that women knew in one anothers' arms.

Penthesilea lowered her head when she spoke of these things, measuring out her words, begrudging them, as if her past were something that she would not surrender, that the strangers could not take from her, even if they held her body. And the slave woman, who sat in silence while the others talked, took pleasure in the captive's stubborn reticence, just as worshipers delight in paintings on temple walls of other celebrants making offerings to the same divinity.

At times the women's promenades took them outside of the palace precinct. They strolled about the city streets—the avenues sweeping up to the palace and the alleys winding near the ramparts. They visited the temple of Thetis, which stood a stone's throw from the northern bastion, a square brick building whose walls tapered into wooden columns that held up a flat roof of the same material. The holy place's front steps led past a wooden-pillared porch into the central chamber. Here, the oak-carved statue of the Goddess stood, on a blue-black rock that had fallen from the sky in the old days. Gold and silver leaf covered the wooden presence from head to toe, and fine cloth threaded with the same metals draped Her body. The Goddess smiled gently on those who came to adore Her: votaries clothed in black and white robes who sang hymns and chanted prayers; humble folk dressed in homespun who clutched little clay figures to lay in the wicker basket at Her feet; foreigners wearing garments of many shapes and dyes—dark men in closely curled beards and fair men in drooping blonde mustaches—who carried vials of perfume or ingots of glass or lumps of amber to place on her altar; nobles in their sunset orange finery and clinking, glittering jewels, who proffered cups and bowls wrought of precious metals, or led slaves shambling forward under the weight of freshly killed animals or fish.

One day, Aegista noticed Penthesilea glowering as she observed the worshipers streaming toward the statue. But, why? Was Penthesilea jealous for the sake of her own goddess? Did the sight of the temple and the sanctuary make her homesick? Did the prisoner want to offer Thetis something? But, what? Penthesilea had nothing, save the tunic she had been captured in.

The next time the women visited the temple, Aegista put the tiny clay likeness of an owl, the bird of prophecy, wisdom, and hope, into Penthesilea's hand and closed her fingers around it. Puzzled, Penthesilea looked at it. Before long she blushed and turned a glance full of love and thanks on Aegista, whose pleasant mask dissolved into a warm smile, until she noticed that Hesione was watching.

Penthesilea joined the procession that crowded toward the Goddess. When it was her turn, she placed the offering in the basket and stood with bowed head for so long that a young priestess came out from behind to ask her to move on, but thought better of it after she spotted Hesione.

The priestess, whose name was name Anteia, and who was
Hesione's second cousin, attached herself to the Amazon's party
as they wandered around Troy. Anteia was a slight woman,
coming up only to Penthesilea's chin, but her irreverent gaze and
sturdy arms, which she held in an arc in front of her, gave away
no weakness.

"We Trojans have always worshiped Thetis," explained
Anteia, "since the beginning, since She carried us here from
Crete, and Idaea came down from the mountain to the sea to welcome us. For the sea was the beginning of all life. The earth
came out of her and the clouds that fertilize the earth; and the
sea gives us food from her depths and carries ships to us to bring
us wealth.

"Thetis is the daughter of the Mother Herself, who brought
Her forth from the deepest chasms of the sea to rule it as the
Triple Goddess: She who makes the seasons—birth, life and
death, red, green, and black—and She who knows what is, what
will be, and what has been. That is why so many people lay
gifts at Her feet. To thank Her for Her bountifulness or to know
what will be. For Her high priestess can tell the future on the
tips of her fingers and read the sacred letters that Thetis has
bestowed upon Her loving children to know Her secret words.

"Fifty priestesses serve Thetis. Each day we dress in black
and white and prostrate ourselves at Her feet and sing hymns to
Her bounty and Her wisdom. Every year, She brings back life,
when the cranes mate in the willows and the apple trees bloom.
Then we put on robes as white as the sea foam and celebrate the
life She gives the earth. For five days we drink the wine of
wisdom and eat the herbs of vision. We intone the secret songs
and dance the nine-stepped crane dance until we drop, worship-
ing Her whose belly brought and brings life to earth. Many come
from all over the land to join our revels, to share the divine ecstasy." Anteia's eyes glittered up at Penthesilea's.

"Every thirteen moons, in the middle of the death season,
when the moon's night is the longest and the cold winds sweep
the land, we put on robes as dark as cuttlefish ink and sacrifice
three black storks to Her. We snuff out the flames that have
burned in the sanctuary lamps all year and wait in silence in the
shadow until the rays of the new sun from the east have crept
from the temple entrance to Her feet. Then white doves fly out
from Her body, because She has once more given birth to the
light, and we ignite the lamps and torches, and parade around
the temple three times, beating the drums and wailing our wel-

come to the returned day and to the birth season that will not fail us.

"When the moon has reached her fullness and receded fifty times, we marry the high priest to Her. For fifty moons he is Her consort. Then we sacrifice a ram to Her and marry him to Her again. It was not like that it in old days: then, there was no high priest, and we married a young man to Her—always the fairest and noblest of the slaves or captives; he lay with the high priestess (who is Her incarnation) for fifty moons; then he ate the sacred leaves and they sent him to the Goddess in Her hidden world beneath the warm sea, and a new young man took his place in this world and married Her once more.

"But that was long ago, you see. In the old days Troy obeyed Her alone, for the queen herself was Thetis' high priestess. She was the chief of the clan of the Owls—for Thetis sent the owl to earth before She did the mortals, and the owl knows when the king will die. The queen foretold the future and ruled over the king's heart and mind.

"But that is no more. For many, many years ago, in the time of our great-grandmothers, the queen of Troy, the Goddess' chief priestess, was Chrysê. Her consort, who was called Teucer, had grown too powerful. The Goddess told Chrysê that the kings had stolen the city and its wealth from Her; that She wanted Chrysê to get them back. Chrysê's lineage and allies held a secret counsel and decided to rise up against Teucer. One of your Amazon queens allied herself with Chrysê, too." Anteia squeezed Penthesilea's hand. "But Teucer learned of the plot and called on soldiers from his own kin and took the queen and her closest friends prisoner. Still, he did not dare kill her, for she was a priestess. Instead he exiled her and set his younger brother over the temple, named him high priest, although the Goddess commands that only a woman of our clan, the Owls, may rule Her household. A few claim that he went against the Goddess' wishes, because Chrysê had no sisters. But it was because he did not trust any woman, or any man loyal to the Owls, to obey.

"And the kings of Troy would have left it that way—with no woman to govern Thetis' house, and instead a man from their own family. But the Goddess punished them for that. For in the time of Teucer's son, Iasion, the rains did not come. For nine seasons the land was dry and no barley grew. For three full turnings the people went hungry, the sheep died, and even the sea pulled away from the shores of Troy and the fish fled. The king and priests sacrificed to Poseidon—imagine, Poseidon!—but of course he was powerless to bring the rain. Then the Goddess spoke to Chrysê's daughter, Astyochê. A sea crow, the owl's friend, perched on Astyochê's left shoulder and sang the grief of the Goddess: that the Trojans did not worship Her anymore in the old ways; that the man priests stole the treasures from Her that the Trojans lay at Her feet; that She grieved for a woman's hand to care for Her. When Astyochê learned this, she stood by the gate and repeated what Thetis had said to her. The women of Troy heard her and promised that they would not spin or weave until the priestess came back. The king, who had grown rich from trading in the woolen cloth they made, could not make them change their minds and had to swear to Thetis that he would call on an Owl woman to be High Priestess over the temple. When he did, the winds began to blow, the sky grew dark, and the rains came. And Iasion kept his oath. But he did not allow his own queen to put on the sacred robe of black and white; instead, he called on her cousin. Nor did the priest he had named step down. And since that time a man of the king's clan has always watched over the temple, counted the treasure that the people give the Goddess and that we priestesses take to keep Her house and to conduct Her worship according to the old ways. Since that time, no woman of my race has worn the diadem of queen and the robes of High Priestess at the same time. The kings will not tolerate it.

"The priests of Poseidon, who have the king's ear, have tried to change the old ways. The priests say that the sun has greater power than the moon. They say that the sun makes the seasons and the year. That the sun divides it into thirteen new moons that do not follow the moon and five short days that the priests claim Poseidon won from the Mother in a game of drafts. But the priestesses know that the moon waxes and wanes twelve times to make the three seasons—from birth to life to death, from seed to plant to barren ground. That she leaves five days at the beginning of the birth-season and five before the cold wind blows, because she loves five, the number of fingers on the hand that tells the future, the number of the star that has no end, the number of the Goddess' sea daughters, the number of open letters in the secret alphabet that we Owl women alone know how to read.

"In the time of Laomedon's grandfather, Deimas, the priests tried to change the way the year is reckoned. But the holy priestesses cried out among the people that the priests wanted to steal five days from them. Men and women stormed the palace. The soldiers did not stand in their way, because their days, too, were being shortened. The king had to give in. It was then that Deimas built a new palace on the hill, far away from the gate.

"The priests have also said that the Great Goddess did not conceive and bring forth Thetis by Herself, although everyone knows that She gave Her birth and form in the deepest abyss of the deepest sea. The priests claim that Poseidon, who rules the sea winds, begot Thetis by tricking the Mother into coming to his cave and raping Her.

"In the time of Laomedon's father, whose name was Ilus, an Achaean king sent him the gift of a statue of Poseidon. The Trojan priests planned to carry it into Thetis' temple. The priestesses cried out in the city that Poseidon was trying to defile Thetis, just as he had tried, in vain, to violate Her Mother. When the Trojan women heard this, they stood around the temple ten deep to protect Her. Some men went with them. The priests could not get the statue through. The king ordered soldiers to clear the way with their spears. But the soldiers were afraid of Thetis' anger and did not charge. The king had to give in.

"The kings have always wanted to take away the priestesses' powers. They have always wanted to take away their sway over the hearts of the Trojans. They have always wanted to take away the might of the Owls and our allies. But they cannot. For many are those who love the Goddess as we do— as you do." Anteia's arms hooked around the Amazon's and her breast pressed against her biceps.

Stammering, Penthesilea pulled herself away. Then she saw Hesione scrutinizing her through narrowed eyes.

After that, Anteia no longer joined them.

Hesione often led them to the walkway on top of Troy's walls. They would circle it and gaze out at the plains to the east and south and at the sea to the west and north. Penthesilea always stopped and stared over the oldest stretch of rampart, the section overlooking the fig trees, where the bastion sloped less steeply than in any other place. One day, Hesione pointed out the leaf-green fields east of the city where Laomedon pastured his horses, and the handful of buildings that made up the stables for which he was reknowned. Penthesilea peered at the fields, her face strained in concentration, as if she were trying to fix her eyes on something there. After a while she raised her glance and surveyed the hills that separated Troy's level country from the mountainous hinterlands that stretched toward the rising sun, toward Themiscyra. Then, sadness clouded her vision but she did not turn it away. She started when Aegista covered her wrist with her hand. Her look met Aegista's, and, each woman's heaviness of heart dissolving for a brief moment, understanding flickered between them like tongues of magic flame. Penthesilea heard movement behind her and looked over her shoulder. Hesione had half-closed her vixen's eyes.

On that day as the sun slipped behind Themiscyra's walls, and the first airs of evening scurried through the streets, Feodissia sat with Telkhinia in the smith's doorway enjoying the break in the midsummer heat. The lanky Amazon put a mug to her mouth and gulped down the beer that foamed over the vessel's edges. Then she gurgled in contentment and placed the empty container at the foot of the stool she occupied, next to her cane. Telkhinia, who held a half-full cannikin between her thighs, beat rhythmically on them and smacked her lips.

Feodissia stretched out her long legs, one of which was wrapped in clean linen. "I'm glad to be up and about," she said. "Looking at walls all day drove me mad."

"But I hear tell you had some good company while you were mending," said Telkhinia. Word had gotten around that Anuphey took every chance she could to steal away from Thalestris' house and sit at her friend's bedside.

"I did, until Antiope made up her mind she didn't like it."

Telkhinia spat out a mouthful of liquid. "Antiope, my ass! Miminousa broke up a few good parties, but, still, to get cut down rescuing the likes of her.... One Miminousa was worth a dozen Antiopes."

"Yup. I don't like Antiope one bit, after the way the Achaeans slipped out of here in the dead of night. How'd they do it, except she showed them the way? And I don't care what she says, that they held a knife to her. She could've run away if she wanted. She had a horse. They were on foot. She could've led them in circles until help came. Instead, three got away, and we lost Miminousa. I don't care a hang what Thalestris plans for Antiope when her own time comes. I don't care to ride behind her."

"They say Thalestris will go to the West sooner than you think. She's very sick. After that, it'll either be Antiope or Melanippe who'll be the boss around here."

"Yup. But Melanippe isn't any better, and I don't much care to ride behind her, either."

"Bah! Melanippe! Looking at you like you're not good enough, and talking to you like you don't know up from down."

"I'd rather ride behind Penthesilea," said Feodissia. "And I'm not the only one. Riders who know what happened when those Hittite deserters surrounded us think the same as me; and so do women who rode with her after those Achaeans."

"Does anyone know what happened to her?"

"Tecmassa says they searched for miles around but didn't find a sign of her or the horses—only her knife, on the other side of the stream from the dead men."

Telkhinia turned her eyes to a spot in front of her feet. It was there that, two moons before, Tecmassa and Marpessa had thrust stakes on whose ends the genitals of Aella's rapists were impaled. Before planting the poles there, the Amazons had zigzagged their horses through the traders' camp brandishing the flesh-tipped sticks and shrieking the Amazon war whoop.

Telkhinia's youngest, Dirce, came out of the smithy and tugged at her mother's sleeve. The lass smiled uncertainly, black rectangles gaping where front teeth should have been. She whispered something to the grownup and scampered back inside.

"Well how'd she do that? She must have climbed over the roofs," Telkhinia beamed. "Anuphey's here to see you. In back of the shop."

Feodissia bolted up. Her legs were still not used to bearing her weight, and she began to topple sideways. Telkhinia rose, caught her by the waist, and handed her her walking stick. Feodissia hobbled rapidly into the shop.

Telkhinia filled her mug again and sat. She sipped her beer and watched the sky's azure modulate into purple silver. After a while she heard the dull thud of hooves. Someone was running a horse up from the gate. The rider turned a corner. A wild mop of red hair bounced against her shoulders. Marpessa rode past and waved hello without slowing her mount.

Marpessa's destination was the palace. Still, following Tecmassa's instructions, she stopped first at the temple and reported the news to Myrtho. A messenger sent by Theseus had arrived at the northeast border and asked for safe conduct into the land. Penthesilea was alive. She was Theseus' prisoner. He had taken her to Troy. The courier begged to speak with the chief of the riders.

Myrtho dispatched word to Ariona. She would be glad that Penthesilea was alive. She had said that Penthesilea was a fine fighter and a good leader. Charope had told her so. Tecmassa had, too.

Myrtho had no doubt that gossip would rapidly bear tidings of Penthesilea's whereabouts to Hippolyta. Hippolyta, however, would not be joyous to receive them. Thalestris was not in good health, and, however she might plan to bequeath Antiope her high station, Hippolyta and others would resist. They wished for Melanippe to assume her place. But Penthesilea was an impediment to these designs: she was Antiope's companion and therefore stood to gain preeminence from Antiope's ascension; what was more, she had no love for Melanippe; at the same time, many riders entertained a high opinion of Penthesilea and would listen attentively to her counsel. No. Hippolyta would not welcome her return. Indeed, she might do everything possible to prevent it.

Myrtho contrived to accompany Thalestris two days later to hear what the messenger had to say.

"The Amazon prisoner is in good health," recited the man, a tall, gaunt-cheeked Achaean named Metion. "Prince Theseus has made sure of that, because of her rank in your household. He's willing to send her back to you."

"What are his terms?" asked Thalestris. Her posture on her horse was erect, but her cheeks were sallow, and yellow-gold flecks tinged the whites of her eyes.

"He wants the three barrels of gold powder."

Myrtho's fingers tightened. How had the Achaeans discovered such a well-kept secret? Myrtho had told nobody about it, not even Iphinoë, whom she planned to succeed her. Had Antiope learned of the gold from Thalestris and betrayed its existence to her redhead? Myrtho darted a glance laden with wrath at Thalestris, who had sucked her lips into a white line and was staring back with no less ire.

Metion, who had taken in every detail of the exchange, added, "He'll settle for nothing less."

"Nothing less?" repeated Myrtho.

Metion looked straight at her. "Prince Theseus will put the prisoner to death, slowly, if you don't send the ransom."

Myrtho felt the color drain from her face.

"When I decide," said Thalestris without sparing a glance for her, "you'll know."

Later that morning Myrtho set foot in the royal hall. Thalestris, who was sitting in her throne, her chin in her chest, straightened up. Antiope, standing beside her, crossed her arms. Celano, who was facing these women, bowed low and slipped behind Thalestris' chair.

The others assembled before long. Ariona, who had demanded the interview; Hippolyta, who had gotten word of it and could not be left out; and Melanippe, who must have been visiting the city.

Ariona stepped forth to say something, but Thalestris silenced her with a gesture. "You know that an Achaean messenger has come to me about Penthesilea's ransom. Theseus has demanded that, in exchange for her life and safety, I send him the three barrels of gold dust that are hidden in a cave under the temple palace."

Hippolyta's eyebrows shot up in surprise. "Three barrels of gold powder?"

"They have been in our possession since the time of Thalestris' mother, the ruler Orythia," said Myrtho. "I remember when they brought them to the temple palace. Anactoria was high priestess then. An Amazon patrol had discovered them in lands belonging to the Goddess. For this reason, a half belongs to Her. A quarter is the chief's, and the rest was to be divided among the Amazons who fought for it."

"And who are those?"

"Four rode in that group—Tanaïs, Alcippe, Leokadia, and Penthesilea, of whom the captive Amazon is the namesake. None is alive now. Alcippe and Penthesilea the elder died defending the treasure; Tanaïs died of a fever years later. All except Leokadia were without issue, and their share reverted to the Goddess. Leokadia, who was severely injured in the action and survived her wounds against all odds, offered her part in thanksgiving for Her special grace."

Hippolyta pulled her shoulders back. "And why," she asked, "have I never heard a word of that discovery?"

"That's the way Orythia wanted it," said Thalestris.

"Orythia understood in her sagacity," said Myrtho, "that knowledge of so great a treasure would invite foreign invasion and cause the Amazons to fight among themselves. That is why only the high priestess and the chief of the riders were to know of it."

"Not anymore," said Ariona. "The only one the treasure is a secret to nowadays is the Amazons. Someone betrayed it to the outsiders. Someone told Theseus that. . . ."

"Penthesilea did," said Thalestris. "Penthesilea's their prisoner. You know what they do to prisoners to make them tell the truth."

"That is not so," said Myrtho. "Penthesilea knew nothing of the gold. I never uttered a word of it to her."

"And I never spoke about it to Antiope," insisted Thalestris. "How else, then, could Theseus hear of it?"

"There's many a rider who'll ask the same question," said Ariona. "And a lot will figure that you told the secret to Antiope and that she blabbed it to that redheaded Achaean. Antiope's given them little cause to look on her with friendship."

"I knew nothing of the gold," protested Antiope.

Hippolyta sketched a wry smile. "Who'll believe the truth of what you say?"

Antiope covered her mouth with her hand.

"I never spoke of the gold to Antiope," snarled Thalestris.

"It's Myrtho's word against Thalestris'," asserted Antiope.

Ariona turned to her, "Don't you know yet that most women will believe Myrtho sooner than Thalestris?"

Antiope looked at Thalestris, expecting her to deny it, but she kept her eyes ahead of her.

"That's right," scoffed Melanippe. "Antiope told him."

"Nonsense," snapped Antiope.

"Antiope's good at betrayal," sneered Melanippe. "After all, it was she who led those criminals to safety."

"How long do you think you can get away with those lies?" asked Antiope.

"Everybody says so," retorted Melanippe.

"Lies! You are lying!"

Melanippe taunted, "And for what? For the sake of her— was it Antiope's itching loins, her dynastic plans, or both?"

Antiope lunged for Melanippe. "Antiope!" growled Thalestris. Celano stepped in the way and seized Antiope's shoulders. Antiope stopped, grabbed Celano's hands, and threw them down. But she returned to her place.

Melanippe's lips parted in scorn; Hippolyta smirked to say, "I told you so"; Ariona crossed her arms and looked from Melanippe to Antiope and back.

"Enough of this!" said Thalestris. "I am your chief and I will tell you my decision without wasting time. I don't see any reason to give the Achaeans what they ask for. They want a ruler's ransom and they can't have it. I won't give it to them. This Penthesilea's just a rider in my household, no more."

"The daughter of no one, a foundling, nothing more," added Hippolyta.

"What do you say to that, Antiope?" jeered Melanippe. "Penthesilea's your comrade in arms. Why don't you stick up for her?"

Antiope put her hand over her mouth.

Hippolyta jerked her nose in the air.

Thalestris continued, "Penthesilea's not an officer in my household, just a rider, with no treasure of her own, whom I took in as a favor to Leokadia."

Myrtho's eyes flashed at the falsehood. Thalestris had asked for Penthesilea to further her ambitions, and Leokadia had sent the child against her will. Nevertheless, Myrtho would gain nothing by disputing the point. She pronounced instead, "This treasure, Thalestris, is not entirely yours to dispose of as you desire. The greatest part of it belongs to the temple. You have no right to say what will become of most of it. Only the Goddess does."

"And of course," said Hippolyta, "the Goddess intends to buy your foundling back by shipping off a ransom fit for royalty."

Myrtho did not alter her expression.

Celano leaned over and began to whisper in Thalestris' ear. Thalestris looked at her lap. Myrtho and Ariona traded worried glances. After a while, Thalestris nodded, and her advisor stepped back.

Thalestris drew her mouth into a bloodless smile. "The gold is not the temple's but the riders'," she said. "You, Myrtho, can insist all you want that it is not and that it belongs to you. But when I tell the Amazons that three parts of the treasure are theirs and that every woman gets a share, they'll believe me. You know they will, because of what each has to gain from it."

Myrtho folded her hands in front of her.

Thalestris went on, "And to make sure that none of the treasure slips away, I'll send a squadron to retrieve it and to bring it back here."

Ariona opened her mouth to protest, but Myrtho laid her fingers on her shoulder.

Hippolyta remained silent as well. She would not talk or act against Thalestris' plans. They suited hers. Thalestris doubtless was aware of that.

Myrtho bowed her head. Only after a moment did she raise her eyes and say, softly, "Of course we votaries shall not resist. How can we? Priestesses have no weapons and are not skilled in the ways of war. But the Goddess will defend Herself. Invading Her sacred ground to take what is Hers is an act of desecration, and She will deny Her blessings to all who dare to commit such an impiety. She will no longer welcome them into Her presence. And should any rider dare trespass, should any rider dare set foot in Her holy sanctuary, She will reject her sacrifices and curse her fortunes and her lineage. Of that I am most certain. And although you, Thalestris, pray to Her for health, She will not easily pardon your sacrilege."

Thalestris grew paler.

"So even if we could take up weapons and make a stand against your force of arms," continued Myrtho in the same quiet voice, "we would not."

She lifted her skirts and swept out.

Chapter 13

Twilight bathed the garden. The shadows at Penthesilea's feet lengthened even as she gazed distractedly at them. The airs stopped moving. A high-pitched chorus began to din in the branches of the trees. Only at this moment after sunset and in the pale silence before dawn did the breezes that scoured Troy's streets stop eddying and fleeing.

A sky-blue rider's tunic, cut like the one she had been captured in, lay on the bench beside her. Damasos the flute player, Hesione's slave, had just brought it to her with the princess's greetings. Glaucia was giving a banquet that night to celebrate the Ripeness and begged Penthesilea's attendance. Hesione had commissioned the garment to show off Penthesilea's looks. Penthesilea was glad to have rider's garb again and yearned to put it on. The long dress they had clothed her in hobbled her knees and ankles. She was tethered to the palace, too. They waited on her and tried to amuse her, but she was trammeled all the same. Once, after she could walk without faltering, she tried to go outside on her own. The guard at the entrance put up his spear and barred the door—"With all due respect ma'am; with all due respect"—until Aegista, breathless and frightened, came to get her. Another time, while Hesione stood chatting with a young officer at the foot of steps leading up Troy's wall, Penthesilea started to climb them, and the fellow bounded up after her and ordered her, if with deference, to come down. It was like that in the marketplace, too. She liked to go there, to get away from the palace, to circulate among the traders and see if anyone had news of home. But someone was watching all the time, from an accommodating distance to be sure, but watching nonetheless. The city's ramparts were a corral within whose barrier she paced in fury. It clawed at her. She longed to break out, to run Tala toward the rising sun.

Tala and Melanthus. Penthesilea shut her lids and once more saw their filthy coats and the blood and welts that the Achaeans had inflicted on them. At least Laomedon's hostlers would take good care of them. The sleek animals that pranced in front of Trojan chariots made her sure of that. Still, Penthesilea wondered at the steeds' short stature—most of them no taller than fourteen hands, not like Melanthus' seventeen and Tala's sixteen. Penthesilea shook her head sadly. How many winters and summers was it now that she had ridden the mare day in and day out? Tala was a good mount, sure footed, alert, smart. A breeder would see that right away, too. They'd cross her with the stallion as soon as she came into heat. She'd drop good foals. They'd have a stable full of tall horses soon enough. But would they have fighters to mount them? To learn to handle horses like the Amazons would take many lifetimes of trying and failing, unless someone taught the Trojans how. Hadn't the Mare Goddess personally instructed the first ruler, Marpasia, and her women?

Penthesilea remembered the silhouettes of her four friends sitting their steeds in moonlight that made the Amazons into streaming-haired goddesses who urged their vaulting beasts toward the land of fate. The dull thud of their ponies' hooves echoed in her head; the odor of horse and leather and women riding together filled her nostrils. Themiscyra. At this season granary floors groaned under the weight of new barley and women hauled fragrant baskets from the orchard to the city. Cleothera and her daughters were plucking bursting grapes from the vines that overran the west-facing slopes. . . .

Longing threatened to drown Penthesilea. She opened her eyes. The ninth full moon was rising. It had twice waxed full since she had been taken prisoner. Any day now the messenger that the Achaeans had sent to Themiscyra would return with word. Would the Amazons pay them the ransom they demanded? And if the women did not, what would the Achaeans do to her? Penthesilea remembered the boat and their savagery and shuddered.

No! That would not happen again. They would not lay their hands on her again. She would escape from them if her ransom did not come. But how? How could she get away? The question whirled around in her head until it hurt. She felt that the answer was right there, that she could touch it if she knew in which direction to reach out. She asked and asked, and asking made her dizzy.

But, once she saw it clearly, how could she slip away without someone seeing her? Someone was always there. Always.

.

Rattling foliage and tenor giggles gave away where the slaves Jason and Damasos were thrashing among the leaves. How could she trust them? How could she trust Aegista, as much as they loved one another? The owners would inflict unspeakable tortures on the poor wretches, if they even suspected that they knew that another slave, Penthesilea, planned to flee, much less aided her or closed their eyes when she bolted. Her stomach tightened at the thought. She could not put them in that danger. She must make sure they were all far away if she fled—when she fled.

But how? How could she carry it off? She knew there was a way but could not see it clearly. She ground the knuckles of one hand in the palm of the other. She hated it here, she. . . .

Footsteps and the cracking of twigs. The slight, ivory-skinned form of Damasos emerged from the trees. Jason stepped behind him. They approached. Damasos picked up the flute he had left on the far end of the bench, wrapped his light brown lips around the mouthpiece, and began to coax the skipping notes of a dance tune from its body. His curly, chestnut locks bobbed in rhythm, and his eyes the color of oiled walnut widened and stared at the heavens. Jason sat down beside Penthesilea.

"Do you like that music?" he asked. "Damasos tells me he has been practicing it for many days. They will play it tonight when Glaucia's dancers perform for you. After all, you are their principal guest."

Penthesilea raised her eyebrows.

"Yes. You will sit at Glaucia's right hand and Hesione will sit at yours. She will pour your first cup. She will spare you no honor. They have taken much trouble."

Jason's clear eyes looked straight into Penthesilea's. "Remember, Penthesilea, Laomedon and Priam also want your friendship."

Jason stood up and walked away.

Penthesilea sat as still as a statue and watched him go. What did they all want? What?

The wind, which had risen while Jason was speaking, began to blow steadily. The birds' chorus fragmented into isolated trills. Damasos had stopped playing. She returned to the palace.

Happy notes and cheerful chattering echoed down the corridor. Delicious aromas permeated the air—sandalwood, violets, lamb, sea bream, women's perspiration. Aegista tugged at Penthesilea's sleeve. She stopped.

"You've gone right past the door," said Aegista. "What are you thinking of? And the way you walk is so angry. Don't be angry. The court ladies are celebrating tonight. This is a great feast for the Trojans."

The instruments grew still and the voices became louder to fill the new silence. Penthesilea turned back and strode into a room illuminated by a score of lamps. At the far end, a dozen banqueters, all women, were seated around a carved table on which stood pitchers overflowing with wine and pyramids of apples, pears, pomegranates, and grapes. Elegantly coiffed heads and bare shoulders turned toward the athletic newcomer. The talk subsided, only to rise again immediately as women commented to their neighbors, and the musicians began another piece.

Hesione, who was seated next to the head of the table, rose. Her face lit up with delight, and she stretched out her arms and glided toward the door. As she stepped forward, the bodice of her ivory-colored gown of soft wool grew slack and tight around her small breasts, and its long skirt undulated the length of her hips and thighs. Penthesilea watched her approach so intently that she started when someone placed a wreath on her head. Hesione came up to her, wrapped her arms around her, and gave her a lingering kiss before leading her across the room. Queen Glaucia stood up. Pleasure came over her countenance. She embraced Penthesilea and extended her manicured, bejeweled hand toward the empty setting at her right. Penthesilea thanked the lady and seated herself. Glaucia took her place again, and Hesione occupied the chair on Penthesilea's right. A slave appeared and placed a shallow grayware bowl in front of Hesione. Another brought a flagon of wine and one of water. Hesione mixed the drink with graceful gestures, poured Penthesilea's goblet and her own, and toasted the guest.

Penthesilea expressed florid gratitude and waited for the queen to speak. Glaucia questioned her with a great show of concern, and Penthesilea smiled and nodded as she answered.

Glaucia stood up. The music stopped and the talkers muted their voices. She took Penthesilea by the hand and presented the other guests to her—Trojan ladies, Agameda, Althaia, Medekasta, Phrontis . . . too many names and faces for a stranger to remember. The lady Agameda, a woman Penthesilea's age, whose jet black tresses cascaded over slim shoulders, held on to her after the welcoming embrace and focused a deep and handsome gaze on her. A fine-linked chain of gold (the love-gift Antiope had given to Theseus months before) lay across the smooth flesh above Agameda's breasts, glistening and darkening as she breathed. Glaucia then presented Medekasta, a fairskinned lady in the decline of her beauty, who tilted back her salt-and-pepper ringlets when she drew away and stared boldly at Penthesilea from under painted lids. Hesione, who was observing the Amazon's progress around the table, raised her goblet and wet her lips. Glaucia led Penthesilea to Phrontis, a carefully groomed woman with blue-white hair and a calm, friendly mien. Phrontis did not rise immediately but looked the young rider up and down, as an aging aunt examines a niece whom she has not seen for years. Once Phrontis finished her inspection, she stood up. She measured a head shorter than Penthesilea and grabbed her ears to pull her head down and brush her brow with her mouth.

"Where is your daughter, Anteia?" asked the queen.

"I do not know," answered Lady Phrontis. "When I sent for her at the temple, they said that a messenger had called her away."

After Penthesilea returned to her place, servants staggered in under the weight of platters heaped with meats and fishes, and others hauled in new pitchers of drink. The wine flowed. The musicians conjured the sounds of heaven from wood and string. The room grew warmer; the talk more animated. Penthesilea ate fully and sipped moderately.

Hesione's talk turned to the women to whom Glaucia had introduced her.

"They are the ladies Glaucia always invites to intimate occasions," said Hesione. "All are great nobles and trace their origins back to the founding queens. All are married to Laomedon's kinsmen and friends. All, I should say, except Agameda, the dark-haired woman who is my age. She was the first one presented to you."

"The one with the gold chain around her neck?"

"Yes. She's married to a nobody, to Phereklos the shipbuilder, who's even taken to sending out traders in his name. But his mother and mother before her were fishwives. That's why he stinks like a fish barrel left out in the sun by the kitchen slaves. But Agameda's father, my noble cousin Isos, lost three ships to pirates in three sailing seasons and the rest of his goods in gambling. So he forced her to marry Phereklos, sold her like a slave girl on the market, and with the vilest threats. No one could help her. They say that Phereklos' treasure room is almost as large as my father's. But what does it matter? Agameda cried for days before her father led her to his house. But since then her tears have dried quite nicely. Quite nicely. She consoles herself. Handsome young men flock around her. She's young, rich, generous to a fault. To a fault. Everybody in Troy knows about her lovers except her husband, of course. She makes a fool of him in the other men's eyes. That's how she gets even and has her pleasure, too."

"Makes a fool of him in the other men's eyes?" asked Penthesilea. "Gets even?"

"In Troy a woman can 'share her couch,' as you say, only with her legitimate husband. If she does with any other man, the husband punishes her for it. Of course it was not like that in the old days. The women lay down with whom they pleased. But now the husbands whip them for it if they want. Other men poke fun at husbands, too, whose wives are unfaithful. They also try to seduce them to humiliate the other fellow. It's part of their pleasure—of Agameda's too."

Penthesilea placed a finger over her lips.

Hesione's eyebrows arced in amusement; she patted Penthesilea on the arm and rested her hand there. Penthesilea stared at it as if she wanted to run her lips across it. She then raised her glance to meet Hesione's, who turned away. Penthesilea looked down. When she looked up, Hesione had focused on the handsome middle-aged woman to whom Penthesilea had just been presented.

"What is her name again?"

"Oh, that's the well-known lady Medekasta. She and Queen Glaucia have the same great-grandmother. Medekasta's older than she looks, you see, and has three grown sons, soldiers all, who serve under their father, Tithonos. He's the commander of Laomedon's guard. He was the tall, fat man who stood next to the king when they led you into the throne room. Glaucia says that Medekasta and Tithonos were consumed with desire for each other when their fathers first arranged their alliance. But, naturally, Tithonos tired of her soon enough, although he did not leave her bed altogether until their third son was born and his descendance was assured. She tried everything to get him back, for she still desired him. Everything—love-potions, charms sewn in his clothing, spells cast over his likeness. But neither her magic nor that of a priestess, whom I dare not name, helped her, at least not with Tithonos, because she did take up with the priestess. Tithonos learned of it. There are no secrets in the temple and, of course, Tithonos' enemies took pleasure in spreading the gossip, for there are no secrets in the palace either. But Tithonos only laughed. He said that nothing serious could go on between women because there was no sword to slide into the sheath. Those were his words. Since then Medekasta has lain with many, many women—free and slave. She goes from one to the other, and leaves them more happily than she lies with them. The men even joke about her, say they should hide all the women in their house when they see Medekasta's chair approach the door. "

"And Lady Phrontis, that's her name isn't it?" asked Penthesilea, indicating the white-haired woman with her eyes.

"Lady Phrontis is my mother's cousin and oldest friend. They played together as girls. She is of as high birth as Glaucia and the high priestess, another royal relation. Like them, Phrontis knows the secrets that the Goddess has entrusted to Her sacred daughters. Laomedon's father, King Ilus, made her marry the chief at Amisos—to secure our eastern border, for they were always raiding from those parts. Phrontis spent five harvests in that provincial seaport, shivering in the wind from the cold sea. She bore two sons to her husband, who died of poison. (Luckily for her, someone confessed under torture to having committed the murder.) They wanted to put the deceased's younger brother on the throne and into her bed. Phrontis, who could hardly stand the older brother, a boor and a ruffian, hated the younger one even more. So she escaped from Amisos. She disguised herself as a boy so as not to be raped, joined a traders' caravan, and managed to get back to Troy after stopping at many settlements along the way. Ask her one day to tell you about what she saw. I hope your Amazons are more civilized.

"Still, her son, Otreus, now rules the little place, and Laomedon thinks that the eastern limits of the land are safe. But it isn't the princeling's kinship with Troy that keeps him from plundering our eastern reaches. What keeps his armies from devastating our cities is the Amazons. You are, after all, our allies. He's afraid that if his army left the land for long, your soldiers would move in."

"I see," said Penthesilea in a neutral voice.

"But let's not talk politics. This is a feast. Did you know that, if we counted descendance from the father's clan, Phrontis would be your kinswoman, and you a relation of the most power-ful families in Troy?"

Penthesilea's face became quizzical.

"Many generations ago," said Hesione, "Queen Chrysê of Troy (my forebear) welcomed your Amazon queen, Sinope, for a winter and spring. One of her suite, the Amazon Nicippe, cou-pled with a noble Trojan man. A boy child came of it, Hippolytus. She left the child here. Phrontis' father, Dames, is of his lineage.

"Trojan women also say that Queen Chrysê and Sinope loved each other greatly, as befits two ladies of such noble fore-bears, and that Chrysê gave Sinope many rich gifts because of the great tenderness that Sinope showed her and the great pas-sion that Chrysê felt."

"I know about their friendship," said Penthesilea. "My mother, Leokadia, told me about it; and before my time, they say that the great bard, Glaucê of the deep-sounding voice, sang of it to the Amazons."

"Naturally," said Hesione, "there are doubters. There are those who say that Sinope did not adore Chrysê with all her heart—that it was only a lie your Amazon queen told so that she could spend the winter in the arms of a rich and beautiful lady and go home with many more gifts than she had carried to Troy."

"That is not true," answered Penthesilea, "and people who say that have no passion in their souls. That is not what we Amazons repeat. That is not the story that Glaucê sang and that many still know by heart."

"We do not know the story that you tell," said Hesione.

"Sinope was the third Amazon chief," said Penthesilea, "after Marpasia and Lampedo. She was a brave woman, whose great-great-grandaughter, Thalestris, now rides at the head of our column."

"Your cousin."

"Sinope rode to Troy with an escort of . . . noble ladies and many gifts to win the friendship of its rulers, Queen Chrysê and her consort."

"We know she brought fine offerings of friendship," said Glaucia, who had focused her attention on Penthesilea. The queen's guests saw this and stopped talking. "My sister, the high priestess, wears bracelets and collars of iron on great occa-sions. And my mother left me an ivory statuette carved in the likeness of your Mare Goddess."

"Sinope fell in love with Chrysê when she first set eyes on her," said Penthesilea, gazing at Hesione, who looked at her lap.

Penthesilea continued, "Chrysê was as beautiful as the springtime morning and as powerful as the Sun Goddess' golden rays. Sinope understood at once that a divinity had put on human flesh to walk among the mortals. And Chrysê had only to exchange a few words with Sinope to prize her deeply, for Sinope was as handsome and well spoken as she was devout in her adoration of the Goddess.

"And so they spent the winter and the springtime in each others' arms, and their conversations were as sweet as honey and as heady as the scent of lilacs. But when the Goddess sent the daylight back to earth, when the rain ceased to fall and Arinna warmed the mortals again, Sinope knew that she had to leave Troy, to leave Chrysê, to lead her women back to her own lands, her own people, and to the deity whom she also worshiped. Perhaps that is why your palace cynics say that Sinope did not truly cherish Chrysê, because Sinope went away. But we riders know that that is not the straight truth. For just as a rider proves her worth in battle, so does a lover prove the depth of her affection in the grief she feels when she is torn from the light of her days and the solace of her nights. For every step, every day farther away from Chrysê made Sinope's tears more bitter and her heart more heavy."

The lady Agameda listened closely, resting her flawless brow on the heel of her hand. The lacquered nails of her free hand caressed the gold chain that Theseus had given her for the presents she had showered on him. "These Amazons," she thought, "are not the hags and primitives my redheaded captain says they are. What else has he not told me?"

Penthesilea continued, "As Sinope was carried onward, the face of Chrysê should have grown fainter in her mind's eye. But it grew brighter, as the sun did every day, and made Sinope thirst for kisses that alone could quench the dryness of her soul. As Sinope approached her home, her breast should have warmed to remember the dear ones who would stretch out their arms to her in joyous welcome. But the cold grip of melancholy tightened around Sinope's bosom and made her shiver with desolation. For how can you flee what you treasure? How can you say an eternal good-bye to the soul you enshrine? How can you sunder yourself from one half of your own spirit?"

Lady Medekasta was so absorbed in the retelling that she forgot to pose. She crossed her arms and rested her chin on her chest. "How wonderful it all would be," she thought, "to be cherished so truly and so faithfully, and myself alone to fill the flesh and spirit of one mortal. This Amazon is young and full of hope and life. Her embrace must make you tremble."

Penthesilea said, "Although the end of day always came, when all living things pause in dark and sleep, Sinope could find no respite from her grief. She lay awake and looked up at the firmament through her tears. There the moon was escorted by luminous attendants from the land of birth and dawn to the land of death and sunset, to where Chrysê was, to where Sinope longed to be, to the West, to where the Goddess puts the souls into new bodies after their deepest repose."

Phrontis, who sat with her hands folded in front of her, had turned her serene brow and kindly expression on Penthesilea and, under their cover, was sizing up the Amazon as she would an adversary. "Well, well, well," thought Phrontis. "No wonder Anteia has a crush on her. She's good-looking enough with her dark gaze and full lips, although the nose is too big for my liking. She's bound to please Hesione, too, with those childish stanzas she's reeling off—passion inspired by the Goddess and undying, faithful desire. What nonsense! The Amazon's even directed two glances heavy with meaning at Hesione, who has, of course, dropped hers demurely, as befits a young lady of royal descendance. As if the color in her cheeks and the fullness of her lips didn't give her away. She even seems to be contemplating some inner vision. Ah yes, it's a good thing no one ever told her that Queen Chrysê seduced Sinope and held her close to further her plans against Teucer and that, after many dreary new moons of smothering sentiment and suffocating palpitation, breathed a sigh of relief when her moonstruck Amazon made up her mind to go back to where she came from. It's best to leave Hesione ignorant for now."

Damasos blinked and rubbed his eyes. They glittered despite his fatigue. Holding a lamp in front of him, he conducted Penthesilea through the palace cellar. Penthesilea's head brushed against the ceiling as she followed her guide among large clay jars, crates, baskets, chests, coils of ship's rope, and timbers that lay on the dirt floor or on pallets. Damasos led Penthesilea up five steps to a concealed door that opened into Hesione's apartment. It was dark. The light that Damasos carried revealed the profile of Hesione sitting motionless in an armchair. She did not turn her head. Damasos departed. Shadows again. Pinpoints of the night sky gleaming through a window illuminated the room.

Penthesilea approached and stood in front of Hesione. Hesione looked up and reached out. Her palms were humid.

"So you came," she said.

"I could not do otherwise," said Penthesilea. She cursed her stupidity as soon as she had uttered these words.

Hesione withdrew her hands and folded them in her lap. "I wanted to," added Penthesilea. "I wanted very much to."

Hesione still did not move.

Penthesilea knelt and whispered, "Since I first opened my eyes and you were there. Do you remember?"

Hesione hesitated and then ran her fingers through the hair behind Penthesilea's ears. Penthesilea took Hesione's wrist, brushed its inside with her lips, and buried her head in Hesione's lap.

After a long while, Hesione got up and led her by the hand to the sleeping chamber. An oil lamp placed on a low table near the bed cast a trembling glow over the couch's expanse. A flagon and two goblets rested on the stand.

Hesione stopped and turned. Penthesilea tried to take Hesione in her arms. Hesione stiffened. Penthesilea stepped back. She did not understand but said nothing. Hesione sat down on the bed, beckoning Penthesilea to settle beside her. She heeded. Hesione poured wine. The women raised their cups to one another. Penthesilea swallowed deeply, while Hesione only wet her lips.

"I do not want to drink too much," she said in a voice whose clarity Penthesilea found clouded by a tinge of . . . of what? Her tone was straight and mocking at once. What was she making fun of?

Hesione put her cup down, took Penthesilea's, and placed it next to hers. She drew Penthesilea close and kissed her with a wide-eyed kiss, tasting the Amazon's mouth slowly, carefully. When they separated, Hesione fixed a surprised gaze on Penthesilea and honeyed fire tingled in Penthesilea's veins. Hesione lowered her head in thought. Then she looked up, tilted her face, and beckoned Penthesilea with a smile.

Penthesilea reached for the shoulder clasp that fastened Hesione's dress. Hesione stopped her. "Let me," she said. "Let me." She undressed Penthesilea and slid off her own garment.

She nuzzled the hollow of Penthesilea's neck. Penthesilea kissed Hesione gently and stroked her lazily. Warmth spread over Hesione's body, and her pulse danced. At the same time, she seemed to contemplate her skin that flushed and heartbeat that throbbed.

Penthesilea bent over Hesione like a worshiper over a book of sacred symbols. The divine flame in Hesione grew and coursed and thrilled. At length she shuddered in the blessed ecstasy and fell back, limp, amazed, weeping.

Penthesilea took her in her arms, rocked her like a child, and whispered, "My sweet, my darling." She was glad that she had pleased Hesione to tears. She dipped her fingers in them and stroked Hesione's lips.

Hesione lolled and sighed, her eyes closed, her face frowning over her own fancies. What thoughts, Penthesilea wondered, was she pursuing so intently? After a long while, Hesione raised herself on one arm and said, "You will be good for me. I know you will." She drew Penthesilea to her again.

The day's new light had penetrated the entrance of the sleeping chamber and the wind grown silent when Hesione curled up against Penthesilea and sank into sleep. Penthesilea listened to the delicate forge of Hesione's breathing and felt Hesione's helpless warmth against her own nakedness. That she had delighted Hesione put Penthesilea's mind to rest, but still she asked herself without saying so if this was what her first night with Abba-Bashti would have been like.

The heat in Penthesilea's woman's flesh kept her awake for many hours.

From then on the two women spent the nights in each other's arms. Penthesilea soon found her way without a guide from her own quarters, which Hesione insisted that she keep, to Hesione's apartments. Sometimes the young women did not leave Hesione's room until the next sunset. Aegista would carry them trays of spiced wine and sumptuous foods. She bathed them and perfumed them.

Penthesilea threw herself into loving Hesione: she conjured forth the hidden music in Hesione's flesh and made her shiver in a rapture and repose in a quiescence that Hesione had not known before and scarcely understood now. One languorous afternoon, she buried her head in Penthesilea's shoulder and confessed this. Then she got up on one elbow and asked, in a voice that was both serious and teasing, "What do I do now?"

Penthesilea opened her arms, but it was not to Hesione.

In long embraces in which the words lover and beloved lost their meaning, Penthesilea and Hesione played out their passion, and their gratitude, in long embraces in which the words lover and beloved lost their meaning. The young women spoke of their ravishments in syllables no other mortal understood. Hesione's kisses were so sweet, her longings so deep and complex, that their enchantments overwhelmed Penthesilea, and she could not bring herself to guard against them. Still, once these moments had passed, her mind wandered to the mountains that stretched to the rising sun, and her longings strayed to someone else, and she was more miserable than before.

Hesione reclined, her hands under her head, one knee bent upward and the other to the side. Penthesilea sat cross-legged, facing her, absentmindedly running the tips of her fingers over Hesione's belly. Hesione said out of nowhere, "It is better, you know, much better. That's what my aunt, Phrontis, told me, too."

"What is better than what?"

"The love of women than the love of men, you adorable one. I don't know what I'll do when Laomedon marries me off."

"Marries you off? Does he have plans?"

"No. Not right now. But I am the king's oldest daughter, and Laomedon will use me to further his own plans . . . and to prevent me from causing trouble for his son and heir, Priam."

"Causing Priam trouble?"

"Naturally. It would be too dangerous to marry me to a noble Trojan, or even to one who had the treasure to buy soldiers with. The sons I'd have by whomever that was would lay claim to Troy and fight the sons Priam had. I'd help, of course. Think of the power I'd have as mother of the king."

"They struggle like that where I come from, too."

"So Laomedon will probably marry me to some foreign prince, the more foreign the better, if he can bring himself to part with me. Ambassadors are forever lining up at the throne to seek father's alliance. He'll marry me to the highest bidder, too. I'm sure of that. He's always hungry for treasure; his wars cost so much. To keep his army he has to keep making more war—so that he can pay the soldiers with the slaves and booty that they take. It's never-ending. But sometimes even the Trojan army can't sack enough cities for father to make ends meet. So I might be packed off to some spot at the ends of the earth to replenish Laomedon's coffers. And to help his schemes. That's the main thing royal daughters are good for in this day and age."

"When will that be?"

"Soon. Soon. Laomedon has waited a long time already. After all, I'm over seventeen. Perhaps tomorrow, or the day after, or next year. There's no telling. Laomedon doesn't tell the women what he's planning."

"And you'll marry whom he chooses and follow your husband, even if you don't want to?"

Hesione frowned and pursed her lips. But the thought was too unpleasant to pursue, and she dismissed it with a shrug of her shoulders. "My father doesn't want me to go," she said. "He says I'm the joy of his life. Glaucia thinks his affection for me isn't all fatherly, and I agree. And he'll do almost anything I ask." Hesione widened her eyes and cooed, "All I have to do is ask for it in the right way." Her demonstration over, she giggled. "So perhaps he'll not want to let me go. Perhaps I'll become high priestess. You could be my acolyte and live in the temple. We could institute new ways of worship. Would you like that?"

"I'd like that very much and know just what to worship."

"Or, if I married a foreigner, you could come along as part of my retinue. As my body slave. What do you think of that? As my," Hesione smirked and drew out the words, "body slave."

Penthesilea wanted to blurt out that she was a freeborn Amazon and no one's slave. But instead, she smiled enigmatically.

Hesione reached for Penthesilea and wrapped her arms tight around her. Her mouth sought the Amazon's and intoxicated her until she thought no more of her captivity.

Penthesilea sat up suddenly. It had been almost four new moons now that she was a captive in Troy, waiting for her ransom, hoping for her freedom. Surely that was time enough for a messenger to carry word to Themiscyra and return. The thought took the sleep from her, and she left the bed of Hesione, who sighed and rolled over but did not open her eyes. Penthesilea tiptoed into the sitting room and stared out the window at the dawning day. She inhaled and shuddered. The air was crisp and chill. Blinding yellow rays fanned into the heavens from behind the gray hills. At their feet lay Troy's plain, sea fog still hugging it, then the looming mass of the wall, the streets below, the ter-

raced slope that led from the plateau on which the city stood to
the strip of flower garden beneath Hesione's window.

Penthesilea saw all at once how she would make her escape
if the ransom did not come. On a night when there was plenty of
moonlight, she would descend the terrace in front of the window,
get to the the oldest section of Troy's wall—the one she had observed when they first led her there, the one whose angle was
the least breakneck. She would lower herself from there to the
fig trees. All she needed was a long rope, and coils of it were
stored in the cellar. Once outside the city, she could scramble
down the plateau's side and head east. How long would it take
to get to the beginning of the mountains so that she could hide?
She'd have to start at midnight at the latest.

Bare feet on the tiles. Hesione pressed against her and her
arms enfolded her. Hesione's skin was toasty from the covers; it
smelled of sweat and desire. She licked the flesh between
Penthesilea's shoulder blades. "What are you thinking of,
dearest baby?" she asked.

"You," answered Penthesilea. Telling lies still put gall and
wormwood in her mouth. She turned and kissed Hesione deeply.
The taste was heavy wine that took away the foulness and
made Penthesilea drunk enough to forget.

As soon as Hesione slept soundly, Penthesilea stole out of bed,
took a lamp, and tiptoed through the hidden doorway to the
cellar. She picked up a length of sailing cord, carried it back to
Hesione's apartments and hid it in the depths of the cedar chest
in which Hesione's winter garments were stored.

Hesione reclined in blissful helplessness; Penthesilea lay
stretched out on her side, her head cradled in Hesione's shoulder. Penthesilea looked down the length of Hesione's body—at
her small, ivory-colored breasts, at her nipples as pink and
tight as rosebuds, at the black hairs that traced a line down her
belly, burst into the luxuriant growth of her pelt, and spread out
in downy fuzz to cover the inside of her thighs. Penthesilea
wondered dimly what it would be like to contemplate Abba-
Basthi's nakedness. Then Penthesilea's glance strayed to her
own thighs. She saw for the first time that they were growing
thick and soft. Her stomach, too, from tight and flat was becoming flabby and rounded. The outline of her ribs was beginning to
retreat behind a layer of flesh.

Aegista tiptoed into the room to announce that Hesione's bath was ready. Penthesilea followed Hesione to her tiled room. Once Aegista had finished washing Hesione, the Amazon lifted the large pitcher of rinse water to pour over her. She found the vessel heavier than before.

She began to frequent the garden again. While Hesione sat on the bench and laughed, she climbed up the trees and hoisted herself through their branches. She began to stride around the city again; while Hesione attempted to keep up, she paced briskly through the streets, bounded furiously up and down stairs, and scaled and descended the shrub-planted incline that led from a lateral thoroughfare to Hesione's window.

They lay under a soft white blanket and stared at each other in the light that filtered through. Hesione's forefinger traced circles around Penthesilea's navel. "I love it," Hesione said. "I love the way it's set so perfectly in the middle of your belly, like an onyx in a bronze ring. And I'm the jeweler." She bent over the object of her adoration, made a great show of peering at it, moistened her lips, and kissed it. She lifted her face and said, "No wonder they envy me."

"They? They? But who knows about us?"

Hesione rolled on her back and snorted, "Surely you don't think that no one knows what's going on between us? My poor darling. Nobody can keep anything secret around here. And they have eyes. They see me. They see us. They know you don't spend the nights in your room. They're jealous, because they see how happy I am. They envy it, of course."

"Who are they?"

"Lady Medekasta."

"What?" Penthesilea lifted herself on one elbow. "What?"

"Don't tell me that surprises you. And my little sister. And half the women around here—even the slaves. And mother."

"Queen Glaucia?"

"Yes. Naturally. But she won't say anything. She sees how you make my body happy. People can tell these things just by the way a woman walks. Don't you know that? She sees how devoted you are to me. How you surround me with your attentions. And she resents it. She didn't marry Laomedon for love, you know. It was a political match. Their bed was only for the production of legitimate offspring. Do you know how dull that is? That's why she envies how you make me happy. You can see that by the way she's treated me since you've been around."

"Maybe you're right," said Penthesilea, who had accompanied Hesione on several occasions to visit the queen.

The morning sunlight crept into the sleeping chamber. Hesione rested on her side like a child in peaceful repose, her knees folded close to her chest and her hands joined under her cheek. Penthesilea lay alongside, her body curved to fit into the angles that Hesione's made. The Amazon's thighs touched Hesione's buttocks, her hand overspread her fleece, her lips pressed against her back. Hesione's ribs moved in and out in indolent cadence. Without warning the bed vibrated, clay smashed against clay, and wood ground against wood. Penthesilea sat up in a spasm, rousing Hesione, who rolled over and said without opening her eyes, "It's just the Goddess shaking the earth a little, adored kitten. Don't be frightened. The palace rests on packed earth."

Hesione filled her lungs and exhaled with a loud whoosh. "I have to get up," she sighed. "How I hate to leave my bed when you're in it. Actually, we'll both have to get up."

"What ever for?"

"Didn't I tell you that father wants to see you?"

"Why?"

"He didn't say. He must want something. After all, he's seen plenty enough of you since . . ." Hesione chuckled. "Since you've become attached to my person."

Penthesilea gripped her harder.

"I'm positive that father is pleased we've become such loving friends. It keeps me away from the boys, you see. It wouldn't do for the King's daughter to become pregnant by someone whom the king didn't choose. Laomedon likes that, especially because he doesn't want any man in my bed. I think he's delighted that you're happy here."

Penthesilea said nothing.

Hesione stiffened. "You are, aren't you?"

Penthesilea put on a smile and kissed the pulse that fluttered in Hesione's throat.

Hesione murmured in satisfaction and went on, "He always asks after the rider from Themiscyra. He wants to know if you like being quartered in the palace, if you like Troy. He once asked if you care for me as much as he does. He even asks if I love my new friend as much as I love him." Hesione drawled in a childish soprano, "'Ooh noo, daddy,' I answered, 'Ooh noo.'"

She tittered. "But still, darling child, don't be surprised if he wants something from you."

"I won't," said Penthesilea, who in three weeks at Hesione's side had observed the ways of the palace.

Everyone withdrew to a respectful distance. Penthesilea approached the throne and bowed in the way that Leokadia had taught her years before—respectful but not servile. Penthesilea stood up straight and gazed evenly at Laomedon. His stare was keen and cruel under his thick brows; it drilled into Penthesilea's own stare, assaulted it, and tried to bend it. She did not flinch. Seeing this, Laomedon relaxed his fleshy lips and beamed like an indulgent uncle. Still, a hardness glinted in the back of his regard that reminded Penthesilea of Celano.

Laomedon nodded once and said, "Welcome, Penthesilea. I see that the stories they tell about the Amazons are true. You are a proud and handsome race."

"Thank you," said Penthesilea without changing her expression.

Laomedon said, "The redheaded Achaean says that your mother is the high priestess of Themiscyra."

"That is not true, Laomedon. It is true that Myrtho the priestess loves me like her own daughter. But still, I am not her child, neither by birthright nor adoption. My mother was Leokadia the rider. She is dead now. She was much loved by Myrtho."

"The way Hesione loves you?" asked Laomedon.

"Yes. Because I was Leokadia's girl, Myrtho loved me like her own."

"The Achaean captain also said that you are the cousin of Themiscyra's ruler and live in her house. Isn't Thalestris her name?"

"That is her name, Laomedon. But I am no kin of hers, although I lived in her palace."

"What is your position in her household?"

"I ride with her daughter, Antiope."

"Thalestris' heir?"

"I have been Antiope's companion for three seasons now. I ride with her in battle."

"To what do you owe this rank?"

"My mother, Leokadia the rider, put me there, because Thalestris asked for me by name."

Laomedon tilted his face to show interest.

"Thalestris wanted to further her claims to the throne by getting Myrtho's support; she also wanted to have someone dear to Myrtho in her power once she was ruler. And so she asked for me. There was no way that Leokadia could refuse."

Laomedon needed no further explanation and asked, "What arts of war and command did you learn in Thalestris house?"

"To ride and shoot the bow. To hurl the double-headed axe and wield the long knife. To know every inch of our hills and valleys. To know the surest ways of ambushing and wearing down invaders, until they regret that they ever set foot in the Amazon domain. And if they still do not understand, to carry destruction and harassment to their own lands, until they sue for peace."

"To ride and shoot the bow," Laomedon repeated. "They say that the Amazon queen who visited my ancestor king Teucer could run her horse full speed past a post stuck in the ground, take aim, and shoot an arrow into it without slowing her mount. At twenty paces, mind you." Laomedon leaned forward and lowered his voice. "It's not a tall tale?" he asked.

"Of course not."

Laomedon raised an eyebrow, only to frown an instant afterward. "Don't you women ever fight hand to hand?"

"Why? Not unless we have to."

"Are you afraid that men will beat you, because they're stronger? Do you fear standing man-to-man and fighting it out?"

Penthesilea remembered her set-to with Pirothous but did not smile, and she answered as if she were explaining a difficult maneuver to a rider whose self-respect she did not wish to offend, "The might of a bear without the slyness of a lynx and the agility of a mountain cat is not strength, Laomedon, but weakness. In our terrain, the Amazons always win, be it over the Kaska savages or the trained soldiers of Amisos."

Laomedon's avuncular, untrustworthy, expression again covered his face. He summoned a tall, clear-eyed soldier who had held himself at ease near the entrance. "This is Ennomos, captain of the palace guard," said Laomedon. "Follow him. He will show you something. After you're done, he'll bring you back here."

A chariot and charioteer waited; two chestnut horses pawed the ground. Penthesilea sprang onto the wagon. It slid sideways when she landed on it. It was only a platform with railing on two large wheels. There was room only for one person behind the driver, who turned and bowed his head in a courtly manner.

He introduced himself as Orthaios, a royal cousin. He was a young man, not more than Penthesilea's age. His small face, large nose, and dark hair reminded Penthesilea of Hesione's. Orthaios was bare-chested; a kilt of fine sky-blue wool surrounded his hips. The ends of his horses' reins were wound around his waist, a short knife threading in and out of their straps.

He turned, snapped the reins, and screamed, "Onward!" His steeds took off at a run, the vehicle lurched, Penthesilea's feet slid out from under her. She grabbed the rail and yanked herself upright. Once she had regained her footing, she observed Orthaios. He stood with his legs apart, his knees flexed, his shoulders leaning backward. As the chariot bounced and pitched, he bent his legs and tilted his trunk to adjust to the jolts and sways. Penthesilea imitated his stance and, after losing her balance and righting herself one more time, got the knack of balancing on planks that plunged and shifted beneath her.

The team sped across the marketplace—faces gaped; through the gate—one guard nudged another and pointed; down the hill—pedestrians scurried out of the way and drovers yanked their donkeys off the road. The ground leveled. Orthaios shook the reins and yelled, "Get! Get!" The team vaulted forward. Orthaios by turns pulled back on the reins and let up on them to keep a steady pressure on the animals' mouths. The cloudless sky and ripe fields through which the chariot fled opened in front of Penthesilea, sped by her shoulders, and closed in back of them. Her heart beat with joy at the freedom.

Orthaios tightened the two leather straps he held in his left hand and slackened the ones he grasped in his right. The leftmost horse slowed; the rightmost lengthened its stride. The team pivoted left. The chariot bumped and skidded after them. They hurried past an emerald green field enclosed by a corral fence. Rope halters attached to its gate whipped around the cross pieces in the wind. Four light brown horses, two full-grown and two that reached their withers, were grazing with lowered heads. The animals' coats glistened like polished bronze in the sunlight and rippled like waters that the noonday breeze skims over. A familiar smell, sweet and acrid all at once, horses and leather and manure, began to fill Penthesilea's nostrils. Three long pine board buildings and a corral came into sight. Laomedon's stables! Penthesilea's throat tightened. Tala must be there.

Orthaios bellowed at the horses to stop and leaned back on the reins wrapped around his waist. The beasts ran on, tugging against them. The harder the steeds resisted, the lower Orthaios bent, until—after losing their match of strength and will—the team halted.

Penthesilea saw that those horses would be no good in the field. They were too hard to control. A chariot and charioteer could not zigzag in and out of enemy range the way a rider could.

Penthesilea jumped down. She noticed that the foam dripping from the horses' mouths was pink. Blood oozed from the cheekpieces that pressed the ends of their lips.

She faced Orthaios and looked inquisitively at the knife at his midsection.

"The knife, madam," said Orthaios, "is that what you are asking about? It's for cutting myself out of the reins if I fall and the horses drag me. When they're frightened, there's no telling what they'll do. They take the bit in their teeth and run; they don't slow down for the harshest cheekpieces and strongest nosebands. That's how Capaneus, the first man ever to guide a chariot, met his end. He was dragged to death by his horses. A storm surprised him while he was driving his team. Lightning struck. The horses panicked and started to run out of control. The chariot capsized. Capaneus was caught in the reins and dragged to death."

Chariots were more trouble than they were worth. Mounted archers could make short work of them. Penthesilea did not voice these thoughts. Instead, she pointed to the team and said, "They've got plenty of fire, those two."

"Fire. That they have, madam. Laomedon has four dozen teams like this one. He takes the pick of the horses from his stables for the army."

A gray-haired fellow with uneven shoulders hailed Penthesilea from the farthest building and told her to come over. He was the hostler who had taken Tala and Melanthus when the Achaeans first arrived at Troy. The man disappeared into the stable as soon as Penthesilea reached the cobbling that surrounded it. She followed him inside, passing a row of chariots reared up against the walls. Above each vehicle hung the tack that belonged to its team—headpieces, reins, and neckstraps. Penthesilea slowed her pace and looked closely at the Trojan bridles, with their broad muzzle bands, barbed cheekpieces, and snaffle bits. A Trojan driver had to crush the beast's nose, rip its lips, and wound its tongue in order to make it do what he wanted. Not like an Amazon rider, with her hands, knees, heels, and voice telling the mount exactly where to place itself.

Two bridles with smooth bits and tiny crescent cheekpieces were suspended closest to the stalls, next to sheepskin saddles. The equipment belonged to Amazon horses, one of whom, Tala, had begun to snort. She had smelled Penthesilea.

The stableman stood next to Tala's stall. Penthesilea approached the mare, blew in her nostrils, and tried to scratch her forehead. Tala jerked her neck back and grunted a rough complaint. Melanthus, who occupied the next station, bared his teeth and shook his withers.

"They're mad at you," chuckled the old groom. "Not that they have any reason. We treat them well. Let me show you." The man fastened a lead rope to Tala's halter, undid the small gate that confined her, and led her outside.

Tala's dull scrawniness had given way to sleek good health, the wound on her fetlock had healed, and her hooves were hard and clean. Penthesilea beamed at the hostler with gratitude; he grinned with pride.

Penthesilea asked, in what she hoped was an offhand manner, "Has she been in heat since you've had her?" Tala might have. Mares came into rut three or four times starting a few weeks before the day of the year and ending a few weeks after the longest one. Tala and Melanthus had been in the groom's keeping since the last days of that season.

"In heat?" replied the stableman. "Can't say as we've had any luck with her. But five of our stock horses have, and we put 'em with that big stallion."

"And they took?" asked Penthesilea.

"Three did, as far as we can tell. But come next season we will put that mare to the stallion every year. With the foals she'll drop and with the rag of colts the stallion will get on the other mares, we'll have a squad of tall ones in four seasons, and plenty of breedin' stock to boot.

"But begging your pardon, ma'am, Laomedon's orders are just to show you the tall horses and send you back."

Glaucia and Phrontis stood in a far corner of the throne room, whispering. They looked up when Penthesilea was ushered in. The moment Penthesilea approached the throne, the knot of men who surrounded it stepped back hastily, leaving only the soldier Tithonos stationed at Laomedon's side. Penthesilea bent from the waist.

"You have seen the horses," said Laomedon. "Are you satisfied that they're well taken care of?"

"Yes, Laomedon."

"My stableman tells me that the stallion has already been put to good use, and that we'll breed the mare to him in the spring. We'll have a race of tall horses in a few years."

"I know."

"So you asked the stableman about that. Have you thought about what I intend?"

The Amazon said nothing.

"Your silence tells me that you have. You know that I want a better breed not just to have faster chariot horses. I want a cavalry. I want mounted archers."

Penthesilea did not reply.

"And do you know what I want from you? I want you to train a contingent of archers to fight on horseback the way the Amazons do. I want you to lead them into battle in my wars."

Penthesilea tightened her lips.

"You stand to gain a lot if you do. More than you know. More than you think." Laomedon lowered his voice. "I'll fill your coffers, Penthesilea. Gold, silver, jewels, ivory, amber, name it. Name it. You'll answer only to me, the king of Troy, and to my commander, Tithonos. All the others will have to make way when you enter this room. You didn't enjoy such rank where you come from. You weren't so important in Thalestris' house. You'll live in my palace, too. You'll have your own quarters. Slaves will wait on your every desire. I'll send Hesione to you. Hesione."

Penthesilea closed her eyes.

"So you agree?" asked Laomedon.

Penthesilea crossed her arms in front of her chest.

"I'll give you one more thing," said Laomedon. He glanced at Tithonos, who shifted on his feet.

Laomedon leaned forward: "I'll give you something more important than all the rest—your freedom, Penthesilea. At the end of ten seasons I'll release you from slavery."

Penthesilea's hands dropped to her side.

Laomedon did not take his eyes off Penthesilea and went on, "The messenger that the Achaeans sent to Themiscyra has returned empty-handed. Yes, empty-handed. The women there didn't want to pay your ransom—not Thalestris, not Antiope . . .

and not Myrtho. Not even Myrtho cares to spend one ounce of her goddess' gold to get you back. Forget about the Amazons; they've turned their backs on you."

Penthesilea's windpipe grew tight, but she fought to give no sign of what she felt.

"But I bought you from your captors instead. You are mine." Laomedon scowled and said, "I could threaten you. You know what I could do. . . ." He relaxed his face and continued, "But I won't. Instead, I'll give you wealth, if you ride for me. I'll give you power. I'll give you pleasure. And I'll give you your freedom at the end of ten seasons. Go, now, and think it over."

He turned his attention to Tithonos. She was dismissed. Penthesilea withdrew from the royal hall. Her head ached and her cheeks burned. Her steps took her to Hesione's apartments. Hesione was not there. Penthesilea went to the window and gazed at the sky. Its coolness descended into her entrails.

Soft footfalls and the rustling of a skirt. Someone took her place at Penthesilea's side. Penthesilea still did not turn.

"Penthesilea."

Glaucia's voice. The Amazon faced her. The queen did not wear her usual, gracious mien. Instead, her lips traced a line as straight and sharp as a blade's edge.

"I learned today," she said, "from Lady Agameda, whose pleasure-man is that redheaded mercenary, that the messenger the Achaeans sent to Themiscyra has returned and that the Amazons did not pay your ransom. Agameda also said that Laomedon bought you for himself."

"That is true, my lady."

"I know what Laomedon wants of you, too. It's not hard to discern his wishes. I've watched him for eighteen seasons. He has desired a cavalry all along. He has offered you treasure and power to lead one. He's offered you Hesione. He told her so while you were gone. He has held Hesione back for years, thinking to use her to his best advantage. And now he has. And he has not threatened you. Not in so many words, although his menaces can be vile and he has slaves who carry them out with great pleasure. No. Laomedon wants your loyalty."

"That is true, my lady."

"Have you asked yourself why Laomedon didn't act sooner? Didn't take you prisoner right away and do away with the Achaeans then and there?"

Penthesilea did not reply.

"Laomedon didn't in the hope that he could seize the treasure sent here to redeem you, have the Achaeans murdered in their sleep, and take you prisoner in turn. That is his way, you know, especially with the Achaeans, whom he despises. Now that there's no hope of capturing that prize, too, Laomedon has devised another stratagem. He's offered a price for the prisoner from Themiscyra, and the mercenaries have accepted it. Naturally. They could hardly refuse."

The queen's flintlike eyes cut into Penthesilea's. "Laomedon's scribes now count two tall horses and one Amazon rider among the things that are his. And if you accept his offer, he'll possess a cavalry, too. I don't envy you at all."

"How can the queen of Troy even think of envy?"

Glaucia sighed and caressed Penthesilea's cheek.

Penthesilea continued, "Laomedon has offered to make me captain of his cavalry and free me at the end of ten years."

"Do not deceive yourself that he will release you when he promises that he will. How could he ever let you go? Supposing that you had failed to teach his men one trick and then led the Amazons against them and destroyed his cavalry? Supposing that you had learned by heart the evolutions of his army and the weak points of his city's ramparts? Do you not see that he will never keep his promise? Kings take oaths only as it suits them and find ways to go back on them just as easily. That is how they become kings and remain so.

"And could you trust a man to keep his word who would not have hesitated to plunder ransom money won by others and have them murdered in their sleep? No. A woman like you must despise a man like him. I do not think that you could obey a man whom you despised."

"But once I get my horse back, I could ride like the wind."

"Do not lie to yourself, Penthesilea. You would not flee so easily. Laomedon has made sure of that. You would not leave Hesione, not now at least. You would not turn your back so easily on her embraces, nor on the wines and meats they carry you at your command, nor on the perfumed baths they pour for you at your bidding, nor on chests full of jewels, arms, and ivory, nor on troops you formed yourself, whom you would love because you did, and who would love you for your skill and bravery and obey your every word. And if you accept Laomedon's offer, he'll make you promise on the altar of your goddess not to run away. Would you so lightly go against a sacred oath? Of course not. That is why he'd make you take it."

Penthesilea said nothing.

"And do you want never again to see the women you shared your childhood and young age with? Those whom you love? Those who love you? Those in Themiscyra who pray every day that you will, somehow, escape from Troy?"

Penthesilea hid behind her silence.

"I, Glaucia, Queen of Troy, could never be a slave, could never trick myself into hoping for better days when the Goddess had no more to give me. No. I would, by my own hand, cheat the victor of them. But you, Penthesilea, you, who could not stand being a captive, although you were treated like a royal cousin, you who are young and freeborn and noble, could you tolerate being a slave? You hated your captivity until my daughter welcomed you to her bed. And once Hesione tires of you, you will hate being a slave. She has before, you know, tired of someone even while he lay in her arms. His name was Herakles. She dismissed him from her bed then and there. She threw him away like a toy she had ceased to find amusing. And she told her women about it, so that the word spread through the palace, and the poor fellow was shamed into leaving Troy. She might do the same to you, you know, once she had enough of you. But where would you go? You would have to face the sneers and jests at your expense. You cannot ignore that she is capable of such a thing. And you, yourself, once you tire of Hesione, what will you feel? What will you do?"

Penthesilea made no answer.

"You do not say a word. You do not blink. You know I speak the truth. And so, although you will command others who will obey you to the death, soon enough you will stop deluding yourself and see how much you hate your thralldom, detest your captivity, and execrate yourself for putting up with it."

Worry rushed into Penthesilea's chest.

Glaucia placed her long-nailed fingers on Penthesilea's forearm. "I know you despise bondage as much as I do," she said. "That is why I have come to speak to you."

Glaucia glanced at the door before saying, "You can go back to Themiscyra if you want. I'll make it possible for you to escape."

Penthesilea's pulse began to pound, but she recovered enough to shake her head in doubt.

"It's not as hard as you think to smuggle someone past the palace guards and through the gates. It's been done before, and more than once—in the huge clay jars they send down to the ships or in a closed chair carried by slaves, part of the queen's party on its way to the temple at the foot of Mount Ida."

What did the queen want in exchange? Penthesilea wondered, then asked out loud, "But how could I ever thank you for the gift of escape?"

Glaucia smiled slightly. "You love and fear the Goddess, as I do. I have seen how devout you are. But Laomedon hates Her and does everything he can to weaken Her power. She does not want him to have a cavalry. She would grieve to see Laomedon stronger."

"So would the Achaeans that he is fighting in the south," said Penthesilea, "and the men of Amisos who harass his sea routes and would plague his eastern border...."

"If they did not fear his allies."

"Themiscyra, my lady?"

"Yes. Themiscyra. The Amazon cavalry."

So that was what Glaucia wanted, a change of loyalty. She wanted Themiscyra's riders to join the men of Amisos instead of fight them. "And the Hittites?" objected Penthesilea. "We pay them tribute and they, too, are allied with Troy. They would not like us to shift allegiance. They have a strong infantry. Our lands are only a few days' march from theirs."

Glaucia laughed and said, "Do not be worried about them. They are too busy killing one another. The king and his brother fight each other for the empire. Every soldier is in one army or the next. They will cause no trouble."

"Not now, my lady, but when their civil war is over, they will."

"And the Amazons will have powerful friends. The same friends who want you to escape from Troy. To be free of it. To return to those you love. And to carry word to your queen that, if she desists from Troy's alliance, they will fill her coffers."

"With the booty from the cities they sack and the slaves they sell?"

Glaucia removed a glittering band made of scores of tiny links from her finger, pressed it into Penthesilea's palm, and held it tight. "When the time comes," said the queen, "I will send a messenger to Themiscyra with a gold ring just like this one and more, much more, for your queen—and for you."

Glaucia swept up her skirts and went to the door. There she stopped and looked back. "Do not speak a word of this to Hesione. She's likely to be unhappy about losing her friend and say something indiscreet. As for my offer, before many days are

out I'll send you word to be ready. I have no doubt you'll go."
She paused and articulated, "No doubt." She left the room.

Penthesilea turned to face the window. The air chilled her skin; her head throbbed.

A little later, Hesione returned to her apartments. She wrapped her arms around Penthesilea. "I'm so sorry," Hesione said. "I wanted to talk to you as soon as you left the royal hall, but couldn't. Aunt Phrontis called me away. She wanted to know what I thought of some wretched gewgaws from the south, but I got away as soon as I could. Father spoke to me while you were visiting his stables and told me what he wants you to do and what he wants me to do." Hesione pressed her body against Penthesilea's. "I'm happy. You have been so good for me. And now, precious baby, you'll be there whenever I want you, or at least in the winter, when you're not off making war for Daddy. Don't take any slave girls with you. Or will you train me to be a horse soldier like the Amazon riders so I can go along? You've showed me so much else."

Hesione gave Penthesilea a kiss so full of passion that the sweetness rushed into Penthesilea's entrails, although she did not want it to, and Hesione led her to bed.

Hesione lay with her lids closed, sighing in contentment. Penthesilea ran her fingers over Hesione's nipples, which had grown soft and flat again, and her belly, which had grown cool and fleshy.

"I can't imagine ever having enough of your thrilling me the way you do," whispered Hesione. "Ever."

Penthesilea raised herself on one elbow. "Of course you will," she said.

"Will what, darling child?"

"Have enough of me, tire of me, send me away."

Hesione opened her eyes. "You're dreadfully foolish, you know."

"I'm not. You've done it before."

"Done what, silly kitten?"

"Tired of someone. Kicked him out of your bed."

Hesione sat up. "Who told you that?"

"Everyone," lied Penthesilea. "They say that you told him to leave while he was embracing you. You just told him to get out. And then you told your servants what had happened, so that everyone knew and made fun of the man."

"Oh, that old thing. That was that muscle-bound idiot, Herakles. Glaucia and Phrontis put me up to it. They insisted. They wanted me pregnant. That overdeveloped pea-brain bored me in bed. You never bore me."

"That's not the point," said Penthesilea.

Hesione put a hand on Penthesilea's cheek, but Penthesilea removed it and repeated, "That's not the point."

Hesione turned her head away. When she faced Penthesilea, the helpless mist that had lately infused her glance had vanished. The fury of her look cut Penthesilea.

"Who said such a thing about me?" asked Hesione. "A slave?" she rasped. "You'd believe a mere slave?"

"I am a slave," retorted Penthesilea.

Hesione paid no heed and said, "And you, Penthesilea. Will you never grow tired of me?"

The accusation held some truth. Penthesilea blushed.

Hesione smirked, but immediately changed her expression. She tilted her face, flashed her dark eyes, and tried to pull Penthesilea down against her. Penthesilea stiffened.

Hesione sucked in her lips and paled. She pronounced in a chilling manner, "You have grown arrogant, my Amazon lover. Not even a day has passed since my father made you an important captain in his household, and you become haughty. You speak to the daughter of the man who owns you as if you now owned her. I do not care for you this way. I liked you better when you were . . ."

"Your slave?" interrupted Penthesilea. "Obeying your every whim? Your body slave?"

Hesione snickered, patted Penthesilea on the head, and said, "You do give yourself airs."

Penthesilea bolted out of bed, threw on her clothes, and stormed out of Hesione's apartments. The Amazon tore through the palace and bounded out of the portal without noticing that the guard there touched his spear to his brow and let her pass. She pounded down the hill, but as swift as her steps were, they could not carry her away from Hesione's presence, or Laomedon's, or Glaucia's. She felt them as a burning spot between her shoulder blades.

Hesione. Kissing Penthesilea with great hunger so that she would make the joy race through her; embracing her with great skill so that she could not bear to spend the night away from her; treating her like a plaything to be kept until it no longer entertained her. It was all Hesione's doing. It was all her fault. . . . The words grated against each other. They were not the straight truth. Who, after all, had seduced Hesione for her own reasons? Who had studied Hesione's flesh until no longing remained concealed? Who had let herself become a prisoner of Hesione's passion for her and of her own for Hesione, so that, more and more often, she was near forgetting the woman her heart really. . . .

A black curtain slammed down, and Penthesilea turned her wrath on Laomedon.

Laomedon. The mighty master of Troy, who now had tall horses and wanted a cavalry so that his soldiers could sack more cities and put them to the torch, could rape more women and sell them into slavery.

Pain slashed Penthesilea's vagina. The smell of fumes and gore turned her stomach. She saw Themiscyra's marketplace at the dying of the day. Swirls of black smoke obscured it; flame orange flashes illuminated it. Women's shrieks and men's yelps echoed against the heavens. Aella ran across her vision and disappeared, then a fat, grim-helmeted man, Pirothous. Unseen, desperate screams bounced against the firmament and fell back on Penthesilea's shoulders with such force that they pushed her breath from her.

She clenched her fists until her knuckles whitened. No! She would never fail the women of Themiscyra, never betray the Amazons, never—even if Laomedon had said that they had turned against her. But had they? Perhaps they had. Perhaps. . . . Penthesilea's knees folded. She stumbled but got a hold of herself and resumed her stride. She must escape. Glaucia wanted to help her get away, to smuggle her out of Troy, but Penthesilea wanted no part of her intrigues, wanted to owe nothing, especially double-dealing, to the hard-eyed woman who in her fury to confound her husband thought nothing of destroying the Goddess's friends.

Penthesilea must flee that night. The moon was a few days from full but still bright enough to make her way by. She thought of the rope that she had hidden in Hesione's apartments. Penthesilea then saw Hesione's hostile look and heard her scornful voice. She would never again open her arms to Penthesilea. She had outraged her, vexed her, and so brought her own plans down in ruins. She had let her temper take her prisoner. And yet no deep understanding drew her to this woman, only her own schemes, only her own loneliness.

"And now if I want to run away, if I want to go home, I'll have to crawl back and beg for forgiveness, lick the dust at her feet, plead to share her bed again."

Penthesilea's insides soured but she lowered her head and fought back the feeling. "There's no other thing I can do but get it over with—tonight, and then I'll leave it all behind for good."

Someone bumped into Penthesilea and nearly knocked her over.

"Why don't you look where you're going?" barked a man with a guttural accent.

Penthesilea woke up. It was the white-robed trader who, months ago, had called at Themiscyra in the same caravan as Abba-Basthi, the merchant who had accused Thalia the farmer of theft.

The noise and smells of Troy's marketplace assailed Penthesilea. She blinked like one awakened from sleep and looked up. Farmers stood chattering with each other and with merchants; hawkers walked around crying their goods; sellers stationed behind stands sang the merits of their wares; donkeys brayed as they were led across the space.

Penthesilea shook her head to rid herself of her thoughts, and, without her knowing it, her scout's gaze swept the crowded space in front of the portal. She started. Something clamored for her attention. She glanced back at the city gate. A short woman with close-cropped black hair and full cheeks was staring at her from eyes set deep in her tanned visage. Pale blue light descended on her.

"Abba-Bashti," mumbled Penthesilea. "Abba-Bashti."

Chapter 14

Penthesilea elbowed her way through the crowd. She crashed into someone—the priestess Anteia—blushed and stuttered apologies, but did not stop and hastened to Abba-Bashti, who broke into a childlike grin. Still, Abba-Bashti's eyes were deeper and sadder than Penthesilea remembered. The two women stepped into the shadow of the gatehouse. Penthesilea took Abba-Bashti's hands. They pressed hers. The women stood staring at one another. Neither was able to unfreeze her lips. Then both spilled out words at the same time. Then they giggled and squeezed each other's fingers.

"You, here?" asked Abba-Bashti in her singing accent. Her voice was clearer than the one Penthesilea had imagined. "I thought it," she said. "They said that someone brought an Amazon to Troy, that many times they saw you in the streets, that you came through the market on a chariot this morning like a great captain. They told what you looked like, and I thought it was you. They say that you now live in the palace, with the king's daughter, that you and she. . . ." Abba-Bashti's voice trailed off.

Penthesilea's cheeks burned, and she lowered her head. She tried to speak but could not make a sound. How could she confess that all the while she had shared Hesione's bed, the desire that swept Penthesilea into forgetfulness had never been for Hesione, not for one day, not for one night? Abba-Bashti would never believe her. Penthesilea let Abba-Bashti's hands go, but Abba-Bashti did not drop them to her side. Instead her dark gaze fixed Penthesilea, and Penthesilea saw that there was no anger in it, only unhappiness.

Penthesilea took Abba-Bashti's hands again and searched for something to say. Finally she asked, "Where is Artatama? Where is Tushratta?"

Abba-Bashti gasped and stiffened. She stammered, "My brother is here. He is alive."

"And Tush. . . ." Penthesilea stopped herself. So that was where the grief came from. Abba-Bashti had lost the child.

Shame darkened Penthesilea's vision. When she could see again, Abba-Bashti was looking at her through glittering tears. Suffering contracted her brows and drew her mouth into a tight line. Penthesilea's heart wrenched to look at her. "It hurts me that you are so hurt," she said.

"I see it," said Abba-Bashti.

Penthesilea closed her eyes. An idea rushed into her head. She gathered her courage and said, "I was taken prisoner and brought here against my will. I am a slave, the king's slave. I am treated like a royal cousin, but I cannot live this way. I plan to escape. Tonight. Come with me. Come with me."

Abba-Bashti frowned. Her forehead wrinkled.

Penthesilea braced herself for the refusal.

Abba-Bashti's features lightened. She inclined her head in assent.

Penthesilea shook hers in joyous disbelief. A question formed in her mind as soon as she did.

"Are you thinking of my brother, Artatama?" asked Abba-Bashti. "What he will do without me?"

"Yes. Yes."

"Do not think too much of that. Now I have no boy baby for him to adopt, and Artatama will have to pay a dowry to marry me to someone again or keep me in his house without a son. It is not so bad for him that I go away. And he will see me if he comes to Themiscyra."

"Are you sure? Please be sure."

Abba-Bashti fingered the tiny likeness of Nanaï that hung between her breasts and said, "I am sure. I promise you."

Penthesilea's heart leaped. She waited until its beating stilled and glanced around her to make sure that no one was within earshot. She explained her plans—to steal out of the palace while all slept and to use the rope she had purloined to lower herself down the fortification. When she finished, she said, "Meet me at midnight by the fig trees at the foot of the west wall." Penthesilea noticed that the shadow cast by the parapet had lengthened. The fall afternoon was almost gone. "I must go now," she said. "I have many things to do."

She pivoted on her heels and bounded off in the direction of the palace. She turned her head after she had crossed the marketplace. Abba-Bashti, who was watching her, touched her fingers to her lips.

Penthesilea stepped lively to the great dwelling. The guard at the door straightened up. She strode into the royal hall. Laomedon was standing in the middle of the room, among a handful of leather-kilted men. Penthesilea walked directly up to him. The soldiers grew silent and moved away, leaving the ruler and the Amazon face to face. She bowed once and said, "I am at your orders, Laomedon. Tomorrow I will see the stable master."

Laomedon beamed. His delight was real this time. Penthesilea begged his leave. She headed for Hesione's apartments, crossing paths with Anteia, who was hurrying in the direction of Glaucia's.

Hesione was not in her quarters. Penthesilea threw herself into an armchair and supported her brow on the heel of her hand. She tried to compose meek words, pleading words, words of self-abasement that would make Hesione open her arms again, but Penthesilea's wishes were like seeds that never germinated, and she sat motionless. Hesione soon returned. Penthesilea did not stir from her distressed posture. Hesione hastened across the room, threw herself at Penthesilea's feet, and buried her head in her thighs.

"Forgive me, love," said the king's daughter. "Forgive me, dearest baby."

Penthesilea straightened herself and eyed Hesione with amazement. Hesione looked up. Her brow was candid, her vixen's eyes repentant, but, but what? Did they hide something?

"I was foolish, darling girl," she said. "I spoke too soon. I should never have said what I said. I could not stand your being cross with me."

An uncomfortable undertone laced Hesione's voice. Penthesilea nonetheless took her cheeks in her hand, bent over, and kissed her forehead.

Hesione raised herself and sat on Penthesilea's lap. She wrapped her arms around the Amazon and pressed her chest against her cheek.

Penthesilea pronounced, "My sweet. My darling."

"You do forgive me then, precious child?" cooed Hesione.

"Your kisses are so good that there is nothing for me to forgive," said Penthesilea. It was now her turn to plead for absolution, and she spoke what she hoped were the correct phrases. "But it is I who beg you to forget how pigheaded I was. I was jealous." The last statement, at least, was true.

She embraced Hesione and gave her a lover's kiss. She thought for a moment that she had gotten outside her body and was looking at herself dallying with the young woman. She remembered all the words and gestures that brought Hesione to ecstasy and blissful sleep. But not yet. The sky was still light. Penthesilea pulled back.

"What is it?" asked Hesione.

"I haven't eaten since this morning."

"I'll have Aegista bring something. Let's not leave this room."

"Let's not," agreed Penthesilea.

It was dark out by the time Aegista carried in a tray. As she bent over to set it on a low table next to the chair Penthesilea occupied, she raised her eyes quickly and just as quickly lowered them. Alarm made their pupils into dark green points. Penthesilea wondered what had happened and resolved to ask her the next morning, but realized that she would be far from Troy by then. She stopped herself from glancing over at the chest in which she had concealed the ship's cord but could not repress a smile.

Aegista tiptoed out.

"What are you smiling at, dearest baby?" asked Hesione, who had pulled up a stool and now sat at Penthesilea's feet.

"Your charms, my sweet," lied Penthesilea.

Hesione's lips told of delight. She poured a goblet of wine and handed it to Penthesilea. She began to carve slivers of meat and place them one by one in Penthesilea's mouth.

When the hunger and thirst had gone from Penthesilea, she sighed with ease and sank back. She would miss this luxury, but. . . . Her mind's eye traced the route she would take that night, down the hill under Hesione's window, through dark side streets to the parapet, and down it to the fig trees. Abba-Bashti would be waiting for her there. Pleasure lit up Penthesilea's face.

"You're always so good-looking when you're lost in thought," came Hesione's voice. "But whatever are you thinking about, sweetest girl?"

Penthesilea sat up straight and gazed at Hesione with desire. Hesione grinned, bent forward, and pressed her brow against the skirt of Penthesilea's tunic. Penthesilea put her arms around Hesione and stood, pulling Hesione up against her. The door opened and the lamps flickered. Hesione wrested herself away.

Ennomos, captain of the palace guard, stamped into the room. He held a naked sword in his right hand and in his left a coil of rope that looked like the one Penthesilea had hidden. Four soldiers followed him. In an instant two had stationed themselves behind the officer and two behind the Amazon.

Penthesilea paled but fought back the confusion that struggled to take over her face.

Ennomos addressed Penthesilea. "You come with me," he snapped. "We don't let slaves escape. We don't let them try. You'll be sorry you did."

Penthesilea forced herself to look evenly at Ennomos, although, out of the corner of her eye she saw Hesione, whose lips were parted and eyebrows raised.

The captain nodded once, and the guards at the window grabbed Penthesilea's arms and locked them behind her. Ennomos did an about-face, left the room, and strode down the corridor. The men who held Penthesilea pushed her behind him. Guards and prisoner passed the entrance of the Queen's apartments. Glaucia, who stood under the lintel, watched Penthesilea being led away. They dragged her to the north tower, manhandled her up four flights of stairs, and threw her into a cell.

The door clapped shut like thunder. Gloom closed in. Weak yellow light radiated from somewhere. Penthesilea waited for her eyes to grow used to the faint glow. It came from a lamp that stood on a low table next to a pallet. She surveyed the room. It did not measure more than four paces by six. Walls of sweating stone closed it in. A single opening cut the building blocks at shoulder height. Planks formed the room's high ceiling. Threatening shadows loomed and vanished with the pulsating of the flame.

The cot. A wool throw had been tossed over it. On the floor by its side stood a clay jug and at its feet a slop bucket. The table. Penthesilea placed the lamp that it supported on the floor and dragged it under the window. She stepped up. The break in the stone was twice as high and wide as her arm. Darkness below, the north wall, a gibbous moon, the tang of the sea, and a chill wind. She stepped down and put the support back. She began to search for a way to escape. The street below lay at too great a distance for her to jump. She picked up the lamp and with her fingertips and eyes examined every stone and every chink in the walls, every plank and every nail in the floor and ceiling. Only a hook above the cot broke the smoothness. (Penthesilea's stomach tightened: what torment did it foretell?)

But nothing offered a means of flight. Nothing. She returned to the bed, seated herself, and pulled the blanket tight around her. She shivered and buried her face in her hands.

Someone had discovered that she wanted to escape and had betrayed her. Now she faced the punishment they meted out to runaway slaves, death by torture. Cold fingers gripped her windpipe. Women who had taken refuge in Themiscyra sobbed when they told of the cruelties dealt to runaways. And seasoned Amazons lowered their voices when they recounted what foreign soldiers did to enemies they took alive.

Who had condemned her? Who had given her away? Who had found the ship's cord and denounced her? Aegista? Was it she who had discovered Penthesilea's cache and showed it to Hesione? Hesione? Had she come upon it and seen what Penthesilea intended? Glaucia? Penthesilea again saw Glaucia watching the soldiers drag her off. If Glaucia had learned somehow that Penthesilea planned to escape, she would not scruple to take the story to Laomedon. After all, Penthesilea had plotted to fly from Troy without Glaucia's assistance, to fly from the debt of gratitude—of betrayal—that she would have to repay if she let the queen smuggle her out. Glaucia would never forgive.

Who had betrayed Penthesilea? Who? The question turned to ashes in Penthesilea's mouth. What did it matter? All that mattered was that she was a slave who had tried to run away and had been caught. Soon Laomedon's men would come for her.

Did they know about Abba-Bashti, too?

Dreadful imaginings pulled at Penthesilea. Cold fingers gripped her windpipe, frigid sweat poured from her body, her teeth chattered, her mouth dried until it choked her. She lay unable to move, trembling so hard that the cot rattled against the floor. Hours later, muffled footsteps behind the door roused her. She started. Daylight poured through the window. Perspiration soaked her garments and urine stained the blanket underneath her. A jailer heaved open the portal, ushered in Aegista, and withdrew. Penthesilea frowned and stared at the floor. Aegista sat beside her and put an arm around her. Penthesilea stiffened.

Aegista dropped it to her side. "Listen, Penthesilea," she said. "I did not give away your secret. I did not."

Penthesilea shook her head violently.

"Look at me. Look at me. I swear it."

Penthesilea drilled her gaze into Aegista's. Aegista's gold-flecked eyes stared straight into hers, did not evade them, did not waver. "It was Anteia who betrayed you," she said.

"Anteia?"

"Why do you think it's strange?"

Penthesilea rested her brow in her hand. Aegista wrapped hers around Penthesilea's waist.

"Hesione found the rope you hid," she said, "not many days ago. But I did not hear of this until yesterday. Hesione saw what you wanted to do with it, but did not tell anybody. I think she was afraid that they would take you away from her. Then, yesterday, you said hard words to each other. She must have spoken bitterness to you, the way they say you ran out of the palace. And you to her, the way Hesione was white with anger after you left. So angry that she got the rope from where she put it and set out to find Queen Glaucia and tell her of your crime. But she could not. She could not. She changed her mind on the way. I know. I was with her. Then, while she was visiting with Glaucia, Anteia came in."

Penthesilea remembered having crossed paths with her in the marketplace and in the palace corridor.

Aegista continued. "Anteia took the queen aside and whispered in her ear. Then she left without even looking at Hesione. Then Glaucia told Hesione how you met that trader woman in the market, the way you talked to her and held her hand, the way she blew you a kiss when you left. When Hesione heard this, the veins in her forehead pounded against her skin and she told Glaucia about the rope, and that you must want to run away from them, from Troy. The ice came into Glaucia's eyes. She ordered Hesione to keep you in her rooms, took the rope, and went to find the king.

"After they took you away, Hesione was sad. She asked what would happen to you, and I told her. She began to cry. She does not want them to spoil your body. So she went to see her father. But when she came back she was as sad as before. He did not promise anything. He did not say he will forbid them to hurt you when they kill you. He did not say he will not."

So they did not know about the woman who was supposed to wait for her at the foot of the west wall. That was good. Still. . . . Penthesilea sucked in her lips.

Aegista reached into a sleeve of her robe, pulled out a tiny vial, and gave it to Penthesilea. "Hesione sends this," said

Aegista. "Drink it. You will not suffer. I must go now. If they see that I have visited you, Hesione will have me beaten so they do not say that the king's own daughter went against his commands."   Aegista kissed Penthesilea's cheek.   "I will cry and miss you," she choked, and turned away abruptly.

After Aegista left, Penthesilea uncorked the vessel and sniffed. A sour smell made her throat contract. They had given her the juice of the poppy. It would make her lids happy with sleep and snuff out the light of this world without her feeling it. She put the container back on the table and stared at it until she did not see it any longer. The thought of disappearing without pain should have consoled her, but the death-dread stole upon her, grabbed her, and pushed her down into darkness. It pinioned her there and crushed her chest. It chilled her stomach, until it heaved and stabbed. It paralyzed her limbs and dissolved her spine. Her hair stuck in her scalp like icy needles.

Then a hand so gentle that it could not be a mortal's touched her shoulder and a voice so kindly that it could be only the Goddess's called her name. Joy like morning rays flooded Penthesilea's heart. The Goddess would carry Penthesilea to the West, for she loved the Goddess with all her words and deeds. And in the West, Penthesilea would see Eriboea again, and Leokadia, and soon enough Myrtho, and Tecmassa, and Abba-Bashti, who might even have wept shining tears for her when she found out how they had killed her. Penthesilea smiled to herself. It pleased her that Abba-Bashti would think that she had died so pitifully.

Something thudded against the wall, but Penthesilea did not care to stir from her daydream and kept her lids shut. The thing clunked a second time. The noise sounded from the outside. She raised herself up with effort, stood, and rubbed her eyes. She dragged the table to the window, stepped onto it, and stared down. Thirty feet below, a cloaked figure swung its arms around its head and then, abruptly, stopped moving. A missile banged against the tower's outside. The object dropped to the street and clattered. The form retrieved it and hurled it upward once more. A small stone disk flew toward Penthesilea. She caught it. A string had been secured to a hole in its center. The person below yanked at the line, and Penthesilea reeled it toward her. Something heavy was fastened to it. Penthesilea pulled arm over arm until a bundle slid over the sill and fell on the floor. She jumped down and took the package to the lamp. Two coils of ship's rope had been lashed together. She untied them. One cord was short and one was long; one must be to lower herself down the tower wall with, the other to descend the city rampart. She untied them. Laced to the end of the smaller roll was the little statue of Nanaï that Abba-Bashti always wore and the lanyard that held it against her chest. Penthesilea loosened the charm, laid reverent lips on it, and knotted it around her neck.

Penthesilea slung the larger coil over her shoulder and un-raveled the other. She made a noose of one end of it and slipped it around the hook over her bed. She tugged until her feet left the floor. The crotchet would hold. She took the free length of rope, hoisted herself onto the windowsill, and pivoted so that she sat with with her legs dangling outside. She slipped the end of the cord over her elbow, under her thigh, and between her knees. She tossed the rest of the line into the void. She put both hands around the rope, turned quickly, and slid over the side. Pain jolted her arms as they took her weight. She pressed the soles of her feet against the outside wall and straightened her back. Straining her arms and searching for foothold after foothold, she inched down the face of the tower.

Penthesilea touched ground, crouched into the fighting pos-ture, and peered around. All was quiet and dark. The city slept. The moon had not yet reached its zenith. Abba-Bashti called softly from the entrance of an alleyway. Penthesilea joined her, kissed her once, and was about to pronounce a thankful farewell, but Abba-Bashti spoke first.

"This way," she whispered, pointing to a stretch of eastern fortification that cast deep shadow.

"What? Where are you going?" asked Penthesilea.

"With you. Out of Troy."

"You can't. You won't be able to climb down the wall."

"I am a stranger here. If they find me before they open the gate, they will know I helped a slave escape. The rope hangs from the window."

"But the wall is too high!" said Penthesilea.

"Quiet! I have no choice. I am not afraid."

They stole along the inside of the parapet to its oldest sec-tion and tiptoed up the stairs leading to its walkway. They stopped when Penthesilea's head reached its level.

The Amazon had long since observed that two soldiers al-ways patrolled the wooden track, circling in opposite directions and crossing each other once each circuit. Shod feet and a spear shaft drummed faintly against the wood, grew louder, and reached a crescendo. A cloaked and helmeted figure passed. Penthesilea sprang, and the man slid to the ground without making a noise. Penthesilea signaled to Abba-Bashti, and the two women lugged the body to a crenel, where it would be out of sight. Footsteps again, this time from the opposite direction. The pair quickly returned to their hiding places. The second soldier appeared. Penthesilea fell on him, and he went down.

While Penthesilea tied the end of the rope she carried around a merlon, Abba-Bashti stripped one unconscious guard of his cloak and the other of a small knife tucked into his belt; while Penthesilea put on the mantle and attached the blade to her waistband, Abba-Bashti leaned over the parapet. She sounded a low hum and straightened up but did not face Penthesilea right away. When she did, her expression was unmoved.

How to get Abba-Bashti down? It would be no use instructing her to lower herself by holding the rope between her thighs and elbow, as Penthesilea had lately done. Still, the western rampart sloped toward the top enough for Abba-Bashti to work her way down by planting her feet solidly. They could take most of her weight, and she could grasp the line for balance rather than hang from it for support.

Penthesilea explained the maneuver at length. "Whatever happens," she said, "don't step on the rope and don't let it slide between your palms or you'll burn them. Are you ready?"

Abba-Bashti was.

Penthesilea tested the cord. She said, "You'll have to go first so I can see that you start out right."

Abba-Bashti took a deep breath and reached for the figure of Nanaï that usually hung against her chest. She did not find the statuette, realized where it was, and kissed Penthesilea between the breasts. Penthesilea's heart fluttered and her knees buckled until she stopped them. She threw the cord over the side and helped Abba-Bashti get a good grip on the line and start down.

"Go slow. Go slow," said Penthesilea as Abba-Bashti's head disappeared. Penthesilea recited a short prayer to the Goddess and followed over the side.

Abba-Bashti and Penthesilea crept south and east along the base of Troy's wall. They clambered down the side of the plateau and picked their way toward the morning hills, trying to keep the constellation of the horse on their right and avoid the huts, sheds, and pens crowded around the plateau. Fog that would swoop down, blind the women, and suddenly clear slowed them so much that it was like walking with weights on their feet. Once, mist that retreated unveiled the guiding stars on their left; they had doubled back without knowing it—for how long they could not tell. Another time Abba-Bashti crashed into the barrier of a sheepfold; dogs yelped and bayed, and the women had to negotiate a slow detour.

The sky in front of them paled and a breeze rose at their backs. It swept away the curtain of haze and revealed a long corral fence stretching to either side and a grassy meadow behind it.

Penthesilea grumbled to herself.

"What is it?" Abba-Bashti asked.

"This is the king's horse pasture. I was counting on getting much farther before dawn."

The air began to gust.

Penthesilea went on, "They'll have sounded the alarm by now. They'll send out messengers. We've got to hide right away. Right away." She pointed to a dark mass, a clump of trees, across the field.

Abba-Bashti slipped through the rails, but Penthesilea did not follow. Instead, she looked over her shoulder, then back at the turf. She had drawn her lips tight. The flat light deepened her eyes.

"What is it?"

"Laomedon's stables are back there," said Penthesilea. She shook her head to chase away some bad vision and added, "And I don't like this wind. It shouldn't be blowing at this time of day."

She slid through the enclosure's bars, and the pair began to dash across the field, the gale propelling them forward.

Abba-Bashti had sprinted halfway across, when the airs stopped pressing her shoulders. Her legs weakened for some reason, and she tripped. While she was pushing herself up, she noticed that the grass was swaying although the wind had died. She darted forward again.

Thunder growled softly. It was like the purring of a cat, but something in it threatened. Where did it come from? The sky was clear. The sound echoed again. It was grumbling at her feet. It came from below and not above.

Without warning the earth snarled, and Abba-Bashti lost her balance as if she were fainting. But she did not black out.

Instead, the earth bucked upward, and she was tossed into the air. She flew through it and thudded onto her back. Shock detonated through her bones, and she lay stunned. The meadow around her dinned. She felt her head splitting at the root. Huge tabletops erupted like toadstools at crazy angles from the pasture, which lurched and swayed and tossed her around like a doll.

When she had stopped rolling, she tried to raise herself, but numbness like sleep glued her to where she lay.

The meadow heaved up and fled from under her like a boat rising to a wave and falling back into its trough. The ground fell away from her feet and she slid down, down, down, until soft soil stopped her fall. She lay looking up. A cleft had opened in the ground and swallowed her. A rain of clods and pebbles battered her face. She covered it with her arms and screamed, but the stridency all around drowned her out. She felt the crevasse palpitate around her. The notion came to her that she must get out or be crushed to death. Like a stunned boxer, she lifted herself on her hands and knees, then staggered upright. She darted her eyes around feverishly. Tushratta. Where was Tushratta? When she could not find him, she lowered her head and stood with her arms dangling.

"Climb!" commanded a voice from she knew not where. "Climb!"

Abba-Bashti clawed at the fissure's walls with her fingers and toes, but they crumbled and fell away. No use. It was no use. The gap throbbed again. She reached for Nanaï, but Nanaï was not there. Abba-Bashti raised her eyes heavenward to beg Her to save her from the madness. Just above dangled a corner of the cloak that Penthesilea had been wearing. Penthesilea lay at the side of the pit, holding the mantle above Abba-Bashti's head. Abba-Bashti wrapped trembling hands around the cloth, and Penthesilea tugged.

At the very moment Abba-Bashti slid over the top to safety, the world stopped moving and the silence of death fell over it. She shuddered, her stomach turned; she could hear the blood coursing through her head. She lay prone. She wondered what had become of her little boy, and then remembered. Dry sobs racked her until her chest hurt. Penthesilea sat down next to her and lifted her into her arms. They tightened around her; their staunchness dissolved her trembling and their warmth gave her heart. Her hiccups of fright subsided. She looked around.

The world had changed. There was no more flat meadow. Heaves of earth pushed out of it and folds rippled through it. The fissure near whose edge they were seated ran like jagged lightning across the field. At the far border, trees lay on their sides like dead animals. In the eastern sky, the sun's brilliant arc was floating up from behind the hills. How could that be? The dawn had been breaking at the moment that the earth went berserk. It had convulsed for what seemed an eternity. But in fact Creation had burst open and knit together again in so short a time that she did not know how to measure it.

She moved her arms and legs deliberately.

"Are you all right?" asked Penthesilea.

"I think so."

After a moment's silence, Penthesilea turned her head toward the west. She whistled in amazement. Abba-Bashti's eyes followed the line of her vision. Countless gray-black swirls—smoke—invaded the sky above where Troy stood. They twisted into a thick column that bent toward the onlookers. The city was in flames. Abba-Bashti gasped.

"Your brother?" asked Penthesilea.

Abba-Bashti nodded.

"Where was the caravan camped?"

"Outside the city. Not far from the west wall."

"The Trojans do not open the gates before dawn, so he is not in there. Do you want to go back and look for him anyway?"

"No. If my brother is dead, there is nothing I can do. And if he lives, he will be angry because I left his protection without his telling me I could and because. . . ." Abba-Bashti had trouble saying, "Because I stole ivory from him to get the rope."

Penthesilea looked away and closed her eyes. She opened them after a while and directed them to where she had said the king's stables stood. She turned back, pouting, and plucked up a leaf of grass. She jerked it along the crack of her lips and thought hard about something.

Abba-Bashti lay a hand across Penthesilea's knee.

"I want to go back to the horses," Penthesilea said. "Mine is there, or was there, along with a black stallion that another Amazon rode." Penthesilea pitched the blade away. "They're probably dead, or their legs are broken, so they'll have to be killed. I must go see. I must."

Penthesilea stood and pulled Abba-Bashti to her feet. An inverted T of hot metal seared Abba-Bashti from her buttocks to her shoulders. She took a few steps. It stabbed her like knives in her bones every time she put one foot in front of the other. Penthesilea slipped an arm around her waist and helped her along.

The two picked their way through shattered ground and up-turned trees to where the three horse barns once had stood. The far stables had collapsed, were heaps of rubble, pine boards and piles of hay strewn this way and that and a few teetering uprights. The closest building still held together, although it tilted halfway down a cleft that had opened beside it. All was silent.

"Where are the horses?" said Penthesilea. She hurried to the farthest ruin and was searching through it, when uneven steps sounded at Abba-Bashti's back. A gray-haired man with one shoulder higher than the other limped toward her. Penthesilea shouted hello and hastened back. A bridle jingled in her hands.

"What's become of the horses?" she asked the man. Abba-Bashti saw that he was their keeper.

"They were all out in the north pasture, fattening up for winter when Poseidon did it to us. I came back to see what was left. Not much. Now my boy and me have to round up the ones that are still good and finish off the lame ones."

Penthesilea's face went white.

The old man turned to go.

"I'm coming with you," said Penthesilea.

"Thank you if you are," said the old man. "We sure can use another hand. You got a sharp knife on you?"

"Yes," whispered Penthesilea. She followed him out of sight.

Abba-Bashti lay down. She did not think she could sleep, but a white, aching slumber dragged at her. She started when she felt herself sinking and opened her eyes. She was afraid to close them again. She pulled herself up and toed among the ru-ins. She came upon a sack of barley flour. The horses' fountain still trickled. She lugged rocks together to make a hearth, gathered dry wood, and after many tries rubbed a spark out of two sticks. She cooked cakes on a smooth stone and waited.

The sky was growing flat when Penthesilea returned mounted bareback on the horse that Abba-Bashti had first seen her riding. Dried blood stained the Amazon's tunic. She jumped down, tethered the animal, and scratched up some barley from the nearest stable. She fed the beast and returned to the fire. She lowered herself with difficulty. She stared into the flames

and did not say a word while she wolfed down her food. Her
face was tired and gray; black circles pulled at her eyes.

Finally, she said, "We've got to move. We've got to get
away from the stables. Laomedon will send someone out to see
what happened to his horses as soon as he can. Probably first
thing tomorrow. Let's go. There's light for a little while, anyway."

Abba-Bashti's bones and muscles, which had stiffened with
time felt as if someone were running a blade up and down them.
Still, she rose and banked the fire.

The last hour of the day was a wall of agony into which she
was cemented. Penthesilea held her up, and she gritted her
teeth and put her entire substance into placing one foot in front of
the other. Walking tortured her so, that she began to daydream
that she had marched past suffering. Her lips sketched a distant smile into which tears rolled without her knowing it. The
light dimmed. She stumbled again and again, Penthesilea always propping her up before she fell. They stopped. It took a
moment to understand that they had. A mud-brick hut loomed
up in front of her eyes.

"There's no one here," she heard Penthesilea say. "It's half
fallen down."

A fire heated Abba-Basthi, a bed of twigs and leaves cush-
ioned her, wool around her gave her comfort. Penthesilea
dabbed a drop of sour-tasting liquid on her tongue and kissed her
forehead. Little by little the razor edges inside her muscles
grew dull, and when she braced against the stabs that she expected, her sinews gave back only a dull remembrance empty of
real pain. Pleasant sensations soon radiated from her belly to
her fingers and toes. Penthesilea slid in beside her. Abba-
Bashti put her head on her shoulder, sighed profoundly, and
plummeted into sleep. The warmth pressing on her breast must
be the baby's.

They moved at dawn. Throbbing beat at Abba-Bashti in
waves that froze her in place, and she could trudge on only between their assaults. The women left the trail and climbed far
up a pine-covered hill. They discovered a small cave on its
sheltered side. Many years before, someone had lived there,
had whitewashed the walls, laid a circle of stones beneath a
small hole in the ceiling to serve as a hearth, and widened the
vestibule so that animals could take shelter there—a stone
trough attested to their presence. But the ashes in the fireplace

were wet and cold, stones and branches had clogged the chimney, earth and moss filled the watering place.

Penthesilea built a fire and disappeared. She returned after dusk balancing a dozen freshly killed squirrels on a stick across her shoulders. She skinned and gutted the beasts and cooked the flesh. She gave the first pieces to Abba-Bashti, who ate them gratefully. Heat and vigor flooded her middle. Once Abba-Bashti finished her meal, Penthesilea put a drop of opium on her tongue and made a bed of pine needles. Abba-Bashti stretched out on it and soon pirouetted down to the center of creation. The perfume of life flowed over her; its blood-hot current lifted her prone body and carried it to repose. She murmured in contentment and rested there. Then, outside of it, a horse neighed. The ground under Abba-Bashti shook. The walls of the cavern into which she had drifted began slowly to throb around her head. The palpitations grew in force. She whimpered but did not have the strength to stir. The spasms touched her skull. She knew that they would crush her and her child, if she did not escape. She wailed and clawed at the side of the tunnel, but her scratching wedged her deeper in it. She screamed, but she was too far under the earth for Nanaï to hear her. She flailed and cried out.

Sturdy arms hugged her close. A loving voice whispered her name over and over again like a magic spell. She opened her eyes. Tears flooded them. Penthesilea kissed the drops that tumbled down her cheeks. Abba-Bashti could not tell at the last whose heart was beating in whose breast. Her breathing slowed, the knots of fright untied, and she gave herself up to sleep again.

The next morning Penthesilea rode off to have a look at the country. She returned that afternoon with a sack of barley for her horse, three clay jugs, and a wheel of goat cheese. She had gotten these goods in exchange for the skins of the squirrels trapped the evening before.

"We're in a safe place," she said, "a long way up from the road, and it doesn't look like anyone comes around here often. That's why I want to stay for a little while, until you feel better about traveling. The trees on this hill are very thick, good for going after game, there's good water not far down the hill, and there's one cabin near the bottom. Someone must live there. Probably hunters. But I didn't see a soul.

"I rode down to the road and went along it for a while. This hill's the second of five that run southwest, and the trail goes

through them from Troy toward the rising sun. I passed at least
a dozen people running away from Troy—from what's left of it.
Nobody knows how many were killed, but they say more died
than got out. And there isn't much of the city standing, either.
Most of the buildings that the earthquake didn't throw over
were burned to the ground in the fire. It was still burning yesterday. All the springs are caved in, so there's no water except for
the river. The west wall fell down, too. I asked about your
brother, but nobody could tell me anything."

"And the king's daughter?" asked Abba-Bashti.

Penthesilea, intent on attaching her horse's halter, said
without looking up, "One wing of the palace came down right
away, but they couldn't tell me which one. And fire gutted the
rest."

"Are you sad for her?" asked Abba-Bashti.

"For Hesione?" Penthesilea pronounced, not turning her
head. "I don't know. I don't."

"The Mother must have been very angry at the Trojans,"
said Abba-Bashti, "to punish them so."

Penthesilea now glanced over her shoulder. Grief made her
eyes into a madwoman's. "Angry at the ones who worshiped
Her, like Aegista? Angry at the ones who didn't hurt anyone
else, like Damasos and Jason?"

The two women took shelter in the cave. Penthesilea trapped
rabbits, squirrels, and badgers for them to eat; she gathered
acorns, hazelnuts, and mushrooms. She went down to the road
and traded the pelts of the animals she had hunted for barley
flour, beer, oil, and medicine—willow bark that she boiled and
gave to Abba-Bashti to drink.

Abba-Bashti passed the afternoons, basking in the autumn
sun, which still gave warmth at that time of day. She spent the
rest of her hours in the cave, near the fire, sometimes slumbering, sometimes daydreaming. She lived in the center of her
body. Its throbbing and stillness commanded the rhythm of her
days. Little by little the pangs came less often, her step covered
more ground, and the tightness that had grayed and withered
her face gave way to healthy tones and full-lipped smiles.

One day, she felt well enough to accompany Penthesilea to
the source, which lay in a clearing a few minutes' walk away.
Here, chilly water trickled out of a glistening black rock into a
bowl-shaped hollow of the same stone. Penthesilea put down
the urn she carried, knelt in front of the basin, and brushed away

the pine needles that had fallen on it overnight. Abba-Bashti looked down. On the liquid's shimmering surface, her head and Penthesilea's mingled and trembled together. The heat flooded Abba-Bashti's face. She turned away.

That night, the health tingling in her bones kept her awake long after Penthesilea had drowsed off, pressed against her side, sighing and frowning in her sleep. Abba-Bashti looked up at the pitted stone ceiling. She had never noticed it before and widened her eyes in surprise. It astounded her, too, that she lay in this place of all places and that Penthesilea reclined by her side. Abba-Bashti saw her again as she had the first time: holding her wiry body erect on her horse, gazing at Abba-Bashti with sad and honest eyes. Then the next afternoon, Penthesilea's tanned profile turned stubbornly toward the sky and her mounted figure disappearing down the road. The morning after that many Amazons rode out of their city and followed the same path. Two days later the news came that Penthesilea had disappeared—was dead perhaps.

Abba-Bashti did not go into the city again.

After a month, the traders resumed their journey through the mountains toward Troy. She had never seen anything like what she encountered on that march—the blue-black slopes that loomed on either side and stretched in front and behind as if they ended only at the edge of Creation; the pale yellow of the morning sky that shifted into pink-white and then to azure as the day progressed; the heartbreaking light green of the mountain grasses and deep emerald of the fir trees; the restless silver sparkle of the water that slapped down from everywhere and always tasted cool and pure. Still, these novelties did not obscure the vision of Penthesilea's brooding face nor take away the sick feeling that she was somehow to blame for Penthesilea's doom.

Only Abba-Bashti's baby, Tushratta—with his toothless gurgles and crimson-faced wails—turned her mind from this gloom. She smiled to think of him, and her lips framed a kiss. As soon as they did, she remembered how the infant fell sick one afternoon, how his face puckered and frowned in suffering that he did not understand, how his little body grew hotter and hotter, and he thrashed and screamed. Near dawn he shuddered one last time and lay still. Abba-Bashti did not believe at first that he had died. Then she sat motionless, afraid to feel. She could not speak. She watched, not comprehending, as they put the tiny body into the ground. They moved on right away. They took her by the arms and led her off. They did not even leave her time to spill her tears into the earth.

Nor did her brother comfort her. The death saddened him, too, but when her eyes sought his, he turned his head. He had lost a boy child; he had lost a son to carry on his life and say prayers for him when his own time came to be laid in his tomb. He could not speak of his grief, and he turned his head.

No one ever died deeply, and Tushratta's soul would find a new home, would lodge in a new body. Still, knowing it did not calm her grief.

Abba-Bashti's heart heaved, and a moan that she tried not to voice sounded softly in her throat. Penthesilea heard her, threw her arm around her waist, and mumbled something that she could not comprehend.

Abba-Bashti did not remember the rest of the journey to Troy. The blackness blinded her even on that afternoon, as she trudged once more up the plateau to Troy's marketplace. She did not see Penthesilea at first, although she was looking for the Amazon they said slept in the princess's bed. Then a flash. Clear light. Sudden silence. She heard nothing but the thump of her heart. Penthesilea noticed her, straightened, and hastened to her. Fire danced in her eyes, and pleasure, and a savage, desperate unhappiness that Abba-Bashti did not remember having seen before.

Would she go with her? Yes, yes, yes.

She waited that night by the fig trees until the sky began to pale. Ten times, a dozen times, she heard something, and her heart leaped—but the sound proved to be the flutter of a bird or a trick of the wind. She hastened into the city as soon as the gates were open. How strangely they looked at her in the marketplace, when she asked about the Amazon. She went to the palace door and asked the guard. He folded his arms and said nothing. She lowered her head and was making her way down the hill when she felt someone tug at her elbow. A plump woman with honey-colored hair (Hesione's slave, Aegista, she later learned) told her that they had thrown Penthesilea in prison and would torture her to death for trying to run away. Abba-Bashti's insides heaved so hard that they hurt, and she started to sob. "But where is she?" she managed to ask. "Where have they taken her?"

Aegista led Abba-Bashti up and around the hill and pointed out the window.

"Tell no one that I spoke to you," she said before hurrying off.

Strength like an immortal's flowed into Abba-Bashti, and, as she thought out the rescue, it was as if another person—cold and clear-headed—were plotting it. She felt no fear for herself, only apprehension that she would be caught and her plan thwarted. She waited calmly until Artatama had gone into the city, put an untrembling hand on the ivory carvings he had brought from afar, and carried them to the ship's chandler to barter for ropes. She did not let herself dwell on what would happen to her if they caught her; she pushed back the picture of the crazed slave woman.

Penthesilea muttered something. Abba-Bashti raised herself on her elbow and stared at her. Penthesilea's eyes were closed, but her brow knotted and unknotted frightfully, and her fists were clenched. Abba-Bashti planted a soft kiss on the crown of her head. Penthesilea bolted up and reached out like a blind beggar. She opened her eyes and stared at Abba-Bashti as if at a stranger. Once she recognized her, she nuzzled her chest and whispered, "My darling, my sweet." She ran her fingers over her belly. Abba-Bashti's flesh stirred the way it had when Tushratta put his lips around her nipples. She caressed Penthesilea's forehead and shoulder. Penthesilea's breathing slowed and deepened, she whimpered and sank into sleep again. Abba-Bashti lay awake and felt the humming in her veins.

The next morning Penthesilea disappeared before dawn to hunt. Abba-Bashti waited until the haze burned off, picked up the water jug and walked to the source downhill. She went along slowly, glad to warm her bones in the fall sunshine. What had Penthesilea called it? Arinna's last love-gift to the earth. Abba-Bashti could not have imagined before she came to this land that she would welcome the sun beating on her head, but now its rays cheered her, as did the strength surging back into her, and Penthesilea's warmth pressed against her at night.

Abba-Bashti turned onto the path that passed in front of the clearing in which the source lay. Bushes trembled and a twig snapped. What was that? Had some animal that had come down to drink heard her steps and bolted? No, it was not the time of day for beasts to be there. Abba-Bashti approached the water and knelt to clear the surface. No pine needles had collected on it. Instead, they littered the ground around the tiny pool. Someone had already removed them. Someone had been there when she approached. The noise had been made not by a beast scampering out of the way but by a person who had come to fetch water and been frightened off. Or perhaps a spirit. No. They did not drink the same liquid as mortals.

Abba-Bashti peered about but saw only the larch and the juniper brush that surrounded the glade. She turned back to her task, certain now that she had frightened someone away from the well. It was strange that another person would run from her. Who ever came to draw water that did not linger and talk a while? Especially in such a lonely place as these woods. She filled the jug and straightened up. She hoisted it on her shoulder and began to walk back to the cave. Once, when she paused to shift the urn from one side to the other, the underbrush rustled.

Abba-Bashti reached the cave and went in to set down the vessel. A soft footfall, more like a timid shuffle, brushed the ground at the entrance. She pivoted. The daylight streaming in outlined the silhouette of a child, whose face Abba-Bashti could not discern in the shadow. Abba-Bashti stepped toward the visitor.

"Come outside, child," she said and walked outside. The creature followed. Abba-Bashti stopped, turned, and stared. The youngster, who came up to her waist, tilted its head upward and gazed back with wide eyes. These, large, deep brown, and set aslant of sharp cheekbones, engraved mistrust and curiosity on a dirt-smudged face—a broad brow, tiny, skewed nose, uneven mouth, and fat lower lip, all framed by black pigtails from which wispy licks shot out in all directions. A filthy robe of gray homespun, whose skirt ended in tatters and whose right shoulder consisted of shreds of cloth knotted together, covered the child's body. Faint green spots mottled the white skin under this bodice—faded black-and-blue marks. Children were always falling down. The creature was so thin that its elbows were thicker than its biceps and its knees than its thighs. Something in their angle from its hips hinted that the child was a little girl, although Abba-Bashti was not sure. The child saw her hesitation and stiffened.

Abba-Bashti examined the gaunt figure for another moment and said, "My name is Abba-Bashti. What is your name, little girl?"

"Proto."

"Do you want something to eat, Proto?"

The girl agitated her head. Abba-Bashti beckoned her inside. Proto perched on a rock and peered at Abba-Bashti like a cat at a bird, while she fetched a cold cake, cut a wedge of cheese, and poured beer into a cannikin. She handed the clay vessel to Proto, who snatched at it so hastily that it dropped on the ground and shattered. The girl cringed. She was terrified.

Abba-Bashti pronounced, gently, "There's another cup for water, I'll get it." She handed Proto the rest of her food and went to fetch the second jar. By the time she had filled it and set it by Proto's side, the poor child had already gulped down her cake and was devouring her cheese. She chewed and swallowed noisily until it was gone. Then she licked her fingers one by one, picked up the new cup, and drank it down to the dregs. She took a deep breath and exhaled like someone who had just escaped a great danger.

Abba-Bashti peered at her with renewed curiosity. The flush of contentment that had spread over Proto's face vanished. Suspicion took its place. She rose and looked anxiously toward the mouth of the cave.

"Please don't go," said Abba-Bashti, who did not understand why the child was so frightened. "Come with me now and sit in the sun."

Proto put her hands behind her back. Her eyes darted from Abba-Bashti's face to the way out.

"Please, Proto. I'll give you more to eat, later." Abba-Bashti proffered her hand. "Please," she repeated in a soft voice. "Please."

Proto narrowed her eyes but nodded and followed.

"Where do you live, Proto?" asked Abba-Bashti, once the two had settled between thick bushes that cut the wind. Proto did not unknit her lips. Still, she could not help glancing downhill.

Penthesilea had described a dwelling near the base of the hill. Abba-Bashti asked, "In the house at the bottom?" She pointed in that direction.

Proto's face told Abba-Bashti that she had surmised correctly.

"That is a house of hunters?" asked Abba-Bashti.

The little girl's countenance confirmed Abba-Bashti's guess.

"Do you live there with your mother and father?" she asked.

"I have been watching you," said Proto.

"Do you live there with your mother and father?"

The child whispered in a fearful voice, "You go to the water every day with a man who sits on a big donkey."

"That is not a man but a woman. She does not wear a long skirt, but she is a woman. And that is not a donkey, that is a horse. You must not be afraid of them. But where are your mother and father?"

"My father is gone."

"When did he leave?"

Proto shrugged her shoulders.

"When will he be back?"

"With deer and rabbits," came the reply.

"Where is your mother?"

Proto seemed not to hear the question.

"Your mother. Where is she?"

Proto looked at the forest and began to sing words that Abba-Bashti did not understand.

"Is she there?"

Proto wagged her head in denial.

"Where is she?"

"She went away with the new baby and will not come back again."

"She will not come back? Who told you? Your father?"

Proto scrambled to her feet and fled into the forest. Abba-Bashti stared at the bushes through which Proto had vanished. She asked herself what she might have done to scare the girl away, but shrugged her shoulders as soon as she had, for she knew that she had done nothing. She closed her eyes and raised her face to the sun. Its warm rays made her fall into a half-sleep. Disappearing children. Disappearing children. . . . She saw Tushratta again, and tears traced a wet line down her cheeks and dropped into her lap. She hugged her knees to her chest and wept until the chill made her start and look up. The sun had descended below the treetops. She sat in shadow.

She rose and walked back to the cave. Tala stood tethered outside, her long neck stretched to the ground, munching her barley. Bright orange light pulsated out of the cavern's entrance. Penthesilea, who had renewed the fire, sat next to it flaying a rabbit. She raised her head and grinned; the flames' reflections danced on her face. She saw Abba-Bashti's, and her smile vanished. She rose, put the animal and knife down, and took Abba-Bashti in her arms.

Abba-Bashti lay her head on Penthesilea's bosom and shivered. Penthesilea wrapped her arms around her and swayed her gently. "It has been hard for you," Penthesilea said.

Her eyes brimming with tears, Abba-Bashti nodded. Then she grasped Penthesilea's neck and raised her mouth to hers. Penthesilea pressed her lips against Abba-Bashti's, and their heat made the blood fill them.

Penthesilea pulled her head back and whispered, "Come, let us eat."

"And lie down," added Abba-Bashti in a hushed voice.

Penthesilea's eyes met hers. Great love deepened them. Abba-Bashti and Penthesilea turned away from each other and spoke no more as they readied their meal, afraid to disturb the thought that enclosed them like a cloud of attar incense.

Abba-Bashti took her place near the fire, and Penthesilea poured a cup of barley beer for her and looked around for the second vessel. Only then did Abba-Bashti remember the acquaintance she had made earlier that day. She was recounting how the girl had run away, when Tala snuffled, and both women looked toward the entrance of the cave.

Proto stood there.

"Come here, Proto, and have your supper," said Abba-Basthi.

Proto scurried to her side. She took Abba-Bashti's hand and gaped at the Amazon. Penthesilea stared back, evenly. The two contemplated one another in silence, until Proto rubbed her head against Abba-Bashti's arm and peeked up at her and back at Penthesilea. Abba-Bashti patted the child's shoulder, and Penthesilea handed her a skewer of meat. Proto grabbed the food, lowered her head, and set to chomping furiously. Penthesilea sat down, and the women began to take their evening meal. Once Proto had eaten her fill, she quaffed the beer they offered her, grunted in satisfaction, and stretched out near the fire. She sighed and in no time began to snore.

Penthesilea and Abba-Bashti, who sipped and chewed without speaking, directed their gaze to their bed and then at one another. They would not be alone that night. Abba-Bashti lowered her eyes. What could she do? Nothing, except laugh at her disappointment and hope Penthesilea took it in good part. Abba-Bashti smiled at Penthesilea, tentatively. Penthesilea shrugged her shoulders.

The women watched the flames die down. Penthesilea banked the fire, and the two slid into their sleeping place and held each other close. Their mouths joined in a deep and soundless conversation.

At length Abba-Bashti made herself turn away from Penthesilea, who plastered her body against hers. Abba-Bashti drifted into a fitful somnolence, unable to plummet into her most profound repose. Nor did Penthesilea's breathing deepen the way it did when she sank into her second life, her life of muttering dreams. Still, Abba-Bashti dozed without knowing it until she heard Proto sigh. She felt her slip in beside her and heard her drop off immediately. She sank into shallow rest again.

She opened her eyes as soon as light crept into the cavern. Proto lay between her and Penthesilea. The child's slow respiration combined with the grownup's in lazy counterpoint. The fire gave no heat; the air was dank, but the bed was warm. Abba-Bashti did not stir.

Penthesilea sprang up and smacked her lower belly. Her movement made Proto sit up. Penthesilea realized that Proto had lain next to her and barked, "You here! No wonder!"

Proto threw her arms around Abba-Bashti. The girl was trembling. Abba-Bashti held her tight.

"You'll be sorry you did that," glowered Penthesilea. Abba-Bashti shook her head in disbelief: Penthesilea had never spoken in that tone.

"Fleas. Don't you understand? The child has fleas."

"And what of it?"

"They're a curse. A curse. They drive you mad. They make your camp a hell. And your stable. They love horses. As soon as they find Tala, they'll make her twitch so that she won't look and listen half the time. We hate them!" Penthesilea swatted her thigh. "I think I got it this time." She yanked off the end of the mantle that covered her legs. A bloody pinpoint decorated her flesh.

Penthesilea bolted up and ordered the others to get up as well. "We're going to have to burn the bed, smoke out our clothes, and wash ourselves." She directed her eyes to the mouth of the cave. Bright yellow light tumbled in with the mist. "Lucky for us it'll be a good day."

The women and child heaped the twigs and leaves that made up their bed on the live embers remaining from the previous night's fire. They stepped outside to let the renewed blaze take its course. Penthesilea bid them wait where they stood. "Don't go near my horse, either of you," she said before disappearing on foot.

She returned toting two large urns. She had taken them from the hunter's cabin downhill. It was only right. The women and child went for water. They entered the cavern again. They put the vessels in the coals and bided their time.

At length Penthesilea said, "Proto goes first. Hand me her clothes when she takes them off."

Proto raised her arms above her head, and Abba-Basthi pulled off her tatters. The little girl's head was big for her body. Her ribs protruded from her flesh and her hip bones stuck out around her belly. Purple marks striped Proto's abdomen and yellow-brown lines her thighs. Abba-Bashti stifled a gasp, and her eyes flickered in the direction of Penthesilea, who was examining the child like someone who did not believe what she beheld.

"Turn around, Proto," said Abba-Bashti, trying to keep the alarm from her voice.

The child obeyed. White, puckered streaks—flesh that had opened and knit together again—hatched Proto's buttocks.

Pity choked Abba-Bashti, and she put her arms around Proto. "Who beat you so?"

The girl put her thumb in her mouth and stared at the entrance of the cave.

"Who hit you so hard, your father?"

The child, who still did not look at Abba-Bashti, nodded.

Abba-Bashti kissed the crown of Proto's head and stammered, "Come, let me wash you."

She gave the rags to Penthesilea. She poured jar after jar of heated water over the girl; she scraped and oiled her body. She reached between her legs to wash there. The color fled from Abba-Bashti's face. Enraged, she lifted her eyes to Penthesilea, who paled and drew her lips tight.

That evening Penthesilea asked Abba-Bashti, "Are you ready to move on now? Can you walk until the snows come?"

"When is that?"

"The moon will wane and wax once more before they do, and then we'll have two weeks more if the Goddess keeps smiling on you."

While Penthesilea spoke, Proto had sidled up to Abba-Bashti and hid her face in her stomach.

"And Proto?" asked Abba-Bashti, stroking her hair.

"Of course she's going with us. How can she not? It's a great blessing for you, you know. The Goddess has given you a girl child to save from danger; and Proto will take your place when you are gone." Penthesilea said all this without looking at Proto.

Penthesilea started downhill before dawn: she hoped to trade the scores of skins she had trapped for the cloth and food the women and girl would need on their journey. Proto and Abba-Bashti took the same direction after noon. Proto wanted to return to the hunter's cabin. Abba-Bashti said no at first; she did not care for the little girl's ever going back and recoiled at the thought of visiting the place herself. But when she refused, Proto burst into tears and sobbed confusedly that she needed something—a doll?—that her mother had given her. Abba-Bashti gave in and accompanied the little girl.

As they made their way through the woods, the poor child did not leave Abba-Bashti for the space of a heartbeat. When the path was wide enough to walk side by side, she clung to Abba-Bashti's hand, and, when the way was too narrow, hung on to Abba-Bashti's skirts from behind. It had been like that since the day before. The dear waif had twined around Abba-Bashti the way a vine snakes around a palm tree. She would run up to Abba-Bashti at unpredictable moments and throw her arms around her with such abandon that once or twice she almost knocked her down. If Abba-Bashti left her sight for more than the time it took to go to the edge of the clearing and back, Proto would call out her name. If Abba-Bashti did not answer, she would come looking for her. The sweet ragamuffin had shared their bed of twigs with Penthesilea and Abba-Bashti the night before, burrowing in between them and snuggling up to Abba-Bashti, for they had only one blanket. Of course, Proto would have done the same, even if they had had enough covers for everyone, and Abba-Bashti would not have had the heart to kick her out, and Proto knew it. As for Penthesilea, she went to sleep without a word.

And yet, when Abba-Bashti asked Proto about her father and mother and the life she had lived down the hill, she would look away or smile coyly and say nothing or answer in words that did not seem to go together and glanced off into nonsense. Still, she gleaned from the child's disjointed phrases, and silences, that her mother had died giving birth to a baby that the father took away—that meant he killed it. Since then Proto had lived alone with the man. While he was home from the hunt, his rape and thrashing wounded and terrified her, but she did not know that it could be different; during the long stretches when he was tracking beasts, she dreaded his return but did not think to run away.

They reached the tiny clearing in which the cabin stood. It was a squat, dull brown rectangle of unbaked brick fashioned around timbers that supported a slanted, thatched roof. Dozens of black pines, tall, with dense, whorled tops, hemmed it in, dwarfed it, and cast deep shadow on it. The dwelling's door, hide stretched over a frame, gaped open. Abba-Bashti bid Proto hang back and poked her head through the entrance. "Is anybody there?"

Silence.

Abba-Bashti stepped into the house.

"Is anybody here?"

The stench of beer, male piss, and unwashed body assaulted her. Something across from her scurried out of the way, a clay object smashed on the ground, and liquid gurgled from the same spot. Abba-Bashti advanced. Vegetable rinds, nutshells, and bones crunched underfoot. Some smelled new; some stank of rot. Light creeping in from behind outlined a low table and bench along the facing wall. An earthenware plate with shreds of flesh on it and little black dots, animal droppings, lay on the board. An upturned drinking cup rolled back and forth next to the vessel.

"Proto," called Abba-Bashti, "take what you came to get, fast, and let's go back. Hurry, now. Hurry."

Proto scampered to a corner and retrieved what proved in the sunshine to be a filthy rag doll stuffed with straw that protruded from gouges in its belly.

Abba-Bashti grabbed Proto's hand and led her away in haste. She did not want to run into the father. And Penthesilea must know right away that he had returned.

New manure and horse tracks farther along the trail meant that she had come home, probably crossing a stone's throw uphill of the hut. Abba-Bashti stepped faster. The hoofprints veered off onto a small path. Abba-Bashti followed them. Proto did not. She planted her feet and pouted.

Abba-Bashti stopped and turned. "You won't come with me?"

Proto dropped her eyes and stuck her thumb in her mouth.

"I'm going to find Penthesilea. Come along."

Proto scowled in distress, as if Abba-Bashti was about to desert her.

"Come with me, then," said Abba-Bashti. She took a dozen paces down the new trail and looked back. Proto had not budged from her place. She resumed walking. She heard Proto run after her and felt her grip her skirt and walk in her tracks.

Abba-Bashti did not take many more steps before a strange feeling teased her ears. She did not pay it any mind at first, but it dogged her. She halted and tried to recognize it. She could not and shrugged it off. It came back. She focused in on it again without being able to make out what it was, then she dismissed it a second time—in vain. It still annoyed her; something was not right. She strained her hearing. Silence. Only silence. She moved on, reflecting on the stillness around her. That was it! No birds sang in the branches. Perhaps a hawk was in the area. She looked skyward but saw only luminous pale blue.

She continued down the path. A dim sound reached her and receded. She walked on. The sound, pitched like a man's voice, became steadier, rose and fell in the distance. She strode more quickly. Wrathful inflections burst and surged. She sped toward them. A man was bellowing in anger. Suddenly Proto let go of her garment and bolted in the opposite direction. Abba-Bashti glanced back. Proto had dropped her doll and was tearing down the trail.

Abba-Bashti rushed toward the disturbance.

The path snaked left. Abba-Bashti took the turn and stood still in her tracks.

Ten paces away, a short, hairy man clothed in pelts stood with his back to her. He held a longbow at the ready. The arrow pointed at Penthesilea, who faced him from atop Tala. Penthesilea darted her eyes from the man to the newcomer. The fellow saw the Amazon glance behind him and hesitated. Abba-Bashti snatched up a fist-sized rock. The man drew back his arm to loose the bolt. Abba-Bashti hurled the stone. It struck him between the shoulders. He lurched, and the arrow flew over Penthesilea's head. Tala charged and knocked him to the ground. Penthesilea heaved herself onto his prostrate form. Her knife flashed. It was over. She stood up. Blood spotted her hands and the hem of her tunic.

"He was drunk, and furious I was here, stealing his game, he said. I think he was fit to be tied, too, because Proto wasn't waiting for him."

"To rape and beat? I don't want Proto to see him."

"Where is she?"

"She knew his voice and ran away."

"We've got to hide him so that nobody comes on him until we're long gone." Penthesilea closed her eyes and pondered something. Then she opened them and looked at Abba-Bashti as if she were seeing her for the first time. "Thank you. Again. I owe you my life."

"You have mine," answered Abba-Bashti. She took Penthesilea's hand and raised it to her lips. Thick, salty liquid smeared them.

The women and child set out for home the next morning at dawn. Penthesilea hoisted Proto onto Tala's back, which was also laden with sacks, urns, and baskets, and led the beast by the halter, while Abba-Bashti walked at the girl's side and helped her sit steady in the saddle. Once they left the hill on whose lee the women had taken shelter weeks before, the travelers lowered their heads and pulled their cloaks tight around their bodies. They headed into the northeast wind, which pushed against them without cease and cut them with its frigid blade from dawn to dusk. Shivering, they trekked toward the rising sun among ice-covered peaks and waters that purled faintly under the rime choking their banks. They huddled where they could at night—in shepherds' huts, and, when they found nothing else, in stone windbreaks built for sheep or goats that had long since been driven indoors.

For countless days that grew shorter and colder, until Abba-Bashti imagined that they would end in utter darkness and motionless frigidity, she trudged on behind Penthesilea. When the journeyers stopped each afternoon, Penthesilea would get a blaze going; stunned and hugging Proto next to her because she needed warmth too, Abba-Bashti would feel the numbness flow out of her into the fire and its warmth flood her belly. She would widen her eyes and look into Penthesilea's with gratitude and longing, and Proto, seeing this, would snuggle closer and butt her head against Abba-Bashti's arm. Penthesilea always managed to build them a dry bed—of hay or leaves or twigs— and, when Abba-Bashti lay down on it, she would long for Penthesilea to press her body against her and caress her and make the ache inside her bloom into happiness somehow. But Proto always wedged between them, and Penthesilea always turned her back.

Thirty-two days after they had set out, the journeyers woke up to clouds that pressed on their heads and air that made them giddy to inhale. The wind had died overnight. Penthesilea frowned as she packed Tala and lifted Proto onto the mare's back. The Amazon began to lead them down the road. She halted before they had gone far and looked back. Worry darkened her brow.

"The snows are here," she said. "And early, much too early. The new moon was only last night. The Storm God will get to Themiscyra before we do. There's no traveling much farther. We'll have to look for a place to stay and wait for the spring."

The trail led them up a ridge and down its northeast side. Before them loomed another peak, a conic eruption from the bare trees that covered lower ground.

Penthesilea halted and stared. Jagged dark green diamonds traced a path up and around the elevation. She pointed to its south side.

Abba-Bashti did not understand.

"Don't you see it?," said Penthesilea, pointing. "From the way it lies, it's a hill fort, between those two stands of pine halfway up."

Abba-Bashti followed Penthesilea's arm and made out a smudge of timber and earth. A plume of smoke rose from it, bent into long puffs, and vanished.

"Let's try for that. We can get there before midday if we hurry. And we're close enough to Themiscyra now. Perhaps whoever holds that place is an ally of the Amazons. If they are, we can spend the winter there.

"And if they're not?"

Penthesilea made no answer.

The wind had risen. Powder was falling at an angle. Abba-Bashti caught some in her hand. Surprised, she examined it— cold flecks that turned to drops of water in her palms.

"There'll be plenty more before the Storm God's done with us," said Penthesilea. "Let's hurry."

They lengthened their stride. The flakes fell thicker and whiter, until a brilliant wall blinded the travelers to all but a few feet of road. The north wind slashed at them. Abba-Bashti groaned and hunched her shoulders. Tala lowered her head. Proto hid her face in her mantle. Penthesilea clenched her fists and stamped one foot in front of the other.

The trail wound to the sheltered side of the mountain. There, the airs no longer cut the journeyers in two. They took a path that led uphill and inched toward a close-growing copse of tall pine. Stepping into it was like walking into a wall of shadow.

A thunderous laughter bounced off the tree trunks, dinned in the boughs, and shook the foliage. Penthesilea froze in her footsteps. The path ahead turned. A hefty Amazon mounted on a parti-color horse came into sight. Her big frame shook with merriment. Her face, the color of dark leather, was contorted in gaiety. Her open mouth revealed a row of brilliant teeth, save an inky rectangle where an incisor had once been. The mirth gusting from her mouth made the air tremble.

She reined in. Her eyes widened. "What's this? What's this? I can't believe it! We've been looking everywhere for you!"

A rider who was at least a head taller came up next to her. Big-boned hands and long legs protruded from her mantle, and a huge chin from her cowl. She gaped at the three travelers, stroked her lantern jaw, and said, slowly, "Where've you been, girl? We were getting worried."

Another woman cut between the two. Her frame seemed slight by comparison. She threw back her hood; flame-red hair splashed over her shoulders. "Well preserve me from evil thoughts! We'd thought you'd departed early for the land of the blessed spirits!"

Tecmassa, Feodissia, and Marpessa had passed the days before in the hill fort of Akmon, an old ally of Themiscyra.

"And from the looks of it, we'll have to spend the rest of the winter here," said Tecmassa. "The snows have come. But I can't say as I mind."

"She never minds," said Marpessa, "when there's a larder full of cakes, a cellar full of beer, and a bed full of charms."

Tecmassa guffawed again. Her bellowing agitated the fronds above the wayfarers' heads.

The three riders led the voyagers to the stronghold. There, servants bathed them in perfumed water and feasted them on cakes and wine. When the time came to bed down, Feodissia took charge of Proto, and Penthesilea and Abba-Bashti retired to the sleeping chamber that they were to share for the winter.

They did not speak as they slid under the bearskin, each one still wrapped in the soft wool robe that Akmon had offered her as a welcoming gift. Penthesilea lay still. Abba-Bashti felt her cheeks heat up with embarrassment, like a child afraid to confess her ignorance.

The silence weighed down on them. Penthesilea breathed fitfully. Abba-Bashti waited in the stillness. Penthesilea did not move. At last, Abba-Bashti touched her friend's hand, timidly, fearing lest she pull it away from her.   Instead, Penthesilea opened it.   Abba-Bashti caressed its hollow. Penthesilea tightened hers around her friend's fingers.

Abba-Bashti lifted herself on her side and kissed Penthesilea's neck. Penthesilea turned to her. Her breath warmed Abba-Bashti's nostrils, and she laid her mouth on Abba-Bashti's and ran the tip of her tongue across the line of Abba-Bashti's lips. They grew full, as if they had tasted warm honey, and Abba-Bashti grasped Penthesilea to her. Penthesilea was trembling.

"What is it?" said Abba-Bashti. The hoarseness of her voice surprised her.

"I cannot believe this," whispered Penthesilea. "I am afraid it is a dream and in the morning I will wake up to my prison."

"It is not. You will not," said Abba-Bashti. "I promise."
"You do?"

"I swear before my Goddess."

Penthesilea pushed herself up and slid her garment over her head.   She hoisted Abba-Bashti by the shoulders until she could slip her long blouse from her body. She opened her arms and enfolded Abba-Bashti in them. Abba-Bashti lay back and pulled Penthesilea down. Penthesilea stretched her body over hers, covering her with the heat and weight of her passion, resting her head on Abba-Bashti's breast so that Abba-Bashti felt her heart palpitating against Penthesilea's cheek. Penthesilea kissed and caressed her; first with hesitation, then with fire.

Like water through thirsty earth, joy thrilled through Abba-Bashti's nipples and woman's flesh. Bliss trembled in her stomach. She was singing her lover's name. Rapture lifted Abba-Bashti up and up until she moaned and wailed and burst into radiance like a pomegranate exploding in the sun. She heard her lover chanting her name as if it were a magic spell. The deep-flavored wine of joy flooded Abba-Bashti's fingers and toes and womb. Then her body ebbed away from her in a slow dance. She turned on her side and hugged her knees to her chest, astounded, mute, glad of her silence. She cradled her head in the crook of her arm. Humming reverberated from deep inside her. Her throat was dry.

Penthesilea fit Abba-Bashti's form into hers and rocked her in her arms.

How long did they stay like that? Abba-Bashti could not tell. At last she rolled over and murmured, "I never knew that I. . . ."

Penthesilea laid a forefinger across her lips. Abba-Bashti nuzzled her head in Penthesilea's shoulder. It was wet with tears. One splashed onto her cheek.

Abba-Bashti raised herself on an elbow and pressed her lips against Penthesilea's brow the way she did Proto's when night monsters made her bawl.

"What is it?"

Penthesilea turned away. Sobbing took her prisoner, shook her, pinioned her.

Abba-Bashti stroked the back of her neck, again and again. Penthesilea's convulsions grew more fitful and ceased. She still cried quietly.

"What is it, my love?" asked Abba-Bashti.

Penthesilea sat up. She gulped in a great lungful of air and pushed it out like an enemy she wanted to drive back. She said, "They all betrayed me in Troy. All of them. Except you. At home, they forgot about me. All of them. Except Myrtho and my three friends. The Goddess failed. . . ."

"Hush. She did not. She failed in nothing. She helped me get you out. You are safe and must no longer doubt Her love. Or mine."

Chapter 15

The party rounded the last homeward curve of the northeast trail. Thermodon's waters rushed downstream; white flowers exploded from the apple trees; cottony wisps hurried across a sky of robin's-egg blue. The sweet perfume of blossoms and the sour smell of soaked earth intoxicated the breezes. Far off, on the summit of the hill, Hebatê's sanctuary gleamed in the morning sun.

"See that?" said Feodissia, who rode ahead with Proto astride in front of her. A mounted figure was heading toward them, doubtless coming to meet them. The women patrolling the northeast had dispatched someone to announce Penthesilea's return.

"I wonder who'll get here first," said Abba-Bashti, who straddled Tecmassa's big-bellied piebald behind her.

"Whoever it is," said Tecmassa, "it might not be to welcome us back. There's some that would call us deserters."

Tecmassa, Feodissia, and Marpessa had stolen out of Themiscyra at the end of the previous summer to free Penthesilea or avenge her death if it came to that. One week away from Troy they learned of the earthquake. They rode as far as the city to search for the Amazon. Survivors said that she had been there when it happened; that she had died crushed or burned like the rest. Disheartened, the members of the search party turned homeward but could not bring themselves to set foot in Themiscyra without first having scoured the roads and byways on the slim chance that Penthesilea had escaped.

Myrtho had put the three up to their mission and filled their purses with gold and silver to carry it out. Ariona had looked the other way when they left without asking her consent. Thalestris and Hippolyta could not have been pleased with their unauthorized absence.

Marpessa explained why, while the women bided the winter. "Neither Thalestris nor Hippolyta wanted you back. Thalestris is afraid you'll favor Melanippe when Thalestris'

time comes and we Amazons have to choose a new chief. And
Hippolyta fears that you'll lend your voice to Antiope's
claims."

"Thalestris' time comes?"

"Yes. She's very sick these days. The drinking has caught
up with her, and she'll not live to see the other side of summer.
She still wants Antiope to take her place. (By the way, did you
know Antiope's pregnant? She'll have dropped her foal by the
time we get back.) Thalestris has the riders to enforce her
wishes when she's gone. That is, if they hold steady and don't
desert. But there's much grumbling among them: many a
woman's of the opinion that Antiope betrayed us. And no one can
say, either, that Thalestris has won the love of the multitudes.
Some are not shy to speak their minds, and Hippolyta has
promised them gold and silver if they go over to Melanippe
when the time comes. Not that most of us who grew up with
Melanippe care for her. But she's Naunamé's daughter, and
that will surely mean a lot when Omaïa summons us to choose a
new leader.

"Still, there are too many riders to count who won't say
what they'll do. So neither Antiope nor Melanippe can rely on
being chosen. Those who follow Ariona will not open their
mouths until Ariona speaks her mind. And she hasn't so far.
And there are those who'll pay heed to Myrtho when she tells
them her opinion. But she, too, hasn't pronounced a single word.
So that whoever wants to win the chiefdom has got to get the
backing of the one or the other. Both is best, needless to say.
That's why Thalestris and Hippolyta would not spare an ounce
of metal when those swindling lads sent a messenger to ask for
your ransom. They didn't want you around: each was afraid
that you'd favor the other. They know that Myrtho will pay
attention to what you say and that Ariona's inclined to listen to
you, too."

"So are a lot of other riders," added Feodissia.

"Don't let it go to your head," said Tecmassa. "Self-interest
speaks loudest and has the last word."

"I'll wager that they'll try to get on Abba-Bashti's good
side, too," said Marpessa.

The approaching rider, Hippolyta, met the party.
Penthesilea nodded but did not smile. The old noble pulled her
horse around and rode side-by-side with her. Penthesilea remained silent.

Hippolyta said, "I thank the Goddess that you've returned safe and sound and have come out to tell you that I do. I rejoice that you've returned to take your rightful place."

"I do not believe you.," Penthesilea said. "Last summer, the Achaeans sent a messenger to tell you the terms of my ransom. You wouldn't agree to pay it."

Hippolyta drew her lips into a thin smile.

Penthesilea continued, "You would have let me die screaming at their hands."

"That was Thalestris' doing and not mine."

"I don't believe you."

"Since then things have turned around for good. Do you not know that Thalestris is at her end?"

Penthesilea kept looking ahead of her.

Hippolyta said, "I have dispatched a messenger to Melanippe. I know she will be pleased that you've come back."

"I don't think so. She's always despised Antiope's companion."

"That was true enough before last summer came. But now she wants your loyalty and strength. You know, of course, Antiope's betrayed the Amazons. The Achaeans were spies, and she led them away with our secrets."

"What's become of Antiope?" asked Feodissia.

"She had a baby boy."

"Too bad."

Hippolyta said to Penthesilea, "Now that Antiope has shown her truest stripe, you'll not have interest in returning there."

"I swore to the Goddess to ride by her side."

"The Goddess knows when oaths have no more force. Antiope has broken the most sacred one of all—to shield the Goddess's lands and daughters from Her enemies."

"I owe Antiope my life."

"And she to you. There's no more obligation."

"I ride for Thalestris."

"Who does not trouble to meet you on the road, nor send her daughter to discharge this obligation. Who dealt you an affront when first the Achaeans came, as did Antiope when they insulted you."

The memory pained Penthesilea.

"You do not have to ride for either of those two. Your debt to them was long ago dissolved. There is a place for you among my women. I want a strong lieutenant to lead my riders."

Hippolyta swept her hand around her to indicate Tecmassa, Feodissia, and Marpessa. "These women, too, are welcome at my hearth. For them, there will be treasure, and for you," Hippolyta paused, "for you, the honors due a noble, birthright Amazon. Leokadia's descendance will be a great one in the city."

Penthesilea lowered her eyes.

"And the next ruler will be pleased that you have done this."

"Unless she is Antiope."

"Do not imagine that Antiope will lead us. Before the summer's over Melanippe will be chief. She'll remember who her friends were, and her foes."

"That is not sure. Many Amazons ride for Thalestris. Enough to make sure that her wishes are carried out."

"It would be folly to count on their loyalty once she is dead, or trust Thalestris' offers when she makes them. And, once Antiope is chief, she'll find you inconvenient. You're a reminder of her treachery, don't forget."

Penthesilea and Hippolyta rode on in silence, until Hippolyta said, "Think on what I have come out here to say. You all have much to gain . . . or much to lose. But do not hesitate too long, my friend. Some say Thalestris will not see the harvest. But others who have seen her at close quarters say she will not live to see the traders at our gates." Hippolyta pivoted her horse, saluted Abba-Bashti with a flourish, and hastened toward the city.

Later that morning, Celano made a deep obeisance and led Penthesilea to the great hall. Thalestris, sunk back in her throne, her face in the shadow, waited for her. "Welcome home, my girl," she said in a hollow voice. "I thank the Goddess you've returned safe and sound to your rightful place."

Penthesilea did not reciprocate but stared at Thalestris until her eyes grew used to the half-light. Thalestris' face, once tanned and healthy, was now yellowish and fragile. Her lips, too, once sensual, were now bloodless. Still, her eyes were more alert than ever, feverishly alert.

Penthesilea kept silent for so long that Thalestris stared at her as if trying to read her mind.

At length Penthesilea said, "You refused to pay my ransom." Thalestris ran the tip of her finger over the line of her mouth. "It was not my doing, but Hippolyta's. I know she rode out to meet you earlier today. But don't imagine that her offers came from her great love for you."

Penthesilea arched her eyebrows.

Thalestris ignored the expression and went on, "When the Achaean messenger came to tell me what they asked, Hippolyta said no. She didn't want to pay a ruler's ransom for a simple rider who's not even a birthright Amazon."

Penthesilea shook her head. "Supposing that it happened the way you say it did. Hippolyta's still not the chief of the Amazons; you are. And even if she were, most of the treasure belongs to the temple, and Myrtho wanted to send it. It was you who objected. It was you who said the gold did not belong to the Goddess."

"What's passed is passed, Penthesilea. I didn't call you here to talk about yesterdays. Things have changed, greatly changed. Now you are back, and I'm pleased you are, whether or not you think so. There's a place for you here, the place you swore to the Goddess to take for the rest of your days—as Antiope's close comrade. And when she's ruler, you will be her lieutenant. We are counting on your loyalty."

"I'm no longer bound by oath to you or Antiope. It's not possible that you don't know that and don't know why."

"Why talk of days passed, when it is the ones to come that matter? Once Antiope takes over, you'll be her right-hand woman. She's generous. You know that well. She'll fill your chests with fine gifts."

"I need nothing except my horse and weapons."

"You'll be mighty among the Amazons. You'll ride at Antiope's side when she leads their column."

"I want only to patrol the northeast passes, as Leokadia did before me."

Thalestris leaned forward. "A woman of your choosing can be steward of this palace and its lands, the way Celano is now. Surely you would like that."

"The riders will not elect Antiope to be their chief. There's much bad blood against her. Many women think that she's a traitor. And Melanippe's the daughter of Naunamé the just. Many's the woman who's still loyal to her."

"Antiope a traitor? Nonsense. Lies. Lies planted by Hippolyta to make women forget that they've much bad blood against Melanippe. What's more, I've got enough riders on my side to win the throne for my own daughter, whether they're called together in counsel or take arms."

"Take arms?" asked Penthesilea. "Against who? Against each other? The Amazons will not do that."

"There is no question," said Thalestris, "that Antiope's more fit to be their chief."

"I am not sure. And I'm not the only one who thinks that."

"You'll regret it if Melanippe's chosen when I am gone," said Thalestris.

"No matter what Hippolyta promises you, Melanippe's a woman who does not forget and does not forgive. Once she's sure that no one will stand in her way, she'll remember you were Antiope's companion, and rode at her side through thick and thin for three years, and rescued her from kidnapers. Don't think she'll close her eyes to that. Antiope's more forgiving . . . although she may not be when she becomes ruler and you've not helped her succeed me. Think about that, Penthesilea. But do not wait too long, for I may lose patience, and so may Antiope."

Penthesilea took her leave.

Penthesilea was making her way across the marketplace when she heard the pounding of hooves. She turned. Antiope reined up next to her, jumped down, and threw her arms around her. "You're alive!" said Antiope. You're safe!"   She pulled back. Tears were rolling down her eyes.

"Tecmassa and. . ," began Penthesilea.

"I know. I wanted to go with them but. . . . You know about Theseus' boy child?"

"Yes."

"Word that you'd come back didn't reach me until this morning in the far pastures. I rode here as fast as I could. They say Hippolyta met you before I could."

"She wants me to ride for her."

"You said no."

"I said nothing."

Antiope was puzzled. "Haven't you seen Thalestris?"

"She's very sick."

"Yes. I'm glad you're back. I need you here."

Penthesilea's glance wavered.

"You're going to ride for me, aren't you? That was always planned. You'll be the most powerful Amazon in the land, after me. And rich. I'll give you—name it, name it."

Penthesilea still looked away.

"They say you brought that trader woman back with you. You know there is a place for her."

Penthesilea did not reply.

"You baffle me, Penthesilea. Look, we've been through much together, and I've always been honest with you, and open-handed, as befits a noble Amazon. You're my steadiest friend."

Penthesilea narrowed her eyes. "You let the Achaeans humiliate me when Thalestris gave the banquet for them. You even laughed along with them."

"I'd drunk too much wine."

"You helped them escape from Themiscyra."

"I didn't know that they were spies then."

"But you knew they were rapists and thieves."

Antiope shrugged and said, "I regret that it all happened."

"Regret that it happened? Is that all it comes to? Regret what some say is betrayal?"

"What do you mean?"

Penthesilea contemplated Antiope for a moment. Antiope did not understand. But would she ever? No. Not likely. Penthesilea bowed, begged her leave, and headed for the temple complex.

Myrtho herself waited at the palace door. Penthesilea bounded up the steps and threw her arms around her. Myrtho held her tight. Both wept. After a long while Myrtho stepped back and through moist eyes scrutinized Penthesilea. She wiped a tear from Penthesilea's cheek and smoothed her hair. She said, "Your face is altered. There's great melancholy in your expression; I have never seen it before. And anger. I have never seen that before, either."

Myrtho's features had changed, too: her hair was turning white; her eyes seemed wearier than they had ever been, and her lips more bitter. She conducted Penthesilea to her sitting room, which a brazier warmed even on this late spring afternoon. She made Penthesilea recount her story from the moment she rode out of Themiscyra almost a year before to the moment she returned earlier that day. Wrath deepened Penthesilea's voice when she retold the cruelties that the Achaeans had inflicted on her. "And the Trojans, when they caught me they would have done me in, slowly, hurt me a lot. But Abba-Bashti rescued me."

"That's not a Trojan name."

"No. She's a trader woman from the southern empire. She came here last summer. That's how I knew her. Then her caravan traveled on to Troy. That's where I met her again."

Penthesilea felt her cheeks redden. She wished that Myrtho would ask no more.

"A trader woman from the south," questioned Myrtho. "And she put her life in peril to rescue you?"

"Yes," Penthesilea managed to say.

"She abandoned her people and accompanied you to your home?"

Penthesilea nodded.

Myrtho's mouth sketched a tense smile. "I see," she said.

Penthesilea told Myrtho about the earthquake and fire that ravaged Troy. Grief choked Penthesilea when she related the violent deaths her friends there must have suffered. "Friends who helped me when I was sick. People who would not harm anyone, who worshiped the Goddess. How could She let this happen to them? How could She allow them to be punished like that when they did nothing?"

"I don't know. There is no answer to that."

"No answer?"

"There is none. We priestesses and priests recount stories about the origins of evil, but they are little more than empty tales."

Penthesilea covered her eyes with her hands and did not speak for a while. Finally, she resumed her story and finished it.

Myrtho now said, "Of course you will not return to Thalestris' quarters."

"That's right."

"It is just as well that you don't. I have learned from a good source that there is a place for you in Hippolyta's house. I am of the opinion that you should accept it. She leads the party that favors Melanippe, and Melanippe will be the next ruler."

"How can anyone be certain?"

"There will no longer be any uncertainty when I pronounce myself on my choice. Enough riders are in my debt to erase all doubt, and I desire that Melanippe take Thalestris' place."

"Is she the Goddess' choice?"

"No. The Goddess has said nothing. Melanippe is my choice."

"I never heard you speak well of Melanippe."

"Yes. I never have. She has given offense to many who were raised with her. Others have little confidence in her integrity. Still, she is not a traitor. And even if young ones do not like her, at least they do not despise and mistrust her, as many do

Antiope. These considerations weigh heavily. It is important, too, that Melanippe has almost enough women on her side to carry the day when the Amazons are convoked in council. Once I declare that she is my choice, the matter will be settled. If I do not, the decision will require more time, and the Amazons most probably will ride against each other. However that may be, Melanippe will still win. It is better to prevent such an occurrence. Once the men of Amisos and the Kaska raiders learn that we are fighting among ourselves, they'll fall on us from every quarter. And if we survive, generations of Amazons will be brought up to hate each other. Thalestris and Hippolyta, Antiope and Melanippe, do not anticipate such things. They do not want to. They cannot, for then they might contemplate the folly of their designs. But I do and I see that civil war is the greatest of evils.

"And I must think of the prosperity of the temple and the riches of the Goddess. I do not wish to spend the rest of my days in conflict with a spiteful ruler, who will conspire against the temple to take away its privileges and lands one by one. Nor do I desire to leave this situation to Iphinoë and all who follow when I am gone. I will let my choice be known when the priestesses make the solstice sacrifice two moons hence."

"And Ariona?"

"She despises both pretenders but will keep silent come what may. She says enough women are sworn to ride for her so that she need not fear Melanippe. I am not in accord. That is why it is best that you ride for Hippolyta."

"I'll ask to ride for Ariona. Leokadia did."

Myrtho drew her lips tight. "But surely you must know that this is not in your best interest."

"I can't bring myself to do anything else."

"Melanippe will not like that, and it is by no means certain that I will be able to help you."

"I'll take my chances. I can't do anything else."

Six weeks later, Feodissia brought the news. The others—Penthesilea, Marpessa, and Tecmassa—had just settled into the camp they maintained near the northeast border, where they were keeping an eye out for the first traders to arrive from that quarter. A large caravan had already appeared from the south.

"Thalestris is dead," said Feodissia, when she took her place next to her comrades. "Sooner than anyone expected, like

Hippolyta told us. And Melanippe didn't waste any time sending her to the West, either."

"Melanippe?" asked Marpessa.

"Yup."

"What happened to Antiope?" asked Penthesilea.

"Let her tell the story from the beginning, will you," said Tecmassa.

"Well, I wasn't there then," said Feodissia, "but Anuphey told me how it started. It seems that Thalestris had been very strange the day before, walking around like she was looking for something, and scared somehow, scared. She called for drink; Anuphey brought it, and Thalestris accused her of trying to poison her. She sent for Antiope; Antiope showed up, and Thalestris sent her away as soon as she got there. She finally drank her regular sleeping potion. They found her dead the next morning. Then, even before many people in the palace knew she was dead, Perseia—you know, Melanippe's friend—barged in the main door on horseback with a dozen riders behind her. Someone must have brought them news of Thalestris' passing right away. And since that door's always barred at night, someone must have opened it from the inside."

"That means," said Tecmassa, "that Melanippe had someone inside."

"Only one?" said Marpessa.

"Anyway, Adrasta and another dozen blocked the downhill entrance and the stable door so that no one could get a horse and run away. Two went right to Antiope's room. She's under house arrest. Only a few of Thalestris' women put up a fight. And not for long right away they saw that the rest didn't raise a hand but acted as if they were waiting for them. As soon as the palace was secured, Melanippe walked in and took over. And no one can find Celano. By the time the sun set Thalestris was smoke and ashes. Not a whole lot of riders dared show up at the funeral, either. I got to town right when the flames were flaring up. Melanippe didn't waste time getting things the way she wanted them, too; because this morning, when I rode out, her lieutenant was already down at the tents talking to the old man who leads the caravan."

"Her lieutenant? Perseia?" asked Penthesilea.

"Not anymore. It was Tomiris I saw."

"Tomiris? But she rode for Thalestris," said Tecmassa.

"Yup. Acting like she had call to do what she was doing."

"I'll wager that Tomiris was the insider who let Melanippe know the minute Thalestris passed," said Marpessa, "and opened the palace door."

"That could be," said Penthesilea, remembering Tomiris' maneuver at the games the year before: Tomiris tried to unhorse Penthesilea so that Antiope would lose to Melanippe.

"So, so," said Marpessa, "Melanippe's dearest companion, Perseia, has been pushed aside in favor of Tomiris. Even after Perseia stormed the palace for Melanippe. Fancy that. Who's the more underhanded of the two, do you suppose, Melanippe, or her new lieutenant, Tomiris?"

"Anyway, there's Tomiris telling the traders something they sure didn't like to hear. They were shaking their heads and whispering one to the other as though they'd just heard the bad news. Melanippe must want a special gift, because those trader men didn't like it at all."

"Didn't Celano make them pay when they first got here?" asked Marpessa.

"Yup."

"What did Myrtho have to say?" asked Penthesilea.

"Nothing that Anuphey told me."

"Not that Melanippe would pay her any mind," said Marpessa. "Myrtho never did express a choice."

"She didn't have a chance to," said Penthesilea.

"That will prove a bad mistake," said Marpessa.

"Still," said Penthesilea, "if Melanippe gave it a thought, she wouldn't ask the traders for another ounce of anything. They've paid enough to Celano, and chances are they'd probably hand the new ruler a gift without being asked, just to stay in her good graces. So there's no use offending them by demanding something they'll part with anyway. We need them, and they need us."

"Sense?" said Marpessa. "Sense? Surely you're not serious, my girl."

Tecmassa swigged at the gourd Anuphey had sent along, smacked her lips, and said to Feodissia, "You'll be more welcome at the palace now that Thalestris is gone."

"Maybe so; maybe not. I mean, I ride for Ariona, don't I? And Melanippe will never get over Ariona's staying out of it."

"If Melanippe thought about it," said Penthesilea, "she'd forget all that and leave Ariona alone. There's no use stirring up more hatred among the Amazons. Now's the time for Melanippe to make friends and heal wounds."

"There you go again," said Marpessa.

Themiscyra's vineyards spread over sunset-facing slopes over-looking the farmlands. The grapes grown there produced a heady, dry, deep red wine that traders carried away to console them on lonely nights, and that Themiscyra's women downed in glee, and plenty on festive days—the inhabitants' daily bever-age being the far less intoxicating small beer.

It was said that the Goddess's handmaiden Kulitta acciden-tally discovered how to make the delicious liquid. It began when Kulitta was a prisoner in the palace of the Storm God, Texobos, who was exceedingly fond of grapes, to the point that He hid them in large clay jugs sealed with wax and marked "poison" to make sure that no one else touched them. Kulitta hated captivity so much that she decided to take her own life. When Texobos was not looking, she opened one of the jars and ate its contents. Instead of dying, she fell into perfumed somnolence; it was in this blissful state that she first dreamed of making her escape. A few days later she fed her captor a large dose of the same venom and ran away while He slept it off. She then told the Goddess how she had disarmed His vigilance, and the Goddess told Her daughters.

Some of Themiscyra's vines were worked by women who gave a part of their yield to Thalestris, some to Hippolyta, and others to the temple. The three slopes that produced the plumpest grapes and most delicious drink were cultivated by Cleothera, her two daughters, and her helpers. Cleothera sent her tribute in kind to Ariona. Cleothera's ancestors had labored on those hills since the time of the Amazon queen Sinope, who had made a gift of her rights to taxes from them to Ariona's great-grandmother Nicippe for having accompanied her to Troy.

The other vintners envied Cleothera: not only did she hoe the best of the descents, but her foremothers had passed on to her the art of picking the grapes on the right day, overseeing their fermentation to the precise moment, and flavoring the first wine perfectly before letting it sit for the winter. Cleothera never paid heed to the malicious gossip of which the jealous made her the butt. Her easygoing character, made better by fre-quent sipping of her own product, and the knowledge that she was welcome wherever she went, made her shrug them off. She was content to prune her vines and turn the soil around them, to pick the grapes and tread on them until she waded in juice, to pour it into bell-mouthed jars and watch its nine-day fermentation closely, to spice it, sweeten it, and rack it before laying it down.

She was a happy woman, known for her hoarse songs and cheerful how-do-you-do's, until two great sadnesses ripped her good nature from her. Her first came two winters before, when her younger child—a full-cheeked, healthy maiden just nearing her first moon's blood—succumbed to the fever that was ravaging Themiscyra. Her second happened that very spring, when her oldest daughter, a well-fleshed woman in her prime, died giving birth to her firstborn, a deformed boy child that did not long survive the mother.

Work in the vineyard lagged that season. Cleothera pruned her vines and turned the earth with slow hands and unseeing eyes; the lack of two women to care for the plants also held up the tasks. Ariona—who needed scores of huge jars of wine for her riders and who traded other scores against the amber, grayware, cloth, and spices that the merchants carried in—began to doubt that she would have all that she required. It was springtime; and every woman was busy; Ariona sent the only one who could be spared. It wasn't enough; Cleothera was still one hand short. But it was better than nothing. Then, just as bunches of tiny blossoms began to burst from the stalks, Abba-Bashti arrived, and Abba-Bashti, it seemed, knew something about cultivating fruits. Ariona dispatched her and Proto to the hillsides right away, and Penthesilea rode off to her station in the northeast passes.

When Abba-Bashti and Proto showed up at the vineyard, Cleothera was not there, but her chief assistant, Dione—a short, long-nosed woman with white hair and alert eyes—rubbed her hands and beamed at the prospect of two more workers to care for the plants. Not many days after that, she chuckled as she recounted to Cleothera how quickly Abba-Bashti had caught the knack of thinning the least promising shoots and securing the ones that remained to the pole around which they were to finish growing, and of trimming the longest tendrils so that the plants would spend their efforts making fruit instead of spreading outward.

Proto thrived. She became adept at pulling the weeds from around the squat growths and upturning the surrounding earth to give them air. She giggled and prattled with the three other girls who had come out to work with their mothers. Still, Cleothera frightened her. The old vintner would look on her with sad eyes that Proto saw as cruel. The girl would shy away, and the grownup's face would grow longer. And when Cleothera was in her cups, something that happened more and more often, her tears terrified the child, who thought it the start of unspeakable brutality and ran weeping to Abba-Bashti. Sometimes now Cleothera snored the morning away, and the others had to toil under Dione's direction. Sometimes, too, Cleothera would disappear before the sun had reached its highest point and stagger back only as it was setting and supper was stewing in the cauldron. By the time the grapes began to turn dark red, the others would not see her for days on end, and Dione took charge of making sure that the baskets were repaired and that the treading trough was scrubbed out for the harvest.

Then, one morning, a woman came from town to announce that they had found Cleothera's body in the river under the bridge, where the currents had thrown it. How she had gotten so far upstream and whether she had fallen or jumped none of those who knew her could tell. Nowadays she was unsteady on her feet most waking hours; but then again the spirits of unhappiness might have done her in.

Cleothera had died without issue—she had no daughters any more, no parents, no cousins—and so the responsibility of awarding the living to another woman fell back on Ariona. She did not hesitate. The vineyard was now Dione's to work, and her daughters, and her daughters' daughters. They would be the tributaries of Ariona and her descendance. It was the natural choice, the only choice. Had not Dione toiled at Cleothera's side since both were girls? And had not Dione been Cleothera's closest friend, although—despite what some women whispered—she had never shared her couch, or at least not for long; and that was so many years before that gossips recalled it only when there was nothing else to wag their tongues about.

Shortly after Cleothera's death, it was Penthesilea's turn to ride back to Themiscyra and report on the scouts' sightings. She started out from camp at first light and rode as hard as she could. She wanted to make her report and get her supplies right away, and then hurry off to the hills and spend the night with Abba-Bashti before hastening back to her patrol. She had not seen her since the moon had waned and waxed. Penthesilea arrived at Ariona's house at noon, and while she and Ariona were making their way on foot to the palace, the latter told her the news of Cleothera's death and Dione's taking over the living.

Melanippe was waiting for them in the great hall, lounging in the large armchair, which had lately been raised on a daïs a step high. Tomiris, who stood by her side, balanced one hand on her hip and draped the other over the back of the throne. Once the newcomers entered, Melanippe straightened up and Tomiris dropped her hands to her side and drew her face into a neutral mien that Penthesilea did not trust.

"Make your report," said Melanippe without offering the customary refreshment.

Penthesilea spoke: "The first caravan that crossed here late this spring on their way to Troy has already come back, two moons early. They'll reach Themiscyra's gate by sunset tomorrow. They stayed in Troy for a few weeks. They say that there's nothing to stay for—no commerce to speak of since the Goddess shook the earth. It ruined the Trojans. Those left were lucky to have the clothes on their back. They built shanties against the walls that were still standing. The only thing they have to trade is some wool. The rest—amber, grayware, lead, everything—the earth swallowed or the fire did. I'm not surprised, either. It was...."

"Finish your report," snapped Melanippe.   Penthesilea searched Melanippe's face.

Melanippe gazed back without recognizing her and commanded,

"Continue."

"Since there was nothing for the Achaean sailors to barter against, most of them didn't bide their time there, either, so there were few Achaean ships for the merchants from the south to trade with. There was a lot of plundering last fall and winter, too: the mercenaries who weren't killed robbed everything they could and cut down anyone who stood in their way. But there's law and order now. One of their princes was out of the city when the earth shuddered, and he's scraped together what's left of his army and taken control of Troy again, although nobody can figure out how he pays his troops to keep them loyal."

"Loyalty's always a problem," said Tomiris.

Ariona raised one eyebrow.

"Did anyone say whether the southern traders will call at Troy anymore?" asked Melanippe.

"None of them can say. There are other ports on the warm sea, but none is so well situated as Troy, none lies between the warm sea and the cold one as Troy does. It's best to ask the merchants yourself."

"I'll do as I see fit," said Melanippe, waving her hand to end the discussion.

A woman entered the hall bearing a tray, flagon, and goblets. She placed them on the table and poured. The Amazons made their libation and drank. It was wine, but not the sweet dark liquid that Thalestris had prided herself on. Instead, they sipped a dryer, lighter mixture that nonetheless tasted familiar.

"This is good wine, is it not?" asked Tomiris.

"Yes," said Penthesilea, who thought no more of it.

"If you say so," said Ariona, who had long ago foresworn strong drink.

"It's from Melanippe's vineyard," said Tomiris. "But not the one the Thalestris collected taxes from. The new one."

"The new one?" asked Ariona.

"Yes," said Tomiris, "the one Hippolyta had her eyes on for many years."

Ariona could not recall which hillside that was.

"The one Dione works now that Cleothera is dead," smirked Tomiris.

Ariona stepped back, crossed her arms over her chest, and shook her head. "You know very well," she said, "that Melanippe's great-grandmother Sinope awarded rights to that vineyard to my great-grandmother Nicippe as a reward for serving her faithfully during their journey to Troy."

Tomiris pursed her lips in amusement.

Ariona addressed Melanippe. "You know very well that it has been in my family since that time."

Melanippe drew her mouth into a slight smile.

Ariona quizzed her with her glance, trying to see if Melanippe was serious about her plans. Melanippe's expression did not change. Ariona realized finally that Melanippe indeed intended to take her land from her. The color left the old Amazon's brow, and she pronounced, "Your ancestor Sinope will look upon your seizure of what is mine as. . . ."

"You're not accusing the high judge of the city of theft, are you?" said Tomiris.

Ariona tensed her mouth to speak, but Penthesilea interrupted. "What you are doing is unjust. The Amazons will not look kindly on it."

"Will they not now?" taunted Tomiris. "Well then, call them together if you want. You have every right to. Of course, there's few outside Ariona's little party who'll pay much mind to what you say. Hippolyta's won't. Nor Melanippe's."

Tomiris spoke the truth. Most Amazons in council would jeer at Ariona's claim, for they were beholden to Melanippe or to Hippolyta. Still, there was another way to prove that tribute from the land went to Ariona. "There are records in the temple," said Penthesilea. "The priestesses must have written the present down. They always do for land arrangements."

Melanippe and Tomiris exchanged glances. Melanippe nodded her consent, and Tomiris hurried out of the hall. The ease with which Melanippe had acquiesced and Tomiris hastened off made Penthesilea uncomfortable and, judging by the look Ariona darted her way, had the same effect on the older rider.

Melanippe poised herself on the edge of her chair, held her trunk rigid, and placed the tips of her fingers on her knees. Ariona and Penthesilea took places at the table. Ariona stared at the board and drummed her fingers against it. Penthesilea pressed her knuckle against her mouth. What was wrong with Melanippe that she should try to ruin a woman whom she would need in battle sooner or later? What would Dione think of the news? Not that anyone ever asked the women of the plow or the women of the tool what they thought of these arrangements. She would now pay her tribute and owe her loyalty to Melanippe and probably would not mind. Her life would be the same. But Abba-Bashti's? Melanippe could contrive to make things hard for her, although Penthesilea had trouble imagining how. Still. . . . The portal opened and closed. Penthesilea started. Steps approached but passed by the entrance of the hall. She sank back in disappointment. Melanippe exhaled scornfully, her lips parting to reveal huge incisors.

More noises from the palace door. Voices. Footfalls. Myrtho and Tomiris entered. Myrtho, whose hands were empty, swept past the seated Amazons. She approached the throne. Ariona rose precipitously and also went up. Penthesilea followed. Tomiris stationed herself beside the chair of state, placed her thumbs and fingers on her hips, and announced, "Not a trace of any record."

Melanippe sniffed in disdain.

Myrtho looked from one to the other as if she were taking their full measure for the first time. Her brow contracted but soon enough grew smooth again. She folded her hands in front of

her and said, "But Tomiris relates the event in an incomplete
fashion. When she presented herself with the request to see the
record of the donation to Ariona's great-grandmother, I went to
the room in which such writings are preserved. But search as I
might, I could not find the tablet that records this gift. I found
it perplexing that I could not. Quite perplexing. I have never
removed the tablet from its habitual place. I have never had
cause to. And no one except Iphinoë goes there. Notwithstanding, I scrutinized every corner of the room in the event I was
mistaken. But it was nowhere to be found. It has disappeared.
And yet I have laid my eyes on it more than once and can assure
you that Ariona's claim is well founded."

Melanippe scoffed.

Myrtho continued, "Not only have I seen the tablet, but
Ariona's title to the wine from those three hills is a matter of
common knowledge and needs no writing to make it true."

"Doesn't it, now?" said Tomiris

"The women will give credence to my assurances," said
Myrtho.

"The women will give credence to your assurances," simpered
Tomiris, aping Myrtho's intonation. In her own she said, "No,
they won't. Who do you think will take your word for it, when
they know how much you dote on Ariona's rider, Penthesilea?
They'll see that you're trying to do both of them a favor, because
Penthesilea's lady friend lives off those vineyards. Melanippe
and Hippolyta will make sure to remind them of it."

Penthesilea and Myrtho were speechless.

But Ariona stepped forward. "That's right, Melanippe,"
she said, "you do have enough riders to enforce your will—for
now. But I'll bet my bow you won't always. Judging from the way
you two take on, I'm probably only the first of a long line of
women you'll harm."

The mole above Melanippe's lip began to pulsate. Tomiris
threw back her head and laughed through her nose.

"I can also tell you," said Ariona, "that what you're doing is
not in your own best interest; yet I know you've not enough of anything but spite in your heart to understand what I say."

Melanippe waved her off contemptuously.

Ariona opened her mouth to reply, but Myrtho laid her
hand on her forearm, and Ariona stopped. Myrtho lifted her
long skirts, inclined her head, and promenaded toward the door.
Penthesilea and Ariona bowed low and followed.

Abba-Bashti and Penthesilea lay under the open sky, the diamond outline of the swan and the winged horse circling silently above, the setting moon outlining the peaks of the iron hills. Abba-Bashti's cloak was spread under their naked bodies, Penthesilea's over them.   Abba-Bashti's head rested on Penthesilea's shoulder, and her respiration cooled the furrow between Penthesilea's breasts. Penthesilea stroked her waist.

"I can't help thinking," said Penthesilea, continuing a conversation they had pursued on and off all night, "that Melanippe would have a chance if she knew how to be kind. After all, she's the daughter of Naunamé the Just, and her cousin Antiope has made many women mistrust her. She's sober, too, and that is something that Thalestris was less and less."

"Melanippe will never have power over the women's hearts," said Abba-Bashti, "because she has none over her own, although I do not see why."

"She eats up her life getting even."

"For what? What more can she want?"

"Our loyalty."

Abba-Bashti exhaled a long sigh.

"If Melanippe decides to get at me through you. . ."

Abba-Bashti did not let her finish. She sat up, lay her finger over Penthesilea's lips, and said, "I'll take care of myself and Proto."

Penthesilea ran the tip of her tongue over Abba-Bashti's index finger. Abba-Bashti leaned forward and kissed Penthesilea with such great love that her flesh ached, and she hugged Abba-Bashti against her. Abba-Bashti put her hands and lips and tongue on her. Like a sheet of the running sea, waters sparkling diamond blue and dawn yellow rushed through Penthesilea and rolled back, and hissed forward and fell away, and again and again, until they thrilled into great columns of blinding foam that crashed against her belly and surged to the tips of her fingers. After the last wave burst and lulled, and Penthesilea lay motionless, her lids closed, her throat dry, Abba-Bashti buried her head in her neck and whispered secret words.

One bird trilled, then a second, then a chorus. Penthesilea opened her eyes. Pale blue from the east was staining the dark velvet above.

The women sighed and got up.

Telkhinia's relations with Thalestris had started as they ended—in grudge and spite. The summer before Thalestris went to the West, she had protected the two Achaeans who raped Telkhinia's oldest girl. When Thalestris first ascended to her station, she had forgotten to seat the smith on her right at the banquet that new chiefs always offered the women of the tool. Telkhinia, who had just taken the place of her mother and was now the most important of them, stormed off and spent the next days sulking at Cleothera's. Thalestris fumed at the public act of insubordination, but Celano reminded her that the Amazons owed their freedom to women who knew how to coax iron out of ore and forge weapons from the metal. That was why such women were always on the lookout for affronts; they wanted to prove that they were beholden to no one. Even so, it was better to offer Telkhinia a gift than risk her continued idleness. And generosity would heighten Thalestris' good name among the artisans—not a bad thing at the beginning of a reign. It took a week for Thalestris to calm down, and she ended up sending Telkhinia a skin of beer and a side of venison. The smith, who had tired of empty hands and a muzzy head, was as quick to let bygones be bygones as she had been to take offense. She lit up her forge that night and took up her hammer the next morning.

Whereas Thalestris had stumbled into Telkhinia's disfavor after she became chief, Melanippe had asked for it before she took over. During the time that she was still a rider of no special rank, she had never stopped to drink beer and trade gossip with the blacksmith when she had business with her, even though every other Amazon did, aside from Hippolyta—and Telkhinia had no use for that one, either. And the few times that Melanippe did say something to the metalworker, she talked down. Telkhinia often wondered where Melanippe had gotten it into her head that her butt was more precious than anyone else's and that—just because Telkhinia paid her tribute to the palace—she was some bootlicking menial. Telkhinia's distaste changed to dislike when Melanippe became ruler: the smith turned the hard feelings that she nurtured against Thalestris on the woman who succeeded her and who, even before she took over, had given Telkhinia no call to wish her well.

Telkhinia took out her ill will in the manner of artisans who know that people can't do without them: since she could not refuse to pay her levy any more than she could turn down the repair jobs that Melanippe sent her, she acquitted herself of her due as slowly as possible. Farmers got their plowshares and scythes before the ruler got her labryses and blades. Harvest time was near and Telkhinia still owed six double-headed axes and as many long knives—one-third of her yearly impost, all of which she traditionally delivered before the midseason's full moon. Added to that, one cauldron and an iron brooch (Melanippe's gift to Tomiris) had yet to be repaired, although they had been in Telkhinia's hands since the summer triangle shone its brightest in the northern sky.

"Telkhinia is holding back on purpose," said Melanippe.

"Maybe you're right," said Tomiris, loath to contradict the woman who had elevated her to the lieutenancy of the territory.

"My enemies have put Telkhinia up to this," said Melanippe.

"She is the friend of Feodissia and Penthesilea. Both of them ride for Ariona. Both of them did not want me to be ruler. Telkhinia will do anything she can to cross me for their sake. So will Myrtho, who also did not speak in my favor. That is why I must stop this. Speak to Telkhinia and tell her that the chief of the Amazons will no longer tolerate her lateness."

When Tomiris entered the smithy, Telkhinia was intent on fishing a twisted billhook out of the coals and did not look up. She placed the red-hot tool on the anvil and pounded on it with hammer strokes that clanged so loud Tomiris thought they were beating on her skull. Tomiris put her fingers in her ears and bided her time. The din died. Telkhinia nodded hello, shoved the implement into the fire, and dove into the rear of the shop. Tomiris crossed her arms. They were dripping with sweat; it was also trickling down her spine. After a while, someone stirred in the rear. Tomiris dropped her hands and readied herself to speak. Telkhinia rushed out from where she had vanished.

"Telkhinia. . ," Tomiris began.

"No time to talk now," said the smith. She snatched up her tongs and yanked the instrument from the fire. "I gotta get this thing on the anvil, now it's redder than a stallion's hard-on. You know what they say about striking while the iron is hot." Telkhinia placed the billhook on the surface and wrapped her fingers around the handle of her hammer. She lifted it above her shoulder and slammed it down again and again, a halo of sparks shooting out from where it crashed down on the instrument. Between blows she shouted to Tomiris, "Something important?"

"Yes," yelled the Amazon.

"Speak up, so I can hear you."

"Yes!"

"Huh?"

"YES!"

"Well then, come back this evening. Don't you see I'm trying to get a job done?"

Tomiris returned at dusk. Telkhinia had gone out, and none of her daughters could say where she had repaired to or when she would come home. Tomiris went back to the palace and reported that Telkhinia had not been there when she went to speak with her on behalf of the chief.

"I call that insolence," said Melanippe.

Tomiris kept her counsel.

"I do not intend to stand for it. I myself will go there tomorrow. Telkhinia will learn not to insult her chief, no matter what anybody else tells her."

The next morning, Melanippe—her face at its most self-possessed—strode into the smithy. Athaia, Telkhinia's middle daughter, was kneeling in front of the forge. She looked up, saw who had come in, and hurried into the rear of the shop. Melanippe had a chance to look around for her goods. Stashed in the farthest corner was a cauldron that she supposed belonged to the palace; but there was no sign of the brooch nor of the weapons that Telkhinia still owed.

Steps and voices came from the rear of the shop. Someone was approaching. Melanippe stood up to her full height. Athaia, holding an empty market basket, rushed out of the living quarters and hastened away. Melanippe joined the tips of her fingers to each other. More footfalls in back. Melanippe dropped her hands to her side. Telkhinia ambled out and, without looking at her caller, mouthed the traditional greeting. Then, before Melanippe was able to make the customary response, Telkhinia had turned her back to her. She took up her bellows, bent over, and began slowly and deliberately to pump air into the fire. At length she straightened up, and—still not sparing Melanippe a glance—put on her leather apron. She now took a few paces toward Melanippe and looked her in the face.

Melanippe's nose turned up and to the left, so that it seemed as though she were looking down at the smith, who was nonetheless a head taller.

The smith placed her fists on her haunches. "Well?" she asked.

"I have come about your back taxes."

"Yeah. What about them?"

"The summer is almost gone."

"You'll get them."

"When?"

"When I get around to it. I gotta lot of things to get in shape before the harvest. You'll get them soon enough."

"When?"

"Like I told you, when I get around to it." Telkhinia did an about-face, stepped to the forge, and picked up her tongs.

Melanippe said, "I want my weapons right away."

Telkhinia extracted a pruning knife from the coals, held it at arms' length, and examined it as if she suspected it of some misdeed. "Other folks are in line before you," she said, not taking her eyes off the blade, "no matter how high and mighty you think you are."

"Those weapons are my due," said Melanippe. Her mole was pulsating, and her voice quavered.

Telkhinia laid the knife on the anvil. "What're you so exercised about? I just said you'll get them."

"It is in your interest to get those weapons to me right away," Melanippe said—steadily this time.

"My interest? Who do you think you're talking to, Melanippe? I' m no servant."

"It will not be wise to go against my word any longer."

"Not wise? And what are you going to do about it if I do, take away my birthday?" Telkhinia grabbed her hammer, bent her head, and began to whack the blade furiously.

Melanippe composed her face and left.

Shortly before noon Thersandra the potter burst into the smithy. Seeing no one stationed at the forge, she shouted Telkhinia's name in a tone so alarmed that the smith came bounding out.

Thersandra spoke right away. "Your daughter, your middle daughter, Athaia. . . ."

Telkhinia stiffened. The girl had been due to come back in time for the midday meal but had not yet shown up.

"They've taken her prisoner."

Telkhinia unfroze and squinted at Thersandra. "Whatever are you talking about?"

"I saw it with my own eyes. I was waiting near the entrance to the palace when Athaia walked into the courtyard and through the door. As soon as she stepped over the threshold, two women grabbed her and dragged her inside. They won't let her out, either."

"What? Have you been into the wine? It isn't even noon yet."

"I'm as dry as baked grayware. I saw it with my own eyes. The one that fetched her—Tomiris, you know that one—stayed behind and began to laugh hard. Seems she fooled Athaia into visiting the palace: found her near the gate and told her that you needed to see her there right away. The minute she set foot inside, they grabbed her."

"Stop joking, will you? Why'd anyone ever want to do that?"

"Ransom."

"Ransom? Have you been breathing too many fumes?"

"No I haven't. I saw it with my own eyes. Tomiris says you're way overdue on what you owe them, that you're holding back on purpose, that they're keeping Athaia until you pay up, because someone put you up to it."

"Someone put me up to it? Keeping her until I pay up?" Telkhinia picked up her hammer and said, "I'll pay them good!" She stormed out of her shop and tore uphill. Thersandra sped behind her. Telkhinia hurtled into the palace courtyard. The great wooden portal slammed shut. She thumped on it with her fist. It did not open. She raised her hammer and battered it with slow, deliberate blows. Their clangor shattered the ears of the women in the vestibule all the way on the other side of the building and made the kitcheners look up and wonder what was going on. Still no one pulled the door back. Telkhinia spit on her palms and whacked harder. Splinters of wood, then jagged lengths of board, flew over her shoulder and littered the courtyard. A shock. Telkhinia's hand felt like it was exploding. The hammer flew from it. A labrys thudded into the door and stayed there. Two mounted Amazons rode to either side of her, picked her up under the arms, and carried her to the street in front of the palace. There they heaved her onto the packed earth. She landed at the feet of Thersandra, whom a score of onlookers had joined. The potter's pale face reddened and her gray lips flushed purple. "Who do you think you are?" she screamed, shaking her fists at the riders.

"Yeah!" shouted several others.

Scowling, Tomiris reined up. Four strapping riders, two of whom had lately tossed Telkhinia to the ground, stationed themselves in front of the potter and glowered.

"Who do you think you are?" asked a woman from the back.

"Yeah!" the others repeated.

"It's no use," answered Tomiris. She paraded her mount among them and stared at each one in succession. She pulled her horse around and spoke to Telkhinia, who had just raised herself to her feet. "The same goes for you," she said. "There's nothing you can do. Come back a dozen times and our answer will be the same. We'll kick you out. That's what Melanippe says, and she means it. So pay up. And tell your friends that, too."

Telkhinia stood up and said, "Who the hell do you think you are? I am not doing another stitch of work, until you. . . ."

"You aren't doing another stitch of work?" mimicked Tomiris.

"Then you aren't seeing your daughter." Tomiris ordered one of the riders to fetch Telkhinia's hammer. She tossed it at her feet and said, "Don't think of leaving this behind. If you don't use it, you won't see the girl."

Telkhinia scooped up the implement and, with lowered head, made her way home. Tomiris and the Amazons smirked.

Midnight's waning moon cast uncertain light on Themiscyra. Silence and sleep pressed down on the city. The palace was a heavy mass crushed to the ground by the stillness.

A horse's snuffle broke it and was swallowed up as soon as it had. A lithe figure slipped out of the tack room window and landed soundlessly on the cobblestones. The woman crept around the corner, stood up, and, hugging the sides of the houses, crept catlike down the hill. She glided into an alleyway so narrow that only someone as slim as she could negotiate it. Noiselessly, she hoisted herself into an opening in a wall, slid inside, and alighted on the floor. The faint sound she made awakened Telkhinia, who had just drifted off, having spent the evening fretting and hating.

"Who's that?" muttered the smith, raising herself on her elbows.

"Anuphey," whispered a guttural voice. She tiptoed into Telkhinia's sleeping chamber.

The smith swung her legs over the side of the bed. "From the palace?"

"With word from Athaia. She's all right. She says not to worry. The serving women won't let anything happen to her. And even Melanippe does not dare harm her. It would upset the women of the tool too much. Your daughter's word is not to do a thing for Melanippe until they let her go. Not a thing. She's a brave girl. She will wait, even if it takes the whole winter. I must go now." Anuphey slipped out as quietly as she had arrived.

The next morning Thersandra asked to speak to Myrtho and, once she had, hastened to Telkhinia's smithy. Soon after that, the smith and her two other daughters put on the long cloaks and drooping hoods of pilgrims, marched up the hill, and—having reached the temple complex incognito—fled unseen from Themiscyra through the cave that began at Myrtho's palace storeroom and ended at Telkhinia's smeltery on the side of the hill.

While Telkhinia and her girls were making good their escape, the artisans' quarter, whose din most days resonated as far as the marketplace, was as silent as the night that had just ended. Thersandra had spread the word of Telkhinia's humiliation. All of Themiscyra's craftswomen had seated themselves in front of their doors and crossed their arms. Shortly before noon Melanippe sent riders to see if anyone was working. Each time an Amazon approached an artificer, she vanished into her shop and slammed the door. Melanippe dispatched her four brawny riders to Telkhinia's with orders to bring her to the palace. She was nowhere to be found. Nor were her other daughters.

Melanippe sent orders for Penthesilea and Feodissia to report to her without delay. Three days later, they ran their horses through the gate and walked them uphill to the palace. The girl who took their horses, ordinarily garrulous and cheery, did not speak, nor did another old friend, the serving woman who conducted the riders to the hall. No one waited for them there. That, too, was out of the ordinary.

Someone escorted Myrtho into the room. She was surprised to encounter Penthesilea and Feodissia. Before she had a chance to speak, Ariona was ushered into their presence. She, too, had not expected to see them.

"But it makes sense, if that's the word for it," she said.

"What do you mean?" said Feodissia.

Ariona recounted the events surrounding Athaia's reclusion, including Melanippe's belief that the four now waiting for her had put Telkhinia and the craftswomen up to their deeds.

"Does Melanippe really believe that we're all plotting and planning against her?" said Feodissia.

"I must confirm that she does," replied Myrtho. "She thinks that I look down on her, because I did not pronounce in her favor before she captured the throne; she distrusts Ariona for the same reason. As for you and Penthesilea, much about you makes her suspicious: you both ride for Ariona and are both Telkhinia's friends. What is more, Penthesilea, who is dear to me, and who never seconded Melanippe's pretensions, counts more friends than she knows among the Amazons—and not only among Ariona's riders. "

"Where are Abba-Bashti and Proto?" asked Penthesilea.

"With Dione at the vineyards," said Ariona.

"It would be folly for us to move them," said Myrtho. "Such a gesture would be interpreted incorrectly, and to our detriment."

"What's got into Melanippe's head?" asked Feodissia.

Before anyone could answer, Tomiris strode into the hall and took her place to the left of the women. Four muscular fighters followed and stationed themselves by the door.

Where was Melanippe? Penthesilea and Feodissia traded puzzled glances. No sooner had they done so than Melanippe sauntered out from behind the curtained door that led to her apartments. She had been listening. She stepped onto the daïs, turned her nose up and to the left. Her upper lip trembling, she pronounced, "I will not waste words with you. I have lost patience. The fall harvest is upon us, and the women of the tool refuse to work."

"That's your doing." said Ariona. "You know how Telkhinia is."

"I do not think so. Telkhinia refused to give me my weapons because you told her not to. And when I called her to task for it, you made sure that the craftswomen put down their tools. And now one of you is harboring her. I don't know where, but have reason to suspect that she is hiding in the temple precinct."

"I swear before the Goddess that they are not there," said Myrtho. "I have no reason to conceal them. We all benefit from the artisans' labors. It is to our disadvantage that they have stopped fashioning the tools for. . . ."

"No!" interrupted Melanippe. "You want a bad harvest so that the women blame me and turn to Antiope."

"Are you kidding?" asked Feodissia. "Antiope's just as bad as you are."

Penthesilea darted a look of alarm at her comrade, who shrugged her shoulders.

"Feodissia's false sincerity does not move me," said Melanippe. "Other matters are of more interest to me right now."

She stepped down from the platform and paced around the women she had summoned. "Listen carefully," she said as she circled, "Listen, all of you. If Telkhinia does not return to her forge, if the artisans do not build their fires and take up their tools, I'll hold you personally responsible, each one of you. Our well-being depends upon a good harvest, and you have interfered with it. That's a betrayal. That's a great betrayal. If I call the riders together and ask their advice, they will agree with me, and it will go hard for you. You have three days starting with this morning's sunrise to get the women back to work. If you do not, there is no telling what the Amazon council will recommend." Melanippe had again taken her place in front of the throne. "You are dismissed," she said.

Myrtho shook her head in pity and Ariona shook hers in weariness. Feodissia gaped at Melanippe in disbelief. Penthesilea's face contracted in concentration. She looked at the floor without seeing it and did not stir until Myrtho called her name from the door. She started, pursed her lips, and stalked out.

"Yes," said the priestess after Penthesilea told her what she had been turning over in her mind. "I know where Telkhinia is hiding and will fetch her."

There was no moon the next midnight. Dimness and silence took over the world. Once, the breeze carried the gurgle of Thermodon's current to the street below the palace. A horse whinnied, but the sound was cut short. Two shadowy figures—one short, one full-grown—slipped out of the tack room window and slid to the ground. Hugging the walls, they spirited downhill toward the street of the artificers.

At dawn puffs of smoke bubbled into the sky from the smithy. Soon a white stream of it flowed heavenward. Clattering rang out from a nearby shop, then banging pounded from another, then crashing boomed from still another. By the time the sun had climbed over the wall, the din beat on the ears of women trudging uphill to the marketplace.

In the palace, their body servant awakened Tomiris and Melanippe with the news. Tomiris snickered in triumph;

Melanippe's eyelashes fluttered uncontrollably. "Athaia is free to go," she said. The serving woman hastened to where Athaia was held. She found no one. She went to the kitchen and looked for the girl. Athaia was not there. She searched and searched and returned to Melanippe's quarters an hour later to announce that no one could find Athaia.

The mole over Melanippe's right lip trembled; her eyelashes beat frantically. "Bring Abba-Bashti to me," she said.

But Abba-Bashti was not in the vineyard. Before dawn she and Proto had hurried to the beginning of the northeast trail to meet Penthesilea, who hastened out of town as soon as the gate opened. As she ran Tala toward Abba-Bashti, she did not give a thought that word of her doings would get around. Still, by the time night fell, women (even those who rode for Hippolyta and Melanippe) wept and roared in amusement as they repeated the story of Penthesilea's sense and nerve and Melanippe's embarrassment.

By the next new moon, the icy wind shooed the patrol back to Themiscyra. Bare branches swirled downstream on Thermodon's dull surface. The apple trees raised gnarled fingers to a flat gray sky. The weightless air dizzied a woman to breathe, and the hill loomed black in the distance. A squadron of riders, their capes flapping, were hurrying toward the patrol in the company of Marpessa, who had ridden ahead to announce their arrival.

"Welcome, girl, welcome!" shouted Ariona, the moment she was within earshot. "We've come to escort you into town."

"Better you than Melanippe," yelled Tecmassa. Abba-Bashti, who rode behind on her horse's croup, gurgled with amusement.

They reached the gate. Smiling women waited on the inside—Telkhinia, Athaia, Megara, Thersandra, Dione, Anuphey, and at least a score of others, including familiar faces from the palace staff and a score of Amazons on foot, from Ariona's house, to be sure, but also from Melanippe's and Hippolyta's. Only after Ariona looked over her shoulder to see how Penthesilea was taking it, did Penthesilea understand that the crowd had come to welcome her back.

"Don't let it go to your head, girl," said Tecmassa.

Chapter 16

Feodissia had left the patrol the day before and headed off to have a look at the Trojan road. She had spent the night in a cave near the limits of the land and now crossed the valley that led to the hill overlooking the river Lycus. The rising sun warmed her cheeks; the scent of new grass turned her head. She filled her lungs with the fragrance and pressed it out with a loud, lengthy, contented hiss. She was glad to get out of Themiscyra after the winter. Riding away two days before had been like throwing off a cloak that slowed your step and made you sweat. She hadn't told Anuphey, though, because Anuphey had nothing to do with it, and there was no use bothering her before riding off for all these months. Not that she ever looked at another woman while Feodissia was out of the city. But she sure did like to go down to the tents. And she got babies—kicking, screaming girl children—almost every year, so that even Tomiris looked the other way when she sneaked out winter nights and climbed into Feodissia's couch. Feodissia sighed again.

Too bad the whole winter hadn't been like that. No. The rest had been pest and trouble. Pest and trouble just about from the day they hung up their saddles for the season to the day they finally got away from it all.

It was Melanippe's doing, too. These days you could tell that beforehand. It could make you wish that Antiope was chief of the riders, except that that one wasn't much better. She still had to live in the palace with all sorts of people watching her and couldn't ride out much except when they took her. So you could almost feel bad for her, especially when you caught a look at that long face of hers. As for that cranky boy baby she'd got, a wet nurse took care of him, and Antiope was glad for that, really glad.

Feodissia neared the edge of the lowland. The mist at her horse's feet twirled into columns and shot skyward. The slender trunks and leaves of mountain ash took shape through the thinning fog.

A couple of days after the patrol had come in for the winter, Feodissia had gone with Penthesilea to the sanctuary, though she'd forgotten why. And thinking about it later, it was a good thing she'd gone, too. Night was falling when they left the temple grounds, and dry snow powdered their hair and shoulders. They crossed the marketplace and headed down the alleyway that led to the street in front of Ariona's house. They'd done it so many times before they didn't need torches.

They'd heard footsteps behind. She and Penthesilea had stopped and turned to say hello. Four husky shapes kept walking toward them. The biggest, who was as tall as Feodissia and much heftier, grabbed her by the front of her cloak with one hand and smashed the heel of the other into Feodissia's jaw. She sprawled backward and banged her head against the ground. Stars burst and blinded her; fire split her forehead from the inside. Something told her to roll sideways, and the big woman landed spread-eagle next to her. Feodissia pushed herself to her feet. Through the clanging in her ears she heard knuckles whack flesh and Penthesilea groan. Someone locked Feodissia's arms tight behind her; they almost ripped from her shoulders. The big woman stood facing her and crashed her fist into Feodissia's nose. Pain tore her face in two; she tasted her own blood. Somewhere else, a fist thudded into soft flesh, and Penthesilea snarled and puked.

Then the riders' had heard running footsteps. "There they are!" someone yelled. The arms crushing Feodissia let go. She blocked another swing just in time and buried her fist in the big woman's solar plexus. The woman yelped and doubled over, and someone jumped her from behind. After more thumps and curses, scraping feet, and shouts, the four attackers ran away, and Feodissia crumbled to the ground. The smell of puke cut into her senses. Next to her, Penthesilea lay on her back, out cold, shuddering; blood and vomit covered her lips and chin.

Adrasta, Perseia, and Lysippe had come to the rescue. Adrasta had seen the four Amazons swagger out of the palace and cross the marketplace. The way they walked meant drink and fighting, and, sure enough, as soon as she and Penthesilea disappeared into the passage, they dove behind them. Adrasta and her friends took off after the attackers.

Tomiris had filled their bellies with wine and put them up to it: That was what Anuphey said, and she was repeating what another serving woman had seen. No one could figure out, though, who'd told Tomiris where Feodissia and Penthesilea were spending the afternoon and the moment they decided to head home. When it came to asking for justice, Adrasta and her friends told Melanippe who the attackers were, but the four swore up and down that they had spent the afternoon in the stable. Then Tomiris said that, yes, she had seen them there. Melanippe said that it was their word against Adrasta's and her friends', and it was dark out so there was no telling for sure; and you couldn't punish anyone because there wasn't hard and fast proof, just accusations.

The heat had run up Feodissia's neck; she opened her mouth to grouse, but raw hurt split her jaw and shut her up. Adrasta took over for her, waving her fist at Melanippe, yelling at her that she'd be sorry—very sorry.

The unfairness riled Penthesilea, too, when she heard about it, even though she wasn't a mite surprised. She hadn't been at the judgment, because she had to lay still in bed until her ribs knit. She had plenty of time to think things over, what with being flat on her back all those weeks. Her talk had gotten slower and there was something in the back of her eyes—she was chafed and up to something. Knowing her, she'd own up when she was ready. But she didn't once talk about paying them back, even when the four who jumped them made fun of her the first time she walked out with a cane.

The wooded height overlooking the river came into view. Patches of fog hid its western slope in places. The sun would burn them off pretty soon.

Adrasta, Perseia, and Lysippe had shown up at the banquet Ariona gave to pass the Longest Night. Adrasta sat at the head of the board between Ariona and Charope. Perseia sat next to Antiope and Lysippe next to Penthesilea, who was out of bed for the first time. After that, Adrasta spent so much time in Ariona's house that riders there began to ask why Hippolyta turned a blind eye to her niece's coming back all the time. Anuphey's palace gossip told them why. It seems Melanippe had gotten on Hippolyta's bad side, too, and Hippolyta wanted to keep a foot in Ariona's door but not spend time with her herself. Something about etiquette had ruffled Hippolyta's feathers, although Feodissia couldn't say what, because she never kept track of those things. Then there was what had happened at the end of the trading season. Hippolyta's riders had caught some robbers red-handed on the southern steppes. Tomiris had ridden out—"with her wondrous winning ways," as Marpessa said—and grilled the Amazons like they were the thieves and not the ones who caught them to make sure that they weren't holding on to more than their share of what they had captured.

Feodissia turned her pony onto the path that snaked up the hill overlooking Lycus. The sun had chased away the last shreds of vapor. She threw off her cloak and gloried in the heat on her neck and haunches. Above her head, shrill notes trilled and big wings flapped. They surged above the treetops, spread out like a wide brown cloak ending in black fingers, banked, and, with slow, powerful strokes, beat toward the valley. It was good to be out here alone.

The worst part of it had come on the Day of the Year. Right after sunset Merope, the temple cook, banged on Ariona's door and, breathless, begged to speak to Penthesilea. Merope whispered frantic words, and Penthesilea bolted up and ran out. She didn't come back until the next morning, either, and her face looked like there was no more blood in it and her eyes like she had laid them on some devil sent to spite her.

It seems that Myrtho had passed out in the middle of the ceremony she was leading the afternoon before. Just as she reached up to put a white cloak on the statue of the Goddess, she fell to the ground like a woman who'd had too much to drink— her face all red, snoring so loud it echoed off the walls, her cheeks all puffed up. When they lifted her up to take her to her palace, her right side was limp—arms, legs, everything. She didn't come to until the morning and then she couldn't move her right arm and leg, couldn't feel anything in them either, and the left side of her face was dead.

Melanippe didn't lose any time. She called Iphinoë to the palace that noontime and named her high priestess, although no ruler had ever done that while another high priestess was still alive. And from what Anuphey found out, Iphinoë didn't even stop to think, didn't even tell Melanippe to hold her horses, but said yes like she had expected it all along. Melanippe sent Iphinoë gifts later in the afternoon, a large cauldron and three big bolts of soft cloth she had bought from a trader the summer before. So you knew whose friend Iphinoë was, and she wasn't Myrtho's. Maybe Iphinoë had been the one who told Melanippe where Feodissia and Penthesilea were spending the afternoon on the day they were mugged.

"Then perhaps she was the one who stole the tablet where Sinope's gift of the vineyard was written down," Penthesilea had said.

Women began to repeat that Myrtho was too fond of wine, that the Goddess had struck her down because She didn't want a drunk to pay Her court and do Her will, and that Melanippe was only doing what She wanted. It was a vicious story, and Feodissia knew who spread it without Anuphey's telling her. The lie bothered the life out of Penthesilea. It also bothered Ariona, because now she wasn't sure what would happen to her. With the loss of Myrtho, Ariona hadn't any friends left except her own women and who knew when they would begin to desert her? After all, that's what Melanippe had done to Thalestris. Even Adrasta showed up less and less. When the patrol rode out two days before, just before the full moon, Feodissia hadn't seen her face since before the new one.

Myrtho had gotten better little by little. The feeling came back to her right side, and then she could move it again. Still, she dragged that foot when she walked and the left side of her mouth was pulled down. "She doesn't talk as sharp as she used to," commented Tecmassa, who had gone to see her one day.

"I wonder when she'll be well enough to travel," said Penthesilea, who was listening.

"Why? You got plans for her?"

"For all of us; I'll tell you when we're out of the city."   And so she did, as soon as the four riders had walked their horses onto the road along Thermodon.

"I don't want to stay here much longer," she had declared. "There's no safe place for us and no place for Ariona and Myrtho. It's only a matter of time before Melanippe does more harm."

"Where would you go if not here?" asked Marpessa.

"Toward the setting sun. Myrtho says there are cities near the warm sea that worship the goddess Cybele."

"You'd want all of us to go?" asked Feodissia.

"Yes. All who wanted to."

"Melanippe won't let that happen," said Tecmassa. "And she sure won't like it if anyone takes treasure out of the city."

"Safety and freedom are more important."

"Only for some women," said Tecmassa. "Not for most."

"And I doubt that most rulers would welcome scores of armed women escorting their own priestess into their city," added Marpessa. "You scarcely have need of a soothsayer to predict the welcome we'd be dealt."

"Yes," said Penthesilea. "But there's more than one way to take refuge in a city. If they don't welcome us, we can win a place to stay. The Amazons have done it before. And those who come with me. . . ."

"With us," the three other riders had said in unison.

Feodissia now reached the southwest-facing flat on the summit and surveyed the river, the track that followed it, and the bridge that passed over it. A double line of goats, their coats glistening, their bells clapping, plodded across the span under the eye of a man and a child. The man looked her way, said something to the child, and began to hurry toward the observer, who, seeing this, guided her horse down the hill and ran it toward him.

The minute she reined up, he poured forth excited words, nodding his head and pointing northwest. She swiveled in that direction so abruptly that her horse reared. She quieted it and, turning back to the man, untied the gourd fixed behind her saddle and handed it to him. Then, without sparing him another glance, she wheeled her mount around and dug her heels into its sides. It sprang forward and started for the hill it had just descended.

Seven long ships from Troy, each rowed by scores of soldiers, had landed at Amisos eight days before. The army there was also preparing a campaign. They had joined forces and would march on Themiscyra. Perhaps they had begun. Feodissia had to get back to the city right away. She hoped she would spot her friends on the trail.

By noon she had descended the hill and begun to cross the valley. Her horse, a spirited four-year-old that she was riding for the first year, swallowed up the distance in easy strides. Its back beating against her flesh lulled her into the pleasing certainty that she would reach Themiscyra before the sun went down. She turned her mount into the northeast trail, which narrowed and snaked almost as soon as the animal set foot in it. She bent over the steed's neck and concentrated on the road before her.

Unexpectedly, she heard the hiss of an arrow. The mount screamed and plunged forward; its legs crumbled. Feodissia threw herself free and landed on her stomach at the same time as the horse thudded onto the ground. An obsidian-tipped shaft whacked into the earth by Feodissia's side. She sprang up and dashed for the hill opposite where the bolt came from. She began frantically to zigzag up. Another arrow whizzed above her head. She kept scrambling.

The warmest part of the next day had passed when Marpessa caught sight of a squad of light infantrymen from Amisos—a dozen of them, six carrying bows and six javelins. The men's raised heads pivoted tirelessly. She melted into the hills and took a roundabout route to where she knew her friends waited.

Tecmassa and Penthesilea rushed off to have a look for themselves. "They'd be fools to come in here only a dozen strong," said Tecmassa, having run an eye over the intruders. "They're from Amisos, so they know better, unless they've got plenty of fighters behind them."

"I'm going farther up the road to see how many," said Penthesilea.

"It's sure and certain they'll be looking out for scouts on horseback."

"I'll go on foot over the hills."

Penthesilea followed the sides of the slopes northward. Before long she heard the feet pounding and weapons clinking. Another detachment, this time a troop of heavy infantrymen armed with long shields and thrusting spears, marched along. Guides stationed at intervals along their line scanned the heights. Penthesilea ducked behind thick pine brush, took up a fallen branch, and nicked it once for each soldier she saw. A column of fighters carrying the figure-eight shields that the Trojans favored rounded the road. After the last man had disappeared, the stick Penthesilea held was covered with notches.

She lay motionless in her hiding place expecting to see another group on the heels of the one she had just surveyed—this time men shouldering pickaxes to dig under the walls and pack donkeys toting battering rams for the attackers to smash down the gate. Instead she heard a horse whinny. That must be another Amazon, probably Feodissia. Penthesilea sprang up and scrambled down the hill. She heard a second whinny, then a third, then a man clucking and shouting—"Get going! Get going!" She dove behind a clump of bushes.

Two foot soldiers from Amisos rounded the trail. Then three-dozen men leading as many horses, prodding them and whistling. Trojans again. Then the same number of archers. Then twoscore donkeys—many with wooden wheels strapped to their sides and chariot shafts tied to them, and still others with platforms secured on their backs. War wagons to carry men to battle. The last of the group rounded the road. Penthesilea waited a little longer but no one else came through. She ran back to where her friends were waiting, described what she had seen, and tossed the stick to Tecmassa, who turned it around in her hand and exhaled a low whistle.

"Weren't the Trojans supposed to be our allies?" she said.

"They've evidently neglected to let us know that they've had a change of heart," said Marpessa.

"At the pace they're setting," said Penthesilea, "they'll get free of the passes before dark and settle in around the city before dawn."

Tecmassa scratched her head and asked, "What good will it do them to establish themselves in front of the city, if they haven't got battering rams and pickaxes to get in?"

"I don't understand that myself," said Penthesilea.

"Nor do I," said Marpessa, "but right now don't feel at leisure to indulge in speculation."

"You're not thinking of leaving them here and hotfooting it to town?" asked Tecmassa.

"Feodissia must have seen them and alerted the city," said Marpessa.

"There's no way to be sure; she hasn't passed this way, so we better not count on it."

All three riders frowned. If Feodissia hadn't been able to warn the Amazons, it was better not to think why right now. Penthesilea lowered her head and wrinkled her brow. Her friends stared at her face but did not speak.

Finally, Penthesilea said, "We'll delay them here. If they get to the river by dark, they can march all night—the moon's full—and take up position around the city by dawn, before the Amazons can mount a defense and call for more riders. But if we stall them in the hills until dark, they won't move out again until light. They won't risk finding their way with horses' hooves to protect. So they won't break free of the northeast trail until dawn. By then the Amazons will have plenty of time to get ready for them. We'll spread the alarm when we're done here."

The riders glanced at the western sky. The sun had descended only halfway down.

The women cut along a goat path that wound through the hills surrounding the trail. Soon, a gust of wind carried the sound of footsteps. The riders had caught up with the leading detachment. They pushed on until they had to be in front of it. Penthesilea and Marpessa guided their horses up a slope that overlooked the road; the women dismounted and took cover behind a boulder. Forty feet below, the trail, which was wide enough only for two persons to march side by side, wound left and disappeared behind another hill.

Tecmassa continued to a point that overlooked the place where the way straightened once more but narrowed to permit only one man at a time to file through. That was where the Amazons wanted to trap and hold the first group until Marpessa had finished.

Steps crunched on gravel. Invaders rounded the curve. All wore leather helmets and wool cloaks studded with brass knobs off of which arrows might glance. All the men surveyed the surrounding heights without cease. The last two foot soldiers, who carried javelins, filed by and began to turn left.

The Amazons got out from behind their cover and drew their bows.

"Hey!" yelled Penthesilea.

A foot soldier looked their way; he widened his eyes in terror and opened his mouth to yell. Instead, he crumbled mutely to the ground. His comrade halted and swiveled his neck but fell before he realized what had happened. Screams sounded from the hidden part of the road. Tecmassa must be shooting.

Two Amisos archers crawled into sight. The women loosed another volley. One man yelped and fell onto his side. The other slithered backward out of view.

"Now?" asked Marpessa.

"Now," answered Penthesilea without taking her eyes off the scene below. She heard Marpessa scramble back to where the horses were concealed and her mount break into a run. Silence. On the trail not a soul moved out of cover. No yelling echoed from behind the curve.

Penthesilea examined the flank and summit of the facing hill, the trail in front, and the slope at her back. It wouldn't be long before the men would send sharpshooting archers after their ambushers. How quickly would Marpessa get to where she was going and how much light would remain after she got back?

Marpessa retraced the path the women had just taken. Clanking and stamping reached her from the other side of the hills, grew to a crescendo, and ebbed. That was the main body of the army. She continued her way until she heard men shouting, horses nickering, donkeys braying. She alighted and crawled to a height above the road.

The first team of chariot horses trotted by. She drew an arrow, took aim, and, silently begging Shaushka to forgive her, let it fly. It whacked into the croup of the leftmost steed, which screamed and reared, jerking up the halter by which its keeper was leading it. The man twisted and lost his footing. At the same time, the beast crashed sideways into its teammate, which pulled away sharply from its groom, who in turn, taken by surprise, let go of its rope. The freed horse scrambled up the facing hillside. Its mate followed, but not before it had bucked, its hooves smacking the muzzle of the animal behind it, which threw its weight to the right, causing its own partner to stumble, then vault forward.

The procession hesitated. Marpessa's bowstring twanged. A horse in the rear of the column stiffened its legs, leaped straight up, and crashed to the ground. The beast beside it whinnied in panic and sprang backward, slamming into the first donkey, which flattened its ears, brayed, and bit the frightened horse in the wither. It plunged sideways at the same moment as the pack animal started kicking in all directions, its followers shying out of the way of its hooves, knocking against one another, jerking free of their handlers, bounding into horses, which neighed in anger, reared, and jumped this way and that. Men barked orders all at once. The procession halted.

Marpessa crawled to the rear of the company and drew her bow taut. The arrow struck a donkey in the hock. The animal bellowed and bolted forward, frightening the others, so that, screaming and squealing, they plunged ahead or capered sideways, their burdens twisting, clanking, falling, tripping some, terrifying others. One sprinted toward the head of the column, then another, then two others, then all rushed into the immobilized horses, which bawled and reared and stampeded down the trail.

"There she is!" came a voice from the base of the incline. A Trojan pointed at Marpessa, and the sharpshooter at his side pulled his arrow back to his cheek. Hers flew first, and she raced to her horse.

The quiet was suspicious. Penthesilea's brow pounded as she surveyed the hill behind her, the one she faced, and the road. Nothing moved. No voice or footsteps reached her ears. She saw no one. Where were the marksmen that the men of Amisos were bound to send after her?

The breeze veered and began to shoo in shreds of clouds. The grasses and bushes rustled. In the distance, Tala whinnied wildly. Penthesilea pivoted her shoulders to have a look. An arrow grazed one and knocked the bow from her hand. She lay stunned. The sharpshooter who had missed her tore down the hill, stopped, and drew his bow again. A heartbeat before he shot, she came to her senses and flung herself to one side. A shaft impaled the ground next to her. She drew her labrys. The man took aim a third time. She hurled before he could let fly. The axe cut into his upper arm. He howled. Crazed, blood running from his wound, he sprang downslope and threw himself at her. She rolled out of the way when he hit the ground. He did not move.

During this time, a second marksman had slithered within striking distance and slid behind pine brush. He narrowed his eyes and fastened them on his prey. Penthesilea stripped the dead man of his quiver and began to scurry back to hiding on hands and knees. Her stalker slipped an arrow out of a sheath suspended from his waist. She snatched up her bow and crept on. He placed the nock of the shaft against the string of his own. She glanced back, saw no one, and inched forward again. He stood, straightened one arm, and pulled back the other.

"Behind you!" screamed Marpessa from the opposite hill.

Penthesilea threw herself flat, and an arrow sang by her ears. She rotated, pulled her bowstring back, and let it go. Her shaft flew wide of the mark. The archer dove for cover at the same time as Marpessa loosed a bolt. It fell short. Penthesilea shot twice in quick succession. Screams then silence. Not to be trusted. Not to be trusted. She had to see for herself. She scurried uphill, careering from bush to rock, wondering if he was taking aim. Once the brush in which he was concealed shook convulsively. That could be a trick. She darted a glance at the hill across the way; a sharpshooter was settling in at Marpessa's left. She had not spotted him. Penthesilea swerved, shot, and swerved again.A bolt shattered against the boulder next to Penthesilea.She dove for another growth. She had a good view of the marksman's refuge. A white flash behind leaves. Her bowstring vibrated. A shriek. She crawled toward her target. The archer lay on his back. A dark stain was spreading over his cloak. He rattled in sharp breaths and wailed them out. His feverish eyes followed Penthesilea as she approached.

"Don't kill me," he murmured.

Penthesilea snatched his knife and quiver and left him there.

As she was crawling toward where she had concealed Tala, noises of shuffling feet and clanking spears and shields wafted toward her from up the trail. That was the heavy infantry. She mounted and followed the goat path to where Tecmassa and Marpessa would be waiting.

Tecmassa squinted down the shaft of a captured arrow. "Not bad," she allowed. "And none too soon, either. I had two left and was going to take off before they sent a sharpshooter after me."

"We've put three archers out of the fight, what about yourself?" asked Marpessa, who balanced an arrow on her finger and lifted her arm straight up and down.

"One sure; a second maybe."

"So there's one, maybe two that remain of this squad," said Penthesilea. She surveyed the surrounding hills. "Where do you suppose they've taken themselves?"

"Up that slope," said Tecmassa, pointing.

Penthesilea turned Tala that way and dug her heels into the horse's flank. The steed launched into a run, and Penthesilea shouted over her shoulder, "I'll be back at twilight."

Tecmassa and Marpessa looked at the shadows on the ground. The light would be flat before you knew it. Then the army wouldn't dare move.

Clanking reached the two, then whinnies, then shouts, then the clatter of running feet and crashing shields.

"The amusement is about to commence," said Marpessa. "Pray, from what spot shall I observe it?"

Tecmassa flashed her patched smile and pointed to a place behind the entrance of the narrow passage.

She let the first man, a scout, enter the pass unmolested. Then an infantryman marched into it. His leather helmet, long shield, and sturdy greaves protected his front. A heavy cloak guarded his back, but Marpessa had a full view of it and loosed an arrow. It pierced the covering, and he fell. The scout turned, and Tecmassa finished him. A third soldier, who was about to set foot in the defile, shouted over his shoulder and raised his shield to parry flying weapons. Tecmassa loosed an arrow at his chest. He spun and slammed to the ground. The soldier behind him stopped short and dug in his heels, only to be propelled forward by yet another armed man, who was pushed by something or someone behind him. Marpessa's bowstring twanged twice in quick succession. Screams now reverberated from where the main body of the army had halted and was waiting to step into the pass one man at a time. From out of sight, shields crashed against spears, wild neighs echoed, frantic whinnies rebounded against the hills, terrified yelps and frightened bellows banged against the sky. A man-at-arms hurtled into the ravine as if shoved. He went down. Another met the same fate, and a third. A dun horse pounded by, its ears flat against its head, its mane fanning out, then a second steed blaring high-pitched screams. A donkey bucked through, bawling with every kick.

The shadows played tricks on you now, but Tecmassa made out a helmeted head emerging from behind the hill on which Marpessa was stationed. Tecmassa had to let two arrows fly before she put the sharpshooter out of the fight. Marpessa also shot; Tecmassa heard someone on the slope to her left howl, but the fellow kept lurching toward her, and she had to finish him.

"Okay?" Marpessa shouted.

The sky had turned royal blue. Tecmassa shouted back, "Okay. Okay." She walked quickly to where she had hidden her big-bellied piebald, which was tranquilly chomping grass and swishing her tail. She swung herself into the saddle and guided the animal down the hill.

Penthesilea and Marpessa were waiting in the twilight.

"Job done?" asked Penthesilea.

"Yup. What about yourself?"

"I didn't see a soul."

The three urged their mounts onto the road and walked them in the direction of Themiscyra. As soon as the moon rose above the hills and lit the path, the riders dug their heels into their horses' flanks and ran them toward the city.

They had almost reached the river, when a deep indigo silhouette—that of a long-armed, long-legged, gawky Amazon—stumbled out of the brush and waved them down.

Twenty Amazons, all that Ariona could muster in one night, dim figures in the fog that billowed up from Thermodon, sat their horses facing the entrance of the northeast passes. The sky began to pale; the mists fled up the hills and fanned outward; the summits took shape against the heavens. Ariona, who waited at the center of the group, nodded, and Charope and Klymene walked their animals to the base of the nearest slope, dismounted, and vanished behind it. The sun floated up and and began its ascent. The last columns of vapor swirled skyward from the waters and spread out into nothing. At length Charope and Klymene climbed into view from behind the peak, waved, and slid down to where their beasts were tethered. The knot of riders untied itself and looped into a semicircle around where the enemy would soon appear.

A dim, shuffling noise, hundreds of footsteps scraping and beating on the road, reached the women's ears from the direction of the northeast trail. Ariona walked her horse along one line of riders and down the length of the other. She had good words for every fighter. When she reached Penthesilea and her three friends, who stood near the river, she stopped and kissed each one on the cheek. She then took up her station in the middle of the Amazon column.

Gradually, relentlessly, the faint sound grew into a throbbing one, and the ground shook under the weight of the still invisible army that marched toward the riders. Finally, four shields emerged, an unbroken rampart of weathered hide, with jagged spearheads above it and leather greaves below it. The Amazons slipped their bows from their shoulders, plucked arrows from their quivers, and placed the nocks in the strings. The women drew the bowstrings to their ears and tilted back. A second row of four men marched into sight. Those in the middle had turned their shields up and stretched them above their heads crosswise to shelter themselves and the men at their sides from the shower of missiles that the Amazons were about to loose. The soldiers positioned on the flanks held their protection outward to defend the column's sides. The next row appeared, five wide this time—three bearing their cover above them and two gripping it to their sides—then the next, which counted the same number of soldiers and kept itself safe with the same tactic.

Ariona waved and shouted, "Hold back! Hold back!" Her orders ruffled like a sudden breeze down both lines of Amazons, but not before five of them had loosed their darts. These arced upward and swooped down, scraping off the shields and clattering to the ground.

More foot soldiers in formation came out of the passes. Ariona pushed the heels of her hands toward the hillsides and then toward the river. The slim crescent of riders broke into two dotted lines that moved away from each other, one flowing toward the banks of Thermodon and the other snaking toward the slopes. Ariona followed the latter and took up position on a height where all could see her.

The file of soldiers in the lead turned toward the city, some men doubling their step and others slowing down, so that their shield wall never opened. Before long, scores of infantrymen marched toward Themiscyra.

Tecmassa, who along with her three friends was observing from her post near the river, whistled through the gap in her teeth and said, "We won't stop them, I'll tell you that. We'll hardly slow them down."

"Someone has given this some thought," said Marpessa.

"They sure know what to expect," said Feodissia.

Penthesilea frowned. "Somebody's told them our tactics."

Brass-circled wheels rumbled behind the entrance; soon a double row of chariots emerged from the passes. Men holding up shields surrounded each horse and wagon. An archer stood on the moving platform behind each driver and hefted a figure-eight shield over the heads of both. A short fellow in a glittering bronze helmet drove the lead vehicle. Instead of an infantryman, an archer balanced behind him. The reinsman's head swiveled this way and that as he surveyed the terrain and the surrounding cavalry. His helmeted face flashed in Penthesilea's direction and stopped moving for an instant.

"That's Priam!" said Penthesilea, drawing back her bowstring. Without taking his eyes off her, he lifted his shield. His marksman raised his bow. Penthesilea and her friends dug their heels into their mounts and wheeled away.

The rearguard of the army stepped out of the entrance, and no more came after them. Ariona, her palms facing the ground, crossed them in front of her, and swept them outward twice, then toward her legs. Like a moving string of pearls, the riders located next to the hillsides cantered their horses behind the last of the invaders, and the Amazons stationed nearest the river ran theirs in front of the columns and took up the position that their comrades had just abandoned. Ariona clenched her fist and jabbed it toward the firmament. "Now!" she shouted.

Women stationed near the hills began to shoot at the greaves of the outermost soldiers, and, whenever an arrow drove home and a man crumbled to the ground, women stationed at their sides unleashed a volley into the gap in the shield wall. But before the riders had a chance to take aim once more, those who marched behind stepped over the fallen bodies and closed up the opening. The women behind the columns rushed in close

and unleashed their bolts. But marksmen placed in the rear returned their volley, and women were spun round like tops and
hurled from their horses. The pursuing Amazons wheeled out of
range.

An arrow loosed from Priam's war wagon flung Ariona to the
ground. In an instant, a dozen Amazon shafts sped toward the
sharpshooter, but none reached him before he had taken cover
behind Priam's shield. Charope, who sat her mount near where
her mother had fallen, howled and ran it to the same position.
The young woman spared the dead one a tearful look and extended her arms toward the city.

All the Amazons began to move in that direction save the
tight-sinewed Klymene, who, laughing at the top of her lungs,
goaded her roan stallion toward the chariots. Bowstrings
twanged and shafts flew toward her, but she zigzagged through
them. She came into range and shot at Priam twice. Her first
arrow flew wide of its mark and her second impaled the croup of
his rightmost horse. The beast fell, yanking down the other,
and the chariot slammed onto its side. But Priam and his archer
jumped free. While Klymene, who yelped in triumph, was
twisting back to the line of Amazons, Priam's sharpshooter
kneeled, plucked an arrow from his quiver, and drew it to his
cheek. The shaft's tip followed her evolutions. She turned and
aimed, but before her dart flew, the sharpshooter's did, propelling Klymene to the side while her mount continued forward.
Klymene dove toward the ground, her hands joined in front of
her head. She landed dead.

The Amazons continued accompanying the enemy host, now
shooting, now swerving. But its protective armor covered it like
the carapace of a deadly beast, and it crept on pitiless and un-
yielding.

Melanippe's bow lips paled when Tomiris, having hastened
back from the Thermodon trail, reported that hundreds of invaders in close formation were marching toward the city without Ariona's being able to slow them. Melanippe surveyed the
sky and the shadows and glanced heavily at Tomiris. It was
much earlier than Melanippe had counted on, and the intruders
had numbers and discipline. She and Hippolyta had been able
to assemble only fifty riders since midnight, although messengers had been dispatched to summon another threescore. Still,
none could arrive before a good part of the morning had passed.
Melanippe glanced back and silently counted the Amazons

gathered behind her. Hippolyta, who stood a few paces away, moved her horse up, and the others followed, surrounding the chief and waiting for the news. Tomiris repeated it.

All heads turned and all eyes looked in the direction of the apple trees.

"It's better not to let them march onto the field," said Melanippe.

Hippolyta took her place at her left, and the women formed two columns behind them and ran their horses to where the Thermodon trail spilled onto the grassy plain. Here they dismounted and waited.

They soon sighted the leather-skinned creature, first as dust raised from the road, then as an indistinct line, then as a shield wall that pushed on without pause or mercy. The soldiers' greaves were like the huge brown legs of a millipede crawling forward, and the riders who harassed it like wasps whose bites could not stop it.

The Amazons formed up in a single file facing the advancing animal, which began to roar like a winter storm, its hundreds of men bawling obscene threats at the top of their lungs. Horses flattened their ears, and riders traded sober glances.

Half the women drew their labryses: they would rush between the spear points and swing their axes down on the foot soldiers, who would turn their hide protection toward the blows to ward them off and in so doing offer an easy target to the women remaining behind. If the soldiers fled forward, they would be picked off; if they ran backward, their flight would disorganize their host long enough for the riders to shoot scores of bolts into their midst before they could regroup.

Booming like the tide, the columns surged within javelin range. Melanippe raised her hand to lead the charge and break the shield wall. Before she could shout her order, the hostile ranks opened like the jaws of a dragon and belched forth a squad of chariots that hurtled toward the riders in a din of grinding bronze like ravenous howling. Archers stationed behind the drivers loosed a rain of arrows. One punched through Hippolyta's cuirasse and drove her backward over her horse's croup. She crashed down, kicked twice, and stopped thrashing.

A war wagon was careering toward Melanippe. She swerved in time, and the bolt launched from it whizzed past her mount's ear, making the beast rear and nearly unseating her. While she was steadying the animal, the chariot, driven by a bronze-helmeted man of short stature, raced by.

More war wagons followed at all speed, geeing and hawing to throw the Amazons' aim off. Bolts rained down like rays from heaven. Women screamed, an axle shattered, horses and bodies thudded to the ground, chariots skidded and crashed. The vehicles, which had run through the Amazon ranks, were now wheeling about and weaving back, the archers behind the reinsmen shooting fast and well and the Amazons tensing their bows and returning their fire.

Dozens—both Amazons and Trojans—lay on the ground. An enemy shaft had pierced through the fair-skinned temples of Oebala and thrust her from her horse. She lay on her stomach, her arms and legs outstretched, her jaw twisted back over her shoulder like a bird wrenched to death, her mist-covered eyes wide with pain and incomprehension, black blood matting her sandy curls. A Trojan arrow had driven between the breasts of Lysippe, pinning her to the midair while her horse kept thundering ahead. She lay prone in the dust, staring at the sky without reflecting its light, her sinews unstrung, the arrow's feather protruding from her sternum, red liquid gushing from it like a spring torrent. An Amazon dart had pierced the belly of the charioteer Orthaios and thrust the dark-locked lad from his wagon. He writhed on the grass, his young face contracted in agony, shrieking like a child beset by nightmares, his hands outstretched, dirty brown gore gushing from his wound, fright and nonunderstanding glazing his regard.

"Back! Back! Back!" screamed Melanippe, rounding up the survivors and leading their retreat.

The invading animal widened its maw and absorbed the chariots it had just vomited forth. It then resumed its deadly progress.

"This way! This way!" shouted Charope, running her horse around the rear of the army, which now stood still at the border of the field. The Amazons who remained of her contingent fell in behind her, overtook the columns, and stationed themselves opposite their flank, not far from the river.

Charope beckoned to Penthesilea, who rode near her. "Hurry to Melanippe," she commanded. "Tell her that we've still got ten women and will harass their left as soon as they begin to swing right."

Penthesilea nodded: once the foot soldiers moved to protect themselves from the onslaught against their shield wall that Melanippe was sure to mount, they would drift toward their weapon side, exposing their left flank to a rain of arrows. Penthesilea dug her heels into Tala's ribs just as the army began to march forward again.

Charope's women trotted alongside the advancing troop, taking care to remain out of javelin range, and so did not see the foot soldiers step over the bodies of all the riders who had left the light of day.

The main force of Amazons—the score that remained of those who had first followed Melanippe and the twenty or so who had arrived from nearby patrols—occupied the middle of the field below the gate. The defenders had split up into two equal contingents, one forming a wide semicircle around the other, a tight group stationed in the center of the arc. Mounted, they faced the enemy, whose columns had halted two arrow shots away.

Melanippe sat her horse among the riders in the middle. They would charge a single location in the shield wall. This time they were ready for the chariots and had stationed enough sharpshooters around the pressure point to make sure that not one wagon that erupted from the ranks would return.

The brown leather skin of the beast rippled, and it began to crawl forward again, the ragged hedge of spear tips above it bristling like a spiked spine. The Amazons waited in concentrated silence, their eyes focused on the creature, which growled as it moved forward and lumbered to within one arrow's shot. Its snarling pained Melanippe's ears. Her legs and hands tightened, but she forced herself to wait before unsheathing her labrys and raising it above her head.

"Charge!" she yelled as she dug her heels into her mare's ribs and surged forward, riders following, howling the Amazon war whoop, waving their axes in the air, falling on the same place in the shield wall, dodging spear thrusts and slamming down their weapons on the soldiers who jabbed at them. Infantrymen thudded to the ground and helmets rang against the earth. Foot soldiers stopped and turned to defend themselves. Amazon archers shot into their immobilized herd. Men shrieked. The mounted fighters sliced deeper and deeper into the beast's innards, as priests do at a sacrifice probing for the victim's liver.

Penthesilea arrived after the raiders had cut through to the foe's entrails and the sharpshooters had drifted to within javelin range of the gash in the ranks. She was trying to spot

Melanippe, when the enemy roared like the sea, and a wave of light infantrymen flooded around the wound opened by the Amazons and poured into it. Once these men had swamped it, shield-bearing soldiers sealed it up. As soon as they had, wheels clanged, hooves pounded, and chariots raced around the flanks of the invader. Priam in the lead, the deadly vehicles flew toward the mounted archers in front, showering arrows on them at the same time as the newly-arrived foot soldiers hurled javelins at the Amazons trapped in their midst. Penthesilea located Melanippe as she was toppling from her mount like a tower falling sideways.

The war wagons swept over the front of the riders' line, raking it with bolts. Penthesilea fired back. Priam's archer somersaulted rearward and crashed onto the field, but Priam's chariot did not slow. Instead, he led the deadly vehicles around to deliver another blow. The Amazons who had not fallen were fleeing in disarray.

It was useless to fight anymore. Penthesilea pulled Tala's head around and ran her toward the bridge. A company of soldiers was also running for it. Penthesilea crouched over the mare's neck and goaded her again and again, crossing over the span before the men reached it. Behind the rider, many hooves pounded on the wooden structure. Once she was out of javelin range she looked back. Perhaps two-dozen Amazons followed. At their back, on the opposite bank of the river, Amisos soldiers watched them flee.

The rout had been complete. Priam controlled the field in front of the city.

Penthesilea looked at her shadow. It was noon.

The riders followed her across the farmland to the grove of plane trees that separated it from the heath and the southern rises. Here the women dismounted, tethered their horses, and sank to the ground. No one spoke. Some peered around to see who had survived; others, who did not have the stomach to count even more friends killed, kept their eyes lowered.

Hooves beating against soft earth made them all look up; Amazons were arriving from the plowed fields. Charope led eight women into the copse, Tecmassa, Feodissia, and Marpessa among them. The newcomers' capes, which were weighted down by water, slapped against their horses' flanks. The women dismounted and found Penthesilea.

"What happened?" she asked.

Tecmassa replied, "You weren't gone but a little while, when they turned their shield wall toward us, and there weren't enough of us to do a damned thing against them. Then they just began walking, pushing us to the river, and we couldn't run left or right because they'd closed up both sides. So we decided to swim. Brr! The water's cold this time of year."

"What happened to Melanippe, anyway?" asked Charope.

Penthesilea told them.

"So it's only a matter of time before they lay siege to the city," said Adrasta, who had accompanied the tatters of Hippolyta's women out of danger.

"They don't have any siege tools," said Penthesilea.

"And from what I saw of them while we were running this way," added Charope, "they're not about to begin. They're settling in. They're building fires."

"Whatever can they be biding their time for?" asked Marpessa.

Penthesilea lowered her head and frowned. Women saw that she was calculating something and grew silent.

After a while, she raised her face. "Let's take advantage of their stopping and sitting," she said.

Chapter 17

Adrasta and nine followers backtracked. They were to hide near the bridge until the time came for them to ride into action. The rest of the Amazons made their way to the stretch of Thermodon that served as a swimming place in the hot months. It was here that Perseia and seven women who had been patrolling the near steppes caught up with the others. Perseia reined in next to Penthesilea, who conferred with her in a low voice. Perseia nodded.

All the riders alighted from their horses. Penthesilea slipped her bow from her shoulder, raised it over her head, and grabbed Tala's tail. Shouting "Get! Get!" she pushed the mare into the river and slapped her croup. Tala crashed into the stream and paddled toward the opposite shore, dragging Penthesilea after her. The icy water covered Penthesilea like a skin of pain. She swam on. She heard one splash after another; the other riders were following. Tala pulled her across; the mare's hooves touched the river bed, and she scrambled onto the bank. Penthesilea stumbled behind and watched her comrades land one by one.

"Look!" someone yelled. Midstream, Charope choked and lunged about while her mount, its tail free of her grip, surged toward the onlookers. Charope's face disappeared beneath the surface, then her hand, then her bow. Penthesilea dove in. A thud sounded behind her. Charope appeared once more and went under, leaving a glimmering circle above where she had disappeared. Penthesilea's beetle-like breaststroke carried her to the spot. She ducked her head, grabbed Charope by the braid, and yanked her up. Feodissia, who had rushed into the current right behind Penthesilea, wrapped her hands around the back of Charope's tunic. They pulled her to the shore. She lay gasping, while Feodissia fetched her mount.

The women took to horse immediately. Perseia, who sat hers next to Penthesilea, leaned over and put her hands on her shoulders. Penthesilea returned the accolade. Perseia pivoted her steed, and the squad she led hastened toward the city.

They were to make sure that no pickets lived to tell that a force of Amazons had crossed the river; then they were to wait for their opportunity to damage the enemy.

The remaining riders fell in behind Penthesilea, who headed for the pasture upstream of Themiscyra. After an hour, the Amazons reached the stand of alder at the foot of the iron hills, forded the rivulet that watered the trees, and dismounted. Penthesilea led them to the goat path that snaked north of the city. Watching their animals' hooves like cats watch mice, the women inched their mounts along the tiny track until they had gone past Themiscyra's hill. Then the riders turned their horses toward the river; they picked their way around the tricky slope behind the city, scrambled down its rock-strewn southern face, and got to a clearing a long arrow's shot from the cave entrance where Telkhinia's furnace stood. Here Penthesilea made them settle to the ground and rest, many having been on horseback since the day before. While the others drowsed, she and Feodissia stood watch, pacing and waving their arms to keep themselves from sinking into sleep.

As soon as the sun had descended halfway down the sky, Penthesilea roused the riders. They rode all the way to the base of the hill and emerged from its wooded cover before coming on pickets. Penthesilea pointed, and two Amazons cantered their horses after them and silenced them. Then Penthesilea gestured again, and Marpessa and Feodissia dismounted at the foot of a hornbeam and crouched over something. At length a stream of smoke rose from between them. Marpessa heaped dry branches on the fire. Feodissia gave her quiver to Marpessa; then Feodissia shimmied up the trunk of the tree and settled on a low branch. Then Penthesilea slipped her bow from her shoulder and turned to the others. Their sturdy faces told her that they were ready.

Shrieking the Amazon war whoop, two dozen riders descended on the enemy from out of nowhere. Soldiers lounging on the grass had time only to raise their heads and gawk before arrows put them down. Other men jumped to their feet and tried in vain to dash out of the way, some tripping over the huge shields that they had picked up to protect themselves. The women ran their horses the length of the sitting army, shooting and screaming and spreading terror. Javelins began to fly at them. Penthesilea heard a horse bellow behind her and a body thud to the ground. She wheeled Tala to the left and headed for the river, where fourteen chariots lay with their shafts in the air while the horses that pulled them stood nearby, their muzzles concealed by feed bags. Archers were scrambling for their weapons, and drivers for their ponies. Arrows whizzed past Penthesilea's ears. A horse whinnied and a woman screamed. Then another.

"Let's go! Let's go!" shouted Penthesilea over her shoulder.

The women raced after Penthesilea, who followed Thermodon's bank downstream until they were out of range. There they stopped and turned. Trojans were harnessing horses to chariots on the double. Penthesilea waited. Once they were hitched up, she raised her arm and goaded Tala into a run. The riders charged again. The chariots thundered out to meet them. Penthesilea kept racing forward. An arrow whacked into the ground, and earth exploded at Tala's feet. Penthesilea now eased the mare's head around and urged her toward the edge of the wood from which the Amazons had materialized a little while before. They fell in behind her. The chariots gave chase. Drivers whistled and bawled; whips snapped; hooves pounded.

The Amazons flew past the hornbeam where Feodissia and Marpessa waited, the one holding her bow and dangling her long legs from the bough, the other counting the arrows stacked in a neat row near the blaze she had built.

"They're about to arrive," said Marpessa, taking up an arrow and holding its head, which was wrapped in wax-soaked cloth, over the flames. The tip of the bolt ignited, and she handed it to Feodissia, who lay its nock in her bowstring, tensed the arc, and loosed the shaft at the first chariot to fly by. Fire soon crackled at the feet of the archer. He yelped in surprise. The driver stiffened. The horse screamed and charged forward, the man pulling back to no avail while the panicked beast plunged and weaved toward the trees, where the Amazons now stood waiting to pick the men off.

A second chariot hurtled past Feodissia, who set it on fire, then a third, and she did the same. The fourth driver, seeing the destruction in store for him, pulled his beast around, but not before Feodissia shot. The flaming chariot careered toward the ones speeding after it and tipped over on its side, so that the horse dragged it into their midst. Ponies reared. Drivers and archers toppled to the ground. Their column crashed to a halt. The Amazons charged again.

Theseus and sixty Achaeans hid near the cave entrance until Penthesilea led the assault on the crippled chariots. Then, lighting torches, the land-pirates vanished into the tunnel and inched along it to the room under the temple kitchen cellar.

Merope was stirring a steaming cauldron when she heard scraping on the cellar stairs. She turned. A grim-helmeted man burst in, grabbed her windpipe so that she could not scream, and jabbed his sword through her belly. She crumbled to the floor. He let her go, went back to the basement steps, and waved down them. Raiders pounded up. Theseus barged in. Pirothous followed. They thrust out of the door, sighted the precinct gate, and ran for it. Here Theseus stationed a squad under Pirothous' command to make sure that no one locked the entrance while Theseus and his men took the city.

In the marketplace Abba-Bashti stood among the crowd surrounding Athaia, who had been watching the battle from the parapet and scurried down to announce that, against all hope, the Amazons had counterattacked and enemy soldiers were on the run. The fear that had pressed on the women's shoulders all day flew heavenward like night mists when the sun rises. Abba-Bashti hugged her little girl so tight that she wriggled away.

Suddenly, the gates of the temple precinct ground open and leather-greaved soldiers brandishing swords and spears and screaming vile words pounded toward the press. The knot of women exploded, and they fled in all directions like a school of fish into whose midst a stone has crashed. The young Theia, Dione's granddaughter, stumbled and fell. The Achaean close on her heels tripped over her and, furious, rammed his spear into her back. Abba-Bashti put her hand over Proto's eyes and yanked her away.

Theseus turned this way and that, located the palace, and pointed his sword at it. Metion and twelve men darted across the space and came up to the door at the moment it banged shut. Two soldiers with axes stepped forward, raised them over their heads, and battered the entrance until it splintered apart. The Achaeans rushed inside.

Athaia sped downhill; Abba-Bashti and Proto tore after her, staying only paces in front of the Achaeans led by Theseus, who raced for the city gate, leaving those in their way lying in pools of blood. Athaia ducked into the street of the artificers and flung herself into Telkhinia's smithy. Pushing Proto before her, Abba-Bashti did the same.

Telkhinia jumped up as soon as she read the terror on the newcomers' faces.

"Bolt the door!" gasped Abba-Bashti.

Telkhinia did so just as the first of the Achaeans rushed by.

"What?" she said in disbelief.

Ragged orange clouds cascaded around the setting sun. Soldiers from Troy and Amisos, now disarmed, sat in circles—except Priam, who held himself apart, hugging his hands to his chest, his face turned to the ground. Wounded men groaned. The dead were piled high. Amazons tended bonfires of spears, shields, and bows. Adrasta's and Perseia's women were crossing the field to join the main column of riders who, bone weary but elated, followed Penthesilea to the gate.

She unsheathed her labrys and pounded on the massive portal with its handle, hoping as she did that Abba-Bashti would be the one who heaved the door open and welcomed her. Penthesilea heard the sickening slurp of a javelin piercing flesh and the rider behind screech and crash to the ground. Someone had launched a spear from the top of the parapet above the gate. A leather-helmeted Achaean was lifting his arm to strike again. Bowstrings twanged. The man grew limp and lurched backward, but someone pushed his body over the wall, and he thudded to the ground at Tala's feet.

Chalcodon!

A shaft hissed toward the women. Tala squealed and shuddered forward. Penthesilea threw herself to one side and hit the earth so hard that she could not move. Feodissia reined in next to her, shouted her name, and, once she was roused, yanked her up onto her horse's croup. Feodissia then dug her heels into her mount's side and followed the other Amazons, who had pivoted their animals and run them out of range.

Chalcodon had toppled against Theseus, who was racing up the parapet stairway two steps at a time. Theseus straightarmed the dead weight and shoved. Then he stretched out on his belly and swept his eye over the field. Once he had, he clambered down as fast as he could and, gesticulating with his sword, stationed a dozen men on the parapet under the mercenary Euneus' command, and marched the remaining two dozen back uphill double-time: he would need them to patrol the streets and keep Themiscyra's inhabitants from cutting off communication among his three detachments.

The full moon cast silver light and deep shadows on the street of the artificers. Two Achaeans stood watch over it. Thersandra's door swung open. Then Telkhinia's. Then Oenanthé's. One soldier nudged the other, who was drowsing on his feet, and, holding their spears low in front of them, the men left their cover and tiptoed through the narrow way to see what was happening. They passed a dark alley. Telkhinia and Thersandra jumped them. They silently sank to the ground, and the women dragged them out of sight.

Telkhinia and Thersandra spirited down the street and scratched on each door. Women toting mallets, augurs, hacksaws, crowbars, adzes, chisels, billhooks, gouges, hacks, nippers, stump spades, wimbles, and sledgehammers tiptoed out of their abodes and, hugging the sides of the buildings to stay under cover, stole into the surrounding byways.

Metion strode into the palace kitchen and rasped that the Achaeans were hungry and thirsty. Anuphey carried them bread, wine, and cheese. Metion made her drink a draft of the liquid and swallow mouthfuls of food. He watched her closely for minutes, then, seeing no symptoms of poisoning, ordered her to serve the provender. She leaned forward to hand him his, and he pushed his open palm against her breast. "Later for you," he gurgled. She dropped her eyes, finished distributing the rations, and hastened out. Malicious laughter echoed after her.

She returned to the pantry and broke into a giggle. Dione was waiting for her there. A jug of cooking oil stood on one of the shelves. It was half empty. Dione had made her swallow the other half before bringing the men their food and drink.

"How long will it be?" asked Anuphey.

"Not long before the sleeping potion takes effect."

"I wonder which one snores the loudest."

"Whoever he is, he won't for long," cackled Dione.

A cloud floated over the moon. Women brandishing axes and crowbars ran for the tunnel in the wall that led to the city gate. A gust of wind swept away the cloud. Arrows hissed down. Two women screamed and toppled over. A third fell silently. The rest dove back into alleys and byways.

Oenanthé heaved a pebble against the parapet. The Achaean patrolling it leaned over to see what the noise was. Oenanthé swung her sling, and, stunned, the man collapsed silently onto the walkway. Telkhinia appeared from out of the dark, then two bricklayer's apprentices carrying a ladder, then Abba-Bashti carrying a rope and a bricklayer's hod, then Athaia leading her little sister, Dirce, by the hand.

The apprentices wrestled the ladder up against the wall and struggled with it until it sat securely. Telkhinia and Oenanthé clambered to the top and stood on either side. Athaia coaxed Dirce up and joined her. Still holding the basket, Abba-Bashti followed, then one apprentice; the other kept watch at the foot. Abba-Bashti secured the cord to the basket, and Dirce stretched out in it. Abba-Bashti and the young women grabbed hold of the line and lowered Dirce down the outside. Just as she touched ground, they heard footsteps coming from both directions on the walkway. Oenanthé let fly a stone, and the soldier approaching her sank down. The second man raised his spear and charged Telkhinia. She sidestepped, grabbed the shaft, and yanked it against her. She smashed her fist into the man's jaw. His knees folded, but she did not let him founder, and lifted him over her head and heaved. Meanwhile the other women had descended the ladder. Telkhinia followed. The apprentices wrested it back from the rampart, lay it on its side, and carried it away.

A pale blue rim outlined the eastern walls.

Marpessa shook Penthesilea awake. Climbing out of sleep hurt her eyes and throat. At the top was Marpessa's face. She had found Dirce near the base of the walls, and the basket in which they had lowered her, and not far from there the body of an Achaean who had fallen to his death. Once the knowledge sank into Penthesilea's aching head, she asked, "Did your mother send you?"

Dirce nodded.

"Did she want you to tell us something?"

"Mother said to. . . ." Dirce cut short her words, pushed her thumb into her mouth, and lowered her eyes.

"Said to what?"

"I forgot."

Tecmassa, who had gotten groggily to her feet, raised her hands to the heavens and stalked away.

Feodissia stepped forward. "Here, Dirce, I can show you a trick."

"You can?"

"Sure enough. Want me to tell you what it is?"

Dirce nodded. Feodissia bent over and whispered in her ear.

"I bet you can't."

"I can, too."

"No, you can't."

"I can, too. But I'm not going to. Well, I will if you say first what your mother wants."

"Promise?"

"Promise."

"Mother said to tell Penthesilea. . . ." By this time a dozen riders had surrounded Dirce.

"What did your mom say?" prompted Feodissia.

"That you can. . . ." The Amazons drew closer.

"I have to pee," said Dirce.

Listeners murmured in disappointment.

"Do it right here . . . dear," said Tecmassa, who had returned.

While more grownups joined the circle around her, the little girl hoisted her skirt and squatted. Like a summer storm's raindrops, her urine hissed loudly, tattooed against the ground, splashed higher and lower, louder and softer. At every change of pitch, at every alteration of volume, the adults grew more tense, until, when at last the sound ceased, they were straining taut to listen.

But the child said nothing. She was only pausing. Soon, a low trickle akin to that of a mountain rivulet gurgled from under her. Her elders, let-down, groaned. Her piss drummed against the turf, dwindled to a ripple, stopped. The mature women heeded with every ounce of attention.

But the maiden did not straighten up. Instead, a thin stream that resembled the spent efforts of a brief but sudden downpour began to fizz against the greenery. Some riders growled and others shushed them, but not one of them budged as the liquid tinkled against the verdure, then plunked spasmodically, then did nothing at all. The eavesdroppers held their breath.

No more leaking. Dirce stood to her full height and beamed. Members of her audience burst into applause; others whooped and whistled; two stamped their feet.

Dirce told them about the cave where Telkhinia smelted iron—how it led to the inside, to the temple kitchen.

Feodissia plucked a blade of grass from the ground and put it between her thumbs. She blew into them. The shrill note fell upon the ears of Achaean guards on the parapet. It worried them. What could the Amazons be planning? A dawn assault on the walls? They dispatched a messenger to Theseus, who was inspecting the temple complex, but the soldier did not get through.

By the time the sky became light, Penthesilea and a dozen women had disappeared into the mouth of the cave, and Charope and Tecmassa were leading the rest of the riders in a show of force in front of the gates to divert the Achaeans. When the sun rose over the temple precinct wall, Penthesilea and her followers had stolen into the palace kitchen, where they found no one except Merope's lifeless form. Perseia and five Amazons hastened on tiptoe into the building to secure it, while Penthesilea pushed open the outside door and stepped into the daylight. No one stood guard, but rhythmic thumping reached her ears from what seemed like downhill. Her comrades at her heels, she crept around to the front of the edifice, the throbbing growing louder as the women advanced. They reached the end of the building and stopped. Penthesilea stuck her head around the corner. The open space between the temple and its dependencies was deserted, except near the gate, where a contingent of Achaeans—at least a dozen—had taken up station. A thick beam barred the portal; its planks and crosspieces crashed and shivered around a single point. Someone was assaulting it with a battering ram. A ladder leaned against the wall framing the entrance; men milled around the scale's base; archers were climbing it. Three reached the top and fired down at the other side. The dinning stopped.

One of the soldiers on the ground glanced back. Penthesilea ducked. Still, she heard him yell "Look!" and then heard feet stampeding toward where she was concealed.

"Here they come!" she shouted and tensed her bow.

Ten fully armored Achaeans, some brandishing swords, some gripping lowered spears, sped around the building and charged the seven horseless Amazons. Penthesilea loosed an arrow at the first man, who held a broad blade in his fist. The missile glanced off his shield. He tore toward her as other soldiers raced by. She drew her labrys. He raised his weapon and struck. She threw herself sideways. The force of his blow hitting the earth made him lose his balance. She wielded her axe. She saw a speartip coming for her abdomen. She parried. The soldier tackled her. Hitting the ground shattered her. The fellow's weight paralyzed her. He drew his knife. She gripped his wrist, raised her knee, and, straining every part of her body, managed to shove him off to one side. She used her hands. She jumped up. Another spearman pounded for her. She raised her weapon but the man suddenly dove forward, his hands outstretched, his arm skidding along the ground. A shaft had driven home. A volley of arrows whizzed past, and one by one the Achaeans toppled or threw down their weapons.

Perseia and her five had not found a soul in the palace, then heard shouts and blows outside, and rushed to the rescue. On their way, they had dispatched the three Achaeans still stationed on the wall.

"Now where do you suppose everyone's gone to?" said Feodissia, who, breathless, her forehead streaked with blood, strode forward from where she had fought. At that moment faint pounding reached their ears from uphill. Feodissia loped toward the sanctuary.

Behind Penthesilea, the other Amazons who had stood the charge—Amynome the juggler, the dreamy-eyed Andromache, and Ido, who loved to gamble—all sat against the wall gasping for breath. Adrasta was sprawled motionless on her stomach. Marpessa lay spread-eagle on her back: she rattled breaths in and out; a dark stain was spreading from beneath her cuirasse to the skirt of her tunic.

Penthesilea knelt beside her. Dark blue was seeping into the ivory of her skin, and circles of black like tarnished bronze surrounded her eyes, which were shut. Penthesilea kissed her brow as she would a sleeping child's. Marpessa's lids parted and, once she saw who it was, her emerald green glance lit up, and her lips, which were the color of wax, traced a smile.

"I can't say as I'm doing well, girl," she whispered.

"Don't talk," said Penthesilea.

"I've got to."

Penthesilea acquiesced.

"Will you do a few things for me, then?"

"Of course."

"Don't send me to the other world without taking a tress of my hair."

"I won't."

"Divide that tress in two. Evenly. Promise me that you will. Evenly."

"Of course I will."

"Put one lock in the purse on my belt. Give it to Arne the sandalmaker. When no one's looking, mind you."

"I'll do that."

"Tell her I won't forget. That I'll wait." Marpessa's breathing was like fall leaves fluttering in the wind.

"Please don't talk anymore."

"But I'm not done," murmured Marpessa, gazing up with feverish eyes.

"Yes?"

"Listen. Listen carefully. Don't tell Arne's sister Scarphe the perfumer about it. Please don't."

"Yes. As you say."

"And Scarphe. For her. Put the other lock in the tiny box in my saddlebag. Give it to her. When there's no one around. Tell her that I'll remember. That I'll be there when she comes. And whatever you do. . . ."

Marpessa raised herself on her elbows and fell back.

Penthesilea leaned closer.

Marpessa wheezed, "And whatever you do, don't tell her sister Arne."

Penthesilea nodded and tried not to smile.

Marpessa widened her eyes and glared, then frowned and sighed, "You. You. The Amazons. . . . You must. . . ." A gasp silenced her; she stared at nothing, hiccuped a flow of blood, and went limp.

Penthesilea gaped at her without saying to herself that she was dead. At length anger shook Penthesilea, and tears stung her eyes, and she sprang up and raised her face to the heavens. She clenched her fists and looked around. Never had the outlines of things cut the background with such sharpness.

Excited voices and the shuffling of feet uphill. There, votaries and servants—some carrying babes, some holding children by the hand—were streaming out of the sanctuary. The Achaeans had locked all the precinct inhabitants in the building at dawn, when the women of the tool began their assault of the walls. Feodissia had freed the prisoners. Penthesilea met them and interrogated their faces.

"We do not know where Myrtho is," said Iphinoë, who walked in front of the newly released women.

Philippis appeared, her lips twisted in alarm. "Myrtho was taken from us," she wheezed, "before they. . . ."

The granary door ground open. Myrtho lurched out, Pirothous plastered against her. His left arm circled her waist. His right pressed a dagger to her.

He saw Penthesilea. "I want safe passage," he roared. "Understand? If I don't get it, I'll kill your high priestess. Understand?" He tightened his hold until Myrtho gasped. He kneed the back of her thighs, and she began to stumble toward the precinct gate, which was now unbarred. She put one foot in front of the other. His step locked with hers.

"Let them go!" pleaded Philippis. "Please, please, let them go!"

Penthesilea tensed her lips to give the order. But the words never escaped her mouth, for at that moment Myrtho swooned, dragging Pirothous forward just as an arrow flew at him. The shaft, which Feodissia had aimed at his neck, drove against his helmet instead. The head armor twisted off and clattered onto the cobblestones. Pirothous spun around and teetered but did not fall. Penthesilea sprinted toward him. He saw her and raced for the sanctuary.

Penthesilea vaulted after him. He disappeared inside. She tore through the door and stopped. She drew her labrys and dagger. Her vision swam in the dim light. She squinted until she could see. She darted her glance around but made out nothing—no human shadow, no movement. She hunched forward to hear better. Rapid breaths echoed against the stones. But from where? She glowered and listened harder. She located it, near the statue of the Goddess, and tiptoed forward. Something bounced against the marble floor behind her. She could not stop herself from pivoting, and Pirothous, who had tricked her, sprang from the shadows and lunged at her back. Penthesilea threw herself flat. His weight carried him past her, and he lost his footing. He regained it at the same time as Penthesilea stood up.

His sword was drawn. He raised it over his head, jumped at her, and slashed. She swung the labrys in time. Her axe pounded against the flat of his blade so hard that her biceps stung. Pirothous' weapon flew from his grip and Penthesilea's from hers. Pirothous snarled and leaped forward. His thumbs slammed into her windpipe; his fingers tightened around it. Fire stabbed her throat and cut her temples. Her eyes glazed with pain; her mouth twisted; she jabbed her dagger up under his arm and felt it sink into where his cuirasse opened for his sleeve. The racking in her gullet stopped. Pirothous sank to the ground.

Feodissia was running toward her. "You all right, girl?"

Penthesilea put her head in her hands and whispered, "Yes."

Feodissia looked at Pirothous' still body. "Is this the one who raped you?" she asked.

"Yes."

Feodissia unsheathed her knife and knelt.

Penthesilea stepped into the open air. Abba-Bashti was helping Myrtho to her feet. Tecmassa, mounted on her big-bellied piebald, was leading two horses toward the sanctuary.

Penthesilea guided her horse through the press toward the palace. Tecmassa rode at her side, Abba-Bashti perched behind. Feodissia sat her mount on the other flank, Proto straddling in front of her. At their heels, Amazons had formed a double file to escort Penthesilea to the great hall. She was their chief. The cortege crept forward with difficulty—women thronged around her waving and applauding, holding their children on their shoulders to see the Amazon who had saved them. She shook hands with those who reached out; she greeted every woman she knew by name.

"Don't let it swell your head, girl," said Tecmassa. "The crowd's not hard to make happy. And just as simple to rile. They'll grumble against you just as easy as they're cheering you now. And so will the riders who're pleased to fall in behind you."

Chattering and disturbance. Anuphey elbowed through the crowd.

"What's this? What's this?" asked Tecmassa.

Anuphey ran up to Penthesilea and grabbed her thigh. Penthesilea halted. "I've come from the palace," said Anuphey. "Antiope has disappeared. So has the boy child with the red hair. We've looked everywhere."

"When did you last see them?" asked Feodissia.

"Last evening."

"And where's Theseus?" said Penthesilea. "No one's seen Theseus." She turned to look at her friends, and all traded heavy glances.

Penthesilea addressed Feodissia. "Pick women and organize a search. I don't want them to reach the border."

Feodissia acknowledged the order, lifted Proto onto Charope's mount, and wheeled hers away. Penthesilea set her animal in motion once more.

Tecmassa, who still rode abreast, said, "Just remember that where you're going few will tell you the straight truth because everyone stands to gain or lose something from the chief of the riders and the high judge of the city. So you'll end up suspecting even their good words. Yup. The only one who'll really let you know what you're worth are the horses. They don't know anything about your rank, and they'll throw you without asking twice, if you don't know how to handle them. No one's going to keep you honest, girl, except yourself."

Abba-Bashti raised her face to the heavens. A broad smile invaded her plump cheeks. Her well-sculpted lips parted. Laughter like crystal rain floated down.